12

THE
FLESH
TAILOR

Also by Kate Ellis

For more information regarding Kate Ellis
log on to Kate's website: www.kateellis.co.uk

THE
FLESH
TAILOR

Kate Ellis

piatkus

PIATKUS

First published in Great Britain in 2010 by Piatkus
Reprinted 2010

A CIP catalogue record for this book
is available from the British Library.

ISBN 978-0-7499-0963-5

Typeset in Baskerville by M Rules
Printed and bound in Great Britain by
MPG Books, Bodmin, Cornwall

Papers used by Piatkus are natural, renewable and
recyclable products sourced from well-managed forests and certified
in accordance with the rules of the Forest Stewardship Council.

Mixed Sources
Product group from well-managed
forests and other controlled sources
www.fsc.org Cert no. SGS-COC-004081
© 1996 Forest Stewardship Council
FSC

Piatkus
An imprint of
Little, Brown Book Group
100 Victoria Embankment
London EC4Y 0DY

An Hachette UK Company
www.hachette.co.uk

www.piatkus.co.uk

For my dad, David Ellis

November. The month of the dead. The month of remembrance and funerals.

Dr James Dalcott had no idea why these things flashed through his mind as he picked up the keys to his new Lexus and looked in the mirror. Perhaps it was the miserable weather outside. Or perhaps his recent discoveries about his family had awakened the demons in his head.

He had decided against wearing a suit and opted for an open-necked shirt and linen jacket. After all, it was only a casual dinner with a colleague and her husband. And he wouldn't have thought that Dr Maritia Fitzgerald was the formal type at all.

He studied his reflection. His face was round, tending towards plumpness and, from the slight strain on his waistband as he'd fastened his trousers, he knew he was doing precisely what he instructed his patients not to do – he was putting on weight. Ever since Roz left him, he'd been living on junk food and drinking more than the government's recommended limit. Fine example he was to the sick and malingering of Neston.

After brushing an imaginary speck off his jacket James picked up the carrier bag containing a bottle of decent Cabernet Shiraz and a box of Belgian chocolates – his

1

offerings towards the evening's entertainment. Although he hardly liked to admit it to himself, he'd rather fancied Maritia when they'd first started working together: she was an attractive, intelligent woman and her West Indian background lent her an exoticism rare in their part of the world. But a colleague newly married to a local vicar is hardly a suitable candidate for dalliance. He'd have to content himself with Evonne, although he regarded her more as a friend than a lover and his instincts told him that there wasn't much future in the relationship. And besides, he still couldn't banish Roz completely from his mind.

James glanced in the mirror again and ran his fingers through his receding fair hair, aware that the strain he'd been under since the break-up of his marriage was starting to show on his face. Once he'd discovered what had happened to his father he knew he had to carry on until he'd uncovered the whole truth but when he'd tried to share it with Roz, she hadn't wanted to hear about what she called 'his obsession'. And yet it was something he couldn't help. Not many people had a skeleton like that in the family cupboard – a grim and terrible set of bones, too horrible to reveal to the world.

It was time to go. James had been brought up to believe that being late was inconsiderate to your hosts. He could hear the rain tapping on the glass in the front door. It was a bad night. November weather, chill and damp. There were times when he wished he'd taken up that job offer in Australia after medical school. But it was too late now. He was stuck with a lifetime of English winters, and a waiting room full of sneezing patients, he thought with a shiver as he pulled on his coat.

He was just about to unlock the front door when he saw a dark human shape behind the frosted glass. He hesitated for a moment, wondering who the visitor could be. Then the doorbell rang, loud and insistent, shattering the silence of the hallway.

When James opened the door he was faced with a tall figure standing hunched in the darkness, hands in pockets, face in shadow.

'I'm so sorry. I'm just on my way out.'

The figure began to move forward and James instinctively backed away, clutching the carrier bag to his chest like a defensive shield. Then he felt the hard metal of the revolver, cold against his forehead, and he held his breath. He'd encountered death before in many guises: peaceful, agonising, messy; sometimes welcome, sometimes railed against. But this time he knew it would be different because the death in question would be his own.

The assassin took a step back, taking aim, and James could only whisper the word 'please' before the revolver was fired and the whole world exploded.

James Dalcott's body jerked and twisted as the bullet entered his brain. Then he fell back and his fingers lost their grip on the carrier bag. The bottle inside smashed as it hit the floor and the red wine oozed slowly out of the bag across the polished wood like a slick of fresh blood.

CHAPTER 1

Transcript of recording made by Mrs Mabel Cleary (née Fallon) – Home Counties Library Service Living History Project: Reminiscences of a wartime evacuee.

Things were getting worse in London so my mum decided to send me away. It must have been hard for her but she kept saying it was for the best. They told us we were going to Devon but I was only nine and I thought it must be just outside London somewhere. My mum told me not to complain and that whatever happened I had to grin and bear it. Dad was away in the army and she just wanted me to be safe.

We were put on the train with labels tied to our clothes and one of the grown-ups told me not to lose the label because if I did I'd never see my family again. I held onto that label for dear life, I can tell you, and when we reached the station at Neston the cardboard was all damp and the ink had started to run. I cried because I was scared that nobody would be able to read it and I'd be lost forever in all those green fields I'd seen out of the train window. I was from the East End of London and I'd never seen countryside before. It seemed so big and frightening with all those lonely farms and woods where terrible things probably happened. If you got lost there I reckoned you could never find your way home.

When I got off the train with all the other evacuees at Neston Station, I was scared out of my wits. I knew that whatever was coming, however awful, I had to grin and bear it. But if I'd known then what I was going to find at Tailors Court, I think I would have stayed in London and risked the bombs.

Dr Maritia Fitzgerald looked at the oven in despair. She was sure she could smell burning.

'We can't wait for him.' Her husband, Mark, stood in the doorway. He had ditched his dog collar for the evening and he looked annoyed.

Maritia knew Mark was right. James was an hour late. Of course he might have encountered an emergency but he hadn't called to let them know and she knew for a fact that he wasn't on duty that night.

There were eight for dinner – seven without James Dalcott. There was the retired senior partner at the practice, Dr Keith Graham, who acted as occasional locum and made himself generally useful – some people could never face the wastelands of retirement. His wife, Honor, was a thin fidgety woman wearing a cloud of bright chiffon and an impatient scowl, who worked as an events officer for Tradington Hall Arts Centre. The Grahams had turned up late, the reason unspecified. But from the strained look on Keith's face, Maritia suspected a marital tiff.

Then there was Evonne Arlis, the practice nurse, a mature blonde of large proportions who had already disappeared twice into the garden for a sly cigarette. Evonne had been invited as company for James Dalcott because Maritia knew they got on well but now she was staring miserably at the empty seat opposite.

As the new senior partner hadn't been able to make it because of his daughter's school play, and the other doctor was away for a second honeymoon in the Maldives, Maritia had invited her brother and his wife to make up the numbers. Wesley was bound to keep the conversation flowing – police work was a subject that fascinated everybody, she'd reasoned. But as she brought the food to the table, she noticed with horror that her guests were sitting in awkward silence. She caught the eye of her sister-in-law, Pam, who seemed to understand immediately.

'It must be interesting working at Tradington Hall,' Maritia heard Pam say to Honor Graham in a determinedly cheerful voice. 'I teach year six at Tradmouth Primary and I'm always trying to encourage an interest in the arts. Do you work much with local schools?'

Maritia couldn't quite make out the reply as she was hurrying from the room to fetch the potatoes but it seemed to be rather terse. Honor Graham was a difficult woman at the best of times and James Dalcott's absence seemed to have dampened everyone's spirits.

As she finally sat down and invited everyone to help themselves to vegetables, she saw Keith Graham lean across the table, serving spoon hovering in midair, and look Wesley in the eye. 'So why is crime becoming so bad around here?

There have been two break-ins at the surgery this year and Honor had her car radio stolen, didn't you, dear?'

Honor, her mouth full of salmon, made a noise that sounded like a grunt.

Maritia froze and glanced at Mark who was sitting at the head of the table with an empty glass in his hand, his eyes half closed, as though he was praying for a miracle.

'I had my purse nicked in Tradmouth last year,' Evonne piped up. She had taken a mobile phone from her handbag and was turning it over and over in her fingers. 'I'm going to give James another call,' she said. 'I hope he hasn't had an accident. I told him the other day that he drives too bloody fast and you know what some of these country roads are like.'

'Yes, I think you should try him again.' Maritia was concerned about James too. His absence was out of character.

As Evonne left the table to make her call, Maritia saw that Keith was still looking expectantly at Wesley, as though he had the power single-handedly to bring law and order to the streets.

Wesley helped himself to another potato and gave Keith an apologetic smile. 'Neston would have dealt with your break-ins. I take it there hasn't been an arrest?'

Keith Graham suddenly looked a little embarrassed. 'They did get somebody as a matter of fact. Young drug addict. But he was let off with a slap on the wrist as usual.'

'Not my department, I'm afraid,' said Wesley. 'I just catch them and hand them over to the courts.'

Keith leaned forward. 'That's the trouble. When you catch them the courts can't do anything.'

Maritia opened her mouth to speak. The last thing she

wanted was for Keith Graham to get controversial at the dinner table. But before she could change the subject Evonne returned with a worried look on her face.

'Still no answer. I wonder if someone should go round to his house . . . just to check that he's all right. He could be ill or . . . I'm still under the limit.' She turned to Maritia. 'Look, I'm sorry to be so rude but I think I'll drive round there and . . .'

Maritia glanced at her husband as he stood up.

'Would you like me to go with you, Evonne? It's a filthy night and I don't like to think of you . . .'

That was Mark all over, Maritia thought with a sigh. Wesley was allowed time off, as was she. But a vicar is never off duty.

Evonne looked relieved, as though a burden had been lifted from her shoulders. She was a nervous driver and most of the people at the table knew it. 'Oh thank you, Mark. That's so good of you. Are you sure you don't mind?'

Maritia saw Mark take a deep breath and force out a smile. 'Hopefully we won't be long.'

'At least finish your dinner first,' she said pointedly.

Mark looked at Evonne who gave a little nod. As soon as he sat down again and began to tackle the food on his plate, shovelling it into his mouth as though he sensed Evonne's anxiety and wanted to be off, Wesley's mobile phone began to ring. He rose from his seat and made for Belsham Vicarage's spacious hallway, pressing the phone to his ear.

When he re-entered the dining room all eyes were on him.

'I'm really sorry, I have to go.'

9

Maritia saw a flash of annoyance pass over Pam's face, there for a second then hidden carefully. She leaned forward and put her hand on her sister-in-law's arm and Pam gave her a martyred look.

'What is it?' Maritia asked.

There was a pause as Wesley weighed up how much to reveal. 'There's been an incident. I'm needed, I'm afraid. The dinner was great, honestly. Just sorry I've got to go.'

'I'll see Pam home then,' said Mark, surveying his empty plate and earning himself a grateful look from his brother-in-law.

Maritia followed Wesley out and after he'd gone, pulling up the hood of his coat against the November drizzle, she stood for a while, quite still in the hall before fixing a smile to her face and returning to her guests.

Wesley would never have admitted it to his sister but he was rather relieved to escape from her dinner party. He'd never liked having to make polite conversation with people he hardly knew and probably wouldn't choose to mix with if he did.

He'd thought it best not to tell Maritia that, according to DCI Gerry Heffernan, the victim was a middle-aged doctor – he'd learned that much from the neighbours who'd found the body: with her colleague's unexplained absence, he hadn't wanted to worry her. Then he suddenly remembered that Mark had agreed to drive the worried Evonne to Dr Dalcott's address. The last thing he wanted was for them to turn up at a crime scene.

He found the house on the northern fringes of the village of Tradington and parked next to a high bare hedgerow that shielded the wide lane from the rolling fields

10

beyond. On the other side of the lane stood a row of three neat, cob-walled cottages fronted by deep gardens and, as he emerged from the car, he saw Gerry walking towards him down the path of the middle cottage. Gerry, a large middle-aged Liverpudlian, was usually ready with a quip but there was a solemn expression on his chubby face.

'Hi, Gerry,' he called out. 'Have we got a name for the victim?'

'Yeah. It's a Dr James Dalcott, local GP. The neighbours in that cottage identified him.' He pointed at the small cottage to the left of the victim's, the one with the lights blazing in the windows.

'What about the neighbours on the other side?'

'No answer and no lights on. Must be out. We'll have a word when they get back.'

'Cause of death?'

'Shot through the head, poor bugger. Didn't stand a chance.' He stood there for a moment, shifting from foot to foot on the muddy ground in an effort to keep warm.

'Look, Gerry, I'll have to make a phone call. I've just been at my sister's. James Dalcott's one of the partners in her practice – he was supposed to be there for dinner but he never turned up.'

'Well, now we know why,' said Gerry as he turned to face the house. The floodlights had arrived, lighting the area of the crime scene through a fine veil of drizzle while the white-clad Forensic team darted to and fro in their well-rehearsed choreography like figures on a stage.

The victim's house was fairly large for a cottage and double fronted, unlike its smaller neighbours. All the lights were on and the front door stood open, giving the place a welcoming look.

Wesley pulled out his phone and called his sister's number. It wasn't easy to break the news over the phone and he didn't have time to go into explanations. That could come later. Maritia sounded shocked and she kept asking him if he was sure it was James, as though she found the whole horrifying scenario hard to believe.

But it was the news that Mark and Evonne had already set out for Tradington that made his heart sink. He tried Mark's number but he was put straight through to voice mail. He called Maritia again to get Evonne's number but again he had no luck, which meant he would have to hang about on the fringes of the scene and turn them away tactfully when they arrived. And that wouldn't be the end of the matter for Evonne. As she'd obviously known James Dalcott well, they'd need to talk to her. Just as they'd need to talk to Maritia and all his other colleagues. Murder sends ripples out into the lives of everyone connected with the victim – Wesley had learned that very early on in his police career.

'Come on, Wes. Let's go and have a look.' Gerry handed him a crime scene suit to put on over his clothes. Gerry had already struggled into his and was standing there looking like a thawing snowman.

Just as Wesley was about to explain about Evonne's anticipated arrival, Mark's car appeared, slowing down before gliding to a halt. As soon as it stopped, Evonne leaped from the passenger seat.

Wesley wasn't quick enough to stop her and even the officer acting as crime scene manager, stationed at the gate with his clip board logging the comings and goings, was helpless in the face of her determined dash for the front door. Wesley heard shouts of 'Oi, you can't go in there,' but Evonne ignored them as she headed for her target.

She was screaming now. 'James. James.' And Wesley could only watch as she burst into the crime scene, depositing fingerprints and DNA everywhere before being held back by a well-built constable, the only one who'd managed to halt her progress towards the body on the ground.

He was suddenly aware of his brother-in-law, Mark, standing beside him, muttering an expletive that would have shocked some of his older parishioners. 'Well, I knew she was worried about him but . . . Want me to take her back?'

'Got it in one.'

'Might be best if she stayed the night with us, after a few stiff brandies.'

'Thanks. We'll speak to her tomorrow when she's had a chance to calm down.'

'Maritia'll look after her. Give her something to help her sleep if necessary.'

The well-built constable was leading her towards them. She was sobbing and he was muttering clichés of comfort into her ears. The officer looked relieved when Mark took charge with professional efficiency.

Once Mark's car had disappeared from sight, Gerry sidled up. 'Who was that screaming bird your brother-in-law had in tow?' he asked.

Wesley told him as he donned his crime scene suit. 'She's staying with my sister tonight – we'll go and have a word first thing. Now let's see what we've got here.'

As they began to walk towards the lights Wesley's eyes were fixed on the open front door. The body of Dr James

Dalcott was lying in the middle of the hallway and as Wesley drew nearer he could see the neat, blackened bullet wound in the centre of the dead man's forehead. A halo of red liquid spread across the parquet floor around the body as blood from the exit wound blended with red wine seeping from the plastic carrier bag the victim must have dropped when he died. Wine for the dinner party – wine Wesley himself had been intended to drink. James Dalcott's eyes were open, staring at the ceiling. He looked startled. But then if he was accosted unexpectedly on his way out of the house, death must have come as a considerable surprise.

'Wesley, Gerry, come in.' Dr Colin Bowman, the Home Office pathologist, had been leaning over the body but he straightened himself up when he saw them. 'Bad business,' he said with a solemn shake of the head. 'I only saw him last week at one of our medical dinners. Nice chap.'

Wesley felt the DCI give him a nudge in the ribs. 'Wes was due to have dinner with him tonight, weren't you, Wes? Only he never showed up.'

Colin looked Wesley in the eye. 'I didn't realise you knew him, Wesley.'

'My sister works – worked – with him. I'd never actually met him but she invited us all round for a meal. Did you know him well?' He asked the question in the hope that Colin might have picked up on a bit of medical gossip on his travels.

But Colin shook his head. 'To be honest I didn't. I know he's separated from his wife but apart from that . . .' Colin stared down at the body for a few seconds. 'Mind you, I can't imagine what he could have done to deserve this. The gun was fired at close range – two feet away at the most. Whoever did this must have looked him in the eye when he pointed the gun and pulled the trigger. Killed in cold blood – that's my guess, gentlemen.'

'Thanks, Colin,' Gerry said. 'So we're looking for a professional? A hit man?'

'Your guess is as good as mine. But I don't think we're looking for someone who acted in the heat of the moment.'

Wesley stepped away from the group huddled around the body and began to wander round the hallway, taking in his surroundings. There was no sign of forced entry, which either meant Dalcott let his killer in or the killer had been waiting there when he opened the door to leave the house, laden with the carrier bag containing the wine. He looked at the body again and saw a bunch of keys lying in the pool of wine and blood, dropped when the victim fell. He'd been on his way out all right, looking forward to – or maybe dreading – a congenial social evening with colleagues, when he met his brutal end.

He caught Gerry's eye. 'I'd like a word with the neighbours who found him. Coming?'

Gerry nodded. 'Nothing much we can do here. We'll leave Colin to it. When can you do the PM?'

'Tomorrow afternoon suit you?' Colin replied.

The crime scene team bustled around performing their mysterious tasks, taking little notice of the two detectives as they made their way outside, shedding their protective suits at the gate. It would hardly do to conduct serious interviews, Gerry observed, in oversized Babygros.

The neighbours who'd found the body lived in the house to the right of Dalcott's. A wooden gate led to a well-kept garden, neatened, pruned and swept for the winter. An old but immaculate Morris Minor sat in the driveway and a welcoming light glowed behind russet curtains. Wesley led the way and rang the doorbell.

The front door opened almost immediately, as though the householders had been waiting in the hall for their arrival. Standing there was a couple, probably in their mid-seventies. He was average height with an unusually smooth face, snow-white hair and a hand-knitted sweater; she was more than a foot shorter with a round face topped by steel-grey curls and a sweater identical to her husband's. It didn't take several years of experience in CID to tell Wesley that this pair included knitting and gardening in their list of hobbies and pastimes.

They looked at him expectantly and his instincts told him he'd struck gold. This was a retired couple with time on their hands: if anyone knew about the day-to-day life of James Dalcott, it would be them.

The detectives were invited in and provided with tea. Wesley guessed that the couple – who introduced themselves and Len and Ruby Wetherall – were rather enjoying themselves in their own way. Things had probably never been so exciting in that small South Devon village since the War.

Wesley saw Gerry give him a small nod. It was up to him to start the questions. 'Can you tell us what happened?' he began.

It was Ruby who answered, leaning forward as if she was about to share a confidence. 'Gave us the shock of our lives, it did. I'm still shaking . . . feel.' She extended a hand to Wesley who dutifully touched the sleeve of her sweater. He couldn't detect any shaking of the limb but he nodded in agreement.

16

'So how did you know something was wrong?' he prompted, trying to steer the interview towards the hard facts.

'We arrived home in the car, didn't we, Len?'

Len hesitated for a moment before nodding his head.

'Then Len said he'd seen James's door was wide open so he wandered over to have a look. You hear about all these burglars nowadays, don't you? We thought . . . Well, he thought he'd better just make sure everything was all right, didn't you, dear?'

'So you went up to the front door?' Gerry asked.

'That's right,' said Len. 'He was just lying there. He had a bag of shopping or something and some liquid was spilled all over the floor. I thought he'd had a heart attack at first. Then I noticed the . . . his head.'

Wesley saw Ruby shudder with vicarious horror.

'Then we called the ambulance and we asked for the police too,' she said. 'It didn't look right, did it, Len?'

'No, it didn't look right,' Len Wetherall echoed quietly.

'Did you notice the door was open, Mrs Wetherall?' Wesley asked innocently.

She shook her head. 'Can't say I did. When we pulled up I was too busy searching for my key, wasn't I, Len? I thought I'd lost it.'

'And had you?'

'No. I found it at the bottom of my handbag.'

'When you arrived home did either of you see anybody hanging around? Or anything unusual, apart from Dr Dalcott's door being open?' Wesley looked from one to the other but Ruby and Len shook their heads in unison.

'Can't say we did,' said Len.

'No, can't say we did,' Ruby echoed.

17

Wesley took a sip of tea. It was hot, strong and welcome. He gave Ruby an encouraging smile. 'What can you tell us about James?'

'Oh, he was a very nice neighbour, wasn't he, Len? Quiet. Friendly.' She glanced at Gerry. 'He was separated, of course. Roz, his wife's name is. And she's a flighty piece.'

Wesley couldn't help smiling to himself. It was a long time since he'd heard a woman described like that. The phrase somehow seemed to belong to an earlier, more innocent age.

'What did she do, love?' Gerry asked, a look of rapt attention on his face.

'Well, she left him for another man and now she lives in Tradmouth. And I heard she's having a baby by this new man. She must be forty if she's a day. I ask you.'

Wesley caught Gerry's eye. 'You wouldn't happen to know her address or the name of the man she lives with?' No doubt the information would be somewhere amongst Dalcott's belongings but a bit of local intelligence would save a lot of time.

The couple looked at each other. 'I don't know,' said Ruby. She looked disappointed at having to admit the limits of her knowledge.

'Does she work?'

Ruby snorted. 'Work? Her? Wouldn't get her hands dirty, that one.'

Her husband opened his mouth to speak, giving his wife a nervous glance as though he was afraid to contradict her. 'She does work, actually,' he said quietly. 'When I went to the dentists in Tradmouth the other week I saw her in an art gallery in the High Street.'

18

'Which gallery was this?' There were quite a few to choose from in Tradmouth High Street.

'It's the one with all those pictures of boats in the window.'

'They've all got pictures of boats in the window,' said Gerry with a hint of impatience.

'It's on the corner near the church. Quite a big place.'

Wesley saw Gerry's face light up in triumph. 'Trad Itions. That's what it's called. Daft name and daft prices. So you reckon she works there, do you?'

Len nodded meekly. 'I saw her sitting in there behind the counter but that's all I can tell you.'

Wesley had the feeling that this particular avenue had been exhausted. 'Is there anything else you can tell us? Anything at all out of the ordinary.'

But the Wetheralls shook their heads, almost in unison.

'Thanks, you've been a great help.'

'We're always happy to help the police, aren't we, Len?' Ruby said smugly.

As they left, Wesley noted the excitement in the woman's eyes. But there are always some, so he'd heard, who enjoy a good murder.

'Better get home and get some sleep, Wes,' Gerry said wearily. 'Early start tomorrow.'

Wesley looked at his watch. Midnight already and the black van had just arrived to take James Dalcott on his journey to the mortuary.

Eight o'clock on a Sunday morning was an hour Tony Persimmon hardly knew existed when he'd lived in London. At eight he would have been asleep after a tough week working at the headquarters of Pharmitest

International. He would have risen at eleven and read the Sunday papers over coffee and croissants. But those days were over. And as Nigel Haynes from the farm next door had specified eight o'clock sharp, take it or leave it, he'd thought it wise not to argue if he wanted the job done.

Tony and Jill Persimmon had known since the moment they set eyes on Tailors Court that it was ideal for their needs. Stone built. Sixteenth century. Plenty of outbuildings. Not too far from Neston. And cheap because it had been owned by an elderly woman who'd lived there for years and let the place go to rack and ruin.

Tony and Jill's priority had been to move in and get the business up and running and the renovations were more or less finished, although there were still some parts of the house that hadn't been tackled – unimportant rooms that could wait a while.

The outbuilding they'd earmarked for the office was just perfect – not too far from the house and large enough for all the equipment. Tony wasn't too sure what its original function had been. A cow shed, perhaps. Or some kind of storehouse. But that didn't matter now. It had already been pointed and plastered beyond recognition and after the modernisation was completed it was destined to be the hub of his consultancy business. And the other outbuildings, once converted, would be ideal for the children's clothing company Jill was developing. The one thing the outhouses lacked was electricity and it was costing a fortune to put in. But it had to be done. No electricity, no business. No business, no income.

This was supposed to be the good life away from the London traffic, crowds, pollution and the threat of violent crime, Tony thought as he watched Nigel Haynes scoop up a bucketload of red earth and deposit it delicately at the side of the trench. They had come to Devon with such plans, such optimism, and at first their stay had seemed like an extended holiday. But now the reality of the more measured pace of life and all the petty inconveniences of isolation was starting to get frustrating. In summer the countryside was gentle and stunning in its green, rolling beauty. But now winter had arrived Tony felt rather unprepared for the harshness of rural life once the tourists had gone.

He turned away, wondering if he could risk a trip to the house to make himself some coffee. Even though Nigel was a local farmer who, presumably, knew what he was doing, Tony was a little reluctant to leave him to his own devices. In London experience had taught him that tradesmen usually needed constant monitoring if disaster was to be avoided and Tony Persimmon was used to being in control. But he also wanted that coffee. He stood there wavering for a few moments, almost tasting the hot liquid, before reaching the conclusion that the few minutes he'd take to get himself a drink wouldn't be long enough for any corners to be cut.

When he tried to call out to Nigel, to tell him that he was going indoors for a few minutes and that he was to call him if there was any problem, however slight, his words became lost in the din made by the digger's engine. Nigel was too involved in his task to look up – either that or he chose not to, which Tony suspected was the case – so Tony walked slowly back to the house, glancing back every now and then to make sure the work was still carrying on without his supervising presence. Nigel Haynes was a tall, wiry man aged around thirty with fair wavy hair, freckles, and a mouth that naturally turned up at the corners; good looking in a rustic sort of way. He seemed pleasant enough, but more than once Tony had had a sneaking suspicion that the man was smirking at him behind his back. Even though Tony was determined to make a success of their escape to the country, there were times when he felt a little out of place; times when he yearned for the impersonal bustle of London where the basics of life were available twenty-four hours a day and there was a coffee shop on every corner.

As soon as he reached the back door of the house the digger's engine stopped, confirming Tony's worst suspicions. He turned round and saw that Nigel had climbed from his seat and was staring down into the ditch he had created. Tony could feel his blood pressure rising. He was paying the man to dig a trench for the electric cable. He wasn't handing over good money – cash of course, not a word to the taxman – for him to waste time like this.

Tony began to retrace his steps. If there was one thing he couldn't abide, it was people taking advantage of him. As he approached, Nigel made no attempt to move and kept staring down into the trench as though there was something fascinating down there.

'Problem, Nigel?' he asked in a businesslike voice. Even though Nigel was a neighbour, he didn't feel inclined to let the relationship get too cosy.

'Could be.' Nigel took off his cap and turned to face him. 'Come and have a look at this.'

Tony hesitated for a moment before leaning over the open trench. The smell of the freshly dug soil reached his nostrils, an unfamiliar scent of rotting vegetation and something else he couldn't quite name. As he squinted down he could see something pale lying against the darkness of the earth. 'What is it?'

'I don't reckon that's animal bone.' Nigel tilted his head to one side. 'Could be a dog, mind. It's a fair size but it isn't a cow or a pig, or even a sheep. I'd put money on that.'

Tony took in the bones lying at the bottom of the trench. 'It must be an animal,' he said with a confidence he didn't feel. After all, what did he know about bones?

He glanced down at his pristine green Wellingtons, thinking that it was about time he got some good Devon mud on them and gained himself some credibility amongst the natives. He jumped down into the trench and began to move the damp earth away from the bones.

'Careful,' said Nigel. 'Don't you think we should . . .?'

But Tony ignored him and carried on digging. He was surprised at how cold the soil felt on his bare hands as he uncovered more bones – surely too many for one individual. And when a skull finally appeared, its eye sockets clogged with earth, he knew this was the worst possible outcome. It could cost him time and it could cost him money. Then another skull emerged next to the first, grinning with crooked teeth as if it was sharing a joke with its companion.

A pair of buried human skeletons was bound to cause a tremendous amount of fuss and bother.

CHAPTER 2

Transcript of recording made by Mrs Mabel Cleary (née Fallon) – Home Counties Library Service Living History Project: Reminiscences of a wartime evacuee.

We were taken to this big hall where we had to wait to be picked. It was a church hall I think because there were pictures of Jesus on the wall and bits from the Bible I remember learning at Sunday School. I remember looking at all the faces of the grown-ups and saying a little prayer that I'd be chosen by someone kind and nice. I tried so hard not to cry but I could feel my lips quivering. I kept telling myself to be brave, that nobody would want a cry baby, and I bit back the tears. When any of the grown-ups came near, I didn't look them in the eye because I was too scared. And in the end, when I looked round, I saw that there were only three of us left that hadn't been chosen and I couldn't stop myself from crying any longer.

Then I heard one of the women who'd met us at the station – she was a school teacher I think, a bit on the bossy side – say that Mrs Jannings at Tailors Court hadn't been well enough to get down but she'd said she would take someone. A little girl. As the other two children left were boys, it looked as if it was my turn and I didn't know whether to be glad or sorry. Maybe, I thought, if they couldn't find me a place they'd send me home and that was where I wanted to be more than anything else. Just then I didn't care about the bombs. I wanted to be back with my mum.

The lady in charge told me I was going to a place called Tailors Court and she said that I'd have to be a good girl because Mrs Jannings was poorly. Then I was taken outside and put in a car. It was so full of passengers and it was such a squash that I had to sit on the lady's knee. Anyway, I was dropped off at this big old stone house – in the middle of nowhere. There was nobody about and it looked creepy, like a haunted house. I'd never seen a ghost and I didn't want to, thank you very much. When I looked at the windows upstairs, I thought I saw a face. Then it disappeared and I was scared. I didn't want to go in there but I knew I had to. Grin and bear it – that's what I had to do.

Then a young man wearing a soldier's uniform came round the side of the house. He looked cruel with thin lips, cold blue eyes and Brylcreemed black hair and he reminded me a bit of a boy called Peter Smith back home who used to bully me on the way home from school until my dad gave him a good belting. I remember feeling scared and wishing dad was there, but I knew he was fighting for his country and I had to be brave too. Chin up, I thought. Whatever was coming I had to grin and bear it.

The next morning Wesley left Pam fast asleep in bed and as he crept out of the house on that damp November Sunday the sky was a pale uniform grey and he realised it was dawn.

He felt tired. Last night Mark had brought Pam home to relieve the baby sitter and when Wesley arrived back at two in the morning she'd been awake and asking questions. Even though Pam had never met James Dalcott, his death had come as a shock. People you're about to have dinner with – people who work with your sister-in-law – aren't murdered like that. Such things belong to the rougher areas of inner cities; to gangs and drug dealers . . . not to a family doctor in a small Devon town.

Wesley had arranged to meet Gerry at the vicarage and as he turned into the drive he looked at the clock on the dashboard. Eight o'clock. He hadn't had time for breakfast so, hopefully, his sister would provide something to keep body and soul together but she was a busy woman – especially on a Sunday which was Mark's busiest day – so he wasn't banking on it. There was no sign of Gerry but punctuality wasn't his greatest strength.

It was Maritia who opened the door, her face tired and drawn.

'Mark's gone off to take early Communion,' she said, fastening the belt of her towelling dressing gown. She glanced at the staircase. 'Evonne's not up yet. She was in a bit of a state last night so I gave her a sedative.'

Wesley took his sister's arm and led her towards the living room. Without a word they both sat down, Maritia curling up on the sofa with her feet tucked underneath her.

Wesley leaned towards her, keeping his voice low. 'Look, I need some background on Dalcott . . . everything you know. Good and bad.'

She turned her head away. 'No privacy in death, is there?'

There was a long silence as she stared at her long, slender hands, wondering where to begin. 'He was a nice man, Wes, and I'm not just saying that 'cause he's dead – he really was a nice man. His patients adored him.' She suddenly looked a little unsure of herself. 'Well, most of them.'

He picked up on her last words. 'What do you mean?'

'Well, there was a complaint. But it wasn't James's fault. It could have happened to any of us. It's what you're always afraid of . . . misdiagnosis.'

'Tell me about it.'

She inhaled deeply. He could sense her reluctance to tell tales about the dead man but if they were to catch his killer, she'd have to overcome her scruples.

'It was about eighteen months ago, around the time I joined the practice. Being the new girl I had to learn most of it second-hand, but it seems that James was called out to attend a young child who had a fever and was generally unwell. He examined him, of course, and thought it was a virus but later that day, the parents called an ambulance and the child was rushed to hospital where it died. Turned out it was meningitis. James didn't make the correct diagnosis but if some symptoms – like the classic rash – aren't there it can be difficult. Anyway, the parents threatened to sue.'

'And did they?'

Maritia shook her head. 'No. They're only in their early twenties and probably not confident enough to play the system. They made do with slashing his tyres and scratching the word "killer" into his paintwork.'

'Did he report it to the police?'

'That's the thing: he felt so bad about the kid, he kept quiet about it. Everyone told him he should do something before it escalated.'

'And did it escalate?'

Maritia thought for a moment. 'No, funnily enough it didn't. It was almost as though they got bored with it all and gave up.'

Or were biding their time for the ultimate revenge, Wesley thought, although he didn't put his thoughts into words. 'What are the parents called?'

'Adam Tey and Charleen Anstice. I know that because she's pregnant again and they've started coming to see me. Always together. It's as though he never lets her out of his sight.'

'Understandable if they've lost one child.'

'Suppose so. Look, they're my patients so I can't really tell you any more.' She suddenly looked worried. 'In fact I've probably said far too much already.'

Wesley touched his sister's arm. 'Nobody's ever going to know it came from you, don't worry. I presume quite a few people knew of their campaign against James?'

Maritia nodded. 'Quite a few. And I wouldn't describe it as *their* campaign. I think it was all Adam – I don't think Charleen had anything to do with it. She's a bit of a mouse – wouldn't say boo to a goose.'

Before Wesley could say any more there was a thunderous banging on the front door. Somehow he knew it would be Gerry Heffernan who'd never believed in making an unobtrusive entrance. He walked out into the hall and opened the door. Gerry was standing there, his plump face solemn. Behind him stood DC Trish Walton, the regulation female presence.

'Is she up to talking?' Gerry asked as he marched in.

'She's still asleep. But I've just been talking to my sister.' He told the DCI what Maritia had told him about Adam Tey, leaving nothing out.

'So not everyone thought the sun shone out of the victim's backside. We need to talk to this Adam Tey.'

'Wesley. I didn't expect . . .' They turned to see a figure walking down the stairs. Evonne was clutching a red silk kimono around her body protectively. Her hair was tousled and without make-up she looked considerably older than she'd done the night before.

Wesley looked up at her, concerned. 'How are you feeling?'

Evonne yawned. 'Not good.'

'Are you up to answering some questions, love?' Gerry asked with none of his usual bluntness.

Evonne hesitated for a moment. 'I'll have to do it sooner or later, won't I? Might as well get it over and done with.'

'That's the spirit,' said Gerry with an attempt at jollity. He turned to Trish. 'How about a cup of tea, love? We all need something to wake us up this time on a Sunday morning.'

At that moment Maritia emerged from the drawing room and directed Trish to the kitchen. Then she put her arm round Evonne's shoulders, led her back into the room and sat her down on the sofa. Evonne gave her a weak

29

smile of gratitude as she sat down beside her. It was clear to Wesley that his sister had appointed herself Evonne's protector for the duration of the interview.

'Sorry, Maritia, I need a cigarette,' Evonne said apologetically.

Maritia nodded and searched for something to serve as an ashtray, abandoning her habit of dispensing health advice in the circumstances.

Wesley waited until Trish had handed round the tea before starting. By now Evonne seemed more relaxed and resigned to having three police officers in the room. The fact that she'd met Wesley socially the night before probably helped matters.

'So what was your relationship with James?' he began gently.

'We were . . . we were close.'

'Lovers?' He caught Gerry's eye warningly. The last thing he wanted was for him to interrupt and shatter the atmosphere of trust.

Evonne glanced at Maritia. Wesley, sensing that she might be more ready to open up if her colleague wasn't there, asked his sister if they could have some time alone. Maritia stood up, placing a comforting hand on Evonne's shoulder and telling her she'd only be upstairs getting dressed if she needed her. As she left the room, Evonne looked a little relieved.

Once Maritia had closed the door behind her, Gerry leaned forward. 'I know this is difficult, love, but we need you to tell us everything you know about James Dalcott.'

Evonne took a deep, shuddering breath and began. James was a caring man and a good doctor. She had always found him attractive but it was only when James's bitch of a wife walked out on him for a younger man that their relationship gradually became more than professional. He wasn't the sort of man to play away from home – unlike a lot of men she'd met. However, there had been no talk of them moving in together. They were more like two people on their own keeping each other company, she told them sadly. Wesley sensed that Evonne would like to have taken the relationship a step further. Perhaps James had hung back. Perhaps he still loved his wife. It was something they'd no doubt discover in the days and weeks to come.

Evonne repeated the story about Adam Tey's half-hearted attempts at revenge. 'But I swear he's the only one who could have anything against James,' she said. 'Everyone loved him. All his patients . . . everyone at the surgery. He wasn't the kind of man to have enemies.' She suddenly sat up straight. 'Adam Tey was upset but his girl-friend's expecting again. If he'd been going to do anything he would have acted before now . . . and he wouldn't risk being arrested now Charleen's pregnant again, would he? It must be a case of mistaken identity.'

Wesley thought that Evonne had a point but he said nothing. 'Is there anything else you can think of? Anything unusual that's happened recently?'

Evonne shook her head. 'No. Except that James has been a bit quiet over the past few weeks. Sort of preoccupied.'

'What with?' Gerry asked.

After considering the question for a few moments, Evonne answered. 'When I asked him if anything was wrong he just said it was family business. I assumed he meant Roz.'

Wesley was about to speak when he was interrupted by

the sound of his mobile phone. He really would have to get himself a less cheerful ring tone, he thought. A jolly salsa was hardly appropriate during a murder enquiry. Slightly embarrassed, he excused himself and left the room to take the call.

DC Paul Johnson's voice on the other end of the line was tentative and apologetic. 'Sorry to bother you, sir, but we've had a call from a householder near Tradington. I know you're tied up with the Dalcott murder but I thought you ought to know . . .'

'Know what?'

'Someone turned up some bones while he was digging a trench for an electricity cable. He says they look human and would someone come and have a look.'

Wesley stared ahead for a few moments. This was all he needed. 'Is he sure they're human?'

'He sounded pretty sure. Said there appear to be two human skeletons in the trench.'

The words echoed in Wesley's mind. Two human skele-tons. A double murder. His heart began to beat faster. If two victims were buried on the site there might be more.

He tried to tell himself that it was probably a couple of animals; that whoever had seen white bones against the dark earth had panicked, thinking the worst. But the more he tried to convince himself that there was nothing to worry about, the more his mind kept creating horrifying scenarios: going back over old missing person cases, the discovery of more bodies, blanket press coverage. The ter-rifying prospect of a serial killer operating on their patch. But he was jumping the gun. Pam had always accused him of being too pessimistic.

'Has anyone gone to have a look?'

'A patrol car's attending the scene. We're waiting to hear back from them but I thought you'd want to know. Just a moment, that could be them now.'

While Paul took the other call, Wesley wondered whether to mention the matter to Gerry. But he decided to wait. The tall lanky Paul, with his enthusiasm for athletics and Trish Walton, was a good officer but he was inclined to be rather cautious, even pedantic. When he came off the phone, however, his voice was deadly serious.

'Yes, that was the patrol, sir. The bones are definitely human and there appear to be two individuals in the grave. Uniform are requesting a CID presence right away. And scientific support's been called. They've requested an archaeologist too, sir . . . to help with the digging. I think that friend of yours from the County Archaeological Unit has been called out.'

'Fine,' Wesley heard himself say. He hadn't seen Neil Watson for a couple of weeks as he'd been up in Exeter catching up on his post-excavation paperwork. 'We're in the middle of interviewing a witness in the Dalcott case but I'll let the DCI know about the development,' he said.

'How soon can you get down to Tailors Court? It's just outside Tradington off the Neston road.'

Tradington again. James Dalcott had lived and died in Tradington. But there could hardly be a link to a pair of skeletons in a field. It was just an unfortunate coincidence. Bad timing.

'I'll be over as soon as I can,' Wesley said before ending the call.

DS Rachel Tracey had been given the job of breaking the news to Dalcott's widow. Somehow she suspected that Mrs

Dalcott wouldn't be a widow of the grieving variety. She had taken up with a younger man and abandoned her boring husband so, who knows, Rachel thought, she might even welcome the tidings of James's death. It would probably solve a lot of her problems.

She'd discovered Rosalind Dalcott's new address from the owner of Trad Itions who'd received her call at seven-thirty that morning. He hadn't seemed pleased at being awoken at such an unearthly hour on a Sunday, especially as he told Rachel that he'd been at a party and only arrived home at three in the morning. She sensed he had bitten his tongue, knowing that being rude to a police officer isn't usually advisable.

Rachel was surprised to learn that Roz Dalcott rented the flat above the shop where she worked. The place had been empty so Roz had moved in there with her new partner which had been a satisfactory arrangement for everyone. They were no trouble, paid some rent and kept an eye on the premises.

When Rachel arrived outside Trad Itions at nine o'clock it was raining and the streets were deserted. In November all but the hardiest of tourists had scurried back to their own towns, leaving Tradmouth to its residents. The building that housed the gallery was tall and half timbered, one of a row of similar late medieval dwellings saved from the attentions of overenthusiastic town planners in the early part of the twentieth century by some good fortune which hadn't extended to its neighbours opposite, which had been replaced years ago by a block of uninspiring flats. Now the row, not far from St Margaret's church, was regarded as one of Tradmouth's jewels. And Trad Itions stood in the middle, a bright display of paintings and prints in its front window.

There was an old oak door beside the shop and Rachel pressed the entryphone button. Before long a disembodied male voice grunted a greeting and as soon as she identified herself she heard a faint buzz. She pushed at the door and as she climbed the steep narrow staircase a door at the top opened slowly to reveal a man wearing a thin woman's dressing gown which strained across his chest revealing an interesting array of tattoos and leaving little to Rachel's imagination. She guessed he was in his early thirties and he was tall with dark hair and a good-humoured mouth. And in spite of the fact that his hair was ruffled and he hadn't shaved, Rachel couldn't help registering the fact that he was extremely attractive. For a second she stood there, lost for words, before holding up her warrant card and asking if she could speak to Mrs Rosalind Dalcott.

'What's she done?' he quipped as he stood aside to let Rachel in. As she brushed past him in the narrow doorway she could feel the heat of his body. Had the proximity been deliberate, she wondered. He looked the sort of man who was confident about his own sex appeal.

She entered the low-beamed living room and looked around. The place had character in abundance but she would have found the oppressive dark wood panelling somewhat hard to live with. Suddenly a woman appeared at the door. She was in her forties and perhaps she would have looked better later in the day, Rachel thought, once she had had a chance to plaster on some make-up. But even then she probably wouldn't have been able to hide the telltale signs of encroaching age: the jowls that had

35

just started to lose their firmness, the spider's web of lines around the eyes, the plumpness around the middle of her body. Her hair was blonde and shoulder length – one thing she could control with a simple visit to the hairdressers. She wore a loose-fitting smock top over jeans and had the dishevelled look of someone who'd dressed in a hurry. Rachel's inner bitch wondered what her new man saw in her. Perhaps she had a sparkling personality.

Then Rachel suddenly realised that the baggy top concealed the fact that Roz Dalcott was pregnant – a mid-life baby.

'Mrs Dalcott?' Rachel said.

'I suppose I still am, technically speaking. Why? What do you want?' Her words were offhand, almost rude.

Normally in situations like this Rachel didn't have to feign sympathy with bereaved widows: she could usually feel for them. But Rosalind Dalcott was different. There was a hardness in her expression that put Rachel on her guard. But she still fixed a solemn look on her face and carried on going through the motions. 'I'm very sorry to have to bring bad news, Mrs Dalcott, but I'm afraid your husband, James Dalcott, was found dead at his home last night.'

Rachel saw the woman slump down on the leather sofa. She looked genuinely shocked, unlike her partner who started examining his fingernails in an attitude of boredom.

'What was it?' she asked almost in a whisper. 'Heart attack?' She gave a nervous half smile. 'That's James all over, killed by pie and chips. That was his favourite, you know. Talk about healthy eating . . . he wasn't one to practise what he preached.' She looked straight at Rachel.

'Look, thanks very much for coming to tell me but . . . Harry'll show you out, won't you, Harry?'

But Rachel hadn't finished yet. 'I'm afraid that's not all, Mrs Dalcott.'

She saw Roz glance at the man she'd called Harry, the father of her child. He looked away.

'What is it? Do I need to identify him or something?'

Rachel cleared her throat. 'His neighbour's already done that but we might need a formal identification down at the mortuary.' She hesitated, searching for the words. 'The truth is, Mrs Dalcott, your husband was murdered.'

Rosalind Dalcott sat there for a few moments, opening and closing her mouth, completely lost for words.

It was Harry who broke the silence. 'How? When?'

'He was shot at his home yesterday evening. Some time between seven o'clock and eight. Where were you then, Mr . . . er . . .'

'Parker. Harry Parker. I was here. We both were. We didn't go out all evening, did we, Roz?'

Roz Dalcott shook her blonde tresses and they fell forward to shield her face. Harry sat down heavily beside her and grasped her hand protectively.

'This is a bit of a shock, Sergeant Tracey. Roz is expecting our baby,' he said with a hint of pride. 'Maybe we could leave this till later, eh?'

Rachel's instincts told her that she'd get nothing out of this pair now, although she didn't really feel inclined to leave them so that they could cook up a story between them. However, it looked as though she had little choice. An accusation of bullying a pregnant woman whose husband had just died violently wouldn't look good if the pair chose to make a complaint. Resigned, she managed to muster a sympathetic smile and promised to come and see them later.

Harry left Roz on the sofa, head in hands, and showed Rachel out.

'What is it you do?' Rachel asked out of sheer curiosity when they reached the foot of the stairs.

'I'm an artist,' he said shyly, wrapping the thin dressing gown more tightly around his body. He hesitated. 'Some of my stuff's in the gallery through there.'

He nodded towards a door to his right. Then, unexpectedly, he unbolted it and led Rachel through into the shop. When she'd arrived her mind had only registered the paintings at the front of the window – bright and attractive depictions of yachts in the Tradmouth sunlight. But Harry was making for some large canvases at the back of the gallery. They were painted in oils, the predominant colour being red, and in the dim light Rachel could see that they seemed to be abstract human figures, or parts of figures. And in a couple it looked as though flesh had been peeled back to reveal the inner workings of the subjects' bodies. They were vivid and they were brilliant. But there was no way Rachel would have fancied having any of them on her wall.

'What do you think?' he asked as though seeking reassurance. 'I used to do the tourist stuff – seascapes and harbour scenes and all that – but . . .'

'They're . . . they're very . . .' She searched for a tactful word. 'Powerful.' She felt rather pleased with herself for finding a term that made it sound as if she knew what she was talking about.

'They were inspired by some drawings I found painted on the plaster behind the panelling in the flat. Don't know

38

how they came to be there. Anyway, I was poking around one day and there they were – the sort of thing you find in medical text books. Odd thing to draw on a wall but . . .'

He suddenly looked unsure of himself. Like any artist, she thought, it seemed he was prone to self-doubt. But that really wasn't any of her business.

'We'll need statements from both of you,' she said, businesslike. 'I'll be in touch.'

As she left she glanced back at the pictures. Her initial impression had been right, she thought: they gave her the creeps.

'Of course, they could have been there years. Centuries.' Dr Neil Watson ran his fingers through his long fair hair. It was rather too early on a Sunday morning for his liking and he had been in bed when he'd received Wesley's call. But for the past few weeks he had been officebound, working on post-excavation reports, so he'd thrown on his digging clothes and climbed straight into his ancient yellow Mini to drive down to Tradington, eager to get his hands dirty again.

'Well, we won't know until you get to work,' Wesley said. 'Sorry I can't give you a hand but I'm not exactly dressed for it.' Wesley, with his archaeology degree, liked to keep his hand in occasionally but one look at all that cold clinging mud, a result of recent record rainfall in the south west, made him glad he'd be a spectator until the bones were safely lifted.

Wesley saw that they had an audience: Tony and Jill Persimmon were standing some way away, wrapped up in scarves and gloves, clinging to each other as if for comfort.

He could hear church bells in the distance, a merry

sound which reminded him once more that it was Sunday morning. But when the police have to deal with suspicious death, one day was much the same as another.

Neil had brought his equipment with him in the boot of his car and his trowels and kneeling mats were now laid out neatly. He wore a crime scene suit too, just in case there was evidence of foul play down in the trench which might become contaminated. Wesley watched while he chatted with some of the Forensic team, discussing tactics. Then, after what seemed like an age, he climbed carefully down into the trench and began to scrape the muddy soil away from the bones.

The rooks cawed and mocked in the skeletal trees, rising in a black cloud at the sound of a distant gunshot – a farmer out after vermin. Wesley watched the birds settle again in the bare branches before returning his attention to the trench. The police photographer was recording each stage of Neil's excavation as the archaeologist worked carefully, searching for any tiny clue that might explain how the bones ended up in their miserable resting place and placing objects carefully in a plastic tray.

'Hello there.' Wesley looked up and saw Dr Colin Bowman striding towards them. Wearing a waxed jacket and green Wellingtons, he could have been mistaken for a prosperous gentleman farmer, if it weren't for the large medical bag he carried. 'What have we got here, then?' He seemed subdued, not his usual cheery self.

'Two articulated skeletons buried about three feet down. Not laid out neatly as far as I can see. In fact I'd say they'd been thrown in there unceremoniously.'

Colin's expression was solemn. 'I'd better have a look. Do you mind, Neil?'

Neil helped him down into the trench and he and Wesley watched while the pathologist made a cursory examination.

'No obvious cause of death,' was the verdict as he climbed back onto the grass. 'And no sign of dental work. If you'd be good enough to lift them after the photographers have finished, Neil, I'll have a good look back at the mortuary.' He turned to Wesley. 'I'll see you this afternoon, won't I, Wesley. James's . . .' His voice trailed off.

'Yes. I'll be there with Gerry,' Wesley answered, trying to hide his dread of what was to come later that day. Although he came from a medical family, he had always been squeamish. The odd one out.

Once Colin had bade them a businesslike farewell and all the recording was complete, Neil lifted the bones carefully and put them onto a waiting plastic sheet. It seemed an age before the two skeletons lay there, whole except for some tiny foot and hand bones which had probably disintegrated during the time they'd lain in the earth. It was a sad sight, all that was left of two human beings lying on a layer of cold plastic that glistened like ice on the sparse grass.

'Any idea how long they've been down there?' Wesley asked when Neil had finished.

Neil bent down and took something out of the plastic tray. He handed Wesley a mud-caked object and Wesley scraped the dirt away with his fingers. Soon the shape emerged from the shroud of soil.

'I found it embedded in the wall of the trench, a couple of feet above the bone.'

'It looks like a badly corroded knife blade,' he said softly. 'What do you make of it?'

41

Neil took it from him. 'Yes, I think it could be a knife or dagger: probably had a wooden handle which rotted away long ago. It certainly looks pretty old but I'll have to get an expert to have a look at it.'

Wesley took the object back and studied it. It did nudge a vague and distant memory – perhaps of something he'd found during his student days. But did it have anything to do with the burials? Maybe not. Maybe some inhabitant of Tailors Court had just lost a pocket knife there many years before. A coincidence.

He looked down at the bones lying on the plastic. From his student days Wesley knew enough about human skeletons to tell from the shape of the pelvis that one of these bodies had been a man in life and one a woman. A couple perhaps. Killed and thrown in a trench to rot. But he needed to know how long they'd been there. And whether it was his job to investigate how they met their end.

His thoughts were interrupted by the cheerful ringing of his mobile phone. It was Gerry Heffernan wanting to be kept up to date with developments. As soon as Wesley had finished giving him the bare facts, there was a long silence on the other end of the line.

'So are these skeletons recent – say less than seventy years old? In other words, are they our problem?'

'Can't say yet, Gerry. Colin's been here but he can't tell us anything until he's examined the bones back at the hospital.'

He heard Gerry mutter something under his breath. 'This is all we need what with James Dalcott.'

Wesley said nothing. The possibility of a double murder was bound to make the headlines and capture the public imagination, even if it happened years ago.

The Forensic team were going about their business in

the trench Neil had just abandoned, taking samples and painstakingly sifting the soil under Neil's watchful eye. Wesley edged up to his friend. 'Well?'

Neil gave him a half-hearted smile. 'I'm going to get some geophysics equipment down here, just to make sure there aren't any more burials.'

It was something Wesley hadn't liked to think about but now Neil had put it into words he had to acknowledge the possibility. He looked round. 'It's close to the outbuilding and not too far from the main house. A random killer dumping the bodies would have chosen somewhere more isolated. There's plenty of woodland around here.'

'Mmm. Once we've established how old the bones are we'll have to find out all we can about the history of the place. House looks pretty old.'

'Well, let's hope the bones are too.'

Neil didn't answer. 'How's Pam?'

'OK,' Wesley said quickly. 'Have you heard about the shooting here in Tradington last night?'

Neil raised his eyebrows. 'No.'

'It was a doctor. One of my sister's colleagues.'

Neil uttered an expletive. 'Do you know who did it? Dissatisfied patient or . . .?'

'We're following a number of leads.'

Neil smirked. 'Don't sound so bloody formal, Wes. You must have your suspicions.'

'It's early days. What about you? What have you been doing with yourself?'

'You know how it is. Where do archaeologists go in wintertime? We've just finished a site assessment of some land earmarked for a new supermarket outside Plymouth and I've been catching up on a lot of post-excavation reports.

But you know me. I can't stand being cooped up in an office doing paperwork so this has come as a bit of a relief. Always happy to help the police with their enquiries.' He looked round. 'I'd better give your Forensic team a hand. Then I'll have a word with the people who own the place.' He nodded towards Tony and Jill Persimmon who were still standing there watching the proceedings.

'They look frozen stiff.'

'Yeah. I want to get inside that house. Look at those wings. I reckon they're Elizabethan but the central section's definitely fifteenth century or even older.'

Wesley smiled to himself. The archaeology of buildings had been Neil's secret passion in their university days, even though most of his work now involved digging things out of the ground.

'If I can manage to get the geophysics equipment over here tomorrow, I might be able to hang around for a few days yet. Sweet talk the owners into letting me have a peep at their roof space,' Neil went on, almost rubbing his hands together in gleeful anticipation.

Wesley glanced at his watch. 'I'd better go and see whether anything's come in on that shooting. And I've got to attend the post mortem this afternoon.'

'Rather you than me. Look, I'll call in on Pam if I get the chance – bring a ray of sunshine into the lonely existence of a policeman's wife.'

Wesley attempted a smile. 'I'd better go,' he said, suddenly reluctant to leave. At that moment he was more intrigued by the skeletons at Tailors Court than he was about the demise of James Dalcott. His mobile began to ring again and when he looked at the display he saw that it was Gerry.

He couldn't put off his departure any longer. Duty called.

The police had already called at the small 1960s terraced house in a cul de sac near Neston Railway Station. But Adam Tey hadn't opened the door. There was no way he wanted to talk to them and Charleen felt the same. They had both sat, still as statues upstairs in the tiny bedroom, listening to the spirited knocking on the front door, waiting with breath held until the callers had gone away.

Now they had summoned the courage to come downstairs, Adam left Charleen in the lounge and stared at the grubby telephone on the hall table, wondering whether to make the call. After a few moments of indecision he picked up the receiver.

He'd toyed with the idea of calling round at Carl's flat because he didn't want to risk Charleen overhearing what he had to say. But Carl didn't always answer his door so a phone call was probably best.

He closed the lounge door carefully. Charleen was in there watching telly. She never went out these days, except to the clinic. It was almost as if she was afraid of what might happen to her out there – afraid that she might encounter something that would harm the baby. And Adam knew things wouldn't get any better once it was born. She had lost one child so this new one was bound to be wrapped in several layers of cotton wool. Adam realised this probably wasn't healthy but he couldn't blame Charleen. But he could blame Dr Dalcott. It was all his fault. And now he'd got what he deserved.

When Carl Utley answered Adam lowered his voice. 'Dalcott's dead.'

Utley put the receiver straight down without uttering a word in reply.

An incident room was being set up in Neston Police Station. It was nearer the scene of Dalcott's death than Tradmouth and there was a free open-plan office, ideal for the purpose. Several officers seconded to the team from Neston endured quips about Neston's New Age tendencies from their Tradmouth counterparts. But Wesley knew that Gerry would stand no nonsense. A respected local doctor had been shot dead in his own home and the culprit needed to be caught and caught quickly.

After Gerry had briefed the team with his usual blend of bluntness and Liverpudlian wit, it was time to attend James Dalcott's post mortem. As Wesley drove to Tradmouth Hospital he didn't feel like talking. But Gerry had other ideas. He wanted to go over what they had so far, which wasn't much.

'The search team found nothing out of the ordinary at Dalcott's house, apart from a dead body, that is. And Rachel's broken the news to the not-so-grieving widow and met the boyfriend,' Gerry continued. 'Our Rach seemed rather taken with him. Says he's an artist – very talented.' He paused. 'How's her love life these days?' Gerry had always been one for a bit of juicy gossip.

There was a short silence while Wesley tried to think up an answer. 'As far as I know she's still with Barty Carter but she hasn't mentioned him recently.' The first time Rachel had met Carter, a city boy trying his hand unsuc-cessfully at running a smallholding, he had threatened her with a shotgun. Even though all that had been forgiven by

Rachel, Wesley himself was dubious about the match, although he'd never have said so to her face.

'Bad sign,' was Gerry's verdict, given with all the authority of a hanging judge. 'Does she reckon the widow or her fancy man could have done it?'

'Their only alibi is each other.'

'Put them at the top of our list then. What about this Adam Tey who blames Dalcott for the death of his kid?'

'Not in, or not answering his door.'

'Another one for the list. For a man who was supposed to have no enemies there seem to be quite a few folk who'd be happy to dance on his grave, don't you think, Wes?'

Wesley didn't answer. They'd reached the centre of Tradmouth and he was searching for a space in the hospital car park. When he had no success he drove to the police station where he knew he'd find a welcome. It was raining now and Gerry gave a token grumble about the walk as both men pulled up their collars against the wind blowing in from the river and headed for the hospital.

'And what about these skeletons?' Gerry asked as they walked quickly towards the mortuary. 'Are they old or what?'

'No clues either way at the moment,' Wesley answered. 'As far as I know the Forensic team haven't found much but Colin's going to examine them later. There was something near the bones that Neil reckons might be a knife blade. Probably very old.'

'Was it with the bodies?'

'A couple of feet away.'

'So it could have nothing to do with the burial.'

'Possibly not. And if it turns out they're recent, we'll

have to pull out the files on every man and woman who've gone missing over the past . . .'

'Don't be so pessimistic, Wes. They might have been murdered by William the Conqueror.'

Wesley smiled. 'Let's hope, eh?'

They'd reached the hospital and Wesley pushed open the plastic swing doors leading to the mortuary. He was used to the place but he still felt a pang of dread in the pit of his stomach whenever he entered those doors and they swished shut behind him, trapping him in with the dead.

Colin seemed to have recovered from his initial shock at hearing of a fellow medic's murder and he invited them to take pre-post mortem refreshments which Gerry accepted, muttering something about dying for a decent cup of tea. He could have chosen his words more carefully, given the surroundings, Wesley thought.

After a refreshing cup of Darjeeling Wesley knew the ordeal couldn't be put off for much longer. As Gerry and Colin made their way to the post mortem room, he followed behind like a reluctant schoolboy making for the headmaster's office. He knew what was coming – he'd been through it so many times before but it never seemed to get any easier. When she'd been studying medicine at Oxford, Maritia used to tease him with tales of how she'd been dissecting bodies. He'd tried not to listen, to think of something else, but he'd still had nightmares.

James Dalcott was waiting for them, lying on a bed of shiny stainless steel. His eyes had been closed now and he looked as though he was sleeping, apart from the dark bullet hole which stood out against the pale flesh of his forehead.

'Forgot to tell you, gentlemen, the widow came in with

a policewoman a couple of hours ago,' Colin said as he prepared to make the first incision in the flesh. 'Didn't seem too grief-stricken. In fact I had the impression that she was more interested in making sure he was dead,' he said with the ghost of a wink.

'Some wives are like that,' said Gerry wistfully, although Wesley knew he didn't speak from experience. As far as he knew, Gerry's marriage to his late wife, Kathy, had been happy and he hadn't embarked upon another relationship until a long time after her tragic death in a hit and run accident.

Colin began work, dictating his notes into a microphone suspended above the corpse. According to Colin's observations, James Dalcott was a fairly healthy fifty-four-year-old man; a little overweight but with no sign of serious disease. Cause of death was a bullet wound to the head. One shot through the forehead at fairly close range. An efficient assassination. The bullet, which had passed through the brain, leaving a larger exit wound in the back of the head, had been retrieved from the scene and sent off for analysis.

Dalcott's killer had stood a couple of feet away and looked into his victim's eyes as he pulled the trigger. It took a great deal of hatred, Colin observed, to do something like that. Either that or a cold-hearted assassin with no ounce of human feeling. And Wesley, his eyes fixed on a steel trolley at the other side of the room, thought Colin had probably got it spot on.

If they discounted the hit man theory, they were left with the possibility that someone had hated James Dalcott enough to make them a cold-blooded killer. Adam Tey and Charleen Anstice had reason to hate the doctor who'd misdiagnosed their child's meningitis. And they weren't answering the door, which meant either that they were spending Sunday away from home, or that they didn't want to speak to the police. As far as Wesley was concerned, Tey was top of their list with the widow and her new partner a close second.

'I'll let you have the full report as soon as possible,' Colin said as he left his assistant to sew up the incisions and clear up. 'Now, about these skeletons.'

Wesley felt relieved. Skeletons he could handle. It was the blood and gore he didn't like. 'What about them?'

'Well, I've made a quick examination. Why don't we have a look, eh?' He began to lead them into the next room – white tiled again like the post mortem room. The two skeletons were arranged on separate trolleys, the bones a grubby beige against the crisp white of the sheets they lay on. Someone, Colin probably, had laid them out properly and Wesley could see immediately that one skeleton, the female, was considerably smaller than the other.

'The female has Harris lines. I noticed them particularly on the shin bones.'

Wesley looked up sharply. 'That's interesting.'

'What are Harris lines when they're at home?' Gerry asked, impatient.

'They're lines in the bones which indicate a halt in growth during childhood and adolescence, say in a time of illness or famine. At some time in this woman's early life she went hungry.' He turned to Colin. 'What about ages?'

'A few of the male's teeth are missing and those that are left are worn but not decayed. And he shows signs of having done manual labour. Don't you agree?'

It was a long time since Wesley had studied ancient

skeletons as part of his degree course but he remembered the basics. At Colin's invitation, he conducted his own cursory examination, while Gerry watched, interested.

The man was around five feet six inches tall and, as well as the wear on the teeth, there were signs of wear and tear on the joints that indicated that he was probably middle-aged when he met his end. Wesley had seen similar skeletons in his student days – manual workers from centuries gone by. And there was something else. A healed fracture of the left arm, the bones set at an awkward angle. This man, whoever he was, had not had access to medical expertise and had probably been in considerable discomfort. There also appeared to be an old injury to the left shoulder area, healed like the arm with the bones fused untidily together.

'So he underwent some sort of trauma at some point in his life, Colin?'

Colin peered at the bones. 'Some years before death, I'd say.' He looked up at Wesley. 'A fight maybe. Or an accident?'

'Or battle?'

'It's a possibility.'

'You mean he could have been an old soldier?' said Gerry. 'The question is, which war?

Wesley ignored the question and turned his attention to the woman's bones. They were smaller, more delicate and the teeth were less worn.

'She was much younger,' Colin said. 'And, as I said, the Harris lines indicate that she didn't receive adequate nourishment while she was growing up.'

'So how old?' Gerry asked.

'Well, from the teeth, I'd say late teens, early twenties.

Her wisdom teeth are just coming through and I don't think she'd ever given birth. No sign of trauma to this one but . . . have a close look, Wesley. Tell me if you notice anything odd,' Colin said as he handed over a magnifying glass he'd taken from a nearby shelf.

Wesley glanced at Gerry who was watching expectantly, full of curiosity. Then he bent over the bones and began to examine them carefully. After a minute of so he straightened up, a puzzled frown on his face.

'Are you thinking what I'm thinking?' Colin asked.

'What is it?' Gerry asked impatiently.

Colin took a deep breath. 'Well, I don't know if Wesley agrees with me but I think there are faint cut marks on some of the bones. I noticed similar ones on the male. It's as if . . .'

'You mean they've been butchered?' Gerry sounded quite alarmed. 'You mean we're talking about cannibalism, here in Devon?' He rolled his eyes. 'I can just see the headlines.'

Wesley caught Colin's eye and they exchanged a smile. 'There's no sign of butchery, Gerry. Besides, the skeletons are complete. It's something else.'

'What?'

It was Colin who delivered the final verdict. 'I can't be sure, of course. There could be a number of explanations but . . . well, it's possible that these corpses were dissected after death.'

One look at Gerry's expression told Wesley that this didn't seem to make things any better.

When Wesley arrived back at the incident room he rang Pam, just to remind her that he was still alive. He felt guilty about leaving her to entertain the children on her own on what should be a day of rest. But then guilt went with the territory. If they could harness guilt as a power source, he thought, all the country's energy problems might be solved.

He had just sat down to read through a batch of witness statements when DC Nick Tarnaby shuffled up to his desk wearing his usual morose expression. Tarnaby had only been with CID for five months, brought in to replace Steve Carstairs who had died in the course of his duty attempting to rescue a murder suspect from the sea, an act which had earned him the status of hero in death. Wesley hadn't liked the swaggering racist Steve and he wasn't sure that he particularly liked Tarnaby either.

He looked up and forced himself to smile. 'What can I do for you, Nick?'

'We've had no luck with that Adam Tey, sir. Nobody at the address we were given.'

This wasn't good news. They needed to speak to Tey and his partner. But it was the weekend so perhaps they were away. Or lying low.

He saw that Tarnaby was consulting a sheet of paper in his hand. 'Anything else?'

'Yeah. I was asked to check out some names and one looks promising.' He put the paper down on Wesley's desk. 'Harry Parker's got a record. Robbery, burglary and threatening behaviour.'

Wesley picked up the sheet and read it. 'Thanks, Nick,' he said to Tarnaby's disappearing back. It looked as if Rosalind Dalcott's new partner was no angel. But did that necessarily mean he'd want James Dalcott dead?

CHAPTER 3

Transcript of recording made by Mrs Mabel Cleary (née Fallon) – Home Counties Library Service Living History Project: Reminiscences of a wartime evacuee.

The soldier looked me up and down but before he could say anything the lady who'd brought me in the car came up and took my hand. 'Hello, Miles, I've got an evacuee for your mother,' she said.

At first he didn't utter a word. He just kept staring at me and it made me scared. Then he said 'She's poorly. Don't you think she's got enough on her plate?' He spoke in a funny way like the other people down there. Not like the people I knew in London.

'I was told she'd take a girl,' she said. I could tell she was cross. 'Anyway, she's got no choice. Everyone's got to do their bit. There's a war on, you know.'

Then the soldier suddenly smiled, all charming and

said that he was sure it'd be all right and that she could leave me there if she liked.

But the woman wasn't having any of it. 'I'll have to see your mother,' she said. 'It has to be done properly.'

Miles wasn't smiling now. He picked up a big long gun that was propped up against the door and for a moment I thought he was going to point it at her. I was starting to feel frightened but he bent the gun in two and balanced it over his arm. 'You'd better go up,' he said. 'But remember she's poorly.'

As I climbed the stairs a pretty lady in a green jersey and trousers came out of one of the downstairs rooms. She looked at me for a few moments then she gave me a friendly smile. I smiled back and gave her a little wave and I thought that if this lady was there I'd probably be all right.

Then I met Mrs Jannings and I cried for the rest of the day.

Neil Watson drove down from his flat in Exeter early on Monday morning. He'd made phone calls the evening before, calling in a few favours, and he'd negotiated the loan of the geophysics equipment which was now sitting in the boot and back seat of his Mini. He'd also managed to persuade a few colleagues to help him. It hadn't been hard to lure them away from their paperwork with the promise of some real archaeology, especially once he'd told them about the skeletons and the knife blade.

He'd felt rather excited the night before when Wesley had called to pass on Colin Bowman's conclusions. The skeletons were possibly centuries old, and the mention of the marks on the bones had intrigued him. Perhaps Colin, with his medical mind on dissection and autopsies, had jumped to incorrect conclusions. Perhaps there was another explanation. If only he could think of one. Perhaps it would come to him on the journey down to Tradington.

He arrived at Tailors Court to find the place deserted, but then his colleagues weren't due for another hour. The trench lay abandoned and covered with a tarpaulin. He knew that the Forensic team had made their examination, taken their photographs and collected their samples but if the skeletons were proved to be old, they would lose interest pretty rapidly. Neil was pretty certain they were old. But if the geophysics survey did turn up any more bodies and those bodies had modern dental work, he would be forced to change his mind.

He walked towards the house in the fine drizzle, zipping up his aged combat jacket. He hoped the Persimmons would have a roaring fire and a cup of hot tea for him. But he knew that there was a strong risk of disappointment. They hadn't looked too delighted about the invasion of police and archaeologists onto their property.

The front door was ancient oak with a huge iron knocker at its centre. As Neil couldn't see a bell push, he lifted the knocker and when he let it fall twice the thunderous noise within the house was loud enough to awaken the dead. While he was waiting for the door to open, he took a step back and studied the house. The central section was mellow grey stone and, even though it must have been altered many times over the years, at its core was a traditional Devon longhouse, accommodating a family at one end and animals at the other. The two stone-built wings that sprouted either side were built in the same material but in a different, more boastful style. At some point in the house's history an effort had been made to push the place upmarket and convert it from a working farm to a home fit for gentry.

The door was opened by Jill Persimmon who looked wary at first. Then her expression changed to one of polite curiosity when she recognised him.

'Oh, you're the archaeologist, aren't you?'

'That's right. Mind if I come in?'

She looked down disapprovingly at his boots and he got the message. He took them off and left them neatly on the doormat before following her into the house.

When he'd received the cup of tea he'd been hoping for, Jill sat down opposite him and leaned forward, as if preparing to share a confidence.

'Those skeletons . . . they are old, aren't they? The last thing we want is to have police crawling all over the place. We need to get the electrics into the outhouse so that Tony can get the consultancy going. And then there's my business. We just can't afford any delays. You do see that, don't you?'

Neil said nothing for a few moments. It really wasn't his problem. But he decided that it was probably safe to put her mind at rest on one thing at least. 'As far as I can tell, the skeletons look old, maybe a few hundred years.'

Jill Persimmon looked relieved. 'So we'll be able to carry on with the work?'

'Well, you'll need a go-ahead from the police but I can put in a word. I was at university with the inspector.' He grinned modestly. 'And I don't know whether it's been mentioned to you but we need to conduct a geophysics survey of the area, just to make sure there are no more bodies down there.'

Jill's pale blue eyes widened in dismay.

'It's just a precaution,' Neil said hastily. 'I've got the equipment with me and some colleagues are arriving soon to carry out the investigation. The whole thing will only take a day or two and it'll save you getting any nasty shocks in the future if you want to put more cabling or pipes in.'

He watched as Jill considered the matter, hoping that this appeal to self-interest would work wonders. And it did.

'I see what you mean,' she said. 'I suppose it makes sense but . . .'

At that moment Tony Persimmon appeared in the doorway. As soon as he saw Neil he was all affability and told him to do whatever needed doing so that they need-n't be bothered again. Neil suspected that behind the bonhomie Tony was secretly wishing he'd never called the police out in the first place. All this was holding up his well-laid business plans. Time, as Neil had heard people say so often, was money.

But before he left the Persimmons in peace, Neil could-n't resist asking the question he'd been longing to ask since he set eyes on Tailors Court. 'What do you know about the history of this place?'

The couple exchanged a look. Then Jill spoke. 'The estate agent told us that part of the house dated back to the fifteenth century. Then a wealthy family made some alterations in Tudor times. I think they added the outer wings. We bought it off a family called Jannings, didn't we, Tony?'

'That's right. Old girl had to go into a home because the place was too much for her. She must have been push-ing ninety.'

'She lived here alone?'

'Yes. The place was in a right state but we saw the potential, didn't we, Tony?'

Neil looked round. They were sitting in the kitchen; obviously one of the first rooms they'd attended to. It was a large low room, the modern take on the traditional farmhouse kitchen. It was newly fitted out and the hand-painted units must have cost a fortune.

'How far have you got with the renovations?' Neil asked as though he was interested. But his mind was racing ahead, wondering about the parts of the place that had so far not been touched.

'Half of downstairs along with three bedrooms and a bathroom upstairs. But now the workspace is our top priority. The rest of the house can wait.'

Neil hesitated, wondering how his next question would be received. But he reckoned he had nothing to lose by being direct. 'Do you mind if I have a look round?'

'Why?' Tony Persimmon asked, suddenly on his guard.

'I've a feeling it might be a very important building, historically speaking.' In Neil's experience, there was nothing like a bit of flattery to oil the wheels.

Tony stood up. 'In that case I suppose I can spare you ten minutes for the guided tour.' He didn't sound too enthusiastic but that didn't bother Neil.

He was shown the modernised rooms first. They were cosy and tasteful, just as Neil had expected. Some original features, such as a grand inglenook fireplace in the living room, had been retained, but the overall effect was rather bland, as if the Persimmons had been sticking religiously to the dictates of interior design magazines.

To Neil, the untouched areas were far more interesting.

The two downstairs rooms seemed dark and dingy with grubby grey-green walls and flaking paintwork. But the fine oak beams, chamfered and carved in places, told Neil that this part of the house was probably Tudor, and definitely high status. Tailors Court was no extended peasant cottage.

Whatever furniture had been in there had been cleared out and the dusty, splintered floorboards awaited the inevitable sanding and varnish. There was a built-in cupboard next to the fireplace in one of the rooms and Neil wandered over to open it. The flowery wallpaper inside looked clean and new. It must have dated from the 1950s, Neil thought. The Janningses' day. But it had been emptied. Whoever had cleared this house out had been thorough.

'Do you know how the place got the name Tailors Court?' Neil asked as Tony led him up a fine oak staircase; chunky, solid and newly polished.

'Haven't a clue,' Tony replied. 'Somebody said it was a corruption of another name but don't ask me what it was.' He smirked. 'I don't think it was ever a tailor's shop if that's what you're thinking.'

'I'm not thinking anything,' Neil said quickly. 'I'm just curious, that's all.'

Tony Persimmon smiled but his eyes gave away his impatience.

'So who cleared it out? The previous owners?'

'There was a load of junk in here so I got a house clearer in. Told them to take the lot, after I'd had a quick look through for anything that could be valuable, of course.'

'And *was* there anything valuable?'

'There was a nice dresser. Sold it to an antiques place in

60

Exeter. And a nice Georgian chest of drawers. Had it restored and polished up and it's now in the drawing room. You might have noticed it. Lovely piece.'

Neil stayed silent as Tony led him from room to room. There was an excellent example of late sixteenth-century wall painting – stylised flowers surrounding a coat of arms – in the room that served as a master bedroom, prominently displayed behind glass. He'd half expected the Persimmons to have covered it with a coat of magnolia. Perhaps he was underestimating them. Or perhaps the local conservation officer had insisted.

Tony led the way to a couple of unmodernised rooms. There were beams here too. And panelling which looked original to the Elizabethan part of the house.

'I'd like to get rid of that,' Tony said as Neil went around examining it. 'Makes the place gloomy.'

'I presume the house is listed?'

'I'm afraid so. Bloody nuisance. If I'd known about all the planning restrictions, I would have thought twice before putting in an offer. I took a loose section of the panelling off just over there by the window. There were some revolting paintings on the plaster behind.'

This caught Neil's attention. 'Can I see?'

Tony walked over to the window wall and lifted off a dusty section of battered oak panelling. Neil stood beside him and peered at the section of wall he'd revealed. Then he wrinkled his nose in disgust. He'd seen similar images in anatomy books – a human figure with the flesh stripped away to reveal the muscles and sinews beneath. It was well painted by a talented hand, but still somehow primitive. The artist was no Leonardo.

Neil looked away. 'Can I have a look at the attic?'

He saw Tony glance at his watch impatiently.

'You can tell a lot about the construction of a house from the roof space.'

'Really? I've never been up there.'

'Got a ladder?'

'No need. There's a little staircase behind a door at the other end of the house.'

'And you haven't had a look?' Neil was rather amazed at the man's lack of curiosity. If the house had been his he would have searched every inch of the place on the day he moved in.

'I suppose the surveyor did. And the house clearers took some rubbish out of there but . . .'

Tony Persimmon walked down the landing and into another untouched bedroom, his footsteps echoing on the bare floorboards. There was a door at the far end of the room that Neil assumed was a cupboard but when Tony opened it, he saw a steep narrow staircase inside. The wood was dusty and splintered and as Neil placed a tentative foot on the bottom step, he hoped that hungry woodworms hadn't made a meal of it. But he had no need to worry – the steps held solid under his weight.

He turned, clinging to the filthy wall. 'Got a torch, Tony?'

He waited a few minutes and when the torch was brought he grabbed it enthusiastically and pointed it upwards. And what he saw made his heart beat a little faster.

'What's up there?' Tony shouted.

'There's a door.' He stood at the top of the steps and pushed at the battered oak panels. There was a large iron latch, riddled with rust and age, but when he eventually managed to lift it, the door opened stiffly with an ear-shattering creak.

He shone the torch around the attic.

It was much larger than he'd expected and, from the doorway he spotted at the end, he guessed there was a series of rooms up here, possibly matching the floor below. This first chamber was empty. As he stepped into the room the cobwebs that festooned the sloping ceiling grabbed at his hair. A fine place for Halloween, he thought as he looked around.

He made straight for the closed door at the end of the first attic room, hoping that it wasn't locked.

To his relief the door opened stiffly but he was mildly disappointed to discover that this room was empty too. He stood there for a while anyway, shining the torch upwards to study the construction of the roof.

Then he spotted yet another door at the end of the room. He walked towards it, his feet scraping on the dusty floor. When he reached the door he tried to turn the rusty iron handle but nothing happened. It was locked.

He swore under his breath and retraced his steps.

Feeling for each rickety rung with his toes, he descended the staircase. Tony Persimmon was waiting at the bottom, shuffling his feet impatiently.

'The far door's locked. Any idea where the key is?'

Tony shrugged. 'The surveyor asked for it but the old lady said it was missing. But when we were clearing out we found a few old keys in the kitchen.'

'Do any of them fit?'

'I haven't had the time or the inclination to try,' he said as though the subject of the attic was starting to bore him. 'But you can try them if you like.'

Once downstairs in the kitchen Tony pulled a small drawer out of the dresser and emptied its contents out onto the worktop. A dozen or so antique keys lay there in an untidy heap and Neil began to sift through them just as Jill entered the kitchen. When she spotted the mess on her worktop a look of irritation passed across her face.

'What are you doing?'

He smiled at her innocently and pointed to the keys. 'Trying to locate the key to that door at the end of the attic. Do you mind if I take these up and try them in the lock?'

'Help yourself,' she said with a dismissive wave of the hand. 'If you do get it open I expect you'll only find the usual mixture of crap and junk in there.'

Neil looked out of the kitchen window and saw a familiar battered van pulling up outside. His colleagues were finally here.

'Mind if I do this later? The others have just arrived so I'd better go and unload the equipment from my car.' His eyes wandered longingly to the keys lying there, temptingly. But duty called.

'James Dalcott had a woman – a nurse at the practice – but he still kept calling Roz every five minutes. When she told him she was expecting, it seemed to get worse. Couldn't let her go. Fucking nuisance he was.' Harry Parker sat back in the uncomfortable wooden seat, completely relaxed, making himself at home.

'Where were you when he was killed?' Wesley asked.

'I told that rather nice blonde detective sergeant everything I know. I don't want to have to repeat myself.'

Gerry Heffernan leaned forward, an unpleasant grin on

his face. 'Oh, we policemen always like things repeated. It must be the food in the canteen, kills the brain cells and knackers our short-term memory.' He paused and looked the man in the eye. 'But you'll know all about police questioning, won't you, Mr Parker?'

Harry Parker opened his mouth to speak then closed it again.

'We know about your record.'

'That's in the past. I've put all that behind me,' Parker said, avoiding Gerry's piercing gaze.

'Robbery, burglary and threatening behaviour.'

'I was young and stupid. And that spell inside taught me a lesson.'

'Some say prison just makes you a better criminal – that it's a university for the thieving classes.'

'In some cases maybe, but not in mine. When I came out I swore I was never going in there again.' He paused and looked Wesley in the eye, as if he judged him to be the more sympathetic of the pair. 'But I have got prison to thank for my choice of career. Had a brilliant art teacher in there who recognised my talents and kept in touch when I got out. Pointed me in the right direction.'

Gerry Heffernan gave him a threatening smile. 'That's very touching. But I bet it wasn't the only thing you learned inside. I bet you met some contacts in there. The sort of contacts who can get hold of a firearm at knockdown prices.'

'I don't know anyone like that.'

Gerry pushed his seat back and the legs scraped against the floor, a sound that put Wesley's teeth on edge. 'Only mix with the Vicar and the Mothers' Union now, do you? Bet you do charity work and all.'

'I did donate one of my pictures to a raffle for the local hospice, yes.'

Wesley saw Gerry looking at him. 'Very nice, isn't it, Inspector Peterson? Restores your faith in human nature.'

There was a brown cardboard file on the table in front of Wesley. He opened it carefully and studied the sheets of paper inside, a frown of concentration on his face. Then he looked at the man sitting opposite him and smiled – more friendly than the DCI. He was playing 'nice cop' today. 'Your conviction for aggravated burglary involved a firearm, Mr Parker. You were carrying a gun when you broke into the premises of a Mr Joseph Hyam. Mr Hyam was a jeweller, I believe.'

There was no answer but Parker's face had turned an unattractive shade of red.

'You threatened Mr Hyam, didn't you? You threatened him with a gun. Where did you get it?'

'A mate. It wasn't loaded. It was just meant to frighten him.'

'But it does mean you are familiar with firearms. You've used them, er, professionally, as it were.'

'I was eighteen. A stupid kid. Look, I've served my time, paid my debt to society or whatever you want to call it. I'm not the same man now as I was then. I'm an artist. I'm going to be a father soon. I wouldn't do anything to put that at risk now, would I?'

'I don't know,' said Gerry Heffernan. 'Your girlfriend's ex must have been a real pain in the arse so I can understand why you wanted rid of him, especially with the baby on the way. He'd have come round pestering Roz all the time, wouldn't he? We've got his phone records, you know. One of the last calls he made was to Roz's mobile phone.'

'So?'

'I think he was making things awkward. Did you know about the call?'

'Yeah. It was just routine, about the divorce settlement.'

'Know what's in his will?' Wesley did his best to sound casual.

Parker looked wary. 'You tell me.'

'According to his solicitor he never got round to making a new one after Roz left him. She gets the lot and the house must be worth a bit.' Wesley looked him in the eye. 'The solicitor wasn't too pleased at being contacted on a Sunday but he did tell us one thing. Last Friday afternoon James Dalcott made an appointment to see him on Monday morning. That's today. He said he wanted to make some alterations to his will. Now the solicitor couldn't remember exactly what was in the original will but I'm sure we can take a guess, can't we? In my will I leave everything to my wife, apart from a few small bequests, and she leaves everything to me. It's the usual thing between married couples and James never got round to changing it. Until now. You see our dilemma, Mr Parker?'

Harry Parker examined his fingernails. There was paint caught in them, red mostly. 'Not really. Roz didn't know about this appointment with the solicitor. Why should she?'

'He might have told her when he called her on Saturday afternoon. If he did, it gives both of you a very good motive for murder. The oldest motive in the book – money. Because James Dalcott died when he did, she'll be a wealthy woman. If he'd made the new will . . .' He let the words hang in the air.

Harry Parker looked uneasy. The questioning was

67

beginning to get to him. It would only take another push, Wesley thought, to crack him. He caught Gerry's eye. It was time to put the nasty cop into action again.

'You killed him, didn't you, Harry? You saw all that lovely money you expected to get your hands on going down the drain. How far had the divorce proceedings gone?'

'Dunno. James was making things awkward, holding things up.'

'Was Roz going to do well out of the divorce settlement or . . .?'

'I suppose she was going to do all right. I think he was going to keep the house and pay Roz a hundred grand. She would have gone for more but she felt a bit guilty if the truth were known. She'd left him and she had no kids so she didn't really feel she could take him to the cleaners.'

'That was very charitable of her,' said Gerry with more than a hint of sarcasm. 'But if he died without changing his will, she'd get a ruddy sight more than a hundred grand, wouldn't she? Now remind me, Inspector Peterson, what are the main motives for murder in the policeman's instruction manual? Let's see if I can remember.' He screwed up his face in mock concentration. 'Now there's getting rid of someone inconvenient, like your girlfriend's estranged husband.'

'And money,' Wesley chipped in. 'Don't forget money.'

'OK, I'll admit we'll probably do all right out of all this. But I didn't kill him. I swear.'

'Our Forensic people'll need to examine the clothes you were wearing on Saturday night.'

Parker looked up. 'They've been washed.'

'How convenient.'

68

'Examine away. You won't find anything.'

As Parker was about to be led away to the cells, he turned to Wesley, probably because he judged him the more sympathetic of the pair. 'James had his dark side, you know. That's one of the reasons Roz said she'd never go back.'

Wesley looked at the man. This was something new. 'What do you mean by his dark side?'

'You searched his house yet?'

'Why?'

'You'll see,' Parker said with a smirk. 'Over the past few weeks he became obsessed by it. It wasn't normal.'

'Obsessed by what?'

Parker smiled and shook his head. 'He wouldn't tell Roz any details but it was like it was haunting him.'

'What was?'

'The past.'

'How do you mean?' Wesley's curiosity was aroused now.

But Parker shook his head again. 'Not up to me to say. If you search his house you'll see for yourself.' He shut his lips tight and walked out of the room.

Suddenly Wesley couldn't wait to get over to Tradington to see what he meant.

As Trish Walton rang Adam Tey's doorbell she looked sideways at Nick Tarnaby who was standing by her side, eyes fixed ahead and hands in pockets. Nick's taciturn manner sometimes made her feel uncomfortable. But she decided to ignore it.

She rang the doorbell again but still there were no tell-tale sounds from inside the house.

Nick Tarnaby turned to go. 'They've probably gone away for a few days.'

'Or done a runner after Dr Dalcott's murder,' said Trish, irritated at her colleague's apparent lack of interest. 'Let's talk to the neighbours.'

Tarnaby grunted. 'Waste of time if you ask me.'

Suddenly Trish's patience snapped. 'Sorry if you've got something more important to do but this Tey character had a grudge against the victim. We've got to talk to him. He could be our killer.'

She marched towards the neighbouring front door and rang the bell. This time it opened almost immediately – too quickly perhaps, as though the neighbours had been watching their efforts to speak to Adam Tey and Charleen Anstice with great interest from behind the net curtains.

Because the house had a neat front garden, snowy lace curtains and fussy ornaments on display in the front window, Trish had been expecting to see an elderly lady at the door. But instead a large, tattooed man stood there, taking up most of the doorway. He was bald and the muscles of his bare arms bulged like oranges in a Christmas stocking.

'You police?' he said in a surprisingly high-pitched voice. A dog began to bark somewhere inside the house. It sounded big and fierce and Trish hoped he wouldn't invite them in.

'That's right.' She held up her warrant card but he didn't bother examining it. 'We've been trying to contact your neighbours. Adam Tey and Charleen Anstice.'

'They're in. I heard them.'

'How long ago was this?'

'Just before you arrived. They had the telly on and they

were talking. These walls are as thin as bleeding paper. You can hear everything. And I mean everything,' he added with a suggestive grimace.

'You're sure they didn't go out?'

'No. They're avoiding you. I'd put money on it,' he added with a self-satisfied smirk.

Trish hesitated for a moment. 'Do I get the impression you don't get on with your neighbours, Mr . . . er . . .'

'I can tell you're in the CID, my lover,' the man said with an unpleasant grin. 'You're right. I don't like them. They keep complaining about my Tinkerbell.'

'Tinkerbell?'

'My dog. They reported her to you lot – said she was a pit bull but she's not. All because she growled at him. He said she'd have gone for him if I hadn't pulled her off. But he was tormenting her. She was only playing. She wouldn't harm a fly.'

'I see,' said Trish quickly. She could hear Tinkerbell flinging herself against one of the inside doors. She sent up a silent prayer that the door wouldn't give – the last thing she fancied at that moment was an encounter with Tinkerbell's slavering jaws. 'Thanks for your help, Mr . . . er . . .'

'Mold. Ken Mold. And if they make any accusations against my Tinkerbell, they're lying. Just you remember that.'

'We will,' said Trish as he closed the door on them.

'So what do we do now?' Tarnaby asked in a voice that suggested to Trish that he'd rather be somewhere else.

'We keep trying. They can't keep this up for ever.'

'Can't they?'

Trish marched back to the car. She unlocked the door and sat in the driver's seat.

Tarnaby lowered himself down beside her. 'We going or what?'

'No. We're waiting.' Trish wasn't giving up until she'd spoken to Adam Tey and Charleen Anstice. She could sense Nick Tarnaby fidgeting by her side so she decided to make conversation to ease the tension and possibly improve relations.

'You're married, aren't you, Nick?'

'Yeah.'

'Does your wife work?'

'She used to. She's had to give up.'

'What did she do?'

But before he could answer, she saw Adam Tey's front door open, just a crack at first, then wider. 'Hold on,' she whispered. 'I think it's our lucky day.'

She saw a man emerge and look around. He was short and skinny and he reminded Trish of a ferret with his small features and pointed nose. He wore a parka coat, the hood up against the November chill. Slowly and casually, she got out of the car. Tarnaby made no move but she wasn't particularly bothered. She reckoned she'd be able to tackle this on her own and when she reported back to DCI Heffernan, it might just earn her a few Brownie points.

She walked towards Tey and smiled. 'Mr Tey. Can I have a quick word? Nothing to worry about,' she lied charmingly. 'I'm Detective Constable Trish Walton and I'm making some routine inquiries. Can we talk in the house? I'd like to speak to your partner too. What's her name? Charleen?'

She handed him her warrant card and let him examine it. It was clear that he didn't know quite what to do in the face of her unthreatening manner. It probably confused him, but that was the intention.

The tactic seemed to work. He handed back her warrant card and began to retrace his steps to the house.

'Charleen's pregnant. I don't want her upset.'

'I promise I won't upset her, Mr Tey. I just want a chat, that's all. You do know what it's about, I take it? You have heard the news about Dr Dalcott?'

It was difficult to make out Tey's reply but it sounded noncommittal. She tried another tactic to put the man at his ease. 'I've met your neighbour. It must be difficult,' she said sympathetically.

Tey looked at her. 'He's a fucking animal. Bad as that dog of his.'

'Tinkerbell?'

Their eyes met and he gave the ghost of a smile. 'Yeah. Bloody stupid name for a vicious beast like that. Went for me it did. If he hadn't pulled it off it would have had my arm off. When the baby's born I'm going to do something about it. I'm not taking any risks.'

'I don't blame you, Mr Tey,' she said with sincerity as he opened the front door. If Tey and Charleen had lost one child, there was no way they were going to see this new one threatened by what they thought of as a killer dog. If Tey was telling the truth, she suspected that Tinkerbell's days were numbered.

Tey led her into a small living room with over-busy wallpaper before walking to the foot of the stairs and calling Charleen's name. After his initial reluctance to answer the door, he appeared to have accepted the situation. And now the police were there in the unthreatening form of Trish Walton, they were going to have to answer the inevitable questions. As Trish sat down, she wondered what she should do about Nick Tarnaby. But she decided to let him stay in the car if he wanted. She knew instinctively that she'd get more out of these two on her own.

Charleen entered the room, her eyes fixed warily on Trish who gave her an encouraging smile. When all three were sitting, perched on a three-piece suite too large for the tiny room, Trish began by apologising for disturbing them.

'I'm sure you'll understand why we have to talk to you,' she said gently. 'Dr James Dalcott has been murdered. Shot.' She watched their faces but their expressions gave nothing away. 'Why haven't you been answering your door? Surely you want to eliminate yourselves from the enquiry.'

'We ain't done nothing,' said Tey quickly. 'I didn't want Charleen upset. I didn't want any bother.'

Trish took a deep breath. 'You knew Dr Dalcott. In fact you blamed him for the death of your child.'

Trish noted the glance that passed between the couple: a blend of pain and fear.

'Yeah. We took Sean to the surgery and Dalcott said it was just a bug going round. Sean got worse and we called the ambulance but it was too late.'

'I can see why you'd be angry with Dr Dalcott,' said Trish. She took a deep breath. 'Look, I don't like having to ask you this but it's a formality. We're seeing everyone who might have had a grudge against Dr Dalcott, you understand?'

It was Charleen who spoke. 'Yeah. But we had nothing to do with killing him. We wouldn't do anything like that.'

'Where were you on Saturday night between seven and eight o'clock?'

'We were both here watching telly. Then about ten we went for a quick drink down the Exeter Arms.'

'Any witnesses? Did anyone call round to see you?' Trish asked hopefully. Somehow she didn't like to think of this pair being hauled off to the police station. But then perhaps it wasn't only a misguided attempt to protect Charleen's feelings that caused Tey not to answer the door to the police. Perhaps they had something to hide after all.

'Loads of people saw us at the pub but we were on our own watching telly.' Charleen looked Trish in the eye. 'And you can't prove otherwise.'

Trish might have explained that, if the police felt so inclined, they could take the place apart to look for any slight forensic link between the couple and the crime scene, but she said nothing. In spite of her professional training, she couldn't help feeling sorry for them. They'd lost a child just as her own brother and sister-in-law had, and she knew only too well the devastation it had caused to their lives.

Charleen broke the awkward silence. 'If he hadn't spent so much time at that bloody private clinic he might have been able to pay our Sean more attention. Working all hours, he was, according to Ken next door.'

Trish leaned forward, all attention. This was something new. 'What private clinic's this?'

'It's over Podbury way. Ken Mold next door's a handyman there. I mean we don't speak to him much these days, not since we complained about that bloody dog. But when we were talking to him he said Dalcott must have made a fortune from the work he did there.'

'And what work was that?'

'No idea,' Adam said quickly.

Trish saw him give Charleen a warning look.

'We've told you everything we know,' said Charleen in a weary whine. 'Look, I'm tired. I want a lie down.'

Trish knew when she was being dismissed. But they'd keep. She stood up and made her way outside to join Nick Tarnaby. When she reached the car she stopped and looked back at the small house, thinking that it hadn't been altogether a wasted journey.

Neil had done his bit, walking up and down slowly with the bleeping machine, careful to keep in a straight line like a ploughman creating a furrow. When he reached the edge of the area he stopped, turned and walked back to cover the next section. It was painstaking work but he wanted to discover everything he could about those skeletons.

Had they been lovers – an older man and a young woman killed by a jealous husband? Or had they been disposed of by relatives for an inheritance perhaps? Had they died as a result of a vendetta or a robbery? Or had their deaths been concealed for some other reason? There were so many possibilities and Neil felt that he couldn't rest until he'd found out more.

He wasn't sure why but the possibility that there might be more bodies buried down there waiting to be discovered kept nagging at the back of his mind. However, at two-thirty, just when the sky turned a deeper grey and it started to drizzle, he handed the equipment to another member of the team and made for the house. Tony and Jill Persimmon hadn't been out to see what was going on, which Neil thought was unusual: most people who have archaeologists working on their land can't keep away.

He passed the kitchen window on his way to the front

door but, seeing the room was empty, he stopped for a moment and stared inside. There was no sign of the old keys on the worktop, which was hopeful, Neil thought. Perhaps the Persimmons' indifference to the house's history had been feigned. Perhaps they had found the right key and were exploring the attic at that very moment. And if so, he wanted to see it for himself.

He rang the doorbell and waited. For an age nothing happened and he looked around at the bare trees fringing the fields. A lazy buzzard circled over a distant copse with murder in its heart – prey would be thin on the ground now winter had arrived and the fields lay dormant, waiting for the spring. He watched as it plunged downwards in pursuit of a small furry victim.

After a while he heard footsteps from within the house, echoing faintly on the bare oak staircase. He straightened his back and wiped his grubby hands on his coat absent-mindedly as the door opened to reveal Jill Persimmon. He saw an expression of impatience flash across her face, swiftly replaced by one of cold politeness.

'I said I'd be back to try those keys.' He gave her what he hoped was a charming smile, impossible to resist.

Jill hesitated for a moment. 'Tony's tied up with work. He's in the middle of bidding for a contract so we haven't really got time for . . .'

'No need to bother him. I can take them up there myself and try them in the lock. There might be something behind that door that could tell us more about the history of this place. If I can get proof that those skeletons are old you won't have the cops crawling all over the place asking intrusive questions,' he added, hoping this would do the trick.

She suddenly looked concerned. 'Have you found more skeletons?'

'The geophysics can only give us some idea of whether the ground's been disturbed. To see exactly what's down there we have to dig.'

She said nothing as she stood aside to let him in and when she'd shut the door she delved into the pocket of her jeans. The three keys she held out were plain and rusty, one large and two smaller. He was tempted to snatch them before she changed her mind but, with an effort of self-control, he took them from her and thanked her politely, saying he wouldn't be long.

'I'll come with you,' she said. 'I suppose I'd better see what's up there.'

Although he would have preferred to do his investigating alone, it was her house so he smiled and said, 'Of course. No problem.'

Jill disappeared into the kitchen and returned carrying a large rubber torch in her left hand. Nothing was said as the pair climbed the stairs and made for the upstairs room containing the staircase cupboard. Neil took the keys and torch from her and climbed the rickety steps, aware of her eyes on him as he once again entered the attic. He passed quickly though the first two rooms and began fiddling with the lock of the mysterious door that had so piqued his curiosity. It was a few minutes before he got the largest key to turn stiffly and he hesitated for a few moments, staring at the door as though it was the sealed entrance to Tutankhamen's tomb; a place containing wonderful things. Then he pushed the door open and stared ahead into the roof space before stepping through the doorway and shining the torch around.

A table with bulbous legs stood in the centre of the room, shrouded beneath a layer of dust, and an array of corroded tools and instruments hung from hooks on the far wall, although Neil couldn't quite make out what they were.

'What's in there?' said Jill tentatively. She had followed him but had stayed on the other side of the door and Neil had almost forgotten she was there.

'Come and have a look,' he called back.

As she entered he realised that he was rather glad not to be alone. There was something odd about this room. Perhaps a sense of evil, although he didn't believe in that sort of thing.

He studied the table. It was old, battered and probably made of oak. The legs looked decidedly Elizabethan and tiny tattered fragments of rotten cloth still clung to one edge.

He walked on tiptoe towards the end of the room where the rusting objects dangled. At first sight he'd assumed they were the tools of a butcher's trade. But on closer inspection, he wasn't so sure. Besides, in his experience no farmer would ever carry animal carcasses on such an awkward journey to the top of the house.

Suddenly he wanted to get out of the place. He wasn't usually over-imaginative but he had an uneasy feeling in the pit of his stomach.

At some time in the long history of Tailors Court, something dreadful had happened in this strange, still attic room. Neil was sure of it.

CHAPTER 4

Transcript of recording made by Mrs Mabel Cleary (née Fallon) – Home Counties Library Service Living History Project: Reminiscences of a wartime evacuee.

Mrs Jannings lay propped up on her pillow and I had to go in to her and say hello. She had long grey hair and her face was pale as death. Her lips were the same colour as the rest of her skin and her eyes were really light blue. My big brother who'd just joined the navy used to tell me ghost stories and laugh when I screamed and wouldn't go upstairs alone. Well, this Mrs Jannings looked exactly like a ghost from one of his stories. She was even wearing a long white nightie.

I stood there in the doorway and the lady pushed me forward saying something like 'Mrs Jannings, I've got an evacuee for you. A little girl like you asked for. Her name's Mabel. How are you feeling?'

The ghost lady – because that's how I'd started to think of her – raised her hand weakly but said nothing. I looked round at the lady who'd brought me and saw that she looked a bit cross and that she didn't know whether to leave me there or not. I hoped she wouldn't.

Then the ghost lady spoke in a little high voice. 'You can leave her. Mary will look after her. We need the help.'

'If you're sure,' the other lady said. I could tell she wasn't happy.

'Get Mary to show her the room,' Mrs Jannings said. 'She'll have to make the bed.' When she looked at me I saw that her eyes were cold and watery. 'Can you cook?'

My mum had taught me to do potatoes and carrots. I couldn't do nothing fancy but I nodded all the same.

'And clean?'

I nodded again.

'Find Mary,' she said, turning her head away from the lady. 'She'll see to her.'

The lady took my hand and squeezed it. Then we went to find Mary.

Wesley and Gerry stood in James Dalcott's living room and looked around. They had edged their way through the hall, avoiding the bloodstains on the parquet floor, the slick of spilled wine, now dried to a sticky mess, and the Forensic team's markings. But, much to Wesley's relief, they had seen no trace of death elsewhere in the house.

'So what exactly are we looking for?' Gerry asked, scratching his head.

'I'm not sure. According to Harry Parker, Dalcott had some mysterious obsession. With the past, he said.'

Gerry grunted. 'Like your mate Neil and his archaeology?'

'I got the impression it was something a bit more . . . sinister.'

The DCI looked sceptical. 'Well, whatever it is, the search team didn't think it was sinister enough to comment on when they went through the place.'

Wesley didn't answer. Gerry had a point. He'd been in a hurry to get there and look through Dalcott's things but now he wished he'd taken the time to visit Roz Dalcott and ask her exactly what her boyfriend had meant by an obsession with the past. He'd been too impatient, which wasn't normally one of his failings.

As he began to search he experienced a feeling of disappointment. All the important papers – phone records, bank details and any personal letters – had been taken off for further investigation. If there was anything unusual or irregular about the victim's financial affairs they'd soon know, just as they'd know whom he'd been contacting in the days before his death. But Wesley had a feeling that there was something else to find – something seemingly innocent that the officers conducting the initial search had overlooked or thought unimportant.

He started to rummage through the Georgian bureau that stood in the corner of the room but found nothing of interest in the top two drawers. However, when he opened the bottom drawer he saw a dark-blue cardboard folder which he took out and opened. Inside were several copies of birth, marriage and death certificates, photocopies of census entries and, enfolding them all, a large sheet of paper folded into several sections. When he carried it over to the dining table and spread it out, Gerry

Heffernan came up behind him and placed a large paw on his shoulder.

'What have we here?'

'It's a family tree. Looks like James Dalcott was trying to trace his ancestors.'

Gerry bent forward to study the paper on the table. 'That's odd,' he said.

'What is?'

The chief inspector scratched his head. 'Look at the names of Dalcott's parents.'

When Wesley looked more closely he saw what Gerry meant. Dalcott's parents' names were recorded as Greta and Robert Dalcott but these had been crossed out and the names Isabelle and George Clipton printed neatly above them.

'Perhaps he discovered that he was adopted,' Wesley suggested. 'Evonne said he was preoccupied by something – family business, he said. She assumed it was Roz but maybe it was this.'

'Look over here. Greta Dalcott, née Clipton, is recorded as his aunt. George Clipton and Greta were brother and sister . . . look.'

Gerry was right. At some point Greta, married to a man called Dalcott, had adopted her brother's child who had taken the couple's name.

'I don't suppose it was that unusual,' Gerry said. 'Perhaps the parents were both killed and the aunt and uncle looked after their son.' Wesley sensed that he'd begun to lose interest.

'But if that was the case wouldn't you think James would have known all about his real parents?'

'We're talking about the fifties here, Wes. People didn't

talk about things back then. They just got on with it. One of my mum's favourite sayings has always been "least said, soonest mended". Different generation.'

Wesley nodded. Gerry was probably right. He began to fold up the family tree when Gerry put out a hand to stop him.

'Hang on.'

'What is it?'

'George Clipton. Why does that name sound familiar?'

'I'm sure I've never heard it before.'

'It might have been before your time, Wes. Before mine too but I'm still sure I've heard it somewhere before.'

'Do you think Parker could have been talking about genealogy when he said Dalcott was obsessed with the past?'

Gerry sighed. 'Who knows, Wes? When a couple are at each other's throats like that any little thing can seem irritating; any interest can be interpreted as an obsession.'

Wesley folded the family tree and put everything back in the folder. Dalcott had no children so there'd be nobody to pass the information on to; nobody who'd be interested in the forebears of James Dalcott. It was rather a sad thought.

He left the living room and climbed the stairs, his eyes avoiding the site of Dalcott's violent death. He heard Gerry's heavy footsteps behind him, treading slowly.

'Has anything interesting been found on his computer?' Wesley asked as he reached the landing.

'Still waiting. You know how Scientific Support like to take their time. I'm not getting my hopes up.'

They didn't feel like talking much as they searched the bedrooms. It was obvious that the cottage had been painstakingly restored and decorated to Roz's taste, even down to the antique locks on the doors which all boasted shiny keys, and it was as if she was still there in spirit if not in reality. There were half-used women's cosmetics in the bathroom and a silk dressing gown that had seen better days hung behind the door of one of the spare bedrooms. She had left things that she couldn't be bothered taking to her new life with Harry Parker. And James had kept these things around him, perhaps in the hope she would come back one day.

'Wonder if she'll move back in here with lover boy?' said Gerry absentmindedly. 'After all, it's all hers now. Might have been a different story if he'd got round to changing the will.'

'Mmm. But is it worth killing for?'

Gerry looked round. 'People have killed for a lot less.'

When they'd finished their search of all the drawers and cupboards, Wesley felt a little disappointed. Somehow he'd hoped to find some clue; a threatening letter from the killer or some secret stash of pornography. But it seemed that Dr James Dalcott had led a worthy, dull and blameless life . . . unless something was discovered on the hard drive of his computer that suggested there'd been some secret wickedness behind the benign façade.

They'd have to wait and see.

Neil had locked the attic room behind him. He'd found the whole experience rather unnerving and he felt that he never wanted to go up there again. Perhaps he was getting too imaginative in his old age.

When he'd left Jill Persimmon in the kitchen she seemed rather quiet, as if the discovery of that room –

85

almost above the bedroom where she slept – had disturbed her too. Neil hadn't discussed the matter with her beyond the bare, obvious facts, but he suspected that, should any more bodies be found in the grounds, the thought of the place being owned by some kind of serial killer might be enough to make the Persimmons sell up and head back to London.

His colleagues were just finishing a section of marked-out grassland fifty yards from the house, just beyond the trench where the two skeletons had been unearthed. He fixed a confident smile to his face and walked over to join them.

'How's it going?'

Chris, the new lad who'd come to the Unit fresh from university, looked up. 'Not bad. How much do you want us to do?'

'All the area up to the hedgerow. That OK?'

'We won't get it all done today.'

'I didn't expect you to.' Neil gave him an encouraging smile.

Chris looked round, a worried look on his face. 'And who's paying for all this? I thought the Unit was worried about funding.'

Neil grinned. 'We are. But this one's down as a possible murder enquiry. If you go into the police control room ours is the first number on their list of contacts – A for archaeologists. And besides that, the Detective Inspector at Tradmouth is an old mate of mine from Uni.'

Neil saw Chris look at him as though he suspected he was making it up.

'Have we any printouts yet?'

'Dave's got something,' said Chris and returned his

attention to his machine. Neil left him to it and trudged across the uneven ground towards a group of people standing chatting by the outhouse.

As he approached, Dave, who had the bearded face and stocky figure of a dedicated real ale drinker, looked up eagerly.

'What have we got?' Neil asked.

'Well, there are a few interesting anomalies.'

This was what Neil wanted to hear. This was something that would potentially keep the paperwork at bay for a few more days.

With the Persimmons' permission Dave was using one of the outhouses as a base. Neil followed him inside. The place was filthy but they'd worked in worse surroundings. At one end of the room was a dusty door half covered with flaking green paint and barred by a pile of old tea chests. Neil had moved the debris and tried the door, just out of curiosity, and when it had creaked open he'd found himself in a windowless room containing an old table, an array of rusted knives and cleavers and a row of meat hooks hanging from the cobwebbed ceiling. Once he'd peeped inside he'd shut the door and never opened it again. He'd assumed it was an old slaughterhouse and now it reminded him uncomfortably of the strange attic room.

He turned his attention to more pressing matters. A laptop screen was glowing on top of an ancient cast-iron boiler. Dave pressed a few keys and they both stared as the results appeared on the screen.

'Look,' said Dave pointing. 'There's where the skeletons turned up and here . . . it looks like the ground's been disturbed. And here too. And there. And there's another one here, slightly smaller than the others. I mean it could be something else, burying rubbish or dead animals, but it's not linear so we can rule out pipes and drains.'

'You're right,' said Neil, squinting at the patterns on the screen. 'It's worth having a look, isn't it?'

'Those are definitely the right size for graves in my opinion.' Dave raised his eyebrows. 'Reckon we might have ourselves a serial killer here?'

Neil didn't reply. He was going over the possibilities in his mind.

'You up to a bit of digging?' he said after a few moments.

Dave nodded. 'Why not?'

Wesley and Gerry were just making for the car when they heard a voice. 'Yoohoo.'

They both turned round. Ruby Wetherall was standing there waving enthusiastically. She looked smart, as though she had dressed up for the occasion and Wesley guessed that having a police constable stationed there to fuss over and keep supplied with cups of tea and home-made cake was rather a treat for her.

Wesley began to walk towards her, Gerry following behind. 'Hello, Mrs Wetherall. What can we do for you?'

She looked from left to right, as though she was afraid of being overheard, before leading them into her house and, once inside, she insisted that they sat down and made themselves comfortable.

'So what is it?' Wesley asked, taking a surreptitious glance at his watch. Chief Superintendent Nutter – usually referred to irreverently as 'the Nutter' by DCI Heffernan who had little faith in his superior's abilities as a crime fighter – wanted an update on their progress. The murder of a local doctor, a respected member of the community, had to be seen to be dealt with swiftly and efficiently, he'd said, ignoring Gerry when he'd pointed out that every victim deserves justice, not just the professional classes.

Ruby touched Wesley's sleeve. 'They've gone. Done a moonlight flit.'

'Who's gone, Mrs Wetherall?'

'Those two men renting the house on the other side of Dr Dalcott's. Said they were father and son.'

Wesley and Gerry looked at each other. The neighbours in the third house in the terrace of cottages had been questioned as a matter of routine but no suspicions had been raised. They identified themselves as Syd and Brian Trenchard, a widowed father and his son, and told the DC who'd interviewed them that they'd moved from Plymouth a couple of weeks ago and were renting the house while they looked for a new place in the area. The son worked in Dukesbridge – something to do with cars – and, as Mr Trenchard senior had recently been widowed, they'd decided to look for somewhere more rural.

In their brief statement they'd said that they'd been out at the time of the murder visiting friends and that they hadn't returned until late that evening. They'd seen and heard nothing and their only dealings with Dr Dalcott had been the exchanging of neighbourly nods.

They hadn't known the dead man and they hadn't behaved at all suspiciously so checking their story was just a matter of routine and hardly considered urgent. Syd and Brian Trenchard had seemed to be low priority.

'What makes you think they've done a moonlight flit,

love?' Gerry asked. 'They might have just gone away for a few days. Can't be easy living next door to a murder scene, as you know yourself.'

Ruby leaned towards Gerry as though she didn't want to be overheard. 'They packed a load of stuff into the car. Looked like all their possessions if you ask me. The place is let furnished so there'd be no need for a removal van. They drove off and I haven't seen them since.'

Wesley caught Gerry's eye. This hardly sounded like proof of guilt.

'I took their car registration number, just in case.' Ruby delved into her pocket and pulled out a neatly folded sheet of paper. She handed it to Gerry with great ceremony. 'There you are, Chief Inspector.'

Gerry stuffed it into his own pocket where, Wesley feared, it would probably get lost amongst all the other scraps of paper that ended up in there.

'Do you want me to look after that?' he asked.

Gerry, always the first to acknowledge that Wesley was far more organised than he was, handed the sheet over.

'How well did you know the Trenchards?' Wesley asked, putting the paper carefully into his pocket.

Ruby licked her thin lips and Wesley suspected she was enjoying herself. 'Said hello a couple of times but we didn't pass the time of day. The father – at least I presume it's his father: you never know nowadays, do you? – always went around in one of those track suits. Big bloke around sixty. Shaved head. The son's in his thirties. Also bald as an egg. Tattoos on his arms. Smaller than the dad. They certainly weren't here when we found poor Dr Dalcott but I saw them come back in their car around ten o'clock.'

Wesley suppressed a smile. 'We know. They've already been interviewed.'

Ruby looked disappointed.

'But you're being very helpful,' Wesley said quickly. He didn't want to discourage further confidences. He stood up. 'Excuse me, Mrs Wetherall, I'll just have to make a call,' he said and left the room.

Finding the Wetheralls' cluttered house rather claustrophobic, he felt he needed some fresh air so he let himself out of the front door, leaving it on the latch, and wandered into the garden. As he pulled out his mobile phone he realised he was standing in a pile of damp and rotting leaves so he stepped sideways onto the mossy grass. He could feel the cold penetrating his shoes but as he made his call his mind was on other things. He had a feeling, just a slight uneasy hunch, that there might be something in Ruby's suspicions. Or maybe a murder next door and a diet of TV detective dramas were making her see assassins behind every tree.

He stood there a while, waiting for the station to get back to him. And once he'd received the expected call he returned to the house, careful to wipe his feet on the doormat.

Gerry Heffernan had settled himself on Ruby's sofa but Wesley knew that his comfort would be short lived. Thanks to Ruby's suspicious mind he'd just discovered that the car used by Syd and Brian Trenchard had been hired in the name of William Smith. And that there was no record of either man having lived in the Plymouth area.

Syd and Brian Trenchard had some questions to answer.

*

91

Neil had moved three feet of earth very carefully, examining every spadeful of soil as he worked. He had only asked Dave to help him. If his suspicions were correct, the fewer feet that trampled on the site, the better.

This was the first anomaly the geophysics had shown up, the one nearest the burials the Persimmons had found. As Neil dug his thoughts kept turning to that attic room. But he knew that if he dwelt on it, it might lead to sleepless nights. Half-seen, half-understood things always held the most horror.

Dave was squatting in the trench they'd created, scraping away at the ground. Neil stepped cautiously into the area beside him and adjusted his kneeling mat before lowering himself to his knees and taking his trowel from his coat pocket. At first they worked without speaking until Dave broke the expectant silence.

'I've got something here.'

From the way he said it, Neil knew that his fears were about to be confirmed. 'What is it?' He leaned across to look at the place where Dave was digging and saw something like yellowed ivory emerging from the darkness of the soil. Bone.

'Could be animal of course,' Dave said, trying to sound optimistic.

Both men carried on digging. Soon another piece of bone appeared beneath Neil's trowel.

'We'll photograph this,' he said quietly, reaching for the digital camera and the measuring stick that lay on a plastic tray at the edge of the trench.

Carefully recording every new bone that emerged from its shroud of Devon earth, they continued in silence.

Then, as the sun began to set and the rooks started

crying from the trees that stretched their bony branches up to the darkening sky, the skeleton appeared, whole and articulated as before. It lay grinning up at them as though it was pleased to have some attention at last; as though it had kept its secrets for many years and now wanted the truth about its fate to come out into the light.

'How many more of them are down there?' Neil said softly and he put down the camera.

Dave sat back on his heels and shook his head.

All patrols were on the lookout for the hire car driven by Brian and Syd Trenchard, or rather the two men who were calling themselves Brian and Syd Trenchard.

When Wesley returned to the incident room at Neston Police Station, the first thing he did was to examine their witness statements. They'd certainly said nothing that aroused suspicion. The two men had hardly known Dalcott; had had no relationship with him whatsoever as far as anybody knew. They'd claimed to have been out visiting friends at the time of the murder and returned to find the floodlit circus of a full crime scene investigation had landed on their doorstep. Bit of a shock, they'd told the officer who'd spoken to them. But now it looked as if they might have been lying. Especially as the address they claimed they were visiting in Morbay didn't exist.

It was five o'clock and dark outside and Wesley could see car headlights passing the window. The view was very different here in the open-plan ground floor office at Neston to the vista they enjoyed in the CID office at Tradmouth – the view over the Memorial Gardens to the River Trad with its bobbing yachts and the steep town of Queenswear on the far bank. He found that he missed it:

he hadn't realised it before, but staring out at the river helped him think.

When his mobile phone rang he looked at the name of the caller and discovered that it was his sister.

'Hi. How are things?' he said.

He heard Maritia sigh. 'Everyone's in shock at the surgery. The receptionists have started a charity collection in his memory. Everyone – all the patients – have been coming in. Some have been in tears. Nobody's talked about anything else all day.'

'How's Evonne?'

'She was here this morning but she had to leave at lunchtime. She was too upset.'

'Understandable.'

'Mind you, Keith Graham . . .' She hesitated.

'What about Keith Graham?' Wesley hoped he didn't sound too eager, but he really hadn't taken to the retired senior partner. Or his wife, for that matter.

'He's covering for a few days – just till we can arrange a locum to replace –' She paused. 'To tell the truth, Wes, he's been getting on my nerves. He's been talking as if James's absence is just an inconvenience; as though he's chosen to go off on holiday or something.'

'Want me to arrest him then?'

His sister gave a small giggle. 'And leave us short-handed with this new virus going round? No thanks. Mind you, there are some in the practice who think he's past it.'

'Including you?'

There was no answer.

'Did you ring for any particular reason?' he asked. It wasn't like Maritia to call for a chat in working hours.

'It might not be important, but I had to go into James's

surgery earlier. I was looking for an instrument and I knew he had one somewhere. I had to look in his desk drawer . . .'

'And?'

'Well, I found something odd. Well, it wasn't really odd – it's just that I didn't know about it.'

'What do you mean?'

'Well, I found some pay slips. They were from this private clinic.'

'The Podingham Clinic near Podbury? He did some private work there.'

'You know about it?'

'I've just found a report on my desk from one of the team. We're following it up.'

'So long as you know.' He could hear the disappointment in his sister's voice.

'Thanks anyway. If you discover anything else, do let us know.'

As he ended the call it occurred to him that it could be useful to have a contact at the victim's workplace. And Maritia had always been observant. If there was anything suspicious, she was bound to sniff it out.

He turned and saw Gerry Heffernan marching towards him. 'So what's this about Trish finding someone who knows Dalcott?'

Wesley picked up Trish's report and held it out. Gerry almost snatched it from his fingers and studied it for a few moments. 'So this Ken Mold lives next door to Adam Tey and Charleen Anstice and he's a handyman at this Podingham Clinic where Dalcott worked part-time?'

'He says he only knew the doctor by sight. If he's telling the truth . . .'

'If Mold was close to Tey and Anstice he might have felt driven to take some sort of revenge for their kid who died.'

'But according to both Tey and Mold there's no love lost between them. Something to do with a dog called Tinkerbell.'

Gerry snorted. 'It might still be worth having a word.' He looked at his watch. 'And tomorrow we'll visit this Podingham place and see exactly what Dalcott did there.'

'I've been wondering that myself. My sister's just called to say she found some pay slips from the Podingham Clinic in Dalcott's desk at the surgery. It doesn't sound as if his colleagues in the practice knew about it. Wonder why he kept quiet?'

'Moonlighting. It always leads to problems. I remember a DC years back who had a sideline as a bouncer at a Morbay nightclub. All ended in tears.'

Wesley's phone began to ring and Gerry plonked himself down heavily in a nearby chair.

When the call was ended Wesley turned to his boss who was sitting with an expectant expression on his face. 'That was Neil.' He paused. 'They've turned up another skeleton, probably female. Neil says the bones look old but we still have to get a team down there, just to make sure.'

Gerry closed his eyes and issued a loud sigh. 'He's sure they're old, is he?'

'As far as he can tell.'

Gerry's eyes suddenly flicked open and a mischievous look passed across his face. 'By the way, Wes, you're in for a treat. I found a message on my desk from the Nutter – he wants you to do a TV appeal about Dalcott's murder. And we're to get a grieving relative for maximum impact.'

'Why me?'

Gerry's lips curved upwards in a wicked grin. 'Have you got to ask, Wes? You're just the right colour to make us look "inclusive". Or at least that's what Nutter says.'

Wesley squirmed in his seat. The last thing he wanted was to be used to make a political point in order to keep Chief Superintendent Nutter happy. 'And where do we find a grieving relative? I don't think Dalcott had any. Only Roz, and she's hardly the distraught widow.'

'It'd be a good way of seeing how she behaves under the spotlight.'

'She's pregnant, Gerry. We don't want to be accused of putting too much pressure on her,' Wesley said quickly.

He saw the DCI shrug. 'What about that Evonne, the practice nurse? She seems more cut up about his death than anyone.'

Wesley nodded slowly. If anyone was devastated, it was Evonne. He looked at his watch. 'I'd better get someone down to Tradington to have a look at what Neil's found.'

'You're not going yourself?'

Wesley surveyed the heaps of paperwork on his desk. 'Wish I could.'

Gerry touched his sleeve. 'If you're staying here let's see what we can find out about George Clipton.'

'George Clipton?'

'Remember? The name Dalcott substituted for his father's on the family tree. I'm sure I've heard it some-where before and I thought we could Google him or whatever you call it.'

Wesley saw that the DCI was looking at him with the innocent enthusiasm of a puppy who'd just been promised a walk. Gerry and computers had never really got on and

he usually delegated their use to colleagues and underlings. Wesley had once suggested that he went on a course
but he'd pretended not to hear.

Wesley leaned forward and typed the name George
Clipton into the computer on his desk. To his surprise a
whole list of sites flashed up on the screen and he selected
the first.

The site was about murderers of the twentieth century
and George Clipton featured prominently.

It seemed that George Clipton had strangled his wife
and had been hanged for his crime in 1957.

CHAPTER 5

Transcript of recording made by Mrs Mabel Cleary (née Fallon) – Home Counties Library Service Living History Project: Reminiscences of a wartime evacuee.

Mary wore a sort of uniform and someone said that she was a land girl but I didn't know what a land girl was back then. I found out later that there were other land girls working at the farm next door but Mary was the only one who lived at Tailors Court. I think the others were billeted on the farm and Mary often said to me that she wished she was with them. She didn't like it at Tailors Court, she said. The place gave her the creeps.

Anyway, on the day I arrived she showed me where I was going to sleep. It was a little room at the end of the house and she told me she slept next door which made me feel a bit better. She laughed a lot and she was the prettiest girl I'd ever seen with fair hair and freckles and a turned-up nose.

Once I'd put my things in my room, Mary told me that Miles slept in the other part of the house. Well away from us. And I felt relieved because I was scared of him, even then.

Wesley arrived home at eight that evening to find Pam nodding off in front of the TV. But after a few seconds she roused herself and gave him a welcoming kiss before directing him to the kitchen where a spaghetti bolognese awaited him in the microwave. Having put the children to bed and prepared most of her work for the following day, she looked exhausted – which was exactly how Wesley felt. However, when she asked about the search for James Dalcott's killer, she sat forward in her seat, eager for information. But Wesley just said it was early days. He didn't feel like discussing the case. Besides, he was hungry.

He took the laptop into the kitchen with him and, as he forked the spaghetti into his mouth, he brought up the list of websites that mentioned George Clipton's crimes. He and Gerry had learned the basic facts of the case back in the office. But Wesley wanted to see what else, if anything, he could discover.

He clicked on a site called 'Murderous Medics' and found that it was dedicated to all those members of the medical profession who had turned to murder. Dr Crippen was there, of course, along with Dr Buck Ruxton, Dr Bodkin Adams, Dr Neil Cream, Dr Harold Shipman and all those other rogue physicians who had used their medical skills to kill rather than heal. As Wesley scrolled through the pages, he was struck by the fact that there seemed to be rather a lot of them. Dr George Clipton, a self-effacing and well-liked general practitioner in a Dorset

it seemed that he had acted in a moment of madness. It would surely have been a true crime of passion and there was no evidence that he had planned his terrible act or that he was ever likely to be a danger to the public in general.

The account of George Clipton's last moments made him feel a little sick. The condemned doctor had gone with the Governor and the chaplain in a sad little procession to the execution chamber where the hangman was waiting. Then his feet and hands were tied, the hood placed over his head and the rope around his neck. In his mind's eye Wesley could see him there, helpless, bound and waiting to be dispatched like a beast in an abattoir, his pounding heart reminding him of the life he would soon forfeit to the all-consuming power of the law.

According to the website, George had claimed his innocence to the last. His last words before the lever was thrown and the trapdoor opened up beneath his feet with a thunderous crash were 'I didn't do it.'

Wesley pushed his plate away and switched off the laptop. The story of George Clipton had disturbed him and he wasn't sure why.

'You all right?'

He looked up and saw Pam standing in the doorway with a look of concern on her face.

'Just looking something up, that's all. Man hanged for strangling his unfaithful wife back in the 1950s.' He paused. 'All the evidence points to James Dalcott being his son.'

She sat down heavily on the chair opposite. 'You sure?'

'Pretty sure. I'll have to do more checking but . . .'

'Surely it can't have anything to do with his murder? I

mean, it was a long time ago. And why would anyone want to get revenge on the son? I presume he was the victim's son as well as the murderer's. She wasn't the wicked stepmother?'

'Oh no. The victim was his mother all right. He was brought up by his father's sister and it looks as though he was never told about his real parents. I don't think he had any idea about all this until quite recently when he started investigating his family tree, then I suppose it all came out. Must have been a shock for him.'

'I never imagined that genealogy could be a dangerous pastime,' she said.

'We don't know whether it has anything to do with his death. In fact the more I think about it the less likely it is.'

The subject exhausted, he began to pack the dishwasher. When he had finished he turned and saw that Pam was watching him. He caught her by the waist and gave her a kiss. She kissed him back and they stayed there for a few seconds, holding each other close. Until the telephone rang.

'Hope that's not the incident room,' Wesley said, squeezing her hand.

Pam broke away, grabbed the receiver and said a cautious 'hello'. After a short conversation she handed it to Wesley, covering the mouthpiece. 'It's Neil. He says it's urgent.'

Wesley took it, giving Pam an apologetic smile, hoping that whatever his friend had to say wouldn't add to his workload.

Somehow he knew that it wasn't going to be a short conversation. Once Pam had retreated into the living room he sat down and listened as Neil spoke in great detail about the geophysics results and the discovery of the third skeleton, interrupting only to ask a couple of pertinent questions. But when Neil got onto the subject of his guided tour of Tailors Court, the anatomical drawings hidden behind the panelling and the strange room in the attic, Wesley could tell from his voice that something about that room had disturbed him – and Neil didn't usually frighten easily.

When he promised to meet him at Tailors Court the next morning, Neil sounded relieved. Maybe he'd just wanted to share the burden of his suspicions. But now they'd become Wesley's problem.

That night he lay awake with all Neil's revelations buzzing round in his head.

It wasn't only the new skeleton that concerned him, but the strange room in the attic at Tailors Court.

He really wanted to see it for himself.

First thing the next morning Wesley called Gerry Heffernan to say he'd be in late. Another body had been found at Tailors Court. And something else – something Neil felt might be suspicious. He was going down there to see it for himself before he made any decisions about which course of action to take.

What he didn't mention to Gerry, because he didn't want to worry him, was that if those skeletons, and whatever was in the attic room, turned out to be less than seventy years old, they might have a massive case on their hands. Something of a scale that would probably require outside help. Wesley sent up a silent prayer that the bones were centuries old and of more interest to Neil than to

Tradmouth CID. But he had an uneasy feeling that this time, his prayers might not be answered.

Gerry ended the conversation by reminding him that he was due to appear on TV that evening – live on the local news programme. Evonne Arlis would be sitting beside him as the token grieving friend to add emotional weight to the appeal for potential witnesses. Wesley curbed a desire to say how much he was dreading it. And he doubted if it would yield any useful results either.

The winter sun was making a feeble effort to shine as he left the house and set off down the main road to Neston. Before reaching the town, he turned off onto a minor road, following a signpost to Tradington. He'd been able to avoid the early-morning Neston rush hour but he still encountered a number of cars and had to carry out the awkward rural ritual of reversing into a passing place several times.

The gates to Tailors Court stood on a winding country lane off the Tradington road and as Wesley steered his way up the drive, he saw that Neil's archaeological team had arrived early and were unloading various items of geophysics equipment out of an assortment of battered vehicles. The search for bodies was still continuing, and Wesley contemplated the prospect with a sinking heart.

He spotted Neil's car parked near the house and pulled up beside it.

As he slammed the car door Neil appeared, seemingly out of nowhere, looking uncharacteristically worried.

'Colin Bowman said to leave the bones *in situ* and he'll come as soon as he can,' Neil said as they began to walk towards the scene of the activity. 'I didn't like to leave them there – always like to lift them as soon as possible, as you know – but . . .' He paused. 'I keep thinking about those cut marks on the first two skeletons. I think this new one's the same. It's a man, by the way. Middle-aged.'

'Anything to date the burial?'

'A few small pieces of pottery . . . Tudor green. And there's some seventeenth- and eighteenth-century stuff in the soil above. No sign of recent ground disturbance. And that knife blade we found near the first burials – the expert I showed it to says it's definitely old; probably sixteenth century.'

Wesley smiled. Things were looking up. 'So if we keep our fingers crossed very tightly, the burials might turn out to be sixteenth century too?'

Neil studied his fingernails and picked at a grubby cuticle. 'If I were a betting man – and in view of the state of the teeth – I'd say they were old.'

'Thank God for that. We've got enough on our plate with this shooting. Now what about this attic room you told me about?'

Neil gave his friend a rueful smile. 'I'll have to use my charms with the Persimmons. I had the awful feeling yesterday that I'd outstayed my welcome.'

'Heaven forbid,' Wesley said under his breath. Neil's enthusiasm for the past could be a little much for some people.

He followed Neil to the front of Tailors Court and when Jill Persimmon answered the door she stood on the threshold, barring the way.

'What is it this time?' she asked.

Before she could say anything, Neil got in first. 'This is DI Wesley Peterson. He's here about the skeletons.'

'Sorry to bother you, Mrs Persimmon,' Wesley said as

he shook the woman's hand. 'More routine investigations, I'm afraid.'

'I thought the skeletons were old.' She gave Neil a puzzled frown. 'I didn't think you needed to involve the police again.'

'As I said, it's just routine,' said Wesley smoothly, sneaking a look at Neil. 'Dr Watson's told me about the attic room he found and I'd be very grateful if I could have a quick look.'

Jill hesitated for a moment. 'Why?'

'If you're busy we can find our own way,' said Neil, taking a step towards the door.

'Well, I am expecting a call.' She went over to the dresser, took a key from a hook and handed it to Neil. 'Just leave it there when you've finished,' she said and disappeared off to the room she was using as a temporary office.

'No problem,' Neil whispered smugly. As he took the stairs two at a time Wesley followed him, noting the exposed beams and the pristine white plasterwork, and when they eventually found themselves in a shabby bedroom, probably untouched since the 1940s, Neil made straight for the far corner and removed a section of dusty panelling.

'Someone's been interested in anatomy,' Wesley said, staring at the newly revealed pictures. 'Funny place to draw them.'

'Mmm,' said Neil. 'But when were they drawn?'

'They look quite fresh.'

'They've been protected by the panelling. They could be any age.'

Neil replaced the section of panelling carefully before

leading Wesley to the bedroom containing the staircase door.

'The room's up here,' he said, his words almost lost behind the creaking of the hinges.

He climbed the stairs and Wesley followed cautiously. The treads looked rickety and he was taking no chances.

Neil unlocked the first door and led Wesley through the bare, cobweb-festooned attic, lighting the way with a torch he'd just taken from one of his combat jacket's many pockets. When they reached the end, he turned the key in a plain oak door and opened it with a dramatic flourish and a horror-film creak.

'What do you make of this then?' he asked as he stepped inside the room and flashed the torch around the walls. Somehow Wesley's presence had taken the edge off the bad feelings he'd experienced there on his first visit.

Wesley took the torch from Neil and walked around slowly, taking everything in. Then he stopped and stared at the rusted instruments hanging on the wall before examining them more closely, touching what looked like a saw tentatively with his forefinger then wiping the contaminated digit on his trousers. 'My dad took me to a medical museum in one of the big London teaching hospitals once and they had old surgical instruments on display,' he said quietly. 'They looked very similar to those, only in much better condition, of course.'

'You reckon this might have been some sort of hospital?'

Wesley grimaced before turning to face Neil. 'I doubt it. Not all the way up here. Are you thinking what I'm thinking about the cuts on the bones?'

Before Neil had a chance to reply he heard a voice behind him. 'What's going on?'

109

Both men swung round. Tony Persimmon was standing in the doorway. Even in the torchlight Wesley could tell that he didn't look pleased.

Wesley stepped forward and showed his warrant card. In his experience people like the Persimmons weren't inclined to argue with the forces of law and order. The aggression vanished from the man's face but he stood his ground. 'What are you looking for?'

'Dr Watson told me about this room and, in view of the bodies found outside in your grounds, I'm just wondering whether to get it sealed off or . . .' It was always best to start with the worst-case scenario and work down.

Persimmon suddenly looked worried. 'We've only just moved in. Even if something happened here years ago it has nothing to do with us. '

'We're well aware of that. But I'll take some samples for our lab.' He took an evidence bag out of his pocket and picked up a fragment of the rotted cloth on the table with the plastic, careful not to contaminate any potential evidence. Then he looked at Persimmon and gave him a businesslike smile. 'Maybe we could talk downstairs? I'd like you to tell me everything you know about the history of the house.'

Wesley thought that Persimmon looked a little relieved as he led the way downstairs. But if it turned out that some dreadful crime had been committed up there in that strange room, the Persimmons were going to have to get used to a bit of police intrusion.

'So that's three bodies down at Tailors Court.' Gerry Heffernan slumped back in his seat. It wasn't as sturdy as his executive leather swivel chair back in his own office at

Tradmouth and it groaned ominously under his weight. Gerry looked alarmed and straightened himself up, searching for the most comfortable position. Wesley knew that he found it hard to think when he wasn't relaxed.

'Three skeletons,' Wesley corrected. 'But Neil thinks they could be centuries old.'

Gerry grunted. 'Well, if he's right, it'll save us a lot of work.'

'I asked the householders what they knew about the history of the house but it seems they haven't taken much interest.'

'Sometimes it's better not to know,' Gerry said quickly. 'I bet they wish they'd never started digging that trench now.'

Wesley smiled. Gerry was probably right. 'But it's not only the skeletons that look suspicious.' He didn't want the boss to be lulled into a false sense of security.

'What do you mean?'

Once Wesley had explained about the pictures and the attic room, Gerry sat in stupefied silence for a while. Then he spoke, a worried frown creasing his chubby face. 'If Neil's wrong and those bodies do turn out to be fairly recent . . .'

He didn't have to finish his sentence. Wesley had been thinking the same thing himself. That attic room up those hidden stairs might have been a scene of butchery – but not necessarily of animals. Maybe a killer had lived at Tailors Court at one time and he had buried his victims in the grounds.

'I've sent a few samples of cloth fragments from that room to the lab. It'll be interesting to see what they find.'

'I take it Neil's still carrying on with the digging?'

Wesley nodded. 'He says there are a number of anomalies on the geophysics survey.'

'And that means?'

'Possible graves.'

'How soon can he get it done?'

'As long as it takes. It's painstaking work. All possible evidence has to be recorded and preserved.'

Gerry sighed. 'Well, he did say those bones had probably been down there quite a while – unlike James Dalcott which is urgent with the press baying for the culprit.' A local morning newspaper lay on the DCI's desk, folded so that the headline couldn't be seen. Gerry pushed it towards him and Wesley opened it out.

'"Police baffled by doctor's shooting," Wesley read out loud. 'Well, they've got that one right.'

'Makes us sound like the ruddy Keystone Kops.' He began to search the heap of files on his desk and when he'd found what he was looking for he handed a sheet of paper to Wesley. 'The ballistics report. Revolver. Webley and Scott: standard World War Two issue for officers and military police. Someone's dad probably kept it as a souvenir. In spite of all the amnesties, there are probably still quite a few lying around in attics and grannies' drawers.'

Wesley studied the report for a few moments then handed it back to the DCI. 'Maybe the TV appeal will produce some results.'

Gerry looked at him and gave his widest grin. 'How are you feeling? Nervous? It's your first time, isn't it?'

'Yes. I'm a media virgin.'

'Only 'cause you've wriggled out of it before. You couldn't escape forever, you know. Not when the Chief

Constable's so keen to show how inclusive and multi-ethnic we are.' He gave Wesley a wink. 'You'll be fine.'

Wesley said nothing. Gerry appeared to be amused by the situation. But he'd appeared on TV several times making statements and appeals for witnesses, so he probably knew what he was talking about.

Gerry picked up a sheet of paper that was lying on his desk. 'Tom from Scientific Support's been through Dalcott's computer files like a dose of salts. Our victim was fond of genealogy and websites listing medical practitioners and their careers. He also looked at sites mentioning the George Clipton case. Apart from that, nothing out of the ordinary and no suspicious e-mails. We need to visit that clinic Dalcott worked at. Did you manage to find out any more about Dalcott's real dad?'

'I looked at a few websites last night. It seemed like an open and shut case, the oldest story in the book. Middle-aged doctor marries pretty young wife. Young wife has baby then gets bored. She starts going round with a lively crowd and having affairs then the older, boring husband snaps, strangles her and bashes her face in for good measure.'

'No mystery, then?'

'Doesn't look like it. Maybe it's got nothing to do with his murder.'

Gerry scratched his head thoughtfully before looking Wesley in the eye. 'There's always the possibility that history has repeated itself, only in reverse. Pretty young wife gets bored with boring middle-aged doctor, finds younger stud then decides to do dull husband in for the insurance or whatever.'

'I'm keeping an open mind,' said Wesley, although Gerry's theory sounded as good as any.

'There's still no sign of these missing neighbours – Syd and Brian Trenchard or whatever they were calling themselves.'

'As the car was hired in the name of William Smith, I think we can assume they aren't their real names. I've asked Paul to contact the owners of the cottage to gain access. Who knows, if we get their fingerprints we might find their real names on the police computer.'

Wesley stood up. 'Do you think we should let the Podingham Clinic know we're coming?'

Gerry looked him in the eye. 'Why make it easy for them to think up a story?' He looked at his watch. 'I've got to see the Nutter in half an hour. Bring him up to date with our progress. Why don't you and Rachel go to the clinic?'

'Are you going to tell the Nutter about Neil's skeletons?'

'I'll tell him that, according to an expert – that's Neil – the bones probably aren't our problem. That should keep him happy for a few seconds. Right, off you go and see what our victim got up to in his spare time.'

When Wesley broke the news to Rachel she seemed keen to get out of the office. Wesley let her drive as usual. Being born and bred there in the Devon countryside, she knew the landscape well and had been driving down the terrifying narrow lanes ever since she passed her test at the age of seventeen years and one month, having practised assiduously on her parents' farm. Wesley sat silently in the passenger seat and, as Rachel steered her way down the main road towards the small town of Podbury that lay between Neston and Dukesbridge, he went over in his head everything he knew about the murder of James

Dalcott. Dalcott had been shot in the head once, execution style, and the ballistics report stated that the weapon was a World War II revolver.

He couldn't banish the idea of execution from his thoughts. But the only suspects with any motive – the ex-wife and Adam Tey, the father of the child who'd died – hardly seemed the sort to end someone's life so coldly and efficiently. Unless they had paid a professional to act for them: it was a possibility they couldn't dismiss easily. He also had an uneasy feeling about the missing neighbours – had they been professional hit men hired to watch the quarry and strike when the time was right? But if this was the case, they'd certainly taken their time about it. And there was the question of Harry Parker's conviction. He'd used a firearm, albeit an unloaded one, when he'd robbed the jeweller, Joseph Hyam, which meant that Harry Parker was likely to have some pretty unsavoury contacts.

'Anything new?' Rachel asked as they reached a crossroads.

Wesley told her about the ballistics report and shared his views on Syd and Brian Trenchard. He saw a smile appear on her face.

'A father and son hit man team. Is that likely?'

He didn't answer. She was probably right. Rachel often was in his experience. And a hit man would hardly hang around for a couple of weeks living next door to the target. He'd get the job done as quickly as possible and make a rapid exit – and he'd probably work alone.

After a long silence she spoke again. 'What does this Podingham clinic do?'

'I'm not sure. I looked it up on the Internet and it didn't give much away.'

'Not cosmetic surgery then?'

As Wesley looked at her he thought he could see an expectant expression on her face and he wondered if she was fishing for compliments. 'No. No facelifts and liposuction as far as I could see. It said something about working in partnership with its parent company, Pharmitest International.'

Rachel frowned. 'Farmitest? Is that something to do with agriculture?'

'No. Pharm spelled with a PH. Presumably some kind of drug company. I looked them up on the Internet too but it was all a lot of corporate-speak and gobbledygook. Is this it?'

They had just spotted a sign informing them that Podbury was two miles away when, as they passed an area of woodland, Wesley saw a pair of large gateposts topped by stone eagles with outspread wings. The iron gates were firmly shut but there was an entryphone arrangement fixed to the gatepost on the right. There was also a discreet and new-looking sign with the words 'The Podingham Clinic' printed on in flowery script.

'Looks like they want to keep the riffraff out,' Rachel observed as she pulled the car up to the gate.

'As long as that doesn't include us.'

Rachel lowered her window and pushed the button on the entryphone. A few seconds after she'd announced their arrival the gates began to swing open very slowly, as if they had all the time in the world. Rachel, irritated, revved the engine. It did no good but Wesley guessed that it made her feel better.

The drive was flanked by tall evergreen trees crowding over the roadway to form a dark tunnel. If Wesley had been driving he would have been tempted to switch on his headlights but after a while they emerged into what passed for the light in mid-November. Before them was a large house – the sort described in exclusive estate agents' brochures as a Victorian gentleman's residence. The area in front of the main door had been covered with tarmac and marked off into car parking spaces. Rachel chose one at random, edged the car in and switched off the engine.

Wesley led the way to the open front door and they soon found themselves in an elegant hall with a chequer-board floor. There was no sign of medical activity; no drip stands; no wheelchairs; and no hospital swing doors. The place still looked fit for its original purpose – the home of a wealthy and tasteful family.

A door opened to their left and a blonde woman in her thirties emerged wearing a pristine white coat over a dark suit. Her shoes looked expensive and Wesley saw Rachel glance down at them with a flicker of envy.

The woman smiled, displaying a set of unnaturally even teeth. 'Welcome to the Podingham Clinic. I'm Fiona Verdun, the administrative manager.' She shook hands with each of them solemnly. 'We were absolutely devastated to hear about Dr Dalcott – that goes without saying. If we can do anything to help the police . . .'

'Nobody from the clinic has been in touch with us,' said Wesley, trying not to make the words sound too critical.

'Well, it was considered, of course. But the truth is, nobody here had anything relevant to tell you. I mean, James Dalcott was a genuinely nice man and we all assumed, I think, that he was killed by a burglar or . . .' Her voice trailed off. It was an excuse Wesley had heard before and he knew that behind all the fine words was a simple fact: nobody had wanted to get involved.

Fiona Verdun led them into what they supposed was her office, invited them to sit and offered coffee. Her manner was charming and Wesley began to suspect that her objective was to prevent them finding out too much about the workings of the clinic. But he hoped he was wrong.

'So how can I help you?' she said, all openness, as she handed them the coffee cups. 'If there's anything we at the Podingham Clinic can do to help your investigation . . .' She gave them a concerned smile, the sort of smile he'd seen before on the faces of politicians at election time.

'What exactly did Dr Dalcott do here?'

'He assisted in our clinical trials department. Part-time of course.'

'Clinical trials? Can you explain that?' Wesley glanced at Rachel and saw that she was sipping her coffee, listening intently.

'We test new drugs here.'

'On animals?' Rachel asked.

Wesley knew what she was thinking. Animal rights campaigners were often willing to go pretty far to make their point.

'No. We deal with the stage after animal research. We use volunteers.'

'Human volunteers?'

She smiled. 'Of course. They've traditionally been students who want to earn a little extra cash but these days we get a whole cross section of people. With the recession and unemployment . . .'

'And Dr Dalcott kept an eye on the volunteers during the trials?'

'We have qualified medical staff on hand at all times.'

The words 'in case something goes wrong' were left unsaid.

'Did James Dalcott administer the drugs on trial?'

'Sometimes. It would have been part of his duties.'

Wesley smiled. She still looked supremely confident. But he wondered whether his next question would change that. 'How often do things go wrong? Has anybody needed hospital treatment as a result of the trials?'

The mask of calm confidence didn't slip. But Wesley was certain he'd seen, just for a split second, a flicker of panic in Fiona's blue eyes.

'I know of no serious incidents involving adverse reactions to the drugs on trial,' she said as though she was reading from a script.

'How long have you worked here?' Rachel asked, catching Wesley's eye.

Fiona took a deep breath. 'Three months.'

'And before that?'

She hesitated. This wasn't a question she'd been expecting. 'I was in PR.'

'So you wouldn't necessarily know if there'd been any deaths or serious incidents before you started here?'

Wesley's question had the effect of breaking through the veneer of charm. She suddenly looked flustered as she searched for a suitable answer. 'No but . . .'

Wesley gave her his most charming smile. 'May we have a word with the person in charge here? As you said, I'm sure everyone here will be happy to help us with our investigation.'

He looked at her expectantly and saw her open and close her mouth. Things weren't going according to her carefully scripted plan. She had been briefed to bamboo-zle anyone asking awkward questions with charm and statistics and send them away happy.

'I'll see if Dr Welman's available,' she muttered as she picked up the telephone on her over-neat desk.

After a brief and awkward conversation, she looked up at Wesley and forced out a professional smile. 'Dr Welman will see you but he can only spare you five minutes. And I'm sure he won't be able to tell you anything I couldn't,' she added with veiled desperation. 'Dr Dalcott only helped out here part-time, you know.'

'Are there many part-time staff here?' Wesley asked.

'A few. Some work full time in hospitals and as GPs. And a couple, Dr Shallech and Dr Brown, are retired but they help with our drugs trials.'

They were led across the lofty hall to a polished mahogany door at the end of a wide corridor. A wooden sign bearing Dr Welman's name was fixed to the centre of the door, the letters formed elegantly in gold. His title was given below the name as 'Clinical Director'.

Fiona looked a little nervous as she raised her hand to knock. Perhaps, Wesley thought, she would be in trouble later for not heading them off. But this didn't bother him. If Dr Welman had information about James Dalcott that he wished to hide, he needed to find out.

The word 'Come' echoed from inside the office. A monosyllabic order. Fiona opened the door and stepped back.

Wesley entered the room first. Dr Welman was sitting behind a monumental antique desk and he stood up as they came in and held out his hand. He was a small man, thin, with sparse grey hair. It was difficult to tell his age which might have been anywhere between sixty and a well-preserved seventy-five. Wesley had expected him to look annoyed at the intrusion but instead his expression was one of polite concern. Standing by the desk was a tall woman in her late sixties or perhaps even her early seventies. Her hair was cut in an immaculate grey bob and a pair of glasses was perched on an aquiline nose. She wore rather a lot of make-up and the residue had settled in the lines on her face, emphasising rather than concealing.

Dr Welman stood up. 'Come in, officers. Do take a seat. This is Dr Shallech. She works here in our trials department.'

'You knew Dr Dalcott?'

Dr Shallech assumed a serious expression. 'Yes, but we often worked here at different times so I wouldn't say I knew him well. But I was shocked to hear about his death, of course.' Her voice was low pitched and rather husky, as though she was a habitual smoker, but Wesley's nose didn't catch any lingering scent of tobacco. She looked at Dr Welman. 'I really must get back to the department.'

She inclined her head politely to Wesley and Rachel before picking a file up off the desk. 'If you'll excuse me,' she said before hurrying out of the room.

When she had gone Wesley made the introductions and, to put Welman at ease, he mentioned that his sister had worked with James Dalcott.

Suddenly Welman's face lit up. 'Peterson? You're not by any chance Mr Joshua Peterson's son are you? James mentioned that he was working with his daughter – Maria, is it?'

'Maritia.'

'He said her brother was a detective inspector.'

'Yes. I broke with family tradition and didn't attend medical school.'

'Your father is one of the most distinguished cardiac surgeons in the country.'

Wesley thought he detected a note of criticism – of mild disapproval that he'd chosen to pursue criminals rather than follow the rest of the family into the medical profession – but he ignored it.

'You're a surgeon yourself, Dr Welman?'

The man behind the desk suddenly looked wary. 'I worked in medical research and took early retirement but Pharmitest wanted someone experienced to administer their facility here.'

'Is surgery carried out here?' Wesley asked innocently.

'We have some facilities for private surgery. Routine procedures mainly. When Mr Powell retired from NHS work, he took charge of our surgical department.'

'Where did you work before you retired?'

Welman cleared his throat as though he needed time to think. 'Various hospitals and universities around the country. I worked in Canada for a while.'

The answer seemed rather evasive but Wesley decided it was time to get down to business. 'James Dalcott's death must have been a great shock to everyone here.'

'A terrible shock, yes. We were all devastated when we heard.'

Welman sounded sincere. Either that or he was a remarkably good actor.

'What can you tell us about him?' Wesley began.

Welman sat back in his chair and considered the

question for a moment. 'I'm sure you'll have heard from your sister that James was a pleasant man and a good doctor.'

Wesley nodded.

'He was very well liked and I shouldn't have thought he had an enemy in the world.'

'What about his work here?'

'He worked for us part-time. We employ a number of doctors on that basis. Dr Shallech whom you just met is retired but she still does a couple of days a week for us.'

'You seem to employ rather a lot of retired staff here.'

'Nothing wrong with that, Inspector. We have a wealth of experience between us and Pharmitest appreciates that.'

'Of course,' Wesley said quickly. 'Is there anything else you can tell us about Dr Dalcott?'

'James did his work efficiently and he was very good with the volunteers. You need someone with a pleasant manner to reassure them and put them at their ease, you understand.' He paused. 'The work he did here wasn't very demanding in the clinical sense – he was here to make sure the correct doses were administered and observe the volunteers' reactions to the drugs they were given.'

'Have there been any times when his medical skills were needed urgently? I'm talking about any occasions when things have gone wrong and he's had to administer emergency treatment.'

Wesley watched Welman's face and guessed that he'd hit a raw memory. 'Oh dear. Yes. Er . . . There was one incident but . . .' The doctor was starting to look flustered.

'What happened?'

Welman took a deep breath. 'I have to consider patient confidentiality.'

'I promise you that if the matter's not relevant, nobody will know you've told us. And besides, we can always obtain a search warrant.' Wesley looked at the man expectantly. In his experience that particular threat usually worked a treat.

'Very well.' He arched his fingers, gathering his thoughts. 'About a year ago we ran a routine trial but one of the volunteers – a young man – experienced an adverse reaction to the drug. It was very rare, you understand. Quite unexpected.'

'And how was James Dalcott involved?'

'He was supervising the volunteers that evening. The young man lost consciousness and his skin began to blister.'

'I take it he was admitted to hospital?' It was Rachel who spoke.

Welman gave her a sad smile. 'We have all the necessary facilities here and, besides, the personnel in A and E wouldn't necessarily know what they were dealing with. We rushed him to our emergency room here. He survived.'

'But?'

'He was left with a severe sensitivity to light. If he goes out in daylight his flesh blisters.'

Wesley pondered the implications of Welman's revelation for a few moments. 'Did he blame James Dalcott for what went wrong?'

Welman rose from his seat and walked over to the window. He stood looking out over the manicured gardens for a while before answering.

'It wasn't James's fault, you understand, but he was supervising. James's was the face he knew so in his mind it was James who was to blame. Of course James acted swiftly once he realised it was all going wrong. There was no delay in putting the emergency procedures into operation. But even so . . .'

'So there's a young man out there who blames James Dalcott for his condition?'

Welman pressed his lips together. 'I suppose you could put it like that.'

'We'll need his name,' said Rachel, her pen poised over her notebook.

Welman walked over to the polished mahogany filing cabinet that stood in the corner of his spacious office. He opened the middle drawer and took out a file which he examined for a few moments before handing it to Wesley.

'His name's Carl Utley. Aged twenty-six. Unemployed. Lives in Neston.'

'Is he married? Partner?'

'He was living with a woman he described as his fiancée when he came to us for the trial. He put her down as his next of kin. But whether they're still together . . .'

Wesley looked at the address. It was on a small council estate on the outskirts of Neston, not far from the railway station, a few streets away from Adam Tey and Charleen Anstice. And not a million miles from Tradington where James Dalcott had met his end. He took the file to the desk, read through it and made a few notes.

When he'd finished he looked up. 'I believe a man called Ken Mold works here.'

Welman frowned, as though he had heard the name before but couldn't quite place it. Then he remembered.

'There's a handyman called Ken. Is that him?'

'Yes. He lives next door to two of James Dalcott's patients. Their child died and they blame James.'

Welman looked genuinely surprised. 'I didn't know about that.'

Wesley smiled. 'We might need to talk to you again, Dr Welman.' He looked at Rachel and nodded. 'I can see you're busy so we'll see ourselves out.' He flashed a smile at Welman who attempted one in return. But his eyes remained wary. In Wesley's experience, the eyes betrayed a lot.

'So what do you think?' Wesley asked Rachel as they walked to the car.

'That Fiona Verdun was full of her own importance. But I think Welman was being fairly straight with us – after all, he didn't have to tell us about Carl Utley, did he?' She nudged his arm. 'I reckon you're well in there with your family connections. You might not have got as much out of them if they hadn't known your dad was a famous surgeon.'

'The medical profession have always stuck together. A bit like the police.'

As they got into the car, Wesley's mobile phone rang and Rachel sat, hand poised over the ignition key until the short conversation was finished.

Wesley put the phone back in his pocket and turned to face her. 'That was the incident room. They've got an ID on the Trenchards. There's a match on the fingerprints in the house next door to Dalcott's.'

'Do we have names?

Wesley told her.

'So we can make an arrest?'

'If we can find them,' he answered as she started the engine.

Neil's team had just unearthed their fourth skeleton, precisely where the geophysics printout had told them it was going to be. It was female this time. Probably young. And again there were no fillings, something Neil knew that Wesley would interpret as a hopeful sign. The more Neil thought about it, the more the situation seemed to bear all the hallmarks of a historical mystery rather than a sordid modern-day crime. But they still had to go through the motions.

However, the increasing likelihood that the skeletons were old didn't mean he could relax. The Persimmons had made it quite clear that all the skeletons had to be lifted. There was no way they wanted to think that every time they stepped out of their front door they were entering a burial ground. Neil hadn't had them down as the superstitious type but sometimes people can surprise you.

He also had another problem. Somehow the local press had got hold of the story – Neil had no idea how – and that morning there had been a reporter waiting in a car parked near the gate. When she'd seen Neil arrive, she'd sprung from the vehicle like a gamekeeper on an unwary poacher, and barred his way, tape recorder at the ready.

After introducing herself as Nuala Johns of the *Morbay Argus* she'd asked him for a statement about the skeletons. Neil, taken aback and unsure what to say, made noncommittal noises about the investigation being ongoing. It was a phrase he'd heard Wesley use and it sounded good.

'But you can confirm human remains have been found?'

He knew she wasn't going to let the matter drop so, as he'd never been a good liar, he said yes. They had found human bones but all the indications were that they were old.

'How many skeletons have you found?'

'Four so far.'

'There might be more?' She could hardly keep the excitement out of her voice. This had all the hallmarks of a good story. 'And the police have been called in?' she persisted.

'Yes. But that's just routine.'

She continued her barrage of questions for a while and Neil felt himself becoming more defensive as he took a step backwards, preparing for flight.

When she eventually gave up and went away he wondered how long it would be before the wolves descended. And when they did, he knew he'd have to think up something more solid to give them; either that or he could answer their questions with a terse 'no comment'. But that would probably make them all the keener.

There had been a small geophysics anomaly on the edge of what estate agents would have described in a brochure as a paddock, well away from the burials they had discovered so far. Neil made the decision to investigate this himself, although he suspected that it was probably some sort of rubbish pit, or maybe the burial of an animal; a well-loved pet dog, perhaps. But it was best to get it dealt with and ticked off on his list of things to do as soon as possible.

Colin Bowman had just left and Neil thought he was showing remarkable patience in the circumstances. He'd agreed that all the bones they found should be recorded properly and sent to the mortuary for examination and yet as Neil began to dig again, he felt a small thrill of excitement. He needed to discover whether the skeletons were connected with the strange room in the attic and those ancient medical instruments. And he needed to know what dramatic events in the history of that prosperous Devon house had led to those bones ending up buried there in the cold, unconsecrated earth.

He felt frustrated that he hadn't yet had time to research the history of Tailors Court and he knew it was time to delegate. His relationship with Annabel who worked in the County Archives was good, if not romantically close, and he was convinced that she would relish the challenge of Tailors Court. He resolved to call her later – when he had a moment.

'Need some help?' Neil looked up and saw Chris standing there expectantly, shifting from foot to foot in an effort to keep warm.

Neil signalled him to come nearer. 'I could do with a hand. Not that I'm expecting to find much here. It's well away from the burials and the geophysics anomaly's smaller. Could be an animal burial. Or a midden. But we have to check it out,' he said as he began to scrape away at the soil.

He continued digging in silence until a small, dirty white shape appeared and suddenly his heart began to race. He froze for a few moments then he began to scrape more carefully.

'It'll be an animal,' said Chris who'd started working a few feet away.

Neil took a deep breath. 'Stop what you're doing and get Dave over, will you? Tell him to bring the camera.'

Chris hurried away. Neil continued scraping the clinging soil away very carefully. When the skeleton was half uncovered he made the decision to put on a crime scene suit and do things by the book. He placed a plastic tray at the side of the trench and asked Dave to take photographs.

Dave stood there, recording the whole thing without a word while Neil carried on working in silence. This skeleton seemed different to the others. The chances were that this was a child, buried in the cold damp earth and forgotten for many years.

'Should we call the police out again?' Dave asked tentatively.

'They'll be getting sick of us,' said Chris who was now standing watching, hands in pockets.

'I know they will but we'd better be on the safe side. And we'd better get Dr Bowman back here as well.' Neil pointed to a rotted shape just next to the skeleton's right hand. 'What do you make of that?'

'It's wood,' Dave answered. 'Half rotten by the look of it.'

'Yes. But what does it look like?'

'Are those wheels? A wooden car? It can't be.'

Neil didn't answer. He started to brush the soil away from the small pelvis then he picked something up very carefully and, once he'd cleaned it a little, replaced it so that Dave could photograph it *in situ*. Then he climbed out of the trench and took his mobile phone from the plastic box.

When he'd made the two calls he stood by Dave and Chris, staring down at what had been uncovered.

Dave spoke first. 'If that's a toy car, it means . . .'

Neil looked up. 'It means we could have a child murder on our hands. I say we wait for Colin and the police.'

'Poor little sod,' said Dave bowing his head.

CHAPTER 6

Transcript of recording made by Mrs Mabel Cleary (née Fallon) – Home Counties Library Service Living History Project: Reminiscences of a wartime evacuee.

They say you can get used to anything, don't they? Even being in prison so I've heard. I had to do a lot of cleaning and polishing and Mrs Jannings didn't allow me out to play till I'd finished. Even though she seemed better she still stayed in her room a lot. I don't suppose they knew much about depression and that sort of thing in those days but I think that's what she had. She never smiled or laughed and I tried to keep out of her way.

Tailors Court wasn't a proper farm because it didn't have enough land but now there was a war on they kept a few pigs and a couple of cows and what land they had was ploughed up and planted with crops. We had to dig for victory after all. Mary worked on the farm next door but her and the other land girls looked after the land and the animals at Tailors Court too.

I liked Mary. She showed me lots of things. How to put rollers in my hair, how to put gravy browning on your legs so it looked as though you had stockings on and how to draw a line up the back of your leg with an eyebrow pencil to make it look like a seam. I'd never had a big sister but I think Mary was the next best thing.

I was glad when Miles went off back to his unit. He gave me the creeps hanging around like that watching me and Mary. Sometimes Mary used to ask me to stay with her so she wouldn't be alone with him and I didn't blame her.

Then one day a car arrived. It was the lady who'd brought me to Tailors Court. She asked me how I was and I remembered my manners and said very well thank you. Then I saw that she had a girl and a boy on the back seat. The boy was crying and clutching a toy car like his life depended on it.

When Mrs Jannings came out she didn't look pleased. And when I ran upstairs to tell Mary, she said there'd be trouble.

From the fingerprints they'd left in the rented house next door to James Dalcott's, it was soon discovered that the two men who'd called themselves Syd and Brian Trenchard were known to the police under the names Syd Jenkins and Brian Carrack. Wesley observed that they hadn't even had the imagination to change their first names, which suggested that they were hardly criminal masterminds.

Jenkins and Carrack had done time for robbery – mainly from security vans – but the most interesting piece of new information, from Wesley's point of view, was that the last time they had been resident in one of Her Majesty's prisons, their fellow guests had included one Harry Parker. Gerry Heffernan – who was no believer in coincidences – had become rather excited when he'd heard this news and sent a patrol car to Tradmouth to pick Parker up.

When Wesley returned to the incident room, he made straight for Gerry's desk and sat down. 'So Roz Dalcott's fancy man was in jail with a pair of armed robbers who were renting a house next door to her estranged husband.'

'And if anyone knows how to use a firearm, it's an armed robber. I reckon Parker paid these two to get rid of Roz's inconvenient husband before he had a chance to change his will.' He sat back with a beatific smile on his face. 'I think we've cracked it, Wes.'

'What about the other things: the Podingham Clinic and the father who was hanged for murdering his wife?'

'What about them?'

Wesley didn't answer. Gerry was probably right. This case was far more straightforward than he'd imagined. A simple case of greed.

Wesley's mobile phone began to ring. He looked at the display and saw that it was Neil.

'We've found a body,' were Neil's first words.

'Is this number five?' Wesley answered with a sigh. Although it was all very interesting, as things were, he really didn't have the time.

There was a long pause. 'This one's different, Wes.'

Something in Neil's voice made him pay attention.

'How do you mean, different?'

'It's a child. And it was buried with a toy car.'

Wesley's mouth formed an O. He looked at Gerry who

was busy sorting through his paperwork, pushing it from one side of his desk to the other.

'A car. Are you sure?'

'Course I am.' Neil sounded a little hurt.

'Have you called Colin?'

'Yes. He didn't sound too pleased. I reckon he thinks it's just another old one.'

'I'll have a word if you like.'

'I've told him already. He's on his way. We've sealed off the trench.'

'I'll be down right away.'

Gerry looked up. 'What is it?'

'Neil's found a child's skeleton at Tailors Court. He says he thinks it's fairly recent. Colin's on his way there now.' He'd just taken off his coat and flung it across a vacant chair but now he picked it up. 'You coming?'

Gerry stood up, knocking a file onto the floor. He left it there. 'Parker should be here soon but it'll do him good to wait. An hour or so in the cells and a few cups of the bilge-water they call tea from that infernal machine concentrates the mind wonderfully.'

When the two men arrived at Tailors Court Colin Bowman was already there, hunched over the trench with Neil squatting by his side. A pair of uniformed constables were standing at either end of the trench like bookends, watching the proceedings with interest and stamping their polished boots on the sparse, yellowing grass to keep warm.

'So what have we got?' said Wesley as he reached the spot.

Neil stood to one side. 'Look for yourself.'

The small bones lay there in the damp earth, the eye

134

sockets in the skull staring up at him. The child had been buried on his or her back and a chunk of rotting wood, with what looked like wheels at each corner, lay by the right hand. Neil had been right. It looked like a roughly made toy car and the sight of it made him feel a little sick. These sad little bones had once been a child – someone's son or daughter.

He addressed Colin. 'Any obvious cause of death?'

'Nothing obvious, I'm afraid. But I can tell you this poor little chap's had an amalgam filling at some time in his life. I'm afraid this one's yours, Wesley.'

'Is it a boy or a girl?' Gerry asked. He was hovering behind Wesley, staring down at the trench.

'Difficult to tell at this age, Gerry,' Colin answered. 'I think he or she is about nine or ten, judging by the teeth.' He didn't say anything for a few moments. 'If I were you, I'd be getting my missing persons files out.'

'So how long has it been there?'

Colin looked at Neil. 'Any ideas?'

Neil bent down and took a small, soil-caked object from the plastic tray at the side of the trench. He handed it to Wesley.

'I found it resting on the pelvis.'

Wesley examined the thing carefully before passing it to Gerry. 'Corroded metal. Looks like a letter S, or a snake,' he said softly.

A middle-aged constable who'd been standing near by sidled up to Gerry and peered over his shoulder, fascinated. He was a large man with a beer belly to match the Chief Inspector's own. 'I used to have one of those when I was a nipper.' He looked at Gerry. 'Don't you recognise it, sir?'

Gerry nodded and turned the thing round in his fingers. 'It's one of those belt clasps shaped like a snake. All the little lads used to have them at one time, isn't that right?' He looked at the constable for confirmation and he nodded obediently. 'You'll be too young to remember them, Wes.'

Wesley took the object from his boss and stared at it. It did nudge a vague and distant memory – cub scouts and climbing trees; carrying penknives in your pocket before the time when the possession of a bladed weapon took on sinister connotations. He rather thought he might have worn such a belt at one time in the dim and distant past. Or perhaps Gerry was right and they had gone out of fashion long before he was born and he recognised it only from old photographs of childhood innocence.

'The toy car and the snake belt clasp point to this being a boy,' Wesley said quietly.

'We need to do a DNA test to be sure,' said Colin. 'Neil, if you can lift and record these bones, I'll examine them properly back at the mortuary.' His face was solemn.

As Neil got down to work, Wesley spoke quietly, staring down at the grave. 'I think the first thing we need to do is to find out more about the people who used to live here,' he said.

'I'll leave that to you, Wes,' Gerry said as he turned away.

'So where are they?'

Rachel Tracey sat opposite Harry Parker in the interview room. There was a small, smug smile on his lips which was starting to annoy her. His solicitor, a serious young man with dark curly hair who looked as though this might well be his first case since leaving law school, sat quietly by the suspect's side. Every so often he had opened his mouth then closed it again, as though he had been about to intervene then thought better of it.

'I've no idea what you're talking about, Detective Sergeant Tracey.' He leaned towards her and she looked away. He was a suspect in a murder enquiry and she told herself she shouldn't find him attractive. She pursed her lips together and gave him a cold stare.

She was relieved when Trish Walton took over the questioning. DCI Heffernan had asked them to keep Parker occupied until his return and had suggested that the female touch might loosen him up a bit. But Rachel really couldn't see it working. Parker wasn't that stupid. Quite the opposite.

'You do know Syd Jenkins and Brian Carrack. You met them in prison.'

Parker gave Trish a charming smile. 'I keep telling you, I've put all that behind me. I'm an artist now and I've got a beautiful fiancée and a baby on the way. Why should I get involved in anything criminal and risk going back inside? It doesn't make sense.'

Rachel exchanged a look with Trish. If Parker had disposed of his partner's husband before he had a chance to cut her out of his will, it made perfect sense. And how much better if somebody else – two old prison acquaintances, for instance – did the dirty deed for him?

'Let's face it, Detective Sergeant Tracey – or may I call you Rachel? – you can't prove anything. And where are these two alleged hit men I'm supposed to have hired to dispose of Roz's ex, eh? And even if you could produce them, there's no way they'd say I was involved.'

'I think my client's told you everything he knows,' the

137

solicitor piped up in a voice that could only be described as timid.

The door opened and a young constable scurried in and whispered something in Rachel's ear. After announcing that she was absenting herself for the benefit of the machine that was recording every word for posterity, she left the room, returning a few minutes later with a sheet of paper in her hand.

She looked at Harry Parker for a moment then sat down. With a charming smile of her own, she went straight for the jugular. 'In your last statement you told us that you and Rosalind Dalcott were in your flat in Tradmouth together on the night of James Dalcott's death.'

'That's right,' Parker replied with confidence. 'We were together all that night.'

'Did anybody borrow Mrs Dalcott's car that night?'

A look of uncertainty flashed across Parker's face, there for a split second then gone. 'I don't think so. Why?'

Rachel took a deep breath. 'A lot of people complain about surveillance cameras and the Big Brother society, Mr Parker, but I must say that there are times when it comes in useful. We've got some hi-tech new traffic cameras up on the main junction on the way in to Neston. Number plate recognition, the lot. A blue Toyota registered to Rosalind Dalcott went through that junction at quarter to seven heading towards Tradington on Saturday evening.'

She sat back and watched as Harry Parker looked in desperation at the young solicitor who was shuffling his feet as though he wished he was somewhere else.

Then he looked up. 'No comment,' he said. And from then on he exercised his right to silence.

*

About fifteen minutes after Wesley left Tailors Court, he had a call from Neil to say that when he'd lifted the child's bones, he'd found a 1939 penny lying just beneath the ribs. This information confirmed Wesley's worst fears: the child met his or her death after that penny was minted. And there was one person in particular he wanted to see.

Tony and Jill Persimmon had provided a forwarding address for Mrs Jannings, the last owner of Tailors Court. Wesley had intended to contact her when the first skeletons were found but, as Neil was certain that they were old, it hadn't been high on his list of priorities, especially with James Dalcott's murder to worry about. But now everything had changed.

Mrs Esther Jannings who, according to the Persimmons, had been widowed during the War and had inherited Tailors Court from her late husband's mother, now lived in a residential home on the outskirts of the large seaside resort of Morbay. But when Wesley telephoned, he was told that she was among a group of residents who'd gone out for the day to do some early Christmas shopping with some of the care assistants and she wouldn't be back till that evening.

Wesley could have delegated the visit to a junior officer but he wanted to see Mrs Jannings for himself. He wanted to ask her what she knew about the strange room in the attic of her old house. And he wanted to see her reaction when he told her about the child's skeleton buried near the paddock.

Gerry groaned loudly and put his head in his hands when Wesley broke the bad news. Even though the prospects of getting a conviction were slim after all this time, the child's bones were definitely their problem now – along with James Dalcott's shooting.

But Wesley found it hard to concentrate on the case as his imminent TV appearance was nagging at the back of his mind, uncomfortable as a toothache. Because of this he wouldn't get to see Mrs Jannings that day but he'd visit her first thing tomorrow, he assured himself as he drove back to the incident room with Gerry slumped in the passenger seat.

Wesley almost made the mistake of turning the car towards Tradmouth but then he remembered they were stationed at Neston for the time being. He glanced at the clock on the dashboard and saw that it was already half past five. He was due at the press conference at six in time for the local evening news and the prospect made him feel a little nauseous. But that wasn't something he wanted to share with Gerry. At that moment he was in no mood for the DCI's words of wisdom.

When they arrived at the incident room, Rachel greeted them.

'He's keeping shtum,' she said. 'Even when I told him Roz's car was seen driving towards Tradington at the relevant time he didn't say a word.'

Wesley gave her a sympathetic look. 'I take it we're talking about Harry Parker?'

She gave him an enquiring look. 'Who else?'

'Have you spoken to Roz Dalcott?'

'She's next on the list. I thought I'd have her brought in in the morning. We don't want to be accused of ill-treating a pregnant widow, do we?'

'Sorry, Rach, what did you say?'

She looked at him, exasperated and repeated what she'd said.

Wesley gave her an apologetic smile. 'Sorry, I'm not quite with it at the moment. They've found the skeleton of a child at Tailors Court and everything points to it having been buried fairly recently. Well, within the past sixty years or so anyway.'

Rachel stood there stunned for a few moments, taking in the news. 'A child. God. I'll ask someone to go through missing persons, shall I?'

'It'll wait till tomorrow, love,' said Gerry who'd been standing behind Wesley with an impatient look on his face. 'I take it our friend Parker's safely in the cells?'

'Yes, but we can't hold him for much longer without charging him.'

'You don't have to tell me that, Rach,' said Gerry. 'But he's our best suspect so far and I think I'll be able to persuade the Nutter to authorise more time. Me and Paul'll have a word with him – see if we can catch him out.' He grinned. 'You've got a prior engagement, haven't you, Wesley?'

Wesley attempted to look cheerful as his eyes met Rachel's. But he felt like a man en route to the gallows.

'Good luck,' said Rachel softly.

'I think they say "break a leg" in theatrical circles,' the DCI said with a chuckle.

Wesley left Gerry to deal with Harry Parker, although at that moment there was nothing he'd have liked better than to conduct the interview himself. He felt frustrated, as though he was missing out. He knew Gerry would bring him up to date with the facts when they next met but somehow it wasn't quite the same.

On leaving the bustle of the incident room, he found himself walking down the quiet, unfamiliar corridors of

Neston Police Station. He looked at his watch. Pam would have arrived home from school by now – she was always in by five unless she had a staff meeting or a parents' evening. He had ten minutes before the press conference so he took his phone from his pocket and dialled his home number. Pam answered after two rings.

'Hi,' she asked breathlessly. 'How's it going?'

He told her. And when he broke the news about the child's skeleton there was a short silence on the other end of the line. 'A child,' she said after a few seconds. 'How long ago?'

'We're not sure yet. But I don't think it's very recent. Not within the last few years.'

He heard her exhale. He knew what she'd been thinking. If there was a child killer around, were Michael and Amelia safe?

He decided to change the subject. 'I'm just on my way to the press conference. It should be on the local news. You'll record it, won't you?'

'Of course.' There was a pause. 'The kids are looking forward to seeing their dad on telly.'

'I'll see you later then. Not sure what time but . . .'

The line went dead and he was left listening to the dialling tone, hoping that she hadn't meant that Michael and Amelia were looking forward to seeing him on television because they saw precious little of him otherwise. But he told himself he was imagining things. He tried his best, as far as the job allowed. But sometimes he longed to be there to share his children's worries and triumphs. His own father had been dedicated to his work and had spent long hours in the hospital. As a result, Wesley had never felt particularly close to him while he was growing up.

Perhaps this had been behind his choice of career: his little rebellion against his family's expectations. He thought of Michael and Amelia with a pang of sadness: the last thing he wanted was for them to feel as he had once felt – as though they came a poor second on his list of priorities. But, as it was, there was little he could do to change things for the time being.

He put the thought out of his mind and continued down the carpeted corridor to the conference room. As he approached he could hear the buzz of voices and he suddenly experienced a queasy feeling in the pit of his stomach. He had faced armed criminals and ruthless killers but this was far more terrifying.

After pushing open the swing doors he walked confidently up the central aisle, aware of eyes watching his every movement. He had known from the outset that the press would probably regard a black detective inspector as rather a novelty, but he found the reality rather daunting; the way the chatter eased as he walked in and the intense stares – most curious but some hostile.

He took his seat beside Evonne Arlis who looked as though she would have flung her arms around him and greeted him like a long-lost friend had it not been for the assembled audience.

'So glad you're here,' she whispered, touching his arm as if for comfort. She was wearing her dark blue Sister's uniform – no doubt someone had suggested it as a way of emphasising that the victim had been a respected healer and all-round blameless Performer of Good Works in the local area. Image was everything.

Wesley leaned over to whisper in her ear. 'How are you?'

She took a deep, shuddering breath. 'Bearing up. I've gone back to work. It's good to keep busy.'

Before she could say any more, Chief Superintendent Nutter, dapper in his flawless uniform, appeared at the door with the Press Officer by his side. Nutter took his seat and, when the Press Officer had finished his introduction, he looked at Wesley expectantly.

The questions went by in a blur of adrenaline and Wesley was hardly aware of the TV cameras pointing at him. Evonne said her piece, breaking down in tears at just the right moment. Wesley was just thinking that it had all gone rather well when a young woman stood up.

'Nuala Johns, *Morbay Argus*,' she announced confidently. 'Why haven't the police made a statement about the bodies that have been found in the grounds of a house near Tradington? I understand four have been found to date. Have you anything to say, Inspector Peterson?'

There was a split second of total silence before the shouting began. A hundred journalists baying for a golden story. Four bodies. This trumped one dead doctor any day. Wesley glanced at CS Nutter who looked like a rabbit caught in a set of monstrous headlights. This wasn't going according to plan.

The Press Officer gave Wesley a furious look. He hadn't been briefed about any skeletons and Wesley guessed that he was the one who'd get the blame for the oversight.

Wesley stood up and waited for the hubbub to die down. His heart was pounding as he cleared his throat, searching for the right words. In this situation the wrong ones could lead to disaster. 'Ladies and gentlemen, it is true that some human remains have been found on private property. However, expert opinion has concluded that these bodies are probably hundreds of years old and there is a team from the County Archaeological Unit investigating the site at the moment. No doubt a report on their findings will be issued in due course.' He flashed Nuala Johns a charming smile, wondering if the insincerity was showing through. 'If the situation changes, of course, the press will be informed as soon as possible,' he added, thinking of the small bones in the fifth grave.

He wasn't ready to say anything about the child's burial yet; not until they'd done more background research. But when it did become public knowledge, he knew now that the press would think all their birthdays had come at once – especially Ms Nuala Johns who had the lean hungry look of an ambitious young woman on the make.

The Press Officer looked relieved as he brought the proceedings to an end. But not as relieved as Wesley felt.

CS Nutter leaned over and whispered in Wesley's ear. 'I think you handled that rather well, Inspector.'

'Thank you, sir. There'll be a full statement when we know more about these new bones we've found at Tailors Court.' The words came out in a rush.

'New bones?'

Wesley realised that he should have kept his mouth shut. The last thing Gerry wanted was the Powers That Be watching his every move until they knew exactly what they were dealing with.

'We're trying to establish the age of the bones at the moment. There's a chance that they'll be of more interest to an archaeologist than a policeman.' He hoped his words had reassured Nutter but he wasn't hanging about to find out. He excused himself, saying he wanted to speak to Evonne Arlis before she left.

She was hovering by the door and she looked a little lost. Someone should be looking after her, he thought to himself, rather annoyed that she was being left to her own devices after the ordeal of the press conference. As he approached he saw her expression change to one of relief.

'Do you need a lift home?' he asked.

'I don't want to be a nuisance,' Evonne said, her eyes scanning the room. 'A police car called for me and brought me here and I was just looking out for the young constable.'

'Don't worry. It's not far out of my way.' She gave him a grateful smile and he felt that warm internal glow that comes from performing a Good Deed.

'To tell you the truth,' Wesley said as they hurried to his car – it had begun to rain again and he'd parked at the far end of the car park – 'I've been wanting to have a word with you.' He unlocked the passenger door and held it open.

'What about?'

Wesley didn't answer until they were on the road to Tradington.

'Now that the initial shock's worn off, I'd like to talk about James.'

'What about him?' Wesley detected a wary note in her voice.

'Is there anything else you can tell us about his life? People he mentioned, places he went; that sort of thing. I presume you knew he worked part-time in a private clinic? The Podingham Clinic near Podbury?'

'Yes, but I was sworn to secrecy. He didn't want anyone else at the practice to know he'd been moonlighting. He joked that he needed the money because Roz was high maintenance. I bet she's been bleeding him white since she walked out too,' she added with disapproval.

146

'You didn't think to tell us?'

She blushed. 'To be honest, with everything that's happened, it slipped my mind.'

'Did he say anything about what he did there?'

'He said it was just routine work; keeping an eye on people involved in drugs trials, taking blood tests and generally being on hand to make sure they were okay. He said it was dull but it was money for old rope.'

Wesley didn't answer. This was more or less what he'd expected to hear.

She suddenly frowned, as though she'd remembered something. 'I was at his house once and the phone rang. He went to take the call in another room.'

'Go on.'

'Well, I could only hear one side of the conversation but I'm sure James said something about someone taking a risk. When I asked him who it was afterwards, he told me it was someone from the Podingham Clinic and it was just routine.'

'Were any names mentioned?'

'I don't think so. He was speaking very quietly so I only heard snatches. I could even have been mistaken. This is it. Just turn right into this road.'

Wesley obeyed and brought the car to a halt in front of a tiny modern cottage on the southern edge of Tradington village, built as token 'affordable housing', neat and compact as a rabbit hutch. It was about half a mile from James Dalcott's place. Very convenient, Wesley thought, for Evonne to comfort the abandoned husband.

Wesley switched off the engine and turned to face her. 'Did James ever mention that he'd been adopted?'

She shook her head.

'So he didn't tell you that his biological father had been hanged for murdering his mother?'

Evonne stared at him for a few moments, lost for words.

'His father's name was George Clipton. He was a GP in Dorset and he strangled his wife because she was unfaithful. He never mentioned the name?'

'No.' She looked rather stunned. 'That might have been why he was so preoccupied. That might be what he meant by family business. I assumed it was about Roz.'

'We think he'd only found out recently. He was only a baby at the time and his father's sister and her husband adopted him. I imagine they thought it best if he never knew the truth.'

'Oh, poor James. Fancy finding out something like that. He must have been devastated.' She hesitated. 'Did Roz know?'

'That's something I need to find out,' he said quietly.

Because of Roz Dalcott's pregnancy and the fact that it was her new partner rather than herself who had the criminal record, they'd been treating her gently – maybe too gently. Trish Walton had visited her a couple of times for a bit of soft questioning but perhaps it was time to get tougher. Rachel had mentioned bringing her in for questioning and suddenly he couldn't wait to hear what she had to say.

'Look, I'd better go.' Evonne opened the car door, suddenly eager to get away.

'Thank you for taking part in the press conference. Let's hope it brings a few witnesses out of the woodwork, eh?'

She gave him a shy smile and slammed the car door.

CHAPTER 7

Transcript of recording made by Mrs Mabel Cleary (née Fallon) – Home Counties Library Service Living History Project: Reminiscences of a wartime evacuee.

The girl was called Belle and the boy was her cousin, Charlie. Belle was about the same age as me with curly blonde hair and she was very pretty. Charlie was about six months younger and he had fair curls too. Mary said he looked like a little angel, but some of the village boys said he looked like a girl. I think Mrs Jannings had been rail-roaded into taking them because the evacuation people knew that she had lots of room at Tailors Court and she had to be seen to do her bit for the war effort like everyone else. Not that she was happy about it.

Charlie was very quiet and Belle used to tease him which only made him worse. At first he used to spend hours on end with the pigs they kept in the outhouse and

Belle said he smelled like them, which was unkind even though she was right. Not that Mrs Jannings ever said anything. I don't think she noticed what was going on under her own roof.

Belle told me Charlie's family had all been killed by a bomb and I felt sorry for him. But when I tried to be friendly he wouldn't say much and then he started following Miles around. Miles was back from the army and Mary told me he was on leave for medical reasons. I didn't know then what those reasons were of course. He didn't seem to be wounded or anything and I could tell by the way Mary said it that she didn't really believe it.

There was a girl used to come and see Miles – Esther her name was and she was a big, plain girl. Mary reckoned she was sweet on Miles and she said she was welcome to him.

One day Miles killed one of the pigs and it made a terrible noise like someone screaming in agony. I can still hear it now, that awful sound, and I had nightmares about it for ages afterwards. Charlie helped him and although he didn't say anything, there was a funny look in his eyes, almost as though he was enjoying it. From that day on Charlie never seemed to leave Miles's side and sometimes it seemed as if they shared a big secret.

But for a long time I never knew what that secret was.

Roz Dalcott put her hand on her growing belly. It was evening now but Harry was still painting in the old outhouse at the back of the shop. When he went in there she knew he wasn't to be disturbed and his single-minded focus on his art was beginning to annoy her – especially when that art was so uncommercial. Who was going to buy those hideous pictures of dissected bodies downstairs in the gallery? People round here wanted something more cheerful on their walls – not something that reminded them of death and decay. And as for the tourists who came flocking in the summer months, they wanted something to remind them of pretty Devon – fishing boats, beach huts and Tradmouth with its jumble of pastel-coloured houses tumbling down to the river. Not blood and gore.

If James hadn't died when he did, she told herself as she felt the baby moving inside her, they'd be in the direst of financial straits. A few days later and he would have changed that will. And she'd have got nothing.

For the first time since the murder she felt relaxed. But the sudden sound of the telephone broke the silence and made her jump. She picked up the receiver.

It was for Harry. A gruff male voice she didn't recognise.

'Who's that?' she asked, trying to sound calm even though all her senses were screaming that this was someone from Harry's shady past.

'Just tell him it's an old friend from the university of life,' the voice said.

Roz hesitated for a moment then she went off to find Harry, her heart beating fast.

The last thing she wanted was for Harry Parker's past to catch up with him.

It was Wednesday morning and Wesley's ordeal by press was over. When he'd returned home the previous evening he and Pam had watched the recorded results over a glass or two of wine. He'd been relieved to discover that he hadn't come over too badly. Even Neil had rung to congratulate him.

Although he was hardly a natural in front of a camera, he was satisfied that he'd done a competent job. He hadn't made a fool of himself but, as he'd said to Pam, he didn't mind in the least leaving media stardom to those who were bothered about that sort of thing. She'd looked mildly amused and said that stars' wives probably saw even less of their partners than police wives did. Then he'd gone upstairs to say goodnight to the children, only to find them both fast asleep.

In spite of all this, he felt unusually happy as he left the house just before eight to drive to Neston Police Station, even though the weather was dank and grey and when he looked down the hill towards Tradmouth, the town was veiled in a thick sea mist. His good mood lasted as he drove inland, slowed by the early-morning traffic, and when he reached the incident room he sat down at the desk he'd been allocated and placed a sheet of paper squarely in front of him. There was no sign of Gerry as yet – probably due to an alarm clock malfunction – so he thought he would take advantage of the DCI's absence to get a few things straight in his mind before the morning briefing.

He began to write. *Visit Mrs Jannings re child's skeleton. Was Dalcott's father definitely guilty? How much does Roz know about it and who was driving towards Tradington in her car on Saturday evening – Parker or Roz Dalcott? Harry Parker's phone records – has he been in contact with Syd Jenkins and Brian Carrack?*

He was just going to add something about Adam Tey and Charleen Anstice when Nick Tarnaby lumbered up to his desk carrying a piece of paper. He muttered something and plonked the paper on top of the notes Wesley had been making.

'This came in first thing.'

Wesley looked up at him. There were dark rings under his eyes and his breath smelled of stale alcohol. 'Heavy night last night, Nick?'

'No.'

Wesley sighed, picked up the sheet of paper Tarnaby had left on his desk and began to read.

Last Friday Mrs Mabel Cleary aged 73 told her daughter she was taking the coach from London to Morbay to meet up with a long-lost friend. Mrs Cleary definitely caught the coach but she hasn't been in touch with her daughter since. Mrs Cleary's been having medical treatment for a heart condition and daughter's reported her missing at her local police station who contacted the Devon and Cornwall force.

'Nick,' Wesley called across the room. 'Can I have a word?'

Nick Tarnaby got up slowly and ambled across the large open-plan office to Wesley's desk.

'Is there any particular reason why you thought I should see this stuff about Mrs Cleary? It looks like a case for uniform to me. And just because this woman hasn't phoned her daughter, it doesn't necessarily mean anything's happened to her.'

Tarnaby grunted. 'It's the other thing.'

'What other thing?'

'The officer who spoke to the daughter said that the mum had been here during the war. She was evacuated here when she was a kid.'

'What's that got to do with . . .?'

'The daughter found a letter from the friend she was

153

coming to see and it said –' He consulted his notebook. '"I often think about the time we spent at Tailors Court."' He lowered his notebook. 'Just thought you might be interested. But if you don't think it's important . . .'

Wesley hesitated. Perhaps he'd underestimated Tarnaby. 'No, you're right. It could be relevant. Thanks. You did well.'

Tarnaby said nothing. He turned and walked away, leaving Wesley staring at the sheet of paper in front of him. Suddenly Mrs Mabel Cleary had assumed a new importance. If Colin Bowman's expected report concluded that the child's bones found at Tailors Court dated from around the time she lived there, Mrs Cleary and the friend she was planning to visit might even be able to shed some light on the young victim's identity. But at the moment she was missing – and, once he'd broken the news to Gerry, finding her might well become one of their chief priorities.

Gerry arrived at ten past nine, yawning and moaning about the traffic, but he soon recovered and gave the morning briefing to a rapt audience. As Wesley listened, making a contribution now and then and drawing the team's attention to the news that had just come in about Mabel Cleary, he felt the urge to get everything down on paper – preferably in neat columns. Gerry, he knew, didn't work like that but Wesley liked to know exactly what was what.

When Wesley visited Mrs Jannings he wanted Rachel with him because she had a rapport with the elderly and she was sharp enough to notice any lies and evasions. But before they set off for Morbay, he wanted to speak to Colin Bowman: the more information he had about the dating of the skeleton when he faced Mrs Jannings, the better.

Colin picked up the telephone on the second ring and his greeting sounded a little more cheerful today, as though he'd recovered from the shock of Dalcott's violent death. When Wesley asked whether there'd been any progress with the child's bones Colin paused before replying.

'There's definitely a filling in one of the molars and, from items found in the grave, Neil thinks the bones were put there no earlier than the late nineteen thirties.'

'I realise that, Colin, but is there any sign of a cause of death?'

'Sorry. There's absolutely no sign of trauma to the bones. But they bear similar cut marks to the ones found earlier on the same site, only some are deeper.' He hesitated. 'At a guess, I'd say the body was clumsily dissected before burial.'

Wesley stood for a few seconds, the implications whirring in his brain. 'Are you absolutely sure? Neil says those other bones are a few hundred years old.'

'I can only tell you what I think.'

'So the other bones might be connected to the child's skeleton? They may all be modern after all?'

'I'm sorry, Wesley.' Colin sounded as though he meant it.

'We could run more tests,' said Wesley hopefully. 'Carbon dating?'

'That's more Neil's department than mine of course. And I believe the results take time.'

'There were those Harris lines on that first skeleton he found,' Wesley said, a hint of desperation in his voice. He paused. 'Although poor nutrition isn't necessarily a thing of the past.'

After a few pleasantries, Wesley ended the call. He wasn't sure how to break the news to Gerry, but it couldn't be avoided for ever.

He looked round and saw that Rachel was walking towards him. She was carrying a heavy coat and a bright pink scarf was already swathed around her neck. As she approached she gave him an enquiring smile. 'Ready to visit Mrs Jannings?'

'I've got to have a quick word with the boss first.'

'Something's wrong. What is it?'

He hadn't realised he was that transparent. 'I've just been talking to Colin Bowman. It's possible that the bones we assumed were old might be more recent. He thinks all the deaths might be linked and we're pretty sure the child's skeleton dates from the late nineteen thirties at the earliest.'

Rachel looked him in the eye. 'Oh dear. And the boss doesn't know?'

Wesley shook his head.

'You'd better go and tell him.' Rachel touched his arm. 'Good luck.' She bent forward and whispered in his ear. 'And by the way, you were brilliant last night.'

She walked away, leaving Wesley with a smile playing on his lips.

He walked over to Gerry's desk and sat down on a vacant chair. Gerry looked up from a heap of overtime forms and grunted. 'I thought you and Rach were off visiting old ladies.'

'One old lady. Mrs Jannings who used to live at Tailors Court. And the interview might be more important than we first thought. I've been talking to Colin.'

He gave Gerry the gist of what Colin had said and waited. But instead of the anticipated explosion, Gerry put his head in his hands.

After a few seconds he looked up. 'So we've got a dead doctor and now it looks as though there might be a serial killer and all.'

Wesley didn't answer.

'Tell you what, you get over and talk to this Mrs Jannings. I want to know chapter and verse on everyone who's lived at Tailors Court over the past sixty years. Every last one of them. And then I want Mabel Cleary found.'

'Is Harry Parker still enjoying the custody sergeant's hospitality?'

'Yes. But we can't hold him for much longer without more evidence. I'm going to have another word while you're out with Rach and hope he makes a slip-up. And I'm having the widow brought in and all.'

'Parker's got the lot – means, motive and opportunity.'

'His place was searched last night and there was no sign of a firearm.'

'What about tests for residue?'

'Nothing so far. But he could have worn gloves and got rid of all his clothing along with the gun, unless his mates from prison did it for him. Maybe he called in a favour. There has to be some reason why they rented the place next door to the victim.'

Wesley stood up. 'I'd better be off.'

Half an hour later he was sitting in the passenger seat of the pool car, looking out of the window while Rachel drove towards Morbay. As they crossed the old stone bridge which spanned the River Trad, much narrower here than downstream in Tradmouth, he could see the tourist boats bobbing on the grey water, tied up for the winter and protected by tarpaulin. Soon they were speeding out of the town through brown-green countryside. Then the straggling villages gradually gave way to suburbia; the sprawl of Morbay that had swallowed fields with its housing estates and business parks. Wesley closed his eyes. He needed time to think.

But before long Rachel announced that they'd arrived at Palm View Residential Home, and when Wesley opened his eyes he saw that Rachel was parking the car in the drive of a large white stucco house set back from the main road behind a leylandii hedge. As he emerged from the passenger door he noted that the only palm tree in sight was a puny specimen in a pot by the front door.

After locking the car Rachel strode ahead of him and rang the doorbell. It wasn't long before the glass door was opened by a girl in a nylon overall who looked as though she should have been at school.

They'd phoned ahead so getting in was no problem. Wesley hoped that Mrs Jannings would be able to help them but if she was like some of the residents they passed in the cabbage-scented corridor he knew they might be out of luck. There were a lot of blank, puzzled stares and one tiny old woman with fluffy white hair had clutched at his arm with claw-like fingers as he walked by and asked him if he knew where Bob was. Wesley apologised gently and said that he had no idea.

When he asked the young care assistant about Bob, she seemed to know all about it. No doubt she'd heard the story many times. 'He was her sweetheart in the War,' she said, matter-of-factly. 'He was American – based in Tradmouth. Went to D-Day and never came back. It's

158

with you being . . s.' She suddenly looked embarrassed. 'You know, black like him. She never married, you know. Never got over it. Poor Elsie.'

Wesley and Rachel looked at each other. In those few words she had summed up one woman's lifetime of heartbreak and mourning.

'Esther's in here,' she said as they reached the door to a large plastic conservatory. The carpet on the floor had a busy red pattern and the chairs set around the walls were cane with orange marshmallow cushions.

A big-boned, strong-looking woman with straight iron-grey hair was sitting in the corner, a walking frame placed in front of her like a protective cage. It was hard to tell her age but Wesley's first, uncharitable thought was that she was rather ugly. But when she looked up he was relieved to see that her eyes were sharp and alert.

He saw Rachel give the woman a charming smile as she sat down beside her on the sofa. He left it up to her to explain the reason for their visit. And as Rachel told her about the skeletons found near the house he watched her face carefully but he saw no reaction apart from a shake of the head.

'I don't know nothing about no skeletons, my love,' she said to Rachel in a tone that didn't invite argument. 'There was never any talk of anything like that and I can tell you that nobody was buried at Tailors Court while I was there and that's God's honest truth.' She folded her arms defensively, daring them to contradict her.

'How long did you live there, Mrs Jannings?' Wesley spoke for the first time, earning himself a harsh stare. 'Mr and Mrs Persimmon mentioned that you were widowed in the War.'

159

'That's right. I got married in 1944. War bride. But my husband went missing in action a couple of weeks after the wedding. My mother-in-law was an invalid so I stayed on to look after her. She didn't die till 1979. Sacrificed my life, I did. No husband. No kids.' Then a smile spread across her thin lips. 'But I got Tailors Court.'

'You inherited it from your mother-in-law?'

'That's right.' The smile suddenly disappeared. 'Not that it did me much good. I had all that inheritance tax to pay and in the end I couldn't manage the place on my own so I sold it to that yuppie couple from London. He said he'd fallen in love with the countryside when he'd come down here for a visit – something to do with his work. They had no idea if you ask me,' she said disdainfully. 'Then my legs gave out so I had to move into this place. It's going to cost me every bloody penny.' She snorted in disgust.

'So when you lived in Tailors Court were there any children there at all?'

She looked at Wesley sideways. 'I've told you, I didn't have no children. Didn't have time. Miles was lost in action. And if you're thinking those bones are his, you're wrong. They never found him so I can only guess that he's still somewhere over in France. In some corner of a for-eign field that is forever England. Isn't that what they say?'

Wesley looked at her, rather surprised. Somehow Esther Jannings didn't look the sort to quote Rupert Brooke. 'I'm sorry. It must have been very hard for you.'

She gave a little shrug of her wide shoulders. 'You carry on, don't you? You've got no choice.'

Wesley knew he should be feeling sorry for this woman but something stopped him: perhaps it was because she seemed more than capable of taking care of herself; or perhaps it was because there was something self-pitying about her that he found distinctly unattractive. He also suspected that she'd avoided answering his question about children with the deftness of a politician so he decided to repeat himself.

'Were there any children staying at Tailors Court while you lived there? Anyone at all, even for a short time?'

She thought for a few moments. 'Well, if you go back as far as the War, there were some evacuees – vaccies we used to call 'em. But they went home when all the danger passed.'

Rachel leaned forward. 'Do you remember them?'

'Vaguely.'

'How many were there?'

'A few. They came and went.'

'Boys or girls?'

'Both as far as I recall. But my mother-in-law preferred girls. She said they were quieter.'

'It's not always the case,' said Wesley with a smile. 'My daughter's a lot more boisterous than my son,' he added, establishing his credentials as a family man to put the woman at her ease.

But Esther Jannings just grunted and looked away.

'Was there a girl called Mabel?'

'How should I know? There were some snotty kids hanging around the place but I never knew their names and I think a few had come and gone before I got wed to Miles. I can't tell you about them cause I was a young girl back then and I didn't take no notice. But I do remember there was a land girl called Mary. Miles used to say she was no better than she ought to be. She was from some big city up north. Manchester maybe.'

161

'Do you know what became of her?' Rachel asked.

Wesley knew what she was thinking. Her mother had been brought up on a farm in the area, had married a local farmer and had acquired an encyclopaedic knowledge of the goings-on in the local farming community over the years. There was always a chance she'd know somebody who knew somebody whose mother remembered a land girl called Mary who was 'no better than she ought to be'. It was a long shot but it was worth a try.

'She got married to the son of the farmer she worked for. Always flashing her eyes at the men, she was. Even at my Miles. Little whore,' she added with a surprising amount of venom.

'Do you know the name of the farmer?' Rachel persisted.

'Haynes. Gorfleet Farm. Got her feet nicely under the table, she did.'

Rachel's eyes met Wesley's and she gave him a small nod. He guessed that she knew the Haynes family – or at least her mother did.

Wesley took over the questioning. 'One of the skeletons we found belonged to a child aged nine or ten. It was buried near the paddock and certain items found in the grave suggest that he or she died after the late 1930s.' He watched Esther Jannings's face for a reaction but he saw none.

'Well, I don't know nothing about that. The paddock's some way from the house so who's to say some murderer didn't decide to dump a body there? It's nothing to do with me.'

'While I was at Tailors Court I went up in the attic.'

She suddenly looked wary.

162

'Have you ever been up to the room at the end? We found a table in there. And what looked like surgical instruments.'

Esther opened her mouth to say something then closed it again. Tight.

'Do you know anything about that room, Mrs Jannings?'

She shook her head.

'You lived in the house. You must know something about it.'

She looked Wesley in the eye. 'It was Miles's room. He told me never to go in there.'

'And you did as you were told?' Wesley asked. Somehow he found it hard to see Esther Jannings as a downtrodden woman.

She nodded. 'I didn't go up there and I never wanted to. That door was kept locked and Miles kept the key.'

'And all the years you lived there after he died, you never went up there out of curiosity?'

'I did not,' she said firmly. Somehow Wesley believed her.

'So you suspected that something . . .' He searched for the right word. 'Something unpleasant happened in there. If you'd just thought he had a model railway up there you wouldn't be looking so scared now, Mrs Jannings. What did Miles do in that room?'

'I don't know. And I didn't want to know.'

There was a long pause and Wesley waited. People, in his experience, could never resist filling a silence. Eventually his patience was rewarded.

'He used to like science.'

'What sort of science?'

163

'Experiments. He used to tell me about them.' She shook her head and suddenly she looked unsure of herself, almost frightened. 'I knew him before the war, you see, and he was . . . But after he came back from Dunkirk with that wound to his head he changed completely. It was like something had been switched on. Something evil. I can't explain.'

'But you still married him?' said Rachel gently.

'He was a man, wasn't he? And my mam reckoned he was a good catch, being the only son and all.' She looked Rachel up and down. 'We can't all be blonde and pretty, you know. Some of us had to take what we could get.' There was a bitterness in her words that made Rachel look away.

'Tell me about the experiments,' said Wesley.

'He never used to be like that when I first met him. Like I said, he used to be nice, and always bright – he got a scholarship to the Grammar School. Then he came back wounded and he'd changed. He started to catch animals. He'd put mice in bottles and see how long it took them to die and . . . the dog had puppies and one of them was weaker than the others: I found him cutting it up while it was still alive. He said he wanted to see what went on inside it.' She looked away. 'It was disgusting.'

'But he'd been brought up in the country. He could have seen any farmer around here butchering livestock any time,' said Rachel with the detached practicality of a farmer's daughter.

'That's not the same, is it? He liked . . . experiment-ing. He said he'd found this book about a man who used to live there who was some kind of doctor – but I didn't want to know. It scared me. I wanted him to stop but he said that if it bothered me, I needn't have anything to do with it. Then sometimes when I went round his mother would say he was up in the attic. And he always needed to clean himself up before he came down to see me.'

'This was before you were married?'

She nodded. 'Oh yes. I only saw him a couple of times a week when we were courting. And we were only married a fortnight before he . . .' She sniffed loudly. 'Before he went missing.'

'So all this started after he was wounded at Dunkirk? It changed his personality?'

'That's right.' She hesitated.

'Is there something else?'

'He must have painted them but I can't see how it was possible.'

Rachel looked at Wesley enquiringly. Esther was beginning to lose them.

'What are you talking about, Mrs Jannings?' she said gently. 'What did you think Miles had painted?'

'Those horrible pictures behind the panelling.'

'What panelling?'

'In the bedroom Miles used to sleep in before we were wed. The room with the stairs leading up to the attic. I started to take the panelling off one day – must have been a few years after the war finished. His mother said it was old and dark and why didn't we use it for firewood and I could paint the room, cheer the place up a bit. But when I saw what was behind it, I put it straight back again. Horrible it was.'

'Tell me about it?' Wesley asked. He knew what was coming but he wanted to hear Esther's version.

'It was drawings of people with their skin hanging off. Showing, you know, their insides.'

'And you thought your husband had drawn them?'

Esther shook her head. 'He couldn't draw a straight line and these were good. I mean they were very realistic. I don't see how he could have done 'em, I really don't. But when I went to take the panels off I found they were really loose so he must have had 'em off the wall at some point.'

'Perhaps he'd found the pictures behind the panels and that began his interest in . . . in science,' Wesley suggested.

Esther thought for a moment. 'It's possible.'

'What do you know about the history of Tailors Court?'

She shook her head. 'I know it's bloody old. And that it's draughty and falling to bits. My mother-in-law told me it was built when Queen Elizabeth was on the throne – not this Queen Elizabeth we've got now, the other one with the big dresses and the red curly hair. A family called Garchard built it and the Janningses only got it in Victorian times. And it wasn't always called Tailors Court.'

'What was it called, do you know?'

She frowned. 'Flesh Tailor's Court. That's it. Flesh Tailor's Court.'

Wesley glanced at Rachel. 'No wonder they changed it,' he said in a whisper.

Rosalind Dalcott had been brought in and it looked to Trish Walton as though she'd decided to play the Grieving Widow – and a heavily pregnant Grieving Widow at that. Not that it washed with Gerry Heffernan.

'We've just released your partner on bail,' Gerry began. 'But we'll want to speak to him again.' He leaned forward, slightly threatening. 'Sooner rather than later.'

166

All of a sudden the Widow abandoned her role and stared at the DCI, dry-eyed and defiant. 'He didn't kill James. You're wasting your time – and mine. I've told you everything I know.'

Trish watched as Gerry gave Roz a dangerous smile. She had seen a similar grimace once on a crocodile at Morbay Zoo when it had spotted a tasty snack. He let the tension build for a few seconds before turning over the photograph that had been lying face down on the table in front of him. It was a still from a traffic camera, enhanced to reveal the car number plate.

'Harry's refused to say he was driving. That means he's landed you right in it. Terrible that – he wants to save his own skin so he leaves you to take the blame. Or was it you driving that car? Did you kill your husband, Mrs Dalcott? Did you point the gun at his head and pull the trigger? Ever fired a revolver, Mrs Dalcott?'

She shook her head vigorously. 'Never.'

'We've got a warrant to search your flat.'

'Well, you won't find anything.'

'Why? Have you got rid of the evidence? Where is it – in the river? Buried under some hedgerow? There are lots of places around these parts to get rid of a gun.'

'Don't be ridiculous,' she replied.

'Well, you can't deny it's your car so what was it doing driving towards Tradington while you and Harry Parker were supposed to be tucked up all cosy in your Tradmouth love nest?' Gerry Heffernan smiled again and waited for a reply.

Roz let out a loud sigh. 'OK. I went round to see James around seven. He'd told me he was going to see the solicitor about the divorce settlement and I was going to try and persuade him to be more generous. I mean, Harry doesn't make a fortune with his art . . . yet. And I'm just paid pin money at the gallery. I needed that money.'

'And now you've got it,' said Trish. 'Let's face it, Mrs Dalcott, your husband died just at the right time.'

Trish saw Gerry glance at her appreciatively.

'But I would never have killed James. I was sure I could make him see reason,' Roz continued.

'And when he didn't you shot him,' said Gerry.

'No. You don't understand.'

'Make us.'

Roz swallowed hard. She looked tired, Trish thought. Perhaps the interrogation was too much for her in her condition. But then she told herself firmly that there was a distinct possibility that this woman was a cold-blooded murderer.

'OK,' said Roz, bowing her head. 'I drove there and when I arrived James was getting ready to go out – some dinner party at one of his colleagues' houses. I said I wanted to talk but . . .'

'But what?'

'He started saying how he was willing to take me back. How he'd forgive me and bring up the child himself. He said we could put everything behind us if I'd leave Harry.' She looked Gerry in the eye. 'He said some awful things about Harry. He said he was a little crook who was after his money. It's not true. Harry loves me.'

'So you told him he was wasting his time?'

'That's right.'

'How did he react to that?'

Roz thought for a few seconds. 'More sad than angry, I suppose. He didn't raise his voice or anything like that.

He just said I was making a big mistake but it was up to me.'

'Did he mention changing his will?' Trish asked.

There was a long silence. 'I didn't know about it till you told Harry.'

Trish glanced at Gerry who gave a slight nod. 'I can't believe he didn't mention he'd made an appointment with his solicitor when you saw him on the night he died. And it must have been so tempting – if he died that weekend, you'd be financially secure for the rest of your life. And with the baby coming . . .'

Roz looked away. 'I know. But I didn't kill him. Even when he started going on about faithless wives running in his family, I just felt sorry for him.' She began to pick at her fingernails: Trish could see that the glossy red varnish was chipping. 'I didn't hate James, Chief Inspector. Far from it. I just found him boring.'

'So you left James for a bit of excitement?'

She didn't answer.

'Did you know about your husband's real parents?'

'Of course. They were at the wedding. But they're both dead now. What about them?'

'Would it surprise you to learn that the Dalcotts weren't James's real mother and father? Mrs Dalcott was really his aunt – his father's sister. His real father was called George Clipton and he was hanged for murdering his wife, James's mother. He strangled her because she was unfaithful to him.'

Trish glanced at the DCI. His words had been brutal and now Roz was sitting, stunned, her hand resting protectively on her bump. 'I take it you didn't know?' she said.

'I'd no idea. Poor James,' said Roz. 'He was obsessed with researching his family history – not that he ever shared it with me. It explains a lot, him harbouring a dark family secret like that. He was probably too ashamed to tell me. That'd be James all over. He was a proud man.'

Trish thought she could detect a reluctant fondness in Roz's voice and this was something she hadn't expected. Perhaps, she thought, there had been some latent affection for the boring husband after all and Harry Parker had had an inkling that his position was precarious. Perhaps that was why he had killed Dalcott – or had him killed.

'How long did you stay in Tradington on the night James was killed?' Gerry asked.

'It can't have been more than fifteen minutes. To tell you the truth, once I started talking to James, I realised I shouldn't have gone. It was upsetting for him and upsetting for me. And he was rather preoccupied. Getting ready to go out, I mean.'

'You're quite sure he didn't mention changing his will?'

'No,' she said without making eye contact.

'And he didn't mention if he was expecting a visitor?'

Roz shook her head, more relaxed now. 'I told him I'd speak to him another time then I left – drove straight back to Tradmouth. No doubt you've got that on tape as well,' she added with a hint of sarcasm.

'Yes we have. But you'd still have had time to shoot him.'

'I wouldn't know one end of a gun from another. And before you ask, Harry was home when I got back and neither of us went out again that evening.' She raised her head and looked Gerry straight in the eye. 'I know for certain that Harry didn't kill James so you can search the flat any time you like.'

'We'll do that, love.'

'Can I go now?'

Trish saw Gerry Heffernan nod. The young police-woman who was sitting by the door of the interview room stood up and guided Roz Dalcott out with the studied concern of a hospital nurse reassuring a patient that the procedure was over and had been successful.

Wesley had met Stella Tracey before when armed robbers had targeted Little Barton Farm and as Rachel led him into the kitchen, her mother greeted him like an old friend.

Wesley sat by the table in the warm farmhouse kitchen breathing in the aroma of a baking casserole as Stella placed a ham sandwich made with home-made bread and pickle, a mug of steaming tea and a slice of her famed fruit cake in front of him. He began to feel a little guilty at enjoying this impromptu lunch. But, as Rachel pointed out, her mother was the fount of all knowledge concerning the local farming community and she would be able to provide more information about the land girl who married into the family at Gorfleet Farm than any police computer system.

It was Rachel who began the interrogation. 'Now, mum, we need some information.'

'Fire away,' said Stella, walking over to the Aga and checking the oven.

'You know the Hayneses at Gorfleet Farm near Tradington, don't you?'

'Of course. I think you know them too. Didn't you meet Nigel Haynes at a Young Farmers' Dance? Oh, it must be over ten years ago but surely you must remember.'

When Rachel didn't answer Stella continued.

'Nigel's due to take over the running of the farm when

his father retires. And he's still single,' she added meaningfully, her eyes flicking in Rachel's direction.

Wesley saw Rachel look away, her bottom lip jutting like a petulant child's. Perhaps, he thought, being back in her childhood home made her feel a little like a teenager again. Or perhaps it was something else – an uncomfortable memory maybe.

Then he remembered why the name Nigel Haynes seemed familiar. In the report on the discovery of the first skeleton at Tailors Court, the driver of the digger had been named as Nigel Haynes from the farm next door.

'Anyway,' he said. 'I believe one of the Haynes sons married a land girl who was working on their farm. Her name was Mary and she was staying just outside Tradington in a house called Tailors Court.' He thought it best not to mention Esther Jannings's comment about her being no better than she ought to be. He wanted to hear Stella's independent verdict.

Stella nodded. 'That's right. Of course it was before my time but I know she came from somewhere up north and she was a land girl during the war. She met John Haynes – he passed away about ten years ago – and she never went back. I think your gran went to the wedding, Rachel.'

'Considering this was all before your time, you seem to know all about her,' Rachel said.

'I keep my ear to the ground.' She looked at Rachel, slightly teasing. 'And I know she had two children. Peter – that's Nigel's father who took over the farm – and she had a girl as well but I can't remember her name. The daughter stayed around here and I think she's got two girls of her own. I did hear that one of them's working for some newspaper.'

'Is Mary still alive?'

'As far as I know she's still going strong. But she'll be well into her eighties now.'

'Do you think she'll be up to talking to us?'

Stella Tracey shrugged. 'You can only ask. I think she still lives with Peter and Brenda at the farm,' she said as she busied herself with clearing away Wesley's empty plate. 'I'd ring them first to see how the land lies.'

Fortunately Stella had the number of Gorfleet Farm in the battered address book that lay next to the telephone on the huge Welsh dresser. The address book sprouted scraps of paper and dog-eared business cards which fluttered out as she leafed through the pages, only to be thrust back in again at random.

Wesley suggested that Rachel speak to the Hayneses as there was already some tentative connection. But she was quick to say that it might be better coming from him and as she watched him make the call, she fiddled nervously with a table mat, turning it over and over in her fingers. Perhaps her mother's presence was making her feel awkward. Or perhaps there was some history between her and Nigel Haynes that her mother didn't know about.

When the call was ended Wesley turned to face Rachel. 'I spoke to Peter Haynes. Mary's in hospital with some sort of infection and she's not up to speaking to anyone at the moment,' he said feeling a crushing disappointment. He'd been hoping Mary would tell them all they needed to know.

Rachel looked at him as though she'd read his thoughts.

'But she is responding to the antibiotics they're giving her and the doctors say it might just be a matter of time till she's on the mend.'

Hoping the doctors had it right, Wesley said a polite goodbye to Stella and followed Rachel out into the farmyard.

173

As they drove away from the farm, Rachel seemed to relax. But she stayed uncharacteristically silent as they approached Tradington. Wesley suspected that, now that she'd enjoyed the independence of sharing a cottage near Tradmouth with Trish Walton, she felt as though she'd become a stranger in her childhood home. She'd cut the apron strings and there was no going back.

It had started to rain again and Wesley looked out of the car window at the rolling fields. Now that winter had arrived, the twisted black wood in the hedgerows looked dead and naked without its veil of greenery. In summer this landscape was lush and beautiful but now it was grey-brown and bare, as though the whole earth was dying.

He glanced at Rachel, tempted to ask her about Nigel Haynes, but something in her expression made him change his mind.

Nobody saw the corpse as it floated downstream towards Tradmouth. The river Trad was swollen at this time of the year – swollen and icy cold. Anybody who fell in wouldn't have stood much of a chance but this body hadn't come to be there by accident or misfortune. It had been placed there carefully to float out to sea on the tide, unseen and unmourned.

But the treacherous currents of the river worked to the commands of nature rather than man and before long the corpse had become entangled in the mooring rope of a small yacht bobbing at anchor in the shelter of Bow Creek. Now it floated there and its black hair spread out, mingling with the dark, clinging seaweed beneath the leaden sky.

CHAPTER 8

Transcript of recording made by Mrs Mabel Cleary (née Fallon) – Home Counties Library Service Living History Project: Reminiscences of a wartime evacuee.

Mary was courting. Full of it, she was. Not that I understood half the things she told me – I was too young for that. His name was John and he lived at the farm next door. He didn't have to go away because farming was a reserved occupation, you see. We all had to eat, after all. John was nice and he'd bring round milk and eggs for us. Sometimes there'd be ham or bacon too and that was a real treat. And besides all that, he used to make us laugh and sometimes he'd do magic tricks for us like producing pennies from behind our ears. I always looked forward to seeing John.

Charlie followed Miles everywhere like a little dog. I thought Miles would tell him to get lost but he didn't seem to mind. And even though I thought it was a bit odd, I didn't say anything.

I didn't have much to do with Miles, even though he was always around, and that meant I didn't see much of Charlie either, although Belle continued to tease him and call him names. She said he was stupid and that he was a nuisance. I said how sad it was that his parents had both been killed in the Blitz but she just rolled her eyes and said he'd come to live with her family and she hated it. I didn't like Belle much. My mother would have said she was selfish.

Then one day I overheard John telling Mary that there were Germans staying in the village. I was a bit scared at first but when I met them, I realised I had nothing to worry about. These Germans were nice and they were just like us really.

Wesley felt rather deflated when he returned to the incident room. He'd pinned his hopes on speaking to Mary, the person who might hold the information he needed to identify the child buried near the paddock, and now he felt the frustration of delay. However, Peter Haynes had said that she was expected to make a full recovery so it was just a question of patience. But that was a virtue he felt he didn't really have time for just then.

'There's someone here to see you, sir.'

Wesley looked up and saw Nick Tarnaby standing to attention in front of him.

'Who is it?'

Nick Tarnaby's thin lips flickered upwards in a suggestive smirk. 'Woman. Blonde. Fit. Says she wants to talk to you.'

'Does this fit blonde woman have a name?'

'She said you knew her.'

Wesley was about to say that he knew lots of women but he was afraid this might have been misinterpreted.

'She's waiting in Reception. Says it's important.'

Wesley sighed and began to put the papers on his desk into some sort of order. Then he stood up and made his way to the front desk, wondering who his mysterious visitor could be. As curiosity got the better of him he quickened his pace.

But his heart sank as he pushed open the swing doors leading to Reception and saw Nuala Johns standing there with her back to him reading a notice warning against leaving valuables in cars.

'Ms Johns. What can I do for you?' he said unenthusiastically as she turned to face him.

He saw her eyeing him as a cat eyes a bird, but it could have been his imagination. 'Well, Detective Inspector Peterson, it is good to see you. I was wondering if you can tell me any more about these skeletons at Tailors Court.'

She inclined her head to one side expectantly and fluttered her eyelashes. Pulling out all the stops.

'I'm sorry, Ms Johns, but as I told you at the press conference, I really can't help you. The bones are still the subject of various tests and –'

'But the child's skeleton's more recent. Have you identified it yet?'

Wesley stared at her and felt the blood drain from his face. 'That information hasn't been released yet. How on earth did you hear about it?'

She gave him an enigmatic smile. 'You're not denying it, then?'

'Well . . .' His mind raced as he wondered how best to handle the question. 'More bones have been discovered on the site and they appear to belong to a child. But that's all I can tell you. They might be hundreds of years old but we won't be able to confirm it until they've run tests and . . .' He decided against mentioning the filling in the child's tooth, or the remains of the toy car and the snake buckle. There was still so much more they needed to know before it was all made public.

She took his elbow and led him to the bench where members of the public waited to show their driving licences or to report missing items. Today, possibly due to an unexpected outbreak of good driving and honesty, it was empty so there was nobody to overhear what they had to say.

'I believe you have a degree in archaeology, Inspector . . . or may I call you Wesley?' She smiled prettily and he wondered what she was up to.

'That's right.'

'That's right you've got an archaeology degree or that's right I can call you Wesley?' She was positively flirtatious now. She'd even hitched her tight black skirt up a couple of inches.

'Both.' Wesley pretended to look at his watch. 'I really don't have much time, Ms Johns. We are in the middle of a murder enquiry.'

'Oh, James Dalcott. I take it that's some sort of revenge killing – I've heard about the complaint made against him. Or perhaps it was a crime of passion? His ex's boyfriend maybe?'

'I really can't comment at this stage.' She was beginning to irritate him. And worry him. If she started printing all this conjecture, she could cause no end of trouble.

'Let's get back to the skeletons, shall we? You do know about Simon Garchard, I take it?'

'Who?' It wasn't a name that had cropped up during the enquiry and he hoped she wasn't a few steps ahead of them.

'Simon Garchard. Physician, necromancer, magician. South Devon's answer to John Dee.' She paused and looked him in the eye. 'You really haven't heard of him, have you?'

'Should I have?'

She stood up. 'Well, if you're not interested . . .'

'Who says I'm not interested? Please. Sit down. Tell me what you know about this Simon Garchard.' He had heard the name Garchard before very recently. But he couldn't remember where. Then it came to him. Esther Jannings had said that a family called Garchard built Tailors Court.

She hesitated for a few moments then resumed her seat. 'When I heard about the skeletons and how they might be old, it rang some bells.'

'What do you mean?'

She gave him a secretive smile. 'I'm a local girl. There were various legends – very vague of course – so I thought I'd see whether there was any truth behind them.'

'Simon Garchard lived at Tailors Court, am I right?'

She looked rather surprised. 'How did you know?'

'Lucky guess.'

'He was the eldest son of Thomas Garchard who added a couple of fashionable Elizabethan wings to the original medieval house. When he died Simon inherited the house but his interests didn't lie in farming or managing the estate. He sold most of the land off to neighbouring landowners and pursued his dreams.'

179

'Which were?'

'Science. He was a pioneer. Or at least he thought he was. Not that the authorities at the time saw it like that. He was said to have snatched newly buried bodies from local churchyards and in 1595 he was tried for killing a woman and hanged.'

'How did he kill this woman?'

She smiled, showing a row of perfect teeth. 'I've got you interested now, haven't I?'

'You didn't answer my question.'

'Her name was Annet Raine, described as a maidservant, and he was accused of strangling her then dissecting her body. It was said he made drawings on the walls at Tailors Court. I don't know whether they're still there but . . .'

'I know all about the drawings.'

'How?'

Wesley didn't answer. 'So Garchard was what, a physician? A barber surgeon?'

Nuala Johns shook her head. 'Oh, there's no suggestion he was qualified as anything. I get the impression he was more of an enthusiastic amateur. But there were some pretty dark stories going round at the time.'

'What sort of stories?'

The answer was another enigmatic smile. She was keeping him tantalised, playing him like an expert fisherman plays a trout.

'This is all very interesting, Ms Johns, but . . .'

'I thought with your degree in archaeology you'd be interested. Were the skeletons at Tailors Court connected with Simon Garchard, I wonder? I don't think the bodies snatched from the churchyards were ever found.'

'How come you know so much about Tailors Court?'

'My grandparents and my uncle and aunt own the farm next door and my grandmother even lived there for a while. And like I said, I've done my research.'

The light suddenly dawned. 'Your grandmother's Mary Haynes.' Stella Tracey had mentioned that Mary had a granddaughter who worked for a newspaper. He felt annoyed with himself for not putting two and two together before.

She smiled. 'Nice deduction, Detective Inspector. The house wasn't always known as Tailors Court, you know.'

'It used to be Flesh Tailor's Court, I believe.'

Nuala's mouth fell open and he gave her a brief, secretive smile. Her smugness had annoyed him and he rather enjoyed taking the wind out of her sails.

But her disappointment didn't last long. 'I suppose the Flesh disappeared with the apostrophe. And it was called Tradington Court when it was first built but the locals renamed it. That's what they used to call Simon. The Flesh Tailor.'

'Because he cut people up and sewed them back together?'

'Something like that, I expect.' She raised her eyes. They were a brilliant blue. Clear and calculating. 'So, Wesley,' she said after a long pause. 'I've told you what I know about Tailors Court so why don't you return the favour?'

She hitched up her skirt again. Wesley looked across at the reception desk and saw that the officer on duty there was watching the pair of them with interest while pretending to sort through a pile of forms.

She fluttered her eyelashes again. They were thick with

mascara and they reminded Wesley of predatory spiders. 'I'm not asking for all your deepest, darkest secrets – although that would be nice. All I'm asking is that you let me have whatever your press officer's going to release before it gets made public.' She pouted like a poor man's Marilyn Monroe. 'That's not too much to ask, is it? And in return, I'll keep you up to date on anything I manage to find out. Just like I did today.'

Wesley pretended to consider her proposition for a while. 'I'll have to think about it,' he said after a few moments.

'You do that. And in the meantime, how about dinner tonight?'

Wesley had assumed that the flirtation was strictly professional – that she was using her feminine charms in pursuit of a good story. But now it seemed that he might have misread the situation. 'I'm afraid I'll have to pass,' he said quickly. 'Sorry.'

'Tomorrow?'

'Sorry.'

He was rather relieved when his mobile phone began to ring. He answered it and told the caller to hang on while he saw Nuala Johns off the premises. She seemed reluctant to go, probably suspecting that the call heralded some new development in the case. But Wesley wasn't playing that game. He waited until she was safely outside before starting the conversation.

Adam Tey was worried about Charleen. She hadn't felt the baby move for a few hours and she was starting to panic. Adam had suggested calling Dr Fitzgerald – or even going down to A and E – but Charleen had put herself to bed. That was when he'd received the call from Carl Utley.

Carl never left the house these days – not since his problem began. Or at least that's what he said. Adam had heard that sometimes he prowled round the area in the hours of darkness, his face shielded with a hood and a scarf. It was like the Phantom of the Opera, Adam thought to himself, only this was in Neston and there was no chance of Carl Utley gaining power of any sort over a beautiful woman.

Adam was relieved when Charleen told him that she'd felt a flutter of movement. He leaned over her and kissed her on the forehead, feeling suddenly protective. After what had happened to their last child she was prone to panic and at that moment he didn't really want to leave her alone. But Carl had said it was urgent so he felt he had to go.

He walked to Carl's flat a few streets away, braving the drizzle, because he'd been cooped up with Charleen for days now and he felt he needed the exercise. He could hear the rumble of a train on the nearby railway track and he suddenly wished that he and Charleen could get away from Neston and begin a new life. But he knew it would never happen.

When he arrived at Carl's flat in the small, brick council block, he rang the doorbell but he had to wait a minute or so before Carl answered. When the door finally opened the narrow hall was in darkness and Carl stood back in the shadows, the hood of his sweatshirt pulled up over his head protectively. As Adam stepped inside, he didn't look in Carl's direction because he knew that Carl had a terror of people staring at him.

Without a word Carl led the way into his sitting room. Dark-blue walls, deep red carpet and dark throws draped over the sagging three-piece suite. The shabby wine-coloured velvet curtains were drawn tightly across and the only source of light was a tiny lamp in the corner that had been fitted with the dimmest bulb available.

Even when Adam's eyes had adjusted to the low light level he still couldn't see Carl properly as he'd positioned himself in a dark corner and pulled his hood forward to obscure his face.

'What did you want to see me about?' he asked. Not being able to see Carl's face was starting to make him nervous. It was like talking to a shadow.

Carl didn't answer for a few moments. Adam could hear his laboured breathing and began to wonder whether he was ill. But then he spoke.

'I've been going there.'

'Where?'

'The clinic.'

Adam glanced at the watch on his wrist. He'd got it off the market and it wasn't reliable but it was too dark in that room to make out the time anyway. 'I don't get you. What are you talking about? Look, I don't want to leave Charleen for long. She had a bit of a scare before and –'

'I've been watching the place.'

Something in Carl's words made warning bells sound in Adam's head. 'Why?'

'You'll see. I found a way of getting into the grounds. There's a piece of woodland at the far side of the house. You can see all the comings and goings from there.'

'And?'

'I had these printed off.' Carl produced a folder and

184

handed it to Adam. Inside there were twenty or so photographs. They were mostly of people arriving at the main entrance to the Podingham Clinic. Adam took them over to the lamp and held them in the dim pool of light as he flicked through them.

'I don't understand. Why do you think these are important?'

'Look more closely.'

Adam began to examine them one by one. Some faces featured regularly, presumably staff, and others only once or twice, sometimes in ones and occasionally in twos, presumably the volunteers paid to test the drugs. The guinea pigs – just as Carl had been once. 'Go on, tell me.'

Carl selected another couple of snaps and handed them to Adam. 'There's a group of people. What do you notice about them?'

Adam found the relevant picture and stared at it for a while. 'Don't know. They arrived in a minibus but the other ones arrived alone?'

'The volunteers usually make their own way there. And they're mostly young and short of cash – students and the like. But this lot were brought there in a minibus and . . . well, they just looked different.'

Adam studied the photographs again. Carl was right. There was indeed something different about the group who arrived by minibus. They were men and women, mostly young but a few were well into middle age. Some looked puzzled, others a little desperate.

'When I was there the staff were all sweetness and light. Even though they did leave me like this,' he added bitterly. 'But the way they spoke to this lot seemed different, like they were being given orders.'

Adam absentmindedly started to go through the pictures again. And when he spotted a familiar face he stopped. 'This is Dr Dalcott.'

'Hardly surprising. He worked there. If he hadn't, I might not have ended up like something out of the Night of the Living Dead.'

Adam frowned. 'Was Dalcott there when those people in the minibus arrived?'

'I think so. Why?'

'Don't know.'

Carl took the photograph of James Dalcott from Adam's fingers and tore it into pieces as Adam watched.

'I don't want a picture of that bastard around the place. He deserved everything he bloody got.'

Adam stared at him for a few seconds. 'I can't argue with you there. So why did you call me? What do you want?'

'Something bad's going on at the Podingham. I saw a stretcher being loaded into a van and there was a shape underneath a sheet, completely covered up like a dead body.' There was a long pause. 'I'd like to finish that place. I'd like to let everyone know what goes on there.'

'Why don't you tell the police?'

'The police and I have never seen eye to eye. Besides, knowing them, they'd do me for trespass. Who are they going to believe – a load of doctors who play golf with the Chief Constable or me? I've got form for burglary and handling stolen goods. They're just going to say I've got a grudge because of . . .' His hand fluttered towards his face. 'Besides, they'll say that if I'm well enough to go and spy on the Podingham place, I was well enough to kill Dalcott.'

'And were you?'

Carl turned away. 'It's time you went.'

Wesley's call was from Colin Bowman. He knew immediately who it was when he heard the pathologist's cheerful greeting.

'Just thought you'd like to know that I've completed my report on those skeletons. Would you like to come over and get it?'

Wesley looked at his watch. Now that he was working at Neston, Colin's mortuary wasn't just a short walk away as it was in Tradmouth. 'I'll come over some time this afternoon. Is that all right?'

'That's fine. They do say that November is the month of the dead, don't they, but I must admit that, apart from poor James and all these bones Neil's been digging up, things are a little quiet around here at the moment.' There was a pause. 'Actually Neil called me an hour ago. They've just found two more skeletons but Neil's pretty sure that they're old.' He paused. 'Which means it's only the child that's fairly recent. Strange, don't you think?'

'Very.'

Wesley wondered whether to tell Colin there and then what Nuala Johns had said about Simon Garchard and the possibility that his murderous exploits might be linked to the bones. But he decided against it. He'd tell him face to face.

When he'd ended the call Wesley closed his eyes. More skeletons. He almost wished that Neil would stop looking for them but, presumably, the Persimmons didn't want any corpses left in the grounds of their new home to be unearthed by an unsuspecting workman or gardener at some point in the future.

He felt like getting out of the crowded incident room. It really was too cramped to accommodate all the officers working on the Dalcott case. And besides, it was modern, soulless, and all he could see out of the window was the traffic flashing past on the main road through the rain-drops on the double glazing.

He suddenly remembered that Trish Walton had cornered him earlier, saying that the boss wanted them both to pay a visit to Roz Dalcott's flat in Tradmouth. This suited him fine. The Persimmons would keep. He was about to look for Trish when he saw Gerry Heffernan looming in the doorway.

'Wes. A word.'

Wesley followed him out into the corridor.

'I hear you've been chatting up sexy blondes down in Reception.'

'One sexy blonde. Her name's Nuala Johns and she's the journalist who was asking awkward questions at the press conference.' He summarised their conversation and a smirk spread across Gerry's plump face.

'She knows which buttons to press, doesn't she? All that stuff about this Elizabethan doctor. She's dangled her bait and now she's trying to get you on her hook.'

Wesley had to acknowledge that Gerry was probably right. Nuala had discovered his interest in archaeology and what better way to reel him in than to tantalise him with a historical mystery? 'His name was Simon Garchard,' he said quietly. 'And there's a possibility that he had something to do with the skeletons at Tailors Court. Neil's found two more, by the way.'

'So I've heard.'

Wesley raised his eyebrows. News travelled fast. 'But there's one skeleton that definitely isn't linked to this Simon character – the kid with the filling. The toy car and the snake buckle have been sent off to the lab but we're still waiting for the verdict.'

'Wonder what the Persimmons think about their garden turning out to be a mass grave?'

'I don't think it's a very good introduction to country life.' He raised a hand as though he'd just recalled something important. 'I almost forgot – the results have come back on the samples of cloth I took from the attic at Tailors Court.'

'Well?'

'Traces of animal blood, which fits with what Esther Jannings said about her husband experimenting on animals up there.'

'Sir.'

Wesley looked up to see DC Paul Johnson's tall athletic body filling the doorway.

'I've been through Harry Parker's phone records,' he said. 'He's been calling a pay as you go mobile number rather a lot. I rang it and a man answered. Then I asked if Syd or Brian were there and whoever was on the other end asked who was speaking – sounded really worried. I said it was the car hire company.'

'And what did they say?'

'I just asked if everything was OK with the car. Courtesy call, I said. And I asked them if they were still at the address in Tradington. They asked me how I got the number and I said it was on our records.'

'And did they believe you?'

Paul shrugged. 'I think they fell for it. He said they were still at the address.'

Gerry looked as though he was about to punch the air in triumph. 'We've got him. Harry Parker's been in contact with Syd and Brian. He lied to us and that puts him right back in the frame. Anything else?'

'The phone I rang has been traced to the Morbay area – Banton.'

'Thanks, Paul. Get in touch with Morbay nick, will you? Ask them to keep a lookout for the car.'

Paul hurried back into the incident room and Gerry followed slowly, Wesley by his side.

They were met by Nick Tarnaby. He stood blocking their way with a sheet of paper in his hand.

'I've talked to Mabel Cleary's daughter about that letter. She faxed me a copy.'

Wesley had been meaning to follow up the Mabel Cleary lead but he hadn't had time. He thanked Nick who grunted in reply and once he'd handed the paper over, he turned on his heels and returned to his desk. Wesley read the letter with Gerry leaning over his shoulder.

'So the friend who's invited her down here is called Pat but no surname and no address.' Gerry rolled his eyes. 'How many Pats do you think live in the Morbay area?'

Wesley didn't answer.

'I suppose we could put out an appeal.'

Wesley considered the suggestion. 'Two girls called Pat and Mabel who were evacuated to Tailors Court during the War. Why not? It's the sort of thing local radio and TV does all the time – human interest. No need to mention the skeletons.'

Gerry snorted. 'Journalists aren't daft, Wes. As soon as the name Tailors Court's mentioned . . .'

'Then we just say the Tradington area. Do we tell them that Mabel's daughter thinks she's gone missing?'

'That could be the story. Where is Mabel Cleary? I'll get onto the press office and tell them to contact the local media.' He looked at Wesley, mischief in his eyes. 'Unless you want to do it.'

Wesley shook his head. He'd had enough of being the focus of media attention for one week. 'I'll leave it to you, Gerry.' He looked at his watch. 'It'll be too late to get it on tonight's bulletins but we'll manage tomorrow's.'

He saw Trish Walton walking towards him, reminding him that it was almost four o'clock – time to go and pay Roz Dalcott and Harry Parker a visit in Tradmouth. But first he'd call in and see Colin at the mortuary to pick up the report.

Wesley drove the ten miles to Tradmouth with Trish in the passenger seat and parked in the police station car park in what he'd come to think of as his own space. When he announced that he was going to walk the short distance to the hospital mortuary, Trish turned a little pale and said she wanted to go up to the CID office to check on a few things. Wesley didn't argue. Mortuaries weren't to everyone's taste.

It was quite dark as he walked past the boat float and the street lights were reflected golden on the black rippling water. The shop windows in the High Street looked bright and inviting and Christmas decorations had begun to sprout here and there amongst the displays like early crops. The Town Council had already strung Christmas lights across the narrow street although they hadn't yet been lit. It wouldn't be long to the Festive Season, Wesley thought – too much food, over-excited children and Pam exhausted with Christmas productions and parties at school. There were times when he thought that Scrooge might have had the right idea after all.

When he arrived at the hospital he pushed open the swing doors that led to the mortuary – situated round the back of the building so as not to alarm the customers.

Colin greeted him with a welcome cup of Earl Grey – just what he needed to keep out the November chill.

'Your friend Neil obviously thinks I haven't got enough to do. I've just taken delivery of two more skeletons,' Colin began in the same casual way as most men would discuss buying a case of wine. 'One female, probably in her early twenties, and a youngish man. The female had borne a child. But Neil did have one piece of good news.'

'What?'

'You mean he's not told you?'

Wesley experienced an unexpected pang of disappointment that he hadn't been the first person Neil chose to share the news with, whatever it was. But then he'd been busy all afternoon – and Colin had been there at the scene. 'No. What is it?'

'He found an Elizabethan coin a couple of inches above one of the new skeletons and he doesn't think the ground has been disturbed since the burial.'

'But the child, Colin. That's still our problem.'

'Ah yes, the child. It's a boy, by the way. The DNA profile's just come back.'

Wesley sighed. 'We've had someone going through our

192

records of all missing children over the past seventy years. There are a few possible candidates but . . .'

'If the child was buried at Tailors Court, it's safe to assume that he had some connection with the place. It's hardly the sort of location a random killer would choose to dump a body. Too far from the road and, even though you can't see that particular spot from the house, it's still too close for comfort.'

Wesley knew Colin was right. The answer to the puzzle had to lie at Tailors Court. But, much as he'd have liked to concentrate on the death of the owner of those small, pathetic bones, the shooting of James Dalcott was being treated as more urgent.

'Want to see the bones? They're all here,' Colin said as though he was offering a special treat.

Wesley felt he couldn't really say no. He followed Colin through two sets of swing doors into a white-tiled room with six steel trolleys arranged in neat rows. Each trolley was covered by a white sheet and beneath each sheet Wesley could make out the lumpy shape of a human skeleton. Colin walked round the trolleys folding the sheets to one side to reveal the bones beneath. The skulls lay there grinning up at them in silent greeting as Colin folded his arms and surveyed the scene.

'Quite a gathering. The only question is, how did they come to be buried without benefit of clergy in the grounds of Tailors Court?'

Wesley decided it was time to share what he'd been told about Simon Garchard with the pathologist. He was a medical man after all, and he'd be able to tell him if what Nuala Johns had told him was nonsense.

When he'd finished Colin nodded solemnly. 'It would

certainly explain a lot of things. The marks on the bones were in the sort of places you'd expect if somebody rather inexpert was attempting a clumsy dissection. And these latest two have had the tops of their skulls removed – a post mortem craniotomy. Whoever cut them up wanted to examine the brains.' He went over to one of the trolleys and examined the bones lying on the crisp white sheet. They were small and delicate. Wesley could tell by the appearance of the pelvis that it was a woman. 'This is one of the new ones brought in today. Again there's no obvious cause of death but I can't help thinking of Burke and Hare up in Edinburgh in the 1820s. They got their victims drunk and asphyxiated them. Then they sold the bodies to the local medical school for dissection.'

'So you think we could be looking at Devon's answer to Burke and Hare?'

'Mind you, according to Neil, they date from the Elizabethan period.' Colin took a deep breath. 'A lot was going on in the medical world during the late sixteenth century, you know. The ideas of the second-century writer Galen – the theory of the four humours and all that – were still very much to the fore, as was astrology, but . . .'

'Go on,' said Wesley. He had a feeling that he was about to learn something interesting.

'Well, dissection wasn't unknown in the middle ages. It began to be used in fourteenth-century Bologna for the purpose of teaching and research. Leonardo da Vinci performed dissections of course and produced some beautiful drawings. And then in the 1540s Vesalius published *The Fabric of the Human Body* which included accurate illustrations of the body's workings and transformed the study of anatomy – he dissected executed criminals in

194

Padua, you know. Then, of course, at the start of the seventeenth century Harvey performed public dissections and discovered the circulation of blood.' He caught Wesley's eye. 'Sorry, Wesley, the history of medicine's fascinated me ever since my student days. Hope I'm not boring you.'

'Far from it. If the bodies Neil found had been dissected, it fits in with what I've heard about Simon Garchard. He had no medical school and no supply of executed felons so he had to get the corpses where he could.'

There was a long period of amicable silence before Wesley asked his next question. 'I notice the child's not here with the others.'

Colin said nothing. He led Wesley through to another bare white room and slid out one of the mortuary drawers. When he gently pulled the sheet aside, Wesley saw the skeleton lying there and his heart lurched. The bones seemed so small, so vulnerable. This child had only been a couple of years older than his own son and the thought disturbed him.

'I've been having a closer look at this one, Wesley. There's no obvious cause of death but look, there are cut marks on the ribs there and there. The cuts on these bones seem deeper and less controlled than the others. Consistent with a very clumsy dissection.'

Wesley bent and stared obediently at the place where Colin's gloved finger was pointing.

'Any clue to his identity?'

'From the coin and the other items found with the body we're looking at the late nineteen thirties at the earliest, probably a little later,' Wesley said 'We're making enquiries, of course, but James Dalcott's murder takes priority.'

195

Colin bowed his head. 'Any progress?'

'We're following a few leads.' Wesley realised he sounded evasive but he really couldn't think of anything else to say. There were so many tantalising possibilities but they had nothing solid as yet. Perhaps he would make a breakthrough when he visited Roz Dalcott and Harry Parker – but he wasn't counting on it.

When he reached the hospital entrance, he found Trish waiting, stamping her feet to keep warm, her hands thrust firmly into her pockets against the damp wind blowing in from the river. When she spotted him she looked relieved.

'Hope you weren't waiting too long,' he said.

She smiled enigmatically but didn't reply.

They walked in silence and when they reached Trad Itions the gallery was still open. They could see Roz Dalcott inside, sitting at an antique desk reading what looked like a magazine or catalogue of some kind. Wesley pushed open the shop door and a bell jangled loudly.

Roz looked up eagerly, expecting a customer to relieve the boredom. But when she saw Wesley standing there with Trish hovering behind, the welcoming smile that was starting to form on her lips turned into a scowl.

'I've already told you everything I know. This is harass-ment.'

Wesley gave her a charming smile. 'Sorry to bother you, Mrs Dalcott, but I'd just like a quick chat.'

Roz rolled her eyes to heaven and looked away. Hers was an expression he'd seen before on many a criminal's wife or girlfriend. It was the look of a woman who's con-vinced that the police are persecuting her wronged partner.

'Is Harry in?'

'He's gone out. It's a free country.'

Wesley glanced at Trish. Their presence was really getting to Roz. Which was probably a good thing.

'We've been going through his phone records. He's been calling a couple of old friends – Syd Jenkins and Brian Carrack. Perhaps you know them as your late husband's next-door neighbours – Syd and Brian Trenchard. Funny how they vanished after James was shot. You see, I can't help making a connection between James's death, their disappearance, and the fact that Harry knows them from prison and he's been ringing them. What do you think?'

She blustered for a few seconds, her manicured fingers flicking nervously through the pages of the catalogue on the desk, playing for time.

'You're making this up,' she said once she'd gathered her thoughts. 'Harry's always saying the police try to trick you. I don't know anything about this Syd and Brian. James mentioned a couple of men were renting the house next door – father and son he said they were – but I don't think he ever talked to them apart from to say hello. And Harry hasn't said anything about knowing them.' She folded her arms over her growing bump and pressed her lips together in a stubborn line.

'What time will Harry be back?'

'You're wasting your time,' she said with brittle confidence. 'He's got nothing to hide.'

Wesley looked round the gallery. He hadn't been in here before. Once he and Pam had got as far as looking in the window but, after one glance at the prices, they'd walked on.

Suddenly a set of pictures in the far corner caught his eye. Blood-red oil on three large canvases. They were striking but it was probably a good thing that they didn't occupy a more prominent position – they were the sort of thing that would have put him off his dinner. He walked over to them slowly, unable to take his eyes off the images of flayed flesh, parted to reveal the inner workings of the body. He'd seen pictures very similar to these recently. Remarkably similar.

'They're Harry's,' Roz said with a hint of pride. 'Brilliant, aren't they?'

He saw that Trish was watching him and when their eyes met, she pulled a face. As an art critic, he thought, her tastes probably matched his own. Although he couldn't fault Parker's technical skill, the subject matter certainly wouldn't be to everyone's liking.

He cleared his throat. 'They're, er, very . . .' He searched for the right word. 'Very visceral.' He hesitated. 'Actually I've seen something similar recently and I was wondering where Harry got his inspiration.' Something told him that Harry Parker must have seen those pictures behind the panelling at Tailors Court. He couldn't believe the similarity was just a coincidence. 'Has he ever visited a place called Tailors Court, owned by a couple called Tony and Jill Persimmon?'

'I've never heard of them. He got the idea from the pictures upstairs – the ones we found behind the panels in the living room. I thought they were disgusting but Harry . . . He said they were powerful and that they got to the root of the human condition.' She sounded as if she was quoting him word for word. 'Harry's work's too good for a little provincial gallery where most of the punters just want pretty views of the River Trad. They should be exhibited in London if Harry's to get the appreciation he deserves.'

After that bravura display of loyalty, Wesley was lost for

198

words. He saw that Trish had turned away from Parker's paintings and had begun to study a set of pretty river-scapes. Roz gave her a brief look of contempt and stood up.

'Can I have a look at the pictures upstairs?' said Wesley innocently. 'I'm really interested.'

Roz hesitated. Then she stood up, walked over to the shop door and turned the sign hanging there round to 'Closed' before leading them upstairs. Wesley could sense suspicion in every guarded movement and he knew that she thought it was some sort of ploy to gain access to the flat. But she probably couldn't think of a valid reason to refuse without making it look as if she had something to hide.

She opened the door to the living room and made for the fireplace. She pushed a section of panelling and, like the one at Tailors Court, it slid back stiffly to reveal the roughly plastered wall beneath. Wesley could see that someone had drawn on the wall – rough sketches of dis-sected human corpses; ribs drawn back to reveal the inner workings of the body; heart and lungs with their attendant arteries.

'I must admit I'm glad I don't have to look at those things all day,' Roz said.

'I'm sure you are,' Wesley replied. He studied the sketches more closely. These were slightly different from the ones at Tailors Court. They were rougher and the pro-portions seemed slightly wrong, as though they had been drawn by a less talented hand.

'What do you know about the history of this place?'

'They've got a local history section in the library if you're interested,' she said with studied boredom. 'Why?

Do you think they were done by some serial killer when he chopped up his victims?' Wesley could hear the heavy sarcasm in her voice. 'I can tell you one thing for certain – they weren't done by Harry. He's got real talent.'

'I'm sure he has,' Wesley replied, resisting the mischievous urge to ask whether his talents also lay in the direction of armed robbery and murder.

There was no sign of Harry Parker in the flat so it seemed that Roz was telling the truth when she said he was out. Wesley's suspicious mind had considered the possibility that she'd been lying to him. There was nothing more to be done until Parker came back. Then he'd have some questions to answer about his old friends Syd and Brian.

As they returned to the shop, Wesley looked directly at Roz. She looked away, uncomfortable.

'We need to talk to Harry. Tell him to call us when he gets back.'

Roz turned the shop sign back to 'Open'. 'And if he doesn't want to?'

'We come and get him. It's his choice.'

She nodded. Message understood.

'What was all that business with those awful pictures about?' Trish asked as soon as they were outside.

'There are some very similar pictures behind some panelling in a room at Tailors Court where those skeletons were found. But I don't think they were done by the same person,' he said before going on to explain about the attic room and Colin's findings on the Tailors Court bones.

'Lee Parsons is checking on missing children,' she said quietly after a few moments. 'But if the child's skeleton really dates back to the nineteen thirties or forties . . .'

'We might never know who he was. Unless we find Mabel Cleary and she can throw some light on the matter.'

Trish said nothing as they walked back to the police station car park.

It was eight o'clock when Wesley arrived back home and Pam was waiting for him in the hall. She looked as though she had news to impart. He gave her a swift kiss of greeting and waited.

'Neil's here,' she said, nodding towards the living room door. 'They've found more skeletons today.'

'I know. I'll just see the kids before . . .' He could smell food and he realised that he hadn't had anything to eat since his visit to the Traceys' farm. He was hungry and the last thing he felt like at that moment was more talk about skeletons – he'd had his fill of the subject at the mortuary.

He hurried upstairs, taking two steps at a time, aware that Pam was watching him. When he looked in on the children he found Amelia fast asleep, curled up with a small frown on her delicate face. Michael, however, was awake and reading. He was a serious, scholarly child, just as Wesley's parents claimed he had been. Wesley sat on the bed and, after a brief conversation about school and a quick story, he said goodnight to his son and crept back downstairs.

When he entered the living room Neil was lounging in an armchair, quite at home. When he saw Wesley he grinned sheepishly. 'I think I've just eaten your dinner. Sorry.'

Pam stood up and touched his arm. 'I'll see what's in the freezer.' From the way she hurried off leaving the two men together, Wesley suspected that she'd had enough of Neil for the time being.

Wesley sighed and flopped down heavily on the sofa. 'If you've found any more skeletons, I don't want to know. I'm off duty.'

'I didn't think policemen were ever off duty,' Neil said before taking a final sip from the half-empty mug of tea in his hand. 'And these are particularly interesting ones because the tops of the skulls were removed post mortem.'

'I know. I've seen them.'

Neil looked a little disappointed.

'How many more skeletons are down there, do you think?'

'Hopefully none. We've investigated all the geophysics anomalies now so . . .'

'Thank God for that,' said Wesley. 'Not that the old ones are my problem. I was just afraid there might be more like the child's – it's a boy, by the way.'

'Poor little bugger. You'll keep me informed, won't you?'

Suddenly Wesley remembered something. Something important that tiredness and the pressure of the case had temporarily driven from his mind. 'I don't know if you've managed to find out much about the history of Tailors Court.' He paused for effect. 'Or rather Flesh Tailor's Court.'

'What?'

Wesley explained, repeating the story he'd heard from Nuala Johns. Simon Garchard and his medical experiments.

Neil's eyes lit up. 'The bones are probably the right age . . .'

'Apart from the child.' Somehow Wesley couldn't get that boy out of his head.

But Neil hadn't heard him. 'If this story about Simon Garchard is true then it stands to reason he'd have hidden the evidence in his garden.'

'And there's more. According to Nuala Johns, Garchard was tried for murder. He was accused of killing one of his maidservants and dissecting her body.'

'He probably ran out of corpses when the village constables made the graveyard more secure – or perhaps there was an outbreak of good health in Tradington and nobody died.'

'Possibly. Anyway, he was hanged. And I saw something else today that you might find interesting.' Wesley went on to tell him about the pictures behind the panelling in Roz Dalcott's flat.

Neil raised his eyebrows. 'So they're the same as the ones at Tailors Court?'

'Similar but not the same. They're not as well drawn.'

'You think they were drawn by someone different?'

Wesley nodded. 'I'm no art critic but I'd say so.'

'Who?'

'Maybe Simon had an assistant.'

'Every Burke has his Hare.'

'Something like that.'

'Tell you what, Wes, we've more or less finished at Tailors Court now so it's back to Exeter to catch up on our post-excavation reports and what have you.' He leaned forward. 'While I'm there, I'll see what I can find out about Simon Garchard. There's bound to be stuff in the archives. I'll get Annabel to give me a hand.'

Wesley grinned. 'Thought you might.'

Neil caught on immediately. 'We're just good friends.'

'And I'm the Commissioner of the Metropolitan Police,' Wesley said with a mischievous grin. Annabel and Neil were opposites – but opposites frequently attract.

He heard the distant ping of the microwave followed by Pam's voice calling from the kitchen. Dinner was ready.

But before he could satisfy his hunger his mobile phone began to ring.

When he finished the call Neil looked at him enquiringly. 'Bad news?'

'Someone doing a bit of night fishing in the Trad has hooked a body. I've got to get down there right away and meet Gerry.'

'Tough,' said Neil, resuming his seat and making himself comfortable.

CHAPTER 9

Transcript of recording made by Mrs Mabel Cleary (née Fallon) – Home Counties Library Service Living History Project: Reminiscences of a wartime evacuee.

The German man was a doctor. There was talk that he'd delivered Mrs Bowe's baby. Mrs Bowe had six already and Mary said that Mr Bowe was away fighting and there'd be trouble when he got back. I didn't know what she meant back then but I do now.

I'd never met a German before and at that time I didn't particularly want to, thank you very much, not after what their bombs had done to our street in London. But when I fell over and broke my leg while I was helping with the harvest at Gorfleet Farm – well, I say helping but I expect I was more of a hindrance if the truth be told – and they said they were sending for Dr Kramer, I was in too much pain to object.

Mary said I made such a fuss but she didn't know how much it hurt. Then Dr Kramer arrived and took charge and I started to feel better. He was small with black hair and a little beard and he spoke very good English with a German accent. I knew – well, everyone knew – that he was staying with Mr Hilton, a retired teacher who wrote books on local history. Dr Kramer had a son called Otto and rumour had it that they were refugees from the Nazis. Somebody said they were Jewish. Dr Kramer was nice and he had a sort of twinkle in his eye. And it was a good job he'd come because one doctor in the village had joined up and the other was well past retirement age and wasn't well at all. You never think of doctors being ill, do you?

But that wasn't long before it happened. And I think it was the stories Otto Kramer used to tell us – the ones he'd heard from Mr Hilton – that started the whole thing off.

Much as Wesley enjoyed Colin Bowman's genial company, his visits to the pathologist's place of work were becoming far too regular for his liking. And the mortuary was the last place he'd choose to visit first thing on a dank Thursday morning.

According to Colin, the body hooked by the unlucky fisherman had been in the water for a week or so and, having suffered the effects of decomposition and the voracious attentions of various river creatures, it wasn't in a particularly good state.

'So it's a woman?' Gerry said, stating the obvious as he stared down at the discoloured corpse lying on the stainless steel post mortem table.

'That much is certain. Five foot two. Longish dark hair, possibly dyed,' said Colin. He had finished his initial examination of the corpse and was preparing to make the

Y-shaped incision in the breast. 'And not in the first flush of youth, I should say.'

'How old?'

'Hard to say exactly. I'd say mid-fifties but she could be a little older.' Colin hesitated. 'No trace of any clothing. Odd that she seems to have been naked when she went in.'

'Very odd,' said Gerry. 'Far too cold in November to go skinny dipping.'

Wesley stood back a little, trying to avoid getting too close to the action. The last thing he wanted to do was to faint again as he did at the first post mortem he'd attended when he'd started at the Met.

'Mind you, you get these naturist health fanatics, Wes,' Gerry continued, oblivious to the odour of decay rising from the body on the table. 'In their eighties some of them. Nothing they like better than to have to break the ice before they do a few lengths.'

Wesley smiled. The scenario seemed unlikely. But this woman, whoever she was, must have been naked for a reason. 'Any sign of sexual assault, Colin?'

'No. But that doesn't mean it didn't happen. Even if a body's fairly well preserved it's often difficult to detect that sort of thing once it's been in the water a few days.'

'Perhaps that was the intention.'

'It's been known,' said Colin solemnly.

He worked in silence for a while. Then when he'd finished, he nodded to his assistant to sew the unknown woman back up again.

'So what's the verdict, Colin?'

Colin pulled off his surgical gloves. 'I did notice one thing of interest.'

'Don't keep us in suspense,' said Gerry.

Colin hesitated. 'There are very faint traces of ink on the torso. Very hard to see because of the immersion in water but . . .'

'Ink? You mean she'd written something on her hand?'

'No, Gerry. It's on her back.' He nodded to his assistant who gently rolled the body onto its side. Colin pointed to the relevant spot and the two detectives peered to see. The marks were hardly visible after all that time spent in the river but they were there all right.

'She can't have done it herself.' Colin paused. 'It rather reminds me of the marks surgeons make before they oper-ate – to make sure they're cutting in the correct place.'

Wesley and Gerry looked at each other.

'So if that's the case, what operation would you say she was going to have?' Wesley asked.

Colin thought for a few moments. 'Something con-nected with the right kidney, perhaps. Although that's just a guess: her kidneys looked healthy enough to me.'

'If she's wandered off from a hospital nearby she shouldn't be hard to trace.'

'I've already made enquiries here,' said Colin. 'She's not one of ours.'

'What about the cause of death?'

Colin thought for a while, staring at the corpse. 'I can tell you what she didn't die of. She didn't drown.'

'You're sure about that?' said Gerry.

Colin looked a little hurt. 'Absolutely sure. This poor woman had a massive heart attack. It's a case of natural causes, gentlemen. Fancy a cup of tea?'

Mabel Cleary's daughter, Sandra, alighted from the coach at the waterfront and looked around. In summer this part of Morbay was teeming with harassed parents and their offspring making for the beach below the concrete promenade with buckets and spades. But today a solitary dog walker, well wrapped up in quilted coat and woolly hat, had the damp beach all to herself. The choppy sea was an uninviting sludge grey and the beach shops and kiosks were firmly locked and shuttered. A week earlier Christmas lights had been strung up along the sea front by the Council and now they drooped forlornly between the lampposts, doing little to relieve the bleakness of the scene.

Sandra fastened the top button of her beige raincoat and shivered. She wasn't quite sure why she'd come but she'd felt that she should be doing something positive. Even if the search was futile, she had to make the effort to look for her mother.

The policeman she'd spoken to over the phone – Nick his name was – had told her about the planned TV appeal. It was a good idea, Sandra thought as she began to walk towards the station, her wheeled case trailing behind her like an obedient dog. She was to take the local train to Neston where she'd be met at the station. Sandra, who didn't know the area at all, had no idea how far Neston was. In her agitation, she hadn't even bothered to look it up in the road atlas her husband kept in his car.

As she waited on the freezing platform for the train, she delved into her roomy canvas shopping bag. It was still there – the transcript of the tapes Mabel had made for the local library. The reminiscences project. But as far as Sandra could tell, there was no clue to her whereabouts in what she thought of as her mother's ramblings. And there was no mention of anyone called Pat so far.

But Pat had summoned her down here to the south west. And Pat was a bit of a mystery.

Nick Tarnaby was leaving the incident room just as Wesley and Gerry returned. 'Everything OK, Nick?' Wesley said to his disappearing back.

Tarnaby stopped and turned. 'Yes, sir. I'm just off to meet Mabel Cleary's daughter at the station.'

Wesley let him go, wondering whether it might have been better to assign someone more sympathetic to the task. But Nick was the only officer free at that moment so there was little choice.

Gerry had marched on ahead and Wesley joined him at his desk. He could see the pictures of James Dalcott on the notice board, photographed in life and death. Near these photographs were details of everyone they'd interviewed during the investigation along with Gerry's scribbled comments – some rather libellous, Wesley thought. But then nobody but the investigation team was likely to see them.

At the other end of the huge board were photographs of the child's bones together with the rotting wooden car, the coin and the snake belt buckle found in the grave. Since Neil had confirmed that the other bones found at Tailors Court weren't CID's problem, their images had been removed. Mabel Cleary's picture wasn't up there yet and Wesley hoped it never would be. He hoped that Mrs Cleary would be found alive and well.

Gerry looked round. 'I'd better say a few words about our corpse in the river. We're doing a check on all hospitals and clinics in the area to see whether they're missing any patients.'

Wesley nodded. It was the only place to start. He

glanced at the notice board again. Soon the unknown woman would join the others in the gruesome picture gallery, unless they could discover her identity soon and eliminate the possibility that her heart attack had been brought about by some sort of foul play.

Gerry gathered the troops to bring them up to date and, as everyone was returning to their tasks, the phone on Wesley's desk began to ring.

When he recited his name a familiar voice answered. 'I've got something for you,' it said tantalisingly with a hint of coquettishness. 'It's something I'd rather not say over the phone so how about lunch?'

'Hello, Nuala. What kind of information are you talking about?' He had no time to play flirtatious games even if he'd wanted to.

'Something good. Something you'll be interested in.'

'Why don't you come to the station?'

'You need to eat, don't you? I'll see you at twelve-thirty in the Star – that's the one in Neston by the river. Don't be late.'

Before Wesley could protest, she put the phone down. He closed his eyes and whispered a couple of expletives. He felt angry with Nuala Johns for being so presumptuous and angry with himself for allowing her to get away with it. Most men would have relished the prospect of lunch with an attractive woman, but Wesley suspected that it might turn out to be a time-wasting ordeal. However, he decided to grit his teeth and meet her as arranged.

He spent the next hour or so sifting through paperwork, trying to get the various cases straight in his head. They seemed to have become entangled somehow: James Dalcott's shooting and the discovery of the child's bones at

Tailors Court. The only connection he could think of so far was tenuous to say the least – the fact that the gruesome wall paintings in Roz Dalcott's flat were similar to the ones at Tailors Court. But he knew that even such nebulous links sometimes turned out to be significant.

When twelve-fifteen arrived he put his coat on. He saw Rachel Tracey watching him.

'Where are you off to?' She liked to keep tabs on the comings and goings.

'I'm having lunch with a beautiful woman,' he said. Sometimes Rachel was so earnest that he couldn't resist a spot of teasing.

'Do I know her?' she said quickly.

He gave Rachel an enigmatic smile and carried on. 'Nick Tarnaby's on his way to pick up Mabel Cleary's daughter from the station.'

'Yes, I know. She's booked a room at the Star so he's taking her there first before bringing her here.'

Wesley was on the point of telling Rachel that he was lunching at the Star. But some mischievous imp inside him was enjoying the thought of her frustrated curiosity so he stayed silent.

'I was talking to the press officer earlier and the local TV people seem keen on doing this Mabel and Pat item on the bulletin tonight,' Rachel continued. 'They'll probably want to interview the daughter – Sandra, I think her name is.'

'Good. It's about time we found Mabel Cleary.'

Rachel hesitated. 'Any chance that she's the woman in the river?'

Wesley shook his head. 'I doubt it. The descriptions don't match.'

'Well, that's one blessing. You'd better not keep the lady waiting,' Rachel said pointedly as Wesley turned to go.

He smiled to himself and pretended he hadn't heard.

It took ten minutes to reach the Star from the police station. It was an ivy-clad Georgian building with an impressive portico situated at a crossroads by the river: one of those small-town hotels with a good reputation that, over the years, had become a hub of social activity: the local choice for dinner dances, wedding receptions and Rotary Club Meetings. Wesley dawdled at the entrance for a few moments before going in. He presumed Nuala intended to meet him in the bar rather than the expensive restaurant – at least he hoped so.

He was just wondering whether he'd bump into Nick Tarnaby and Mabel's daughter, Sandra, while he was there, when Nuala arrived, walking slowly down the road towards him as though she had all the time in the world. Wesley felt a stab of irritation but he forced his features into a businesslike smile and extended a hand, determined to keep the encounter on a professional footing.

Nuala's skimpy jacket and mini-skirt left little to the imagination and her only concession to the autumnal chill was a pair of Ugg boots. As they shook hands her eyes met his and she smiled a smile that would have made most men's pulses beat a little faster. But Wesley was well aware that she was an ambitious journalist out for nobody but herself. Given half a chance she'd destroy his career to get a good story.

'Let's find a seat,' he said as he stood aside to let her lead the way.

They ordered their food at the bar and when they were settled with their drinks – Nuala with a dry white wine and Wesley with a head-clearing orange juice – Nuala

213

edged a little closer. Wesley stared ahead, focusing his eyes on the hand pumps on the bar.

'Relax,' she said, touching his arm.

'Sorry, it's been a busy week. I presume you know about this elderly woman who's gone missing?'

Nuala grunted. 'Mabel Cleary? That's old news.'

'They're doing a TV appeal tonight. You know the sort of thing – does anyone know where she is? And who is the Pat she came down here to see?'

'I think James Dalcott's a much sexier story than some wrinkly who's chosen to go walkabout,' said Nuala taking a sip of wine. 'Any developments?'

'You'll be the first to know, I promise.' Wesley picked up his drink.

'And those skeletons at Tailors Court? Now that's a really sexy story. I'm working on a big feature about it.'

'You might want to talk to Neil Watson. He's in charge of the excavation so they're more his concern than mine.'

'Oh, Dr Watson.' She giggled. 'You're old pals, I believe. Dr Watson and the Great Detective. Where have I heard that one before?'

'That's an old joke, I'm afraid. And yes, we have known each other a long while. We were at university together.'

'Doing archaeology.'

'That's right.'

'So have you found out any more about the child's skeleton?'

Wesley was about to put his glass to his lips but he lowered it. 'We're not ready to make a statement about that just yet. As soon as . . .'

'You rang my uncle, didn't you? You wanted to speak to my gran.'

214

Wesley had almost forgotten that she was the grand-daughter of Mary Haynes from Gorfleet Farm, right next door to Tailors Court. She hardly looked the sort to belong in a farm setting.

'Did you know that the new owner of Tailors Court used to work for Pharmitest – the company who own the Podingham Clinic where James Dalcott worked part-time? How's that for coincidence, eh?'

This was news to Wesley. But then why should Tony Persimmon have thought it worth mentioning?

'How did you find out?'

Nuala gave one of her irritatingly smug smiles. 'Easy. I Googled him. Don't you have computers down at the police station?'

Wesley didn't answer. Such a link had never occurred to him and he felt a little annoyed with himself. But before he could think up anything to say in his defence, Nuala changed the subject.

'You work with the Tracey girl, don't you? Rachel, isn't it? I used to see her around sometimes.' She gave a know-ing smile. 'Bossy little piece. I can imagine she'd enjoy slapping the handcuffs on. I think there was something between her and my cousin Nigel at one time. Not that he's ever said anything about it.'

Wesley raised his eyebrows. He'd sensed that there was some history between her and Nigel Haynes. But Rachel wasn't one to broadcast the ups and downs of her rela-tionships so the details would probably remain shrouded in mystery.

But Nuala seemed to have become bored with the subject of Rachel. 'So why do you want to speak to my gran?'

'She was living at Tailors Court during the war. She came down here as a land girl, I believe.'

'That's right.'

'How is she?'

'Gran's pretty indestructible. She's due out of hospital any time now. Do you think she might know something about the child's skeleton?'

'Has she ever talked about her time at Tailors Court.'

'Not to me she hasn't. I think she was too busy snogging in haystacks with granddad and a few assorted GIs to notice much of what was going on around her.' She grinned. 'Snogging – that's a delightfully old-fashioned word, isn't it? These days it'd just be fucking.'

Wesley saw that she was watching him, trying to gauge his reaction. But he kept his expression neutral. It was time to steer the conversation away from Mary's love life. 'You said you had something to tell me.'

She leaned forward conspiratorially. 'I've got hold of some information about James Dalcott and I thought I'd be a public-spirited citizen and share it with the police.' She drained her glass and put it down. 'Buy me another drink and I'll tell you what it is.'

Wesley didn't feel inclined to argue. He went to the bar and by the time he returned their food had arrived – sandwiches for him and something piping hot with a thick crust for Nuala. She ate a few mouthfuls of pie hungrily before putting her knife and fork down.

'James Dalcott was the son of a murderer,' she said before taking another sip of wine.

'I know.'

Nuala's expression of disappointment when he uttered those two words gave Wesley a frisson of satisfaction.

After a few more sips of wine she spoke again. 'You can't know. It was all hushed up. I had the devil's own job researching his background. I had to get hold of birth and adoption certificates and –'

'And you thought the police were too dim to do all that themselves?' He was trying hard not to gloat. 'We found out pretty early on.'

'And you don't think it's relevant?'

'To be honest I can't see a connection. Can you?'

Nuala looked quite crestfallen for a few seconds. Then she bounced back. 'That body-snatching I told you about – Simon Garchard . . .'

Wesley was about to take another bite of his tuna sandwich but he stopped in midair and put it back on his plate.

'I found something about it in the churchwardens' accounts of St Petroc's church, Tradington. Dated 1594.' She began to delve into her handbag. 'Here, I took a copy.'

She handed Wesley a few photocopied sheets. The handwriting was difficult to decipher but after a while he found that he could just about make out the words. '*The graveyard has lately been disturbed and the body of Ralph Printon, the blacksmith, was stolen by evil doers.*' An entry dated two months later on the next sheet told a similar story. '*The churchyard has again been desecrated and the body of Mistress Lettice Venmore who lately died in child bed stolen by villainous persons. Prayers have been offered for the safe return of the remains.*'

There was another entry, almost identical, on another sheet. Three weeks after Mistress Lettice Venmore's mortal remains vanished, the 'villainous persons' were at it again. One of the victims was Harry Batch, the late landlord of the Courtenay Arms in Tradington Village. The name of the pub was familiar to Wesley – he had had a rather good lunch there with Pam the previous summer. And at the same time the grave of a young woman called Alys Tye, a pauper, was similarly desecrated.

He handed the sheets back to Nuala. 'Very interesting. But what's it got to do with me?'

'All these bodies went missing when Simon Garchard was in residence at Tailors Court. If he fancied himself as a doctor and he needed bodies for dissection, where better to get them from than the local churchyard? I found the accounts for Belsham church as well. They lost the bodies of two young women – that's six in all – and none of them were ever found. How many has Neil turned up at Tailors Court?'

'Six,' Wesley answered quietly.

'I think if you give Neil the details of all those missing corpses, he'll be able to match them to his skeletons.'

'But wouldn't it have been a bit obvious?' said Wesley, trying to hide his excitement at the likely solution to Neil's mystery. 'Presumably Simon Garchard was an intelligent man who'd know better than to foul his own doorstep.'

'You'd think so. But the Garchards were gentry so per-haps nobody dared to say anything. You know the story of Elizabeth Bathory?'

'Remind me.'

'She was a Hungarian countess who systematically tor-tured and murdered hundreds of young women but, because of her social position, nobody spoke against her. It was decades before she was found out. And then only when she went too far – just like Garchard did when he killed the maidservant.'

Wesley nodded wearily.

'Things like that happened all through history,' she

continued. 'Wealth has always allowed certain people to buy others and treat them like possessions.' She looked him in the eye. 'Look at slavery. That affected some of your ancestors, at a guess?' She inclined her head, waiting for a reaction.

'Yes. Greed can make men sink pretty low,' he said quietly.

'Or the desire for power, or knowledge. Dominion over nature.'

Wesley looked at her curiously. She'd clearly thought all this out. Perhaps he'd underestimated her. 'So how long after these bodies went missing was Garchard tried for murder?'

'About eight months.'

'Perhaps people's patience finally ran out. Maybe he was suspected of this body-snatching but nothing could be proved. Then the maidservant died and they grabbed the opportunity to nail him once and for all.'

Nuala didn't answer. There was a long silence while she finished her meal and Wesley watched her tucking in hungrily. She was probably one of those women Pam always said she envied, he thought. A woman who could eat like a horse and stay as thin as a supermodel.

'It might be interesting to see what was said at his trial,' Wesley continued. 'Perhaps when I get the Dalcott case out of the way.'

Nuala looked up. 'It'll be in Latin, won't it?'

'My Latin's a bit rusty but I can still get by,' he said, suddenly feeling a little smug that she'd underestimated him. 'But I've got rather a lot on at the moment.' He took a last bite of his sandwich and pushed his plate away. 'I'd better be going.'

To his surprise Nuala reached out and took hold of his arm as he stood up. He looked down and saw her slim, ringless hand resting on his sleeve.

'Don't go. We're still getting to know each other.'

He picked up the hand gently. 'Sorry. If you discover anything else . . .'

'I don't suppose you're free tonight?' she said. She had inclined her head to one side and there was a definite invitation in her blue eyes. 'I'll probably have found out lots more about Simon Garchard by then.'

'Sorry. I'm tied up.'

'Then untie yourself.'

'Another time maybe.'

She pouted in mock disappointment and Wesley wondered whether to make a throwaway remark about his wife not seeing much of him. However, he stayed silent. Some instinct told him that if she thought he was unavailable, the flow of information might dry up completely. He gave her an apologetic smile. 'Maybe.'

As he left the bar he didn't look back. And when he reached Reception the sight of Nick Tarnaby with a middle-aged woman drove all thoughts of Nuala Johns out of his mind.

Gerry Heffernan put down the telephone receiver and sighed. This was getting him nowhere. No hospital in the vicinity had mislaid a female patient – or any patient come to that. He clenched his fist and gave the desk a half-hearted punch. But before he could put more effort into venting his frustration, he heard a voice. 'Sir. Could I have a word?'

He looked up and saw Trish Walton standing there. All

of a sudden he felt glad of the company. It could be lonely at the top sometimes and Gerry was a gregarious man.

'Hi, Trish, sit yourself down. What can I do you for?'

She smiled dutifully at the feeble joke. 'I've been checking out any private hospitals or clinics that our mystery woman from the river might have used.'

'And?'

'I tried that clinic where James Dalcott worked. The Podingham Clinic.'

Gerry leaned forward expectantly. From the tone of Trish's voice he could tell that she hadn't altogether drawn a blank. There was a glimmer of hope somewhere.

'The person I spoke to, a Fiona Verdun, said the premises were sometimes used by surgeons to operate on private patients but that it was usually fairly minor procedures.'

Gerry looked at her puzzled. 'So?'

Trish hesitated. 'It's probably nothing. But I just got the feeling she sounded a bit evasive.'

Gerry thought for a moment. The Trish Walton he knew wasn't prone to flights of fancy. She was level headed and maybe even a little unimaginative. If she thought something was wrong it was probably because it was true.

'So what wasn't she telling you?'

'She seemed too anxious to dismiss the surgery they did there as trivial but I'd like to find out more.'

'We'll probably need a warrant. And it's hard to get a warrant on a hunch. I should know, I've tried it often enough.'

Trish smiled. 'I've got an idea. You know these drugs trials? If I went along as a volunteer, I could get the feel of the place.'

Gerry looked at her in alarm. 'Oh no, Trish. I'm not going to let you do anything like that. That bloke called Carl Utley ended up . . . well, we don't really know how he ended up, do we? We haven't seen him yet.'

'I know one of the other DCs has been trying his number regularly and a couple of them have visited his address several times. They said there was no sign of life – perhaps he's away.'

'I think it's about time we made a real effort to have a word with Mr Utley,' said Gerry. 'As soon as we make contact I'll pay him a visit.'

He suddenly felt like getting out of the office. And he was keeping his fingers crossed that Carl Utley would soon give him the perfect excuse.

'Mrs Ackerley?' Wesley offered his hand and Sandra Ackerley shook it weakly. 'I'm Detective Inspector Peterson. I believe your mother left for Devon a week ago.'

'That's right.' She glanced at Nick Tarnaby who was standing glumly by her side, hands in pockets.

'I've tried everyone who knows her but nobody's heard of a Pat who lives round here. What are you doing to find her?' She gave Nick Tarnaby a sideways look. 'This young man here doesn't seem to know what's going on.'

'Let's talk about your mother, shall we?' Wesley said, smoothing the waters. He turned to Nick. 'It's OK, Nick, you get back to the incident room if you like.'

Tarnaby hesitated for a moment then slouched out of the hotel foyer and disappeared through the swing doors into the rainy street outside. Wesley knew Nuala Johns was still in the bar so he looked around for a suitable haven. He spotted a door marked 'Residents' Lounge'. Sandra was booked in to the hotel for the night which made her a resident so he led her towards the closed door, glancing at the bar entrance and hoping that Nuala wouldn't emerge and break the spell. He could tell Sandra was ready to talk. And he needed to learn everything he could about Mabel Cleary.

The Residents' Lounge was reassuringly old fashioned; painted in dark red with glowing mahogany furnishings, it had the feel of a gentlemen's club, a warm refuge from the bustle of the outside world. Once Sandra had made herself comfortable on a well-worn Chesterfield sofa, Wesley sank into a neighbouring armchair.

'I suppose they'll be putting the Christmas decorations up soon,' said Sandra absentmindedly.

'They get earlier every year,' said Wesley. It was something he'd heard his mother say often and he felt the familiarity of the subject would establish some rapport.

But he was wrong. She burrowed in her handbag, pulled out a clean tissue and dabbed at her eyes. 'I want mum home for Christmas. I can't even begin to think what it'd be like without her. You've got to find her. I won't be fobbed off with excuses.'

Wesley leaned forward. 'Don't worry. We'll find her.' He hoped he was right and he hoped she couldn't see through the mask of forced optimism.

He decided to get one of the key questions out of the way first. 'Er, this might sound strange but has your mother been in hospital for surgery recently?' He wanted to make absolutely sure she had no connection to the corpse in the river.

'No. Why?'

'And she's had no health problems at all?' It was possible that she'd been keeping something from her daughter;

223

that she'd travelled to Devon far away from home to have treatment secretly so as not to worry her family.

'She has a heart condition – angina – I have to keep an eye on her to make sure she's taking her medication and living healthily. She can be difficult at times – defiant like a small child – so she needs to be watched. But apart from that . . .'

'We've seen the copy of the letter she received from Pat. I don't suppose you've managed to find your mother's address book?'

Sandra shook her head. 'She must have taken it with her.'

'And you're sure she got on the coach to Morbay?'

'Oh yes. I gave her a lift to the coach station myself. I had a word with the coach driver – asked him to keep an eye on her. And she said she was being met at the other end so I didn't think there'd be any harm in letting her go. I told her to keep her mobile on at all times but . . . well, she's gone and switched it off.'

Wesley knew most of this already. Someone from uniform had already spoken to the coach driver. Mabel Cleary had alighted at Morbay coach station. But he hadn't seen where she went after that.

'I presume she hasn't done anything like this before.'

'Of course not. If she had, I wouldn't have let her go.'

'And did she ever talk about Devon? Or mention anybody she knew here?'

Sandra started to pick at a jagged nail. 'I knew she'd been evacuated down here but she used to change the subject whenever I mentioned it.'

She delved in the large canvas bag she was nursing on her knee and brought out a cardboard file. She handed it to Wesley. Inside he found a sheaf of typed A4 paper with the logo of Home Counties Libraries in the front. *Reminiscences of a Wartime Evacuee.*

'I found this in her flat. There's a lot about where she stayed. It was a place called Tailors Court. It's the name Pat mentioned in her letter. There's no mention of a Pat in here but the library say it's not finished – she made more recordings but they haven't been transcribed yet so . . .'

Wesley sat in silence for a few moments. He longed to snatch the file from Sandra's fingers and find out exactly what Mabel had to say about Tailors Court. But he had more questions to ask first. He decided on the straightforward approach. 'We've made some interesting discoveries at Tailors Court recently. I don't know whether you've read about it in the paper or . . .'

'I never read the papers,' she said quickly. 'Haven't got time.'

'Some skeletons have been found in the grounds.'

Sandra's hand went to her mouth.

'They seem to date back to the sixteenth century. Apart from one. The bones of a child – a boy – were found some way away from the others. And from certain items found in the grave, it appears they date from around the time your mother was there. You see why we're so concerned.'

Sandra sat for a while, stunned. 'You think mum witnessed something and someone's silenced her?'

It was rather a melodramatic way of putting it but that just about summed up Wesley's suspicions perfectly.

'It's a line of enquiry we'll be following up. I take it you've read that file?'

'Yes. I read it on the train. It's all about how she got sent to Tailors Court and who she met there.'

'May I?'

She handed him the file. 'She mentions a character called Miles who sounds a bit . . .' She searched for the right word.

'Suspicious?'

'Strange. But he was in his twenties then, according to this, so he'll probably be dead now.'

Wesley nodded. Miles was the name of Esther Jannings's husband who, according to his widow, had died shortly after their wedding. But even if Miles hadn't been dead, it was unlikely that he'd still be fit enough to go round murdering people to stop them talking about something that happened over sixty-five years ago – even if that something was the murder of a child.

Wesley stood up. 'I'm sure you'll be comfortable here, Mrs Ackerley. This place has a very good reputation. I'd better get back to the incident room. Somebody will be along to see you later.'

Sandra frowned. 'You'll find her, won't you?'

'We'll do our very best,' said Wesley.

Rachel sat at her desk, staring into space and trying to decide whether to call the Hayneses to ask how Mary was.

She felt the blood rising to her face as memories flashed through her brain – memories that made her heart freeze with embarrassment. The consumption of too much strong cider at a friend's seventeenth birthday party on a summer evening in Tradington Village Hall. Flirting with Nigel Haynes and leading him outside. The warm July night and the damp grass that left stains on the back of her dress. The lovemaking, uncomfortable, barely enjoyed and hardly remembered in the fermented apple fog.

Afterwards Nigel had seemed to take it for granted that they were going out together but Rachel had just wanted to forget all about what happened so she'd refused to take his calls and had avoided him until he gave up.

The unaccustomed loss of control and the vague memory of vomiting on the grass in front of him still made her heart shrivel with shame. But she couldn't put off facing Nigel Haynes for much longer. She kept telling herself that it was a long time ago and that he probably wouldn't even remember and this thought gave her the courage to reach for the receiver.

But before she could pick it up the telephone rang. She reached over to answer it but when she heard silence on the other end of the line, punctuated by what sounded very much like heavy breathing, she almost slammed the receiver down again. But something made her stop and listen and after half a minute or so a husky voice asked if that was the police.

'Yes. This is Neston Police Station. Dalcott enquiry incident room.'

'I want to speak to a detective.'

'I'm Detective Sergeant Tracey. What can I do for you?'

There was another long pause, as though the caller was gathering his thoughts. Or at least Rachel assumed it was a he – it was rather hard to tell.

'Dalcott worked at a clinic,' the caller said. He seemed to have lowered his voice but Rachel was reluctant to ask him to speak up.

'Which clinic are you talking about?'

There was another long silence.

Rachel decided to go for it. 'Is it the Podingham Clinic?'

Another pause. 'How did you know?'

Rachel resisted the urge to say something facetious like 'We're detectives, it's our job to know.' Instead she uttered a formal 'It's come up in our enquiries.'

'Yeah. Right,' said the voice on the other end of the line. 'So you know about the place already?'

'I'm sure we don't know everything. If there's something you'd like to tell us, we'd be very grateful.' She tried her best to sound grateful but it was something she couldn't quite manage.

She heard the caller take a deep breath. 'There's something going on there. I think there's been a murder.'

Her eyes scanned the open-plan office, all embarrassing recollections of Nigel Haynes now forgotten. She could see Gerry Heffernan sitting at his desk and she waved frantically in his direction. When she caught his attention he stood up and began to walk towards her. He had understood. She pressed the speaker button on the phone as Gerry perched his large frame on the corner of her desk. He looked at her enquiringly and she cleared her throat.

'Can you tell me who's been murdered?' She glanced at Gerry. He was sitting quite still with his head cocked to one side, listening carefully.

'Dunno. I just know someone's dead.'

'Can you tell me how you came by this information?'

'I just saw it, didn't I? With my own eyes.'

Gerry was making enthusiastic hand signals – he wanted to talk to the caller himself.

'Look, I'm passing you over to DCI Heffernan. He's in charge of the Dalcott case and –'

Before the caller could answer Gerry took the receiver and introduced himself. Through the speaker Rachel heard the caller emit a wary grunt of acknowledgement. It would be up to the DCI to establish some trust.

'Look, if there's something dodgy about that clinic, I want to find out what's going on. I don't like talking about something like this over the phone so can we meet up?'

'I don't go out.'

'Well, I'll come to you then. No problem. Where can I find you?'

The caller hesitated. 'As long as it's clear that I had nothing to do with Dalcott's murder.'

'Why should we think that?'

No answer.

'What's your name?'

The line went dead.

'I'll get someone to trace the call,' Rachel said, preparing to move away.

'No need, love. I know who it was.'

Rachel saw a wide grin spread across the boss's plump face. He beamed at her benevolently.

'Who's been avoiding us? Who had a bad experience at the Podingham Clinic which he blamed on James Dalcott?'

Rachel felt annoyed with herself for not catching on quicker. But then she'd had a lot on her mind. 'Carl Utley?'

'Let's get over there, shall we?'

'So what's all this about a murder at the clinic?'

Gerry winked and reached for his coat.

As he was walking back to Neston Police Station Wesley looked down at the file he was holding. Mabel Cleary's memories of a childhood spent with strangers. He'd already had a peep at the introductory section which explained that the library service where Mabel lived had started the project to record the memories of people who'd lived through the Second World War. The people involved were given equipment to record their reminiscences. Then the results were transcribed and kept in the library, available as a living history resource for future generations. Wesley thought it was an interesting idea. And important. Too many fascinating memories of momentous events had died with their witnesses.

He checked the time. He had just passed a wholefood café housed in the ground floor of a tall Elizabethan building at the end of Neston's steep narrow High Street. It had a chalked menu outside and the facia was painted in vibrant African patterns. He hadn't told Gerry Heffernan what time he'd be back so he reckoned he wouldn't be missed if he went into the café and read Mabel's account of her wartime years over a cup of tea. It would be preferable to the incident room with its ringing telephones and the eternal possibility of interruption.

He went inside, sat down at an empty table and ordered a pot of Darjeeling from a young woman dressed in rusty black with an interesting array of facial piercings. Once the tea was poured, he took the papers out of the file and began to read.

Mabel's memories made for easy reading. The fact that they had been transcribed from the spoken word somehow made the prose more vivid. As Wesley turned the pages he almost felt that Mabel was there sitting opposite him, telling her story.

He made a mental note of the characters in the little

drama. The pale and sickly Mrs Jannings, the rather sinister and possibly damaged Miles, Mary the pretty, vivacious land girl, the other evacuees – Belle and Charlie – and an assortment of people who lived round about including Otto Kramer, the son of a Jewish refugee.

He'd reached the final sheet of paper and when he'd finished reading he felt disappointed. As Sandra had said, the transcripts weren't yet complete: there was, as yet, no mention of a Pat and, far from revealing the identity of the victim or the killer, the last page proved to be about the Kramers who had taken refuge in the village, their presence having created quite a furore. Although this was interesting from a sociological point of view, it wasn't really what Wesley had hoped to find. He'd hoped for a clue to the identity of the boy's bones. But, over his years in CID, he'd come to learn that vital evidence doesn't often come so easily.

There was a mention of Charlie owning a wooden car but then lots of boys would have done in those days. Charlie was a possible victim but, on the other hand, he might still be alive and well.

There was, however, one interesting fact concerning the Kramers: Mr Hilton, the man they were staying with, was described as a local historian and Otto had apparently taken great pleasure in teasing the children at Tailors Court with what he'd learned about the former resident, Simon Garchard, back in the sixteenth century. It probably meant nothing, Wesley thought. But it was interesting all the same.

But then he looked more carefully at the last page. At the foot of the paper was the first line of a new section. It began 'One Sunday after church John Haynes came

231

round to fetch Mary. That was when he found the blood-stained knife.' And then, frustratingly, the narrative stopped.

Wesley began a frantic search through the sheets, almost knocking over the tea in his agitation.

But there was nothing there. How John Haynes had found a knife and what happened next had to remain a mystery for now. Until Mary Haynes was in a fit state to throw light on the matter.

Or her granddaughter, Nuala Johns, knew more than she'd already told him.

Even though it was only three o'clock in the afternoon, the darkness had already begun to close in. There were no lights on at Carl Utley's address but the neighbours who lived on the opposite side of the landing – a very young couple with a baby and a harassed look on their plump, pasty faces – told Gerry and Rachel that it was always like that. However, they often heard somebody moving about in there and it gave them the creeps.

Rachel thanked them and tried the door bell again but there was still no reply. She'd had the mysterious call traced but as it was a pay as you go mobile, she was none the wiser. She just hoped Gerry's instincts were correct and they'd got the right man.

'Utley's got form for burglary and handling stolen goods, you know,' Gerry said casually, seemingly quite unconcerned at their lack of success. 'Nothing recent though. Not since the incident at the Podingham Clinic clipped his wings.'

'So what do we do now?'

Gerry looked round. 'Do you know, Rach, I'm a bit

worried about this bloke. I mean, he's not answering his door and something might have happened to him. I vote we look for a way in.'

Rachel hesitated. 'Is that wise, sir?'

'He's called us to report a murder and now we can't get hold of him. Of course it's wise.'

Without another word Gerry took out his wallet and extracted something that looked like a credit card from its leathery depths. He grinned at Rachel. 'Don't worry, love. It's only a Huntings loyalty card – out of date.' He slipped the card down the edge of the lock and there was a satisfying click as the door opened half an inch.

When he pushed at the door with one finger it opened silently.

'Oh dear,' he said theatrically. 'He's left his door open. Now we wouldn't be doing our duty if we didn't just have a quick check round to make sure everything's all right, would we?'

Gerry Heffernan stepped through the open doorway into the darkness and Rachel followed close behind, stepping into the unknown.

CHAPTER 10

Transcript of recording made by Mrs Mabel Cleary (née Fallon) – Home Counties Library Service Living History Project: Reminiscences of a wartime evacuee.

Dr Kramer's son, Otto, used to play with us sometimes. He and his dad were living with Mr Hilton and I think this made me a bit jealous because I wished I had my dad there. I probably said some horrid things to Otto and called him names and if I could see him again I'd say I was really sorry. Children can be so cruel, can't they?

Belle was much worse though. She was really nasty to Otto. But all that changed when Otto started telling his stories – the ones about Tailors Court. He told her how it used to be called Flesh Tailor's Court because a body snatcher had lived there. He'd dug up bodies in the churchyard and then he'd cut them up in the attic. I told him the stories made me feel sick but Belle didn't care a bit. She just wanted to hear more.

Gerry tried to flick the light switch but nothing happened. It was pitch dark and the only sound he could hear was the rain pattering on the windows.

He could see a faint glow coming from underneath the far door. It could have been from the newly lit street light outside. But, on the other hand, it could mean that their efforts weren't in vain. Gerry pressed on, his large form colliding every so often with jutting items of furniture.

But slowly his eyes adjusted and he could make out the shapes that loomed out of the darkness. A hallstand laden with coats, a vacuum cleaner and some sort of table.

All of a sudden the door at the end began to open slowly and Gerry froze. He felt Rachel touch his shoulder but he didn't know whether she was reassuring him or herself. Both probably.

A dark figure stood in the doorway blocking out the faint dribble of light. It was impossible to see the figure's face but it was tall and thin. A slight stoop gave the impression of someone elderly but if this was who Gerry thought it was, he was only twenty-seven years old.

Gerry decided to speak first, just to get any misunderstandings out of the way. 'Is that you, Carl? Sorry, but your door was on the latch so when we couldn't get a reply we took the liberty of . . .'

'There's no way I'd leave my door open. You broke in.' The accusation sounded more weary than angry.

'Well, anyway, we're here now,' the DCI said lightly, glossing over his transgressions. 'This is DS Tracey. You spoke to her on the phone earlier, about the Podingham Clinic. You told her you'd witnessed a murder.'

Carl Utley made no move to deny that he made the call or to acknowledge Rachel's presence.

'That's why we were worried about you, Carl. Your average murderer doesn't like being seen so he sometimes tries to get rid of witnesses, if you see what I mean. So when there was no answer . . .'

Carl retreated into the far room, leaving the door wide open. Gerry and Rachel followed. The room was lit only by a single red-shaded lamp in the corner and Carl pulled up the hood of his dark top as he sat down on a beanbag in the centre of the floor so that his face was in shadow.

Gerry perched his large form on the edge of a sagging armchair. 'Why did you call us, Carl?'

'Dunno. Seemed like a good idea at the time.'

'But now you're not so sure?'

Carl didn't answer.

'Come on, Carl,' he said quietly. 'I think it's time you told us everything you know.'

For a minute or two Carl said nothing. Gerry's eyes had become accustomed to the lack of light now and he could see Rachel standing by the door. She was swaying slightly as though she was preparing to make a quick getaway.

Then Carl's voice broke the heavy silence. 'I've done nothing wrong.' The statement was followed by a split second of hesitation. 'Well, they'd say I was trespassing but . . .'

'I'm willing to turn a blind eye to a bit of trespassing, Carl,' said Gerry. 'I'm investigating a murder and that's all I'm interested in at the moment. So come on – what have you got to tell us?'

Carl turned his face away, as though he felt more comfortable holding a conversation that way. Gerry watched him, wishing he could see his face and wondering whether the effects of the disastrous drugs trial were bad enough to murder James Dalcott for.

Carl began talking, almost in a whisper. 'I've been borrowing my dad's van and driving to the clinic. There's this wall that runs all round the grounds and it's easy to climb so there's no problem getting in. They've got security lights and that near the building but there's lots of trees and woodland: plenty of places to hide.'

'How often do you go?'

'About twice a week. Sometimes in the day but mostly at night.'

'Why?' Rachel asked. Gerry had been about to ask the same question. He wanted to know why the place held such an attraction. If something bad had happened to him in a place like that, he'd probably be careful to avoid it for the rest of his life.

'Why?' Carl's voice sounded strained, as though the question had brought an array of uncomfortable memories bubbling to the surface of his mind. 'You know what happened to me there?'

'We've heard you took part in a drugs trial and you had some unfortunate side effects.'

Carl stood up. 'Unfortunate?' he hissed at Rachel who took a step back. 'Unfortunate? I'll show you how "unfortunate" it was.'

He moved fast, making for the light switch by the door. When the light flicked on Gerry couldn't help blinking with the unaccustomed brightness. Then he looked at the figure standing still and straight by the door. The hood of his top was now pushed back to reveal his face and Gerry's mouth opened to let out an involuntary gasp which he managed to stifle at the last moment.

The young man's flesh was raw and shiny, red and mottled like salami and it looked as though it had healed badly, twisting the features out of alignment. The watery, bloodshot eyes were half closed. Gerry couldn't imagine what kind of test could have left him in that state. But he knew that if he himself had been so badly disfigured, he'd have fought for generous compensation by any means at his disposal. And he'd probably have been tempted to wreak revenge on those responsible as well.

'You're not saying anything. That's how most people react. They just stare, like people watching a car crash.'

Gerry took a deep breath. 'I hope they gave you a lot of compensation.' It was the only thing he could think of to say.

Carl Utley snorted. 'Compensation? You're joking. According to them I signed something saying I took part at my own risk. I can't remember signing anything like that.'

'You sure they weren't lying?' asked Rachel quietly.

'They showed me a form with my signature on it and they told me it meant I had no legal claim against them if anything went wrong. When I first went there I signed so many things and I bet it was in the small print and some of it was fucking small, I can tell you. They gave me a grand as a "goodwill gesture" they said.'

'I know what kind of gesture I'd have made,' said Gerry with feeling.

'They kept me in there – said I'd had the best private care.'

'I'll bet.'

'Then when I was better and I started kicking up a bit of a fuss they said I was banned from going anywhere near the place. They said they'd call the police.'

'And did they?'

'I've been careful not to let anyone see me. I've got quite good at that since . . .'

Even though Gerry felt for the man, his sympathy didn't blind him to the possibility that Carl Utley was a suspect. 'So why do you keep going there?'

Utley shrugged. 'I've got a lot of time on my hands and I keep thinking that one day they'll make a slip-up. One day I'll see something that . . .' He turned away.

'You could go to the newspapers,' said Rachel.

'They said they'd take me to court if I did – something else that was in the small print.'

There were a few moments of heavy silence before Gerry spoke again. 'What about Dalcott? Did you blame him for what happened?'

Carl sat down on his beanbag and appeared to consider the question for a while. 'Dalcott gave me the injections so yeah, I do blame him. But that doesn't mean I killed him.'

'But you think he was responsible?'

Carl shrugged his shoulders stiffly and sighed. 'I did. But when I really think about it, maybe that's just because he was the one I saw most. I remember he was bloody worried when I started to react badly. I was a bit out of it but I'm sure I remember someone saying they should get me to Morbay Hospital.'

'But you didn't go there?'

'No. Maybe if I had . . .'

'You think Dalcott stopped them sending for an ambulance?'

Carl looked confused. 'I don't know.'

'Maybe it was him who wanted to send you but he was overruled. Perhaps someone higher up than Dalcott didn't like the idea of Morbay Hospital nosing into what the clinic was up to.'

'I don't know. Like I said, I was out of it.'

'I met a Dr Shallech there. A woman – quite elderly. Retired and working there part-time.'

Carl shrugged. 'I never met her.'

'What about Dr Welman?'

Carl shook his head. 'He was the one who told me I couldn't sue them for compensation. Slimy bastard.' He raised his hand and Gerry noticed for the first time that he was wearing gloves. 'And don't forget that Dalcott was hardly whiter than white to start with – he killed my mate's baby.'

'Would that mate be Adam Tey?'

'That's right. How did you –?'

'He's already been interviewed.' Gerry knew it was time to put sympathy aside and start asking awkward questions. 'You seem to be pretty good at sneaking around at night without being seen. Were you in Tradington last Saturday night?'

'No.' The word was emphatic.

'Where were you then?'

'Here.'

'Witnesses?'

'A couple of models and a lap dancer. What do you think? Looking like this, I don't tend to attract much company if you see what I mean.'

'Ever fired a gun?'

'No. Unless you count a water pistol.'

'We can do tests for gunshot residue.'

'Be my guest.'

Gerry knew he wasn't going to get him to admit anything so he decided to move on. 'So let's get back to why you rang us about the Podingham Clinic. You mentioned a murder.'

'That's right.'

'Why don't you start at the beginning?'

'Well, I don't know if it was a murder. Might have been another experiment gone wrong.' Carl suddenly sounded a little unsure of himself. 'I was watching the place like I said before and I saw a stretcher being loaded into a van – not an ambulance, a plain van. There was something on the stretcher – all covered up with a sheet. Like a dead person.'

Gerry looked at Rachel. 'It might have been an undertaker's van.'

'Yeah. But why should someone die in a place like that?'

'It's a clinic,' said Rachel. 'We've been told they do minor operations there – maybe one of them went wrong. Anyway, people die in all sorts of places. Doesn't necessarily mean it's suspicious.'

'You didn't see them. They looked as if . . . as if they had something to hide. And a few days earlier I'd seen some people arriving in a minibus. Not the usual types who took part in the trials. I've got pictures to prove it. Here.' He reached out and picked up a pack of photographs then handed them to Gerry. 'There was just something about the whole set-up that seemed wrong. Don't ask me why but . . .'

'When was this?' said Gerry, flicking through the prints.

'About a week ago. I don't keep track of dates.'

'OK, Carl, we'll check with the Coroner to see whether any deaths have been reported at the clinic recently.'

'You do that. But people with something to hide don't usually tell the Coroner what they're up to, do they?'

The sarcastic venom of Carl's words made Gerry feel uncomfortable. It was always possible that the man was making up the whole story to gain some sort of twisted revenge. Gerry didn't blame him in the least, but wasting police time was a crime. And at that moment, with James Dalcott's murder and the child's skeleton at Tailors Court, time was the one thing they couldn't afford to waste. At least, according to Colin, the naked woman in the river appeared to have died of natural causes. But who she was and how she got there was still a mystery they had to solve.

Utley looked Gerry in the eye. 'So are you going to look into it?'

Gerry glanced at Rachel. From the expression of doubt on her face, he guessed that her thoughts matched his own.

'These pictures prove nothing, I'm afraid, Carl. Pity you didn't get one of this dead body you said you saw.'

'I didn't have my camera with me.'

'Look, Carl, if you're having us on . . .'

'I know, I know – I'll be up for wasting police time. But I'm not. I saw what I saw. I swear.'

'We'll need a statement. And we'll need you to come down to the station to answer some more questions.'

Carl Utley bowed his head and said nothing. And he stayed silent all the way back to Neston Police Station.

Wesley was sitting at his desk. It was difficult to think in the noisy open-plan office with telephones trilling over his colleagues' chatter, punctuated by the occasional expletive whenever one of the office computers decided to misbehave itself.

Something Nuala Johns had told him was nagging at the back of his mind. Tony Persimmon had worked for Pharmitest International and Pharmitest International owned the Podingham Clinic. He leaned over and typed Persimmon's name into the search engine and, sure enough, there it was: Tony Persimmon had been Pharmitest's Regional Head of Strategy – whatever that was – for four years until his resignation six months ago. It was a tenuous link which probably meant nothing but it might still be worth checking out.

He put his head in his hands and closed his eyes. But the thought of Tony Persimmon conjured terrible images of those dissected human bodies sketched with such care and detail behind the panelling at Tailors Court – along with the cruder copies similarly concealed in Roz Dalcott's flat.

He needed to know what they meant, and whether they had any connection at all with his case. He picked up the telephone on his desk and punched out Neil's number. It was about time he indulged in a spot of delegation, he thought. And besides, Neil would enjoy finding out all he could about the former occupants of the building that now housed Trad Itions. He'd be doing his friend a favour really, he told himself.

When the conversation ended and he replaced the receiver, he felt rather pleased with himself. He had set Neil on the quest to find out all he could about Simon Garchard, the 'Flesh Tailor' of Tailors Court, and he had given him the extra task of looking for any connection with the property in Tradmouth. Had Simon owned the house? Or had it been occupied by somebody connected with Simon and his sinister activities? He knew it might take some time but, once his interest was captured, Neil tended to worry at a historical puzzle like a determined terrier.

Earlier he'd called the Hayneses at Gorfleet Farm and discovered that Mary was home from hospital at last and making a good recovery – almost back to her usual sharp self. He needed to talk to her about what had gone on at Tailors Court during the war years and about the possible identity of the little boy who'd been buried there near the paddock. But he wanted to be sure she was up to speaking to him so he resolved to ring again tomorrow. The boy at Tailors Court had been under the earth there for years and the Dalcott investigation took priority.

A voice behind him made him jump.

'Sir. We've got them.'

Wesley swivelled his seat round and saw Paul Johnson standing there, all six foot two of him. He was wearing a look of triumph, like a border collie who'd just put a herd of sheep into a pen.

'Got who?'

'Syd Jenkins and Brian Carrack. They were picked up at an address in the Banton area of Morbay about an hour ago. The local patrols had been keeping a lookout for the car they were driving like we asked.'

Wesley stood up. Sitting looking up at Paul was giving him a crick in the neck. 'Good. Have they said anything yet?'

'They're asking for a solicitor.'

'Always a bad sign,' said Wesley with a smile. Paul always

seemed to take his duties – and life for that matter – seriously but he was an asset to CID, unlike some.

He looked at his watch. Gerry was chivvying out Carl Utley but he was bound to be back soon, possibly with Utley in tow. 'The boss'll probably want to talk to them himself. Get them taken down to the cells. It won't do any harm to leave them to stew for half an hour or so.'

Paul gave him a solemn nod and hurried out, passing Gerry Heffernan who was steaming in with Rachel bobbing behind him.

'Carl Utley's in Interview Room two,' Gerry announced. 'He's going to make a statement.' His gaze lighted on Trish Walton who looked up nervously from her computer screen. 'Trish, you and Rach can do the honours. The female touch.' He hesitated, looking Trish in the eye. 'He's not exactly a pretty sight but don't stare, eh? He's a bit sensitive.' He turned and grinned at Wesley. 'Wes, you and me are going visiting the sick. We're sending a team over to the Podingham Clinic. I've arranged a search warrant 'cause, from what Utley said, they'll have a pack of tame lawyers lurking in the undergrowth.'

When Gerry was in this mood it was usually hard to get a word in edgeways, so Wesley said quickly, 'Paul's just told me they've found Carrack and Jenkins. They're in the cells demanding a solicitor.'

Gerry, who had been about to walk away, stopped in his tracks. Wesley could almost hear his brain working, weighing up the wisdom of delay. Eventually he delivered his verdict. 'Good. We'll speak to them while we're waiting for the warrant.'

'They've already had plenty of time to cook up a good story,' Wesley pointed out pessimistically.

'They're experienced crooks, Wes. They've already got more stories than the public library. Come on.'

Syd Jenkins and Brian Carrack were on the premises and the clock was ticking. Gerry was to take Syd while Brian had been allocated to Wesley and when they reached the respective interview rooms they exchanged knowing smiles and split up.

Wesley gave Brian Carrack a businesslike nod as he entered the room and switched on the tape. He was an unprepossessing little man, probably in his late twenties but it was hard to judge. He was bald with a sharp-featured face and he reminded Wesley of a rodent; a rat, perhaps.

'Mr Carrack. We've been looking for you.'

'Well, now you've found me. I don't know why I'm here. I've not done nothing.'

'So why did you leave the cottage you were renting in Tradington?'

'There'd been a murder next door, hadn't there? We weren't going to hang around. We might be next.'

'And who would want to murder you?'

'Well, we were the targets, weren't we? Stands to reason.'

'How do you work that one out?'

Carrack looked over each shoulder theatrically, checking for any assassins who might have secreted themselves in the interview room. Wesley tried hard to keep a straight face. Brian Carrack had been watching far too many gangster movies.

Carrack leaned forward and spoke in a whisper. 'You tend to make enemies inside, if you know what I mean.' He touched the side of his nose.

246

Wesley sat back. He could smell the man's breath and it wasn't pleasant. 'Why did you come down to Devon, Mr Carrack?'

'Fancied a holiday, didn't we?'

'At this time of year and under false names?'

Carrack shrugged. 'Why not?'

Wesley pretended to study the notes in front of him. 'You were inside with a man called Harry Parker. He's living with the estranged wife of the man who was shot. Is Harry the reason you're down here?'

'No comment.' The answer was swift. Wesley had hit the jackpot.

'Come on, Brian. We'll find out sooner or later so you might as well tell us now. How much did Harry pay you to kill his girlfriend's husband? Must have been a tidy sum because, according to your record, you've never gone as far as killing before. Because James Dalcott died when he did, Harry's lady friend will inherit rather a lot of money. Were you doing your old mate Harry a favour? Did you owe him?'

'No.' Brian Carrack sounded quite outraged. 'It was nothing like that. I never owed Harry nothing.'

'You see, Brian' – Wesley leaned forward as though he was about to share a confidence, trying to ignore Carrack's halitosis – 'you've got means, motive and opportunity – and if you don't come up with a better story I reckon, once the Forensic team have done their bit, that we'll have enough to charge you with James Dalcott's murder. My boss is talking to your mate, Syd. And DCI Heffernan always gets at the truth in the end. He's famous for it.' He looked Carrack in the eye. He could tell the man was weakening. It would just take one last push.

'Come on, Brian, do yourself a favour and tell me exactly what happened.'

Brian Carrack put his head in his hands and he sat there like that in silence for a whole minute. Wesley said nothing. The man needed time to consider his options.

Carrack suddenly looked Wesley in the eye. 'I need you to promise that we won't be charged with anything.'

Wesley raised his eyebrows. 'You know I can't do that till I know what I'm dealing with. I can't turn a blind eye to murder.'

'I've not murdered no one. I'm not a violent man, Mr Peterson, and neither is Syd,' he added self-righteously. 'Same goes for Harry.'

'Good honest crooks.'

'You've seen our records. We might have used threats but we've never harmed a soul.'

'You've scared the hell out of a few souls in your time, though.'

Brian gave a nervous grin. 'All talk, Mr Peterson. We never hurt no one.'

Wesley picked up a pen and turned it over and over in his fingers. He needed to know what Syd Jenkins had said for himself. He needed to consult Gerry. He stood up and announced that he was leaving the room for the benefit of the tape that was whirring in the machine at the end of the table. A minute later he was standing in the corridor with Gerry, comparing notes.

It appeared that the older man, Syd, had come up with a similar story. There was no way they were involved in the shooting of James Dalcott. They'd never fired a gun – even though they'd used replicas to terrify hapless post-masters and the guardians of security vans. They'd used

248

the threat of violence but had never carried it through. They had their standards.

The two men exchanged conspiratorial smiles before returning to their respective victims. Crooks weren't the only ones who could hatch effective plots.

'I've had a word with the DCI,' Wesley began as he resumed his seat at the table. 'Your friend Syd's been very cooperative. Why don't you give me your version? The truth would be nice. He's told the DCI what you were up to, by the way.' Which wasn't exactly true but Carrack couldn't know that. He tilted his head expectantly and waited.

There was another long period of thought as Carrack considered his options. At last he looked up, a worried frown on his pasty face. 'OK. I'll be straight with you, Mr Peterson. Me and Syd have always kept in touch, like. And one day Syd saw something in the paper about Harry having some art exhibition – he'd always been keen on painting inside. So I thought, well, artists are always short of money, aren't they? And me and Syd haven't had work since we last got out. It's not easy living on benefits, Mr Peterson, believe me.'

Wesley assumed his most sympathetic expression. 'I'm sure it isn't, Brian. So what happened?'

'We got in touch with Harry and asked if he was interested in a bit of ready cash. He jumped at the chance – said he had a high maintenance bird and there was a baby on the way. I asked if he knew anywhere we could stay and he said there was an empty holiday place next door to his bird's ex. Nice place – quiet, like. The owner was pleased to let it for a few weeks at this time of year, I can tell you. Times are hard.' He gave Wesley a rueful smile.

'But you left the cottage sooner than planned?'

'Too right we did. There was no way we wanted to hang around.'

'What was this job exactly?'

'Now you promise we won't be done for conspiracy or whatever it is?'

'You never actually did anything, did you?'

Brian's small grey eyes lit up. 'That's right, Mr Peterson. I mean, they can't do you for thinking, can they?'

Wesley smiled. They could easily do them for conspiracy and hiring a car using a false licence but it was probably best not to mention that for now. 'So tell me what you were planning?' he said.

'Big store in Morbay. We're getting near the run-up to Christmas now so the takings'll be up. We were going to go in at closing time just before the security van arrived and whip the lot. We had it timed to perfection we did.'

'Were you using firearms?'

'Replicas. I'd never touch the real thing, Inspector Peterson. Honest to God, shooters frighten the life out of me, they do.'

'So where are these replicas now?'

'Left luggage locker at Morbay station. And that's where they've been since we arrived down here. We weren't going to pick them up till it was time to do the job.'

'And the shooting of James Dalcott?'

Brian Carrack shook his head vigorously. 'That had nothing to do with us. When the filth started crawling all over the place, we scarpered as soon as we'd given them a statement and that's the truth.'

Wesley knew Brian Carrack was a robber, an incorrigible

criminal and a liar. But something made him believe what he said.

'Did you see anyone calling at James Dalcott's house around the time of the shooting? Or maybe you saw someone hanging about, or an unfamiliar car parked nearby?' It was a long shot but he had to ask the question.

He'd expected the answer to be no but sometimes in life, you get a pleasant surprise.

'Yeah. I did as a matter of fact. I just happened to be looking out of the window, doing the nosy neighbour bit, when I saw Harry's bird drive up in a neat little motor – hatchback. We'd never been introduced, like, but we'd visited Harry's place once and we'd had to hang round outside till she left. Bit older than Harry but still fit, if you know what I mean. Lucky old Harry.' He licked his lips in a way that would probably have made Rachel Tracey feel like landing a punch.

'We know about her visit. How long did she stay?'

'About ten minutes.'

'And did you hear a gunshot at all?'

He shook his head. 'I think I heard one but it might have been some farmer out after those bloody crows. You often hear shots round these parts – like the bloody wild west at times.'

'Was this around the time Harry's girlfriend visited?'

'Can't remember. Don't think so.'

'Did Dr Dalcott have any other visitors after that?'

'I'd gone into the back kitchen by then. But I did hear a car. A diesel engine.'

'But you didn't have a look to see who it was?'

There was a long silence. 'I did go into the front and

251

have a quick peep. I couldn't see a car but if they parked it down the lane . . .'

'But you did see someone?'

'It looked like an old bloke – all muffled up in a long coat and some sort of hat, I reckon.'

'An elderly man?' Wesley said. This wasn't what he'd been expecting at all.

'I didn't get a good look at him, mind. I wouldn't know him again.'

Wesley switched off the tape and hurried from the room. This was something Gerry Heffernan would want to know as soon as possible.

When Gerry Heffernan heard about James Dalcott's elderly visitor, he rubbed his hands together with glee and observed cheerfully that this was the best lead they'd had all day.

Wesley took a deep breath. 'Yes but who was it?' He hesitated. 'When I pressed him, he even said it could have been a woman.'

'That's a lot of help,' Gerry said with a grunt, his sudden optimism squashed. 'Could have been anyone then – might even have been Mabel Cleary,' he added, half joking.

Wesley raised his eyes to heaven. 'Let's face it, Gerry, anything's possible.' The myriad possibilities whirling in his head were making him tired. He felt he needed a rest, just to gather his thoughts. But there were too many things to do.

'What did you make of our two friends in the cells?'

Wesley considered the question for a few seconds. 'They hardly look like Public Enemies Number One and Two but you never can tell.'

'All their clothing's being tested for gunshot residue but there was no sign of a firearm when their place was searched.'

'It's not hard to fling a gun into the river,' said Wesley.

Gerry ambled away just as the phone began to ring. Wesley picked up the receiver. They were still waiting for the warrant to search the Podingham Clinic and he hoped that this would be the call to say it was ready.

But instead a female voice said hello. He recognised it at once.

'Hello, Evonne. What can I do for you?'

'I've been thinking a lot about what happened, going over everything again and again in my mind.' The words came out in a rush, as though she'd been rehearsing what she wanted to say. 'I've just remembered something James said to me the day before he . . .'

'What was it?' Wesley sat up straight, listening intently.

'It was something about a photograph. It was after surgery on the Friday and we'd been talking about the dinner party at your sister's. I'm afraid I wasn't paying that much attention because I was thinking about everything I had to do at the weekend and . . .'

'Go on.'

'Look, I can't swear to it but I'm sure he said he'd come across an old photograph and he needed to ask someone about it. I'd almost forgotten about it because it didn't seem important at the time but since then I've been going over everything and . . . do you think I'm just clutching at straws?'

'A photograph? You're sure it was a photograph?'

'I think so. But before you ask, that was all he said. He didn't say who or what was in the photograph. He did seem a bit worried about it, looking back. Do you think it might be important?'

'I've no idea,' Wesley replied.

What Evonne had told him was tantalisingly vague. But a nagging feeling in the back of his brain told him that it could be the breakthrough he'd been looking for. Now it was just a matter of finding the photograph James Dalcott mentioned. And he wasn't sure where to start.

He ended the call and was just making for Gerry's desk to tell him about the possible new development when the phone on his desk started ringing again and he almost stumbled over a trailing computer cable in the race to answer it before the caller rang off. He grabbed at the receiver and uttered a breathless hello. But when he heard the voice on the other end of the line his heart sank. This was all he needed.

'Hello again,' said a confident and slightly flirtatious female voice. 'You sound as if you've been having fun. Didn't know they went for heavy breathing down at the nick.'

'I've been rushing to answer the phone.' He felt a little annoyed with himself for not being able to think up a witty riposte – Gerry Heffernan would have come up with something, no problem. 'What can I do for you, Ms Johns?'

'Ms Johns? We are formal today, Detective Inspector Peterson. I wondered if you fancied meeting up for a drink?'

Wesley picked up a pen and began to doodle on a sheet of paper on his desk, the result being a neat row of grinning skulls. 'Er . . . if you've got some information for me, perhaps it would be best if you came to see me here or . . .'

'Do you know the White Horse near the castle?'

The answer was a wary yes.

'See you there at seven.'

'I'm sorry. I can't –'

The next thing he heard was the dialling tone and he cursed under his breath. The woman was so presumptuous. Did she think he had nothing better to do than to be at her beck and call?

As the phone rang again he felt the pencil he was holding snap in his fingers.

This time it was Pam, asking what time he thought he might be in because her mother said she was calling round that evening with some news. Pam sounded wary and Wesley couldn't blame her. Her mother, Della, was in the habit of striking up relationships with unsuitable men and the latest specimen was an unemployed musician who, according to Pam, was using what little energy he could muster to milk Della's bank account. He used to worry about Della, but now he was almost past caring. As he'd told Pam many times, her mother was a grown woman.

Even though he knew Pam needed his support, he heard himself saying that he had to meet somebody – a possible witness – and he might not be back till eight-thirty or nine. He heard her sigh and experienced an uncomfortable pang of guilt as she put the phone down. But Gerry Heffernan's arrival proved a welcome distraction.

'We've got the warrant, Wes,' Gerry said as he hurried into the office, rubbing his hands with anticipation. 'I'm sending Paul and Trish and a few uniforms. There's nothing like the sight of a police uniform to put the wind up the guilty.'

Wesley felt a little disappointed. He'd been hoping to

take part in the search of the Podingham Clinic himself. The place intrigued him. But he knew his colleagues were more than capable. Besides, he had an appointment with Nuala Johns.

'I've just been talking to Evonne Arlis,' he said, and quickly filled Gerry in about the photograph Dalcott had mentioned.

'Did he seem worried about this photograph, or did he say what was in it?'

Wesley shook his head. 'That's all she can remember. I know Dalcott's house has been searched but a photo probably wouldn't have been considered important so I'd like to have another look round myself. And we could ask Roz Dalcott if she knows anything about it.'

Gerry sighed. 'Tomorrow, eh?'

'And I've discovered that Tony Persimmon who lives at Tailors Court used to work in London for Pharmitest, the drug company that uses the Podingham Clinic for its trials. And Dalcott worked at the Podingham.'

Gerry hesitated. 'If this Persimmon was based in London he wouldn't necessarily have known Dalcott, especially as he was only there part-time. But it's worth checking out. You never know.'

They were moving towards the door when Trish Walton hurried into the incident room. 'The TV people have been in touch about tonight's appeal: Mabel Cleary's daughter Sandra's quite happy to take part.'

'Let's hope it produces something useful,' said Wesley with feeling.

While some of the team were at the Podingham Clinic with the newly obtained search warrant, Rachel Tracey was going through some statements. Being left behind had irked her a little at first. But Gerry Heffernan told her that she was needed in the incident room and, besides, it was a foul day outside so perhaps she was in the right place after all.

The phone on her desk rang and when she answered the voice on the other end of the line sounded vaguely familiar, although for a few moments she couldn't place it.

'Is that Rachel?'

'Speaking. Who's that?'

'It's Nigel. Nigel Haynes.'

She felt her cheeks start to redden and she turned away from her colleagues, fidgeting with the pen in her hand. 'Hello, Nigel. What can I do for you?' She tried to sound businesslike.

'It's been a long time.'

'Yes, it has.'

Nigel cleared his throat. He sounded as nervous as she felt, which she found rather gratifying. 'Er . . . I wondered when you were planning to come to the farm, to have a word with Gran. Inspector Peterson rang earlier and I told him she'd just come home from hospital but . . .'

'How is she?'

'That's just it. She's made a remarkable recovery and she's saying she wants to talk to the police.'

'That's great,' said Rachel, trying to focus on the investigation.

'But . . . well, I think it might be best if she spoke to you alone. After all, she knows your family and . . .' There was a long pause. 'Look, why don't you come over?'

Rachel looked around the room. The only things she had to deal with on her desk were routine reports and they could wait an hour or so. And Mary could be an important witness to whatever had gone on at Tailors Court all those years ago. She might even have information that could help them put a name to the dead child.

'I'll be with you in half an hour,' she heard herself saying.

There was a short silence on the other end of the line before Nigel spoke again. 'I'm looking forward to it,' he said as though he meant it.

She took a deep, calming breath and looked round but Wesley was nowhere to be seen. She found a scrap of paper and scribbled a note which she left on his desk. She was saving him a job, after all.

DC Paul Johnson straightened his back and presented the search warrant to Fiona Verdun like a ceremonial scroll. She examined it and looked at the assembled officers.

'And what do you hope to find?' she asked with weary sarcasm. 'We've already had a couple of detectives here asking about Dr Dalcott.'

'This concerns another matter, Miss,' said Paul stiffly.

Fiona picked up the telephone on her desk. 'The police are here, Dr Welman. They've got a search warrant.'

After a short silence she replaced the receiver and fixed her eyes on Paul, a businesslike smile on her lips. 'He suggests I show you around. As you'll no doubt appreciate this is a clinic and we have patients here for minor surgery. There are also volunteers undergoing drugs trials. Dr Welman says it would be inappropriate for your officers to wander round the place freely but he's keen to cooperate in any way he can. If you'll follow me.'

She led the way down a long corridor, through several

sets of swing doors, until they reached what looked like a hospital ward with individual rooms each side. Nurses in starched uniforms, no longer *de rigueur* in National Health establishments, bustled to and fro, throwing suspicious glances at the newcomers.

'What kind of operations do you do here? Cosmetic surgery?' Paul asked, earning himself a contemptuous look.

'No. It's routine stuff. Hernias, varicose veins, that sort of thing.'

Paul noticed Fiona's eyes flicker nervously as Trish Walton began to wander off down the passage. He saw her disappear into one of the side rooms, emerging after a few moments with a fixed smile on her face.

At that moment a man appeared. He was small with grizzled hair and a heavily lined face. He might have been in his sixties or maybe even older and he was wearing surgeon's scrubs and an angry expression. 'What the hell's going on?'

'If I can have your name, sir?' said Paul with infuriating politeness.

'This is Mr Powell,' said Fiona quickly. 'He uses our facilities here for his private patients.' She turned to the surgeon. 'I'm sorry, Mr Powell, but these policemen are here with a search warrant.'

Powell cleared his throat. 'I take it this is connected with the death of James Dalcott?'

'Not exactly, sir,' said Paul, wondering how much he should give away. 'Certain serious allegations have been made. A witness saw what they thought was a dead body being taken from these premises and there's been no report of any death to the Coroner.'

259

Powell smiled with his mouth but not with his eyes. 'I assure you, Detective Constable, that there have been no deaths here. When did this so-called witness see this imaginary body?'

'A week ago, sir.' Paul was starting to feel a little less sure of himself now.

'This is ridiculous. May I ask who made these allegations?'

'I'm afraid I can't tell you that, sir. If we can just have a look around . . .'

'I don't suppose I can stop you. But I insist that you don't disturb my patients.'

'We'd like to ask them some questions,' Trish said firmly.

'That's impossible. They're recovering from surgery and the last thing they need is an interrogation,' Powell snapped. 'Besides, very few of them speak English so you'll be wasting your time.'

As he turned on his heels and stalked off, Paul caught Trish's eye. They had a job to do.

'Perhaps we can start off in the office,' said Trish. 'All your records are on the computer, I presume?'

'Our computers are down at the moment,' said Fiona.

The words 'how convenient' popped unbidden into Paul's head but he said nothing. Fiona's statement had sounded casual but the way she was clenching her hands told him that she was probably lying.

They began to walk round the hospital wing, a little unsure of what they were looking for. Paul guessed that if there had been a death here, any evidence would have been disposed of long ago.

Powell had been telling the truth when he'd said that few of the patients spoke English and when Paul and

Trish tried to communicate they were answered by nervous stares and shakes of the head.

'We'd like a word with Dr Welman now,' he said to Fiona when they'd drawn a blank. 'And then maybe the drugs trials.'

'Very well. Dr Shallech's on duty this afternoon. I'm sure she'll be glad to answer your questions.'

'A lot of Mr Powell's patients seem to be from abroad,' said Trish.

'He has a lot of overseas patients,' Fiona answered tersely before leading them down another series of brightly lit corridors towards Dr Welman's office.

After a brief knock Fiona opened the office door. Paul, who was standing at her shoulder, saw the doctor look up and caught the momentary panic in the man's eyes. When they entered the room Paul saw that he was leaning over an electric shredder, feeding documents into its hungry jaws.

'I'd be grateful if you stopped that, sir,' said Paul with all the authority he could muster.

But Welman fed another sheet into the machine before he stood up, a satisfied smile on his face. 'Just getting rid of some old papers,' he said calmly. 'Nothing important.'

Paul knew from the self-satisfied expression on Welmans' face that, if there had been any evidence of Carl Utley's claims about the Podingham Clinic, it had now been shredded into tiny pieces.

The search proved inconclusive but as they left Paul looked back. The man who'd been introduced to them as Mr Powell was standing in the main hallway with Fiona Verdun. He had grabbed her by the arm and his face was close to hers. Paul couldn't hear what they were saying but he didn't have to because the body language said it all.

Gorfleet Farm was a full half mile from Tailors Court but, in the countryside, that counted as next door. The farmhouse was four-square Victorian with a jumble of out-buildings filled with machinery and winter feed. As Rachel climbed out of the driver's seat she could hear cattle lowing plaintively in one of the outbuildings and the faint aroma of slurry made her wrinkle her nose. This was a working farm just like Little Barton and as Rachel strode towards the house the familiarity of the surroundings made her feel a little more relaxed.

A pair of border collies came rushing across the wet cobbles to greet her, tails wagging furiously. She bent to stroke them, murmuring words of endearment, then suddenly they dashed towards the house.

Nigel Haynes had emerged from the front door with the dogs at his heels, the collar of his well-worn waxed jacket turned up against the weather. She saw him hesitate when he saw her. Then he walked towards her, a shy smile of greeting on his face.

'How are you, Rachel?' he said quietly. 'I've not seen you for a long time.'

'I've been . . . I've been rather busy.' She straightened her back. Down to business. 'I'm here about those bodies that were found at Tailors Court.'

'Do you know how old they are yet?' His eyes met hers and she saw that they were green flecked with brown, something she'd forgotten till that moment.

She looked away, focusing her gaze on the dogs who were sitting obediently by their master's side. 'We're still working on that one,' she answered, trying to sound efficient. 'But we think one of the skeletons might be fairly recent – say fifty or sixty years old.'

Nigel Haynes stood silent for a few moments. 'Old Mrs Jannings was always a bit odd but I'd never have had her down as a serial killer.'

'We don't really know what happened yet. I was hoping your grandmother could help us. How is she?'

'Almost back to her usual self. She had a water infection and it made her confused. At one point we feared it was Alzheimer's. She kept calling me John – that's my granddad – and talking about evacuees. The War's been on her mind a lot.'

'I wonder if that's because she heard about the skeleton?'

'She might have overheard mum and dad talking about it.'

Rachel thought she could see uncertainty in Nigel's eyes. Perhaps he was finding the encounter as uncomfortable as she was.

But then he spoke. 'It is good to see you again, Rachel.'

'And you,' she heard herself saying automatically, unsure whether she actually meant it.

'How's life in the police? Detective Sergeant . . . that's quite impressive.'

'It's a dogsbody really. But it's . . . interesting.'

'I'm sure. I'd better take you to see Gran. That's what you've come for, after all.'

Nigel took off his mud-caked green Wellingtons and led her through a hallway lit by an unexpectedly ornate chandelier into the small homely parlour where his grandmother was enthroned on a high armchair. There was a half-empty mug of tea on the tripod table by her side and she appeared to be flicking through a copy of *The People's Friend*. She was a plump woman with fluffy white hair and a determined mouth. When Rachel and Nigel entered, she looked up, alert to the new visitor.

'You're Rachel, aren't you? Stella's girl? Our Nigel said you were coming. Come along in, lass. Sit yourself down.'

Rachel did as she was told. Somehow she'd expected Mary still to be bedridden but, with the aid of strong antibiotics, she seemed to be back to her old sharp self.

'We were worried about you, Gran,' Nigel said, taking the old woman's parchment hand.

'Thought I was going gaga, they did.' Mary giggled like a schoolgirl and Rachel suddenly caught a glimpse of the high-spirited land girl; the girl Esther Jannings had described as being 'no better than she ought to be'.

'It'll take more than a few germs to get rid of me,' said the old lady defiantly. 'Now go and put the kettle on. Get Rachel here a nice cup of tea.'

She gave the young man an obvious wink and Rachel had an uneasy feeling that the Haynes clan were reading a hidden meaning into her visit. Nigel was still single and, as far as they knew, so was she.

Rachel looked up and gave Nigel a shy smile. Time and shame had marred her memory of him but now he seemed thoughtful and attractive in a solid sort of way. She only hoped that he had forgotten the toe-curling embarrassments of the past.

'You know I joined the police, Mrs Haynes,' she said as soon as he'd left the room. 'I'm a detective now.'

'Stella's very proud, so I hear.'

Rachel forced out a smile. Her mother had never told

her that she was proud of her police career. On the contrary, Rachel had always had a nagging feeling that she rather disapproved of her only daughter doing something so potentially dangerous and Mary's remark came as a surprise.

She gathered her thoughts. 'I hope you don't mind, but I'd like to ask you some questions.'

Mary's bright blue eyes lit up. 'I never thought I'd be helping the police with their enquiries at my age.'

'Now, Gran, don't you go making any confessions without a solicitor present.'

Rachel looked up. Nigel was standing in the doorway and she saw a concern in his eyes which belied his jocular tone. He was being protective of the old lady and she found herself liking him for it.

'You want to ask me about Tailors Court, is that right?'

'It would really help us if you could remember, Mrs Haynes. When you were staying at Tailors Court during the war, there were some evacuees.'

'Oh aye. I remember the vaccies. Mrs Jannings wasn't too pleased about having a load of kids landed on her but those days you didn't have much choice. You had to do your bit.'

'Do you remember the children?'

'Oh, let me think. There were three girls I think. Belle, Mabel and . . .'

'Pat?'

'That's right. Pat. You've been doing your homework.'

'Any boys?'

'Now Mrs Jannings didn't like boys much but there was one. A lad called Charlie who I always thought was a bit strange. I heard he'd been in some dreadful air raid and seen his family killed but people didn't talk much about things like that in those days. All swept under the carpet it was.'

'What do you remember about him?'

'He was a funny little thing. He was Belle's cousin, you know, but there didn't seem to be much family feeling there.'

'What about the others?'

'Pat and Mabel were OK. Pat didn't come till a bit later but they used to go round together . . . cut Belle out. Not that I can blame them. That Belle was a spiteful little minx. Sly, if you know what I mean. Do you know, Rachel, the older I get, the more I remember about when I was young – sometimes it seems more real than what happened last week.' Another giggle.

'You've heard about the child's skeleton found at Tailors Court?'

'Our Brenda mentioned something. I thought all those bones were old. I thought some archaeologist had dug 'em up.'

'There was one skeleton that wasn't with the others. It was a little boy, aged around nine or ten. He had a filling in his teeth and he was buried with what we think was a wooden car.'

Mary's hand went to her mouth and she sat for a while in silence. Rachel knew better than to interrupt her contemplations.

'The little lad, Charlie. He just upped and vanished one day. I remember my John was a bit worried and he said we'd better look for him. But before we had a chance Belle told us he'd gone to another billet a few miles away so we never thought any more about it. It happened sometimes, kids changing billets. It was a bit of a relief when she told me, to be honest.'

'A relief?'

'Well, around the time Charlie went my John found a knife with blood all over it. And he saw him with blood all over his hands.'

'Saw who?'

'Now he was one I never fancied meeting on a dark night. They said he was all right but I had my doubts. He might have recovered physically from Dunkirk, but I thought Esther was daft taking him on and, if you ask me, it was lucky for her that he was killed when he was.'

'So John saw Miles Jannings with blood on his hands?'

When Mary nodded, Rachel felt a little thrill of triumph.

CHAPTER 11

Transcript of recording made by Mrs Mabel Cleary (née Fallon) – Home Counties Library Service Living History Project: Reminiscences of a wartime evacuee.

I went to Otto's house for tea once and met Mr Hilton, the man the Kramers were staying with. He was a retired schoolmaster and he looked like a mad professor in a film with his wild white hair and his bow tie. He gave us squash and biscuits and took us into rooms with more books than our public library back home.

He got one of the books down and read it to us. It was all about Tailors Court and how there'd been a murder there. In the olden days a doctor called Simon Garchard had snatched the bodies from the churchyard and then he'd murdered a maid and chopped up her body. He got hanged but Mr Hilton said he shouldn't have been. I said why not if he'd been a murderer but Mr Hilton just winked at

me and touched the side of his nose. Then he said some-
thing about things not being as they seemed. I don't know
what he meant but after hearing that story I didn't sleep
for days. I told Belle, hoping she'd be scared, but she said
it didn't bother her and maybe the ghost of Simon
Garchard would get me and slit me open.

She said Miles had shown her and Charlie the room
where it happened. Then one day she dared me to go into
the room. But I never told anyone about it. Not even Otto.

When Paul and Trish reported their findings at the Podingham Clinic Gerry felt disappointed. No solid evidence of anything untoward had been found but they still had a dead woman in the mortuary and, even though Colin insisted that she'd died of natural causes, there was still the question of the pen marks on the skin – and Carl Utley was willing to swear on a stack of Bibles that he'd seen a corpse being removed from the clinic.

Also the fact that Dr Welman had been caught destroying records rang alarm bells in Gerry's head and he'd instructed Paul to bring the shredder and its contents back to the incident room. If he was feeling particularly cruel, he might give one of the underlings the job of reassembling each sheet. He'd wait to see who wasn't pulling their weight that day, he thought mischievously, before allocating the job.

He looked up and saw Wesley approaching, a faraway look in his eyes, as though he had something on his mind.

'I want to have another look through James Dalcott's things,' Wesley said with a decisiveness that Gerry found surprising. 'We've not really covered the George Clipton angle, have we? Clipton was Dalcott's father – and he was hanged for murder.'

'You saying someone was out for revenge? One of the victim's relatives?'

Wesley shook his head. 'That doesn't make sense. James was the victim's son as well as the murderer's.'

'Any ideas on this old bloke Brian Carrack saw visiting James Dalcott on the night he died?'

'If you want my opinion, he's playing with us, Gerry. Anyway, it was dark and remember how badly lit that lane was.'

Gerry had to concede that Wesley was right. Brian Carrack was probably making the whole thing up.

'OK. You go and search through Dalcott's belongings if it makes you happy. But remember the place has already been searched and time is tight.'

Wesley began to move towards the door. 'I won't be long.' He hesitated. 'I'm meeting Nuala Johns later.'

Gerry raised his eyebrows. 'Oh aye? Just you be careful. I've come across her type before. Given half a chance she'll have the words out of your notebook and the clothes off your back. Does your Pam know about this assignation?'

'It's not an assignation. It's purely in the line of duty.'

'That's what they all say.' Gerry raised a warning finger. 'Watch your step, that's all I'm saying. And don't forget about the TV appeal. In fact why don't you get back here in time for the finish – see what comes in?'

Wesley looked mildly irritated. 'Is that necessary? There'll be plenty of people –'

'I need someone to sort the wheat from the chaff. Besides, it'll give you a valid excuse to get away from that Nuala so I'll be doing you a favour. You'll thank me in the morning.'

Gerry Heffernan gave Wesley a knowing wink before he swept from the room.

Wesley was on his way to James Dalcott's house but the knowledge that Tony Persimmon might have known James Dalcott through the Podingham Clinic kept nagging away in his head like a buzzing insect. And he knew the only way to get rid of it was by paying Persimmon a call at Tailors Court. Besides, he wanted to see the place again so this new angle gave him the perfect excuse.

When Jill Persimmon let him in she directed him to the room Tony was using temporarily as an office. He found the man there, relaxed in jeans and sweatshirt, sitting in front of a laptop computer.

Wesley cleared his throat and Tony looked up. For a split second he looked annoyed at the intrusion, then he rearranged his features into a mask of polite cooperation.

'What can I do for you, Inspector? I take it this is about our skeletons?'

'Not this time. I believe you worked for Pharmitest International. Did you know James Dalcott?'

Tony Persimmon didn't answer for a few moments and Wesley waited. He intended to let Tony fill the silence.

'I worked at Pharmitest's head office in London but I had to come down here from time to time to check on the trials at the Podingham.' He gave a weak smile. 'I rather fell in love with the countryside round here – that's how I ended up at Tailors Court.'

'Did you meet Dalcott at the clinic?'

'Yes, I did as a matter of fact.'

'And what was your relationship with him?'

271

'There was no "relationship",' he said quickly. 'He was just a problem that needed solving.'

'A problem?' Wesley had hardly expected such honesty. He sat quite still and listened.

'I don't work for the Pharmitest dollar any more so I suppose it's OK to tell you.' There was a pause while Persimmon gathered his thoughts. 'James Dalcott was threatening to make waves. One of the drug trials had gone tits up – a bloke was left scarred for life. Dalcott thought the company should have been open about the whole incident and the victim should have been given a huge payout. My masters disagreed. We had words.'

'So you bore him a grudge?'

Tony shook his head. 'No way. It was business, pure and simple. I just had to make sure Dalcott kept his mouth firmly shut and I succeeded – using only legal niceties, incidentally.' He sat back in his seat. 'I got out of Pharmitest soon after – got sick of the whole business to tell you the truth. And if you think I killed Dalcott, you're barking up the wrong tree. I had no reason to wish him any harm: I'd left Pharmitest and, like I said, our dispute wasn't personal in the first place. Anyway, I hadn't seen him for months – not since the unfortunate business. Look, if anyone bore Dalcott a grudge it'd be the poor sod who was left scarred. Or even Welman – he doesn't like people who don't toe the line and Dalcott came dangerously close. Welman tends to take these things personally . . . unlike me.'

'James Dalcott lived nearby. You must have seen him around the district?'

'We move in different circles, Inspector. I haven't seen him since I left Pharmitest and that's the truth.'

272

'I'll be sending someone along to take a statement.'

Tony Persimmon sat up straight, bristling with indignation. 'Look, I resent being treated as a suspect. I haven't seen James Dalcott for several months and you'll just have to take my word for it. I've told you everything I know. Now, if that's all . . .'

Wesley knew when he was being dismissed.

He was unsure whether to believe Persimmon's claim about not seeing Dalcott. Surely in a place like Tradington, their paths must have crossed. But Tony Persimmon would keep.

He drove the short distance to Dalcott's cottage and stood at the gate for a while taking in the scene, putting himself in the mind of the killer who had walked up the garden path and shot a man at close range on that dark, damp evening six days earlier.

He could see the neighbours' car standing in the drive next door but he wasn't in the mood for another encounter with Ruby and Len Wetherall so he pulled up the collar of his jacket and opened Dalcott's gate gently, ensuring that it didn't shut with a crash behind him and bring the Wetheralls rushing to their net curtains. The killer would have done the same, he thought as he hurried up the path to the front door – he or she wouldn't have wanted to be seen. But Forensic had assured him that no discernible fingerprints had been left: the murderer had worn gloves but, given the cold November weather, this would hardly have looked suspicious.

He had the key to the front door so he let himself in. As it was no longer considered necessary to have a constant police presence at the scene, the place was deserted and, once the front door was closed to exclude the outside world, Wesley stood quite still in the rapidly fading light, drinking in the heavy silence.

When he'd lived in London he'd never been able to experience this absolute quiet. There would always have been the distant rumble of traffic or an aircraft humming overhead. But here in the countryside was pure darkness and complete silence. And it made him uncomfortable, especially here in the very hallway where a man had died so violently. And reminders of death were all around: the smears of grey aluminium powder left by the fingerprint people and the small stickers used to mark out spots of possible forensic interest. Then there was the dark stain of dried blood in the place James Dalcott had fallen and the slick of red wine from the broken bottle, now dried to a sticky mess.

As Wesley switched on the light to banish the ghosts he could have sworn he heard a sound from upstairs, a soft padding across a bedroom carpet perhaps. Or perhaps it was his imagination.

He decided to ignore it. Empty houses, especially empty houses where a murder had taken place, were inclined to make the senses work overtime. He opened the door to what he knew from previous visits was the drawing room. It was almost dark so he flicked on the light and took a deep breath.

The contents of the bureau in the corner of the room had been pulled out and strewn all over the carpet and his heart began to beat a little faster. Someone had taken advantage of the fact that the police guard had been removed to conduct a rather chaotic search.

The police team had searched for any papers or letters that might throw light on the murder but had found nothing out of the ordinary. If the killer had made his own search, it might mean that something important had been missed. On the other hand the intruder might have just been an opportunist thief targeting an empty house – but all his instincts still screamed that it was James Dalcott's killer.

He walked out of the room on tiptoe and when he reached the hall again he stood and listened. Somewhere upstairs a door opened and closed softly. The intruder was there in Dalcott's house with him. He hadn't been imagining things.

He took his mobile phone out of his pocket and began to dial Gerry Heffernan's number but before he could finish, he heard a crash and footsteps. Whoever it was had decided to make a break for it. He started to climb the stairs, two by two and when he reached the landing, he was faced with a row of doors – all of them shut tight.

Wesley, being methodical by nature, decided to start at one end and work his way along. He turned to his left and opened the first door. It was a bathroom and it was empty. Standing by the basin he dialled Gerry's number again and when the DCI answered he outlined his predicament, briefly and in a whisper. Gerry promised to send back-up. Wesley only hoped it would be soon. Perhaps he shouldn't have come alone but hindsight is a wonderful thing.

In the meantime, he was determined to discover the intruder's identity. He stepped out onto the landing and opened the door of the adjoining room cautiously. The curtains were closed and the room was in total darkness so he felt for the light switch on the wall by the door. There was either no bulb in the main light or it had failed so he searched his coat pocket for the small torch he usually carried and shone its beam around the room. He remembered from his previous visits to the crime scene that this was James Dalcott's bedroom. It was spacious but rather untidy: Dalcott had been a man alone and a busy man alone at that.

Summoning his courage, Wesley opened the door of the huge fitted wardrobe but when he flashed the torch inside he saw nothing but suits, shirts and trousers hanging in rows. As he pushed the contents of the wardrobe to one side, he heard a door bang. Then he realised it was the door to the room he was in. He disentangled himself from the clothes and stumbled towards the door, dropping his torch on the way. And when he turned the door handle nothing happened. It was locked.

He had noticed on his previous visits that all the doors had keys. When Roz and James had bought the house they'd had all the original features restored, down to the brass locks on the Victorian doors with gleaming reproduction keys to replace the ones that had probably been lost over the years. He hadn't envisaged that the intruder might take advantage of Roz Dalcott's attention to period detail and now he was trapped in there until Gerry's back-up arrived and he cursed his stupidity.

The front door banged shut in the distance. His quarry was gone, leaving only silence. He slumped down on the bed and put his head in his hands before turning on the bedside light and calling Gerry to tell the back-up to get a move on.

He heard the DCI laughing on the other end of the line. 'It's us who should lock up the villains, Wes, not the other way round. We'll have to get you sent back to Bramshill for a refresher course.'

When the chuckling died down, Gerry promised that a

patrol car was on its way and, with any luck, they might bump into the intruder on his way out. They were due a bit of good fortune.

As Wesley sat there he used the time for a little constructive thinking, eliminating all the suspects who couldn't possibly have been there to lock him in. Syd Jenkins and Brian Carrack were out of the frame. But that still left plenty of others. And yet there had been no strange car parked in the lane. If the intruder had come by car, he'd parked some way off, perhaps in the village centre, and walked the rest of the way.

Then his mind turned to the photograph Evonne Arlis had mentioned. He stood up, switched on his torch again and shone it into the recesses of the wardrobe. He wasn't quite sure what he was looking for but he harboured an optimistic hope that he'd know it if he saw it. With a deep sigh, he walked across the room and switched on the second bedside light. The photograph could be anywhere in the house – if that's what the intruder was after, it might even be in his pocket by now.

But if he himself had anything he wished to keep safe and private, he'd probably keep it in his bedroom.

He lowered himself to the floor and lifted the blue cotton valance which concealed the ugly base of the divan bed. The divan had a built-in drawer on this side for storing bedding which wouldn't have been obvious to the casual observer. The officers who'd carried out the initial search would surely have noticed it, he thought. But it would do no harm to have another look.

When he pulled out the drawer he saw a pile of folded bed linen. He had a rummage around and at the very bottom was a pillowcase that felt curiously stiff to the touch. His pulse quickening, Wesley felt inside and drew out a cardboard folder. It contained a transcript of George Clipton's trial for the murder of his wife and, as Wesley flicked through the pages, he saw that certain sections had been highlighted. Beneath the transcript lay a photograph of a couple Wesley recognised from the police records he'd seen as George and Isabelle Clipton. And standing slightly apart from the pair was another man. He was youngish, possibly only in his twenties, and he wore a tweed jacket similar to Clipton's own. His wavy fair hair was short and his expression was rather distant, almost aloof. Isabelle Clipton wore a full-skirted flowery summer dress, nipped in at the waist. She was extremely pretty in a china doll sort of way, Wesley thought, but there was an unmistakable hardness in her eyes – or perhaps he was just imagining it because he knew how she behaved towards her husband before he strangled her. He turned the photograph over and saw that there was writing on the back. *George and Isabelle with Liam.*

He suddenly heard voices and the sound of heavy footsteps on the stairs.

'In here,' he shouted and waited for the door to open.

Gerry Heffernan sat back in his chair. Along with some others in CID he'd found Wesley Peterson's short incarceration rather funny at first. But his amusement had abated when he learned that Wesley's captor hadn't been picked up by the patrol cars he'd sent to prowl the area.

It seemed that the intruder had broken in by smashing a pane of glass in the back door and turning the key that had been left in the lock. Gerry resolved to have a word with the search team about basic home security. The neighbours, Ruby and Len Wetherall, had seen and heard nothing. Once they'd closed their curtains at sunset and switched on the TV, they became oblivious to the world outside – or so they claimed.

But Gerry had other things to think about, such as the need to tie up their investigations at the Podingham Clinic. Carl Utley was hardly an unbiased witness, but Gerry was still certain that his story contained some element of truth. And even though their mystery corpse in the river had died from natural causes, he couldn't forget what Colin said about the faint ink marks on the torso. Together with all this, Tony Persimmon's links with the clinic and his dispute with James Dalcott only added to Gerry's building suspicions that something was going on at the Podingham – and that whatever it was could have led to a bullet being shot into James Dalcott's brain.

Even though the clinic was on his mind, he was surprised to receive the news that Fiona Verdun was at the front desk wanting to speak to the officer in charge.

He looked at his watch. He had plenty of time before Sandra Ackerley's TV appearance produced a hoped-for torrent of information about Mabel Cleary's disappearance, so he strolled down the corridor to the front desk, wondering what Fiona Verdun could possibly want.

He found her in Reception, sitting upright on a plastic-covered bench. She stood as he approached and clenched her hands nervously.

'Miss Verdun? I'm DCI Heffernan. What can I do for you?' He knew he sounded hopeful but, in his experience, a spot of optimism never did any harm.

She glanced round. She seemed jumpy, as though she suspected there were spies hiding in the corners.

'Shall we go somewhere more private?' Gerry said.

The answer was a nod.

He led Fiona through the door to the heart of the police station, stopping to punch the security code into the electronic lock.

'Now then, love,' he said once they were comfortably settled in Interview Room two. 'What would you like to tell me?' He took his dog-eared notebook from his jacket pocket and searched for a pen. Eventually he found one in the top pocket of his shirt and gave Fiona an avuncular smile.

She took a deep breath. 'I've just left the Podingham. Walked out.'

'Oh aye? Why was that?'

'I had a row with Mr Powell. Told him I didn't like what was going on there.'

'We've had the place searched and we didn't turn up anything that –'

'You wouldn't. Welman and Powell covered their tracks well. And Pharmitest turned a blind eye.'

'To what?' He waited expectantly, watching her face.

After a short silence she spoke again. 'Powell and Welman bring in people from abroad; sometimes eastern Europe, sometimes further afield. They get paid for donating a kidney. It's big money for them I suppose but . . . Powell has a long list of wealthy patients in need of a transplant. Supply and demand. Market forces.'

Gerry stared at her for a few seconds. 'Go on.'

'A friend of Welman's brings in the donors illegally on his yacht. They're brought ashore at night and taken to the clinic. They stay there for a couple of weeks to recuperate then they make the return journey. Look, I've never had much to do with Powell's side of things and I've only just found out what's been happening. I was told Powell just used the facilities for routine private surgery. I knew there were sometimes foreign patients but Welman told me the clinic had some arrangement with a doctor abroad.'

Gerry ignored her protestations of innocence, although he suspected they were sincere. She'd probably believed what she was told because it was easier that way. 'Who else at the clinic is involved?'

'The staff aren't encouraged to ask too many questions. It was one of the nurses in the surgical unit who told me. She got worried when the police started sniffing around. She hadn't been happy about it for a while.'

'And now you've decided to blow the whistle?'

'You could put it like that.'

Gerry leaned forward, taking her into his confidence. 'A woman's body was found in the River Trad with ink marks on the torso. Our pathologist thinks they could be the sort of marks a surgeon makes before an operation. Is our mystery woman one of Powell's patients?'

Fiona gave a little nod. 'The nurse I talked to said there'd been an incident. One of the donors lied about a heart condition and she died just before she was due to go into theatre. She was in the country illegally.'

'So they couldn't risk reporting her death to the authorities?'

Fiona shook her head. 'Powell said he'd sort it – report the death – but the nurse didn't know what had happened to the body. She'd assumed it had been taken to one of the hospital mortuaries – she'd no idea they'd just dumped it in the river.'

'Her, not it.' Gerry spoke sharply. 'The patient who died was a woman. Do you know her name?'

Fiona stared at him for a moment then shook her head. 'Look, when I found out what they'd done I had to tell someone.'

Gerry picked up the phone. Welman and Powell had to be brought in for questioning. After a short conversation, he returned his attention to Fiona. 'Did Dr Dalcott know about all this?'

Fiona's eyes widened. 'I shouldn't think so. Dr Dalcott and Dr Shallech work in the drug trials unit which is completely separate.' She hesitated. 'But if he found out somehow . . . Is Mr Powell going to be arrested?'

'Concealing a death and dumping a body in the river is a crime, love. Not to mention the illegal transplants. It's up to the Crown Prosecution Service what they want to charge him with. And I should think the General Medical Council will be interested and all.'

She gave a weak smile, a shadow of her old, confident self. But then she'd had a shock.

'You've done the right thing, love,' he assured her, then, after an awkward silence, asked, 'Have you anything else to tell me about James Dalcott?'

She considered the question for a few seconds. 'A week or so before he died he took a day off. A personal matter, he said. He asked me if I'd ever been to Looe.'

'Looe?'

'In Cornwall. It's only about an hour away. I told him it was a nice place.'

Gerry frowned. Looe hadn't been mentioned before as far as he could remember. Or had it? He'd have to read over the files again.

When Gerry stood up Fiona spoke again. 'Do you think Dr Dalcott's murder might be connected with what was going on at the clinic?'

'I've no idea, love. I take it you're not thinking of going back there?'

She looked a little smug as she shook her head. 'No way. I've just had a text to say I've got a job at a health spa in Plymouth. I'm going to manage the place at double the salary.' She gave him a sly smile as he summoned a constable to show her off the premises. He ought to have known she'd time her revelations about the Podingham Clinic to perfection.

Looe. It might mean nothing but it was worth checking out.

Wesley was very tempted to cancel his meeting with Nuala. But she had said that she had some information so he told himself that he'd probably be neglecting his duty if he didn't go. However, he resolved to be careful. And if things got sticky, he could always cool her enthusiasm by going on about his children, he thought with a smile.

After returning to the incident room to report his findings to Gerry and receive the news of Fiona Verdun's revelations, he drove over to Tradmouth police station because he was yearning for a bit of peace and quiet away from the bustle of their temporary Neston base. He sneaked up to his own office on the first floor and settled down with a cup of tea from the machine in the corridor to study the transcript of George Clipton's murder trial, focusing his attention on the sections that Clipton's son, James Dalcott, had highlighted in fluorescent green.

The highlighted paragraphs seemed to be extracts from

witness statements. The largest section concerned the testimony of Dr Clipton's locum, Dr Liam Cheshlare, who had only been with the practice a couple of weeks when the tragedy occurred. He had been on friendly, but not intimate, terms with the deceased, Mrs Isabelle Clipton, and he assured the court that Ned Longdon, odd-job man and regular at the local hostelry, who claimed to have seen him arguing with the victim earlier that day in woodland near her home, had been mistaken. They had met by chance and they'd been sharing a joke, nothing more, and surely the jury wouldn't take the word of a notorious local drunk over that of a respected professional man. It seemed back then in the 1950s the jury had agreed with Dr Cheshlare and had duly disregarded Ned Longdon's testimony.

Then there was the evidence given by Isabelle's friend from the bridge club – the one she'd allegedly spent so much time with. Only half the time that Isabelle claimed to have spent with Betty Cox, Betty had been otherwise occupied with her golf-professional lover. Betty told the court that Isabelle had seemed preoccupied just before her death; perhaps even a little frightened.

The nanny's low opinion of her charge's mother and the disapproval of this starchy but seemingly sincere young woman – a Miss Enid Buchanan – was almost palpable. Mrs Clipton, she claimed, had ignored poor little Jimmy most of the time and had rather too many racy friends for her liking. Isabelle Clipton was an unfit mother who'd paid little attention to her poor little Jimmy – in the nanny's statement the child was always referred to as 'poor' and 'little' as if those were his additional Christian names. After a good deal of prompting by the defence counsel, the nanny admitted that Mrs Clipton seemed to be afraid of something or someone – and that, in her opinion, this something or someone wasn't necessarily Dr Clipton, whom she usually treated with something approaching contempt. But the police in those days didn't follow this up as fully as Wesley himself would have done. The prosecution made its case that George Clipton was a cuckold, driven to strangle and disfigure his wife out of jealousy. And George Clipton was hanged by the neck until he was dead.

It was the nanny who had found Isabelle's body, lying in the quiet lane behind the house. The prosecution claimed that Dr Clipton had encountered his wife there – perhaps he'd even gone out looking for her. A quarrel had ensued which ended when the doctor had finally snapped, placed his hands around his wife's slender neck and squeezed the life out of her. Liam Cheshlare, the locum, had heard the Cliptons having 'words', as he put it, on a number of occasions. The young man was horrified at what had happened, of course, but somehow not really surprised.

Wesley pulled the photograph out from under the file. The three people: George and Isabelle Clipton and Liam. Now he knew who Liam was – Dr Liam Cheshlare – and he couldn't help wondering whether the young doctor was still alive. He would ask one of the team to trace his whereabouts – he'd like to speak to someone who'd actually been there.

He had to face the fact that the evidence against George Clipton seemed pretty solid, if a little circumstantial. Perhaps he'd got it all wrong. Perhaps the tragic history of James Dalcott's parents had nothing to do with his death after all.

He stared at the photograph. There was something

about the young man in the background that looked vaguely familiar. He might even have seen him somewhere recently, many years older, his face and body afflicted with all the indignities and infirmities that come with age. He closed his eyes, trying to remember, but it was no use. And there was always a good chance that he was mistaken.

He read through the papers again, thinking that there might be something he'd missed – something important. Then he recalled something that made him smile. Enid Buchanan – Nanny Buchanan. When Pam had been pregnant with Michael she had bought an assortment of books on baby care and studied them closely, treating the advice as holy writ . . . until she realised that most of that advice conflicted. Wesley had teased her about one she particularly liked – a book by a woman called Nanny Buchanan. The name had conjured for him a mental picture of a stout woman in an old-fashioned starched nurse's uniform pushing a pram the size of a small car around a London park. Nanny Buchanan – firm but fair with a belief in the benefits of fresh air and cod liver oil.

Somehow he had imagined that James Dalcott's old nanny would be long gone – married maybe, with the attendant change of name. But if she was indeed the author of the book Pam had bought . . .

He had been feeling confusion, and maybe even despair, but now a fresh excitement coursed through his body. He picked up the telephone and punched out his home number. Pam answered after the third ring.

'Hello again.'

'Hi.' There was a pause. 'Don't tell me, you forgot to say that you're not going to be in till after midnight.'

'It's nothing like that,' Wesley said quickly. 'Look, have you still got that book about baby care? Nanny Buchanan?'

'Why?'

'Have you got it?'

'It's probably on the bookshelves in the dining room with all the other books I've been intending to give to the charity shop.'

'Can you find it for me?'

There was a pause. 'Why? Has someone brought an abandoned baby into the police station and you need some helpful hints?'

Wesley smiled. 'I'll tell you when I see you. Can you get it for me – please. I wouldn't ask you if it wasn't important.'

He heard a loud sigh on the other end of the line. 'OK.'

'I need the publisher's address – it's usually on one of the front pages.'

He could almost see Pam rolling her eyes. 'I have seen a book before. Hang on.'

He could hear a few distant bangs and crashes as Pam made her search. He could also hear Michael chattering away to his sister, playing some imaginary game, and he suddenly realised how much he missed the children. When this investigation was over, he'd take a few days off. And then Christmas would creep up on them like some stalking beast and he'd become involved in his annual struggle against youthful materialism; a struggle he usually lost.

He heard Pam's voice. 'I've found it. The publisher's an outfit called Flowerdew Publications. Want the address?'

'Please.'

She recited an address in London. Soho, Wesley

thought. Somehow he hadn't associated Nanny Buchanan with such a worldly setting.

'What year was it published?' he asked, fearing that Flowerdew might have gone out of business or been swallowed by one of its larger rivals in the meantime.

'Ten years ago. It was all the rage when Michael was born. There was even a TV series but I don't suppose you'd remember.'

'Is there anything about Nanny Buchanan herself? How old she is? Where she lives? Her experience?'

'Oh yes. I'll read it out to you.' She cleared her throat. '"After training as a nurse, Enid Buchanan worked as a nanny to numerous families, including many in the public eye. In her popular TV series, she shared the knowledge gained from her years of experience with the nation's young mothers and she is a great advocate of the need for calm and routine in a young child's life. She was made an OBE in 1995 and she now lives in a picturesque cottage on the Cornish coast".'

It took Wesley a few seconds to take in the information. She'd worked for families in the public eye – he'd lay money that the publishers didn't mean the Cliptons, who'd been in the public eye for all the wrong reasons: that was something the nanny had probably kept quiet about in the course of her long career. But the thing that made Wesley's heart beat a little faster was the fact that Nanny Buchanan lived in Cornwall. According to Gerry, James Dalcott had mentioned Looe to Fiona Verdun before taking a day off. Was there a chance that he'd been planning to visit his old nanny? She'd been there, part of the Clipton household at the time, so she must have seen and heard things that went on in that house that the

Cliptons wouldn't want to be common knowledge amongst their neighbours.

He thanked Pam profusely and promised to be home at the arranged time before making a couple of calls. Five minutes later, he was relieved to discover that Flowerdew Publications was still in business in the heart of Soho. Fortunately the editor was working late and she was able to assure him that Nanny Buchanan was still alive and well and enjoying her retirement in Looe in Cornwall. In fact she had a new book coming out in the spring – *Nanny's Nursery Recipes*. The editor described the nanny as a spry old bird. Indestructible was one of the words she used. Wesley only hoped she was right. Now it was confirmed, he knew it hadn't been a coincidence that James had mentioned Looe to Fiona Verdun. If James Dalcott's murder was connected with the Clipton case and he had visited Enid Buchanan because she was a potential witness, then she herself might well be in danger. And he needed to get to her before the killer did.

After the editor had passed on Miss Buchanan's phone number she told him, with what sounded like admiration, that she was away at the moment, visiting friends in Austria, and she was due back tomorrow. Wesley thanked her and ended the call, rather relieved that Nanny Buchanan was safe in Austria for the time being. As soon as she returned, he would pay her a visit in the hope she'd be able to shed some light on her former charge's death.

He tried the number the editor had given him, just in case Miss Buchanan had decided to return early from her holiday or there was a relative or friend looking after the house who could throw any light on recent events. But there was no reply. He'd just have to be patient until she returned from her travels.

He wanted to share his new discovery with Gerry Heffernan but when he tried his number there was no reply. He examined his watch: it was getting late and it was almost time to meet Nuala Johns. He felt a momentary thrill of danger, there for a split second then swiftly suppressed. Then his mobile started to ring and when he took the phone from his pocket he saw that it was Neil calling.

'What are you up to?' were the archaeologist's first words. 'I've just spoken to Pam and she said you wouldn't be back till late.'

'I've got to meet someone.'

'Who?'

He thought for a moment and realised that Neil could solve a few potential problems. 'A journalist called Nuala Johns.'

'I met her at Tailors Court.'

'If you're free why don't you come with me? I'm hoping she might have some more information on the history of Tailors Court.'

This was the bait and Neil fell for it. 'What time are you meeting her?'

'Seven at the White Horse near Neston Castle. How's your research going?'

'That's what I was ringing to tell you. I've found out who was living in that Tradmouth town house at the end of the sixteenth century – the one where your victim's wife has a flat. I've had Annabel going through all the rent rolls and –'

'Who was it?'

'A Philip Tanner. Physician.'

'That explains the anatomical drawings on the walls behind the panelling, I suppose.'

'And there's something else. Something very interesting.'

'What's that?'

'I'll tell you later. See you in the White Horse at seven.'

He rang off leaving Wesley staring at the receiver.

Pat Beswick wriggled her feet into a pair of fluffy slippers and took a sip of tea. It was just time for the local TV news. She enjoyed the local news: it wasn't all doom and gloom like the main news – wars and bombings and famines. Not that the local version had been too cheerful recently what with that poor doctor being shot. You'd never think anything like that would happen in a place like Tradington.

And then there'd been those bones at Tailors Court. She must have walked over them countless times – walked over graves. If she'd known that they were lying there all those years ago, it would have given her nightmares.

She put her steaming mug of tea down on the table by the side of her chair and picked up the remote control. Sure enough the local news headlines were on, read by that nice young presenter who reminded her so much of her great nephew. She listened with rapt attention. The latest on the Tradington shooting – police were trying to trace an elderly person who'd been seen nearby on the night of the murder. A doctor had been arrested for his part in a racket involving illegal organ donations at a private clinic near Podbury. A row had blown up over a lap dancing club in the heart of Plymouth. Devon was certainly joining the wicked world these days, she thought as she took a restorative sip of tea.

The newsreader had been replaced on the screen by a woman and Pat settled back into her chair as she introduced the next item.

'During the Second World War hundreds of children

from London and other cities were evacuated here to Devon for safety. Most arrived by train and were billeted with families, attending local schools.'

Pat sat forward and used the remote control to turn up the volume.

'For most of these children, it was the first time they'd been away from their families and it must have been a bewildering and often frightening experience. For many it was their first taste of country living, a true culture shock after the dirt and noise of the big city. They had the freedom to explore the fields and farms and an opportunity to make new friends. So it was for two little girls from London – Mabel and Pat who were evacuated to the village of Tradington near Neston.'

Pat put down her tea and sat quite still, straining to hear every syllable.

'After all these years, Mabel decided to visit her old friend, Pat. And that's where our story becomes a bit of a mystery. Here's Mabel's daughter, Sandra, to explain.'

The camera panned round to a middle-aged woman with a worried frown on her face. 'My mum left home for Devon on November 12th and she caught a coach from London to Morbay. Now I know she was seen getting off at Morbay but I've not heard from her since. I know she received a letter inviting her down from a friend called Pat who she was evacuated with, but unfortunately I don't have Pat's address. I'm sure mum's OK but I'm getting a bit concerned so if her or Pat are watching or if anyone knows . . .'

Pat flicked the TV off and stood up just as a dark figure appeared in the doorway. 'What is it? What's the matter?'

'They're onto us,' Pat replied.

*

292

Wesley was relieved to see that Neil had reached the White Horse before him. In fact he was already sitting with Nuala Johns who was wearing an expression of polite attention. As soon as she spotted Wesley Nuala turned away from Neil and watched him as he wove his way through the tables towards her.

'I thought you were never coming,' she said, half accusing, half flirting. 'What are you having to drink? And don't say "not while I'm on duty". What'll it be?'

'Half of bitter, please.'

She looked disappointed. 'Not a pint?'

'I'm driving.'

She shrugged and made her way to the bar. Wesley sat down by Neil. 'What's new?'

'I was just sharing a few pieces of historical information with the lovely Nuala. She's done rather well finding out about old Simon Garchard's body snatching – Devon's very own Burke and now I reckon I might have found his Hare. At Garchard's trial a Philip Tanner gave the damning evidence. He said he'd seen Garchard with the maidservant, Annet Raine. Garchard denied it. He said that even though he'd dug up bodies to dissect, he'd never actually killed anybody. He claimed that Tanner had talked about wanting to get hold of a fresh corpse but the jury thought he was just trying to shift the blame.'

'What do we know about Tanner?'

'He was described as Garchard's apprentice at the trial and after Garchard was hanged, he set up shop in Tradmouth. He's described in various documents as a physician but there's no mention of him having attended any of the universities that trained physicians at the time.'

'So both he and Garchard were enthusiastic amateurs rather than professional doctors.'

'Looks that way.'

'So we can assume that Simon Garchard drew those pictures at Tailors Court – possibly from life if he was dissecting the bodies from the churchyard.'

'And don't forget Annet Raine's murder. Apparently her half-dissected corpse was found in an outhouse by another servant who raised the alarm.' He wrinkled his nose. 'Garchard denied all knowledge and said he carried out all his autopsies in the attic but Tanner said he'd seen him carrying the body in there. His evidence hanged his master.'

'So it was his word against Garchard's?'

'Not quite. There was another witness who –'

Before Neil had time to continue, Nuala returned. She was carrying Wesley's drink and she put it down in front of him with a flourish.

Before he could thank her she started to speak. 'Neil's been telling me about Philip Tanner. I'm thinking of writing an article about him – even a book.' She sat down, a look of triumph on her face. 'The murderer's apprentice. Think that's a good title?'

'Brilliant,' said Neil. 'Body snatching. Murder. Can't go wrong.'

She turned to Wesley. 'What do you think, Inspector? Reckon it'll be a best seller?'

'It wouldn't surprise me,' Wesley answered quickly. 'What did you want to see me about?'

He saw Nuala give Neil a swift glance as though she wanted to be rid of him. 'I'd found out about Philip Tanner but your friend here's beaten me to it.' She gave a disappointed pout in Neil's direction.

'Neil was just telling me about Philip Tanner giving evidence at Garchard's trial. And did you say there was another witness, Neil?'

'Yes. Another maidservant called Elizabeth Ryde. She confirmed Tanner's story.'

'That's that, then,' Nuala said, downing the last of her pint. 'Garchard got his just deserts.' She touched Wesley's arm. 'Got anything for me on the child's bones yet? I believe Rachel Tracey's been interrogating my gran.'

'And you think you're entitled to first pickings, eh?'

'I didn't say that,' she snapped.

Wesley raised his hands in mock surrender. Nuala was an ambitious woman and she resented the police getting the juicy story before she did. Part of him admired her for it, and part of him hated the cold calculation behind it.

'If you ask your gran nicely I'm sure she'll tell you.'

'That's the point. Now she's clammed up. She says it's a police matter.'

Wesley said nothing. He hadn't seen Rachel since her chat with Mary. Now he suddenly wanted to know what, if anything, the former land girl had revealed.

He made a great show of looking at his watch. 'I'm sorry, Nuala, I have to go. I'm sure you and Neil have a lot to talk about . . . Simon Garchard and all that.' He smiled at Neil who suddenly looked a little fearful, as though his friend was leaving him alone with a man-eating tiger.

Gerry had told him he'd be needed in the incident room to deal with the aftermath of Sandra Ackerley's TV appearance so he hurried back to Neston Police Station, his collar up against the fine drizzle that had just started to fall. He was glad to get away from Nuala. He found her presence disturbing ... and maybe, although he was reluctant to acknowledge it, even a little exciting. When he reached the incident room he put her firmly out of his mind and looked around for Rachel.

She was nowhere to be seen but he learned from Gerry that she'd rushed to the TV station to make sure Sandra Ackerley was OK. She hadn't had time to share what she'd learned from Mary Haynes but she'd promised to have a full report on Gerry's desk first thing in the morning.

Wesley felt a little deflated. Somehow he'd convinced himself that Mary held the key to the whole case. He sat down at his desk and put his head in his hands. Every lead he followed seemed to end in frustration. Even Nanny Buchanan was cavorting about in Austria instead of answering police questions. And if you couldn't rely on good old Nanny, who could you rely on, he thought with a bitter smile just as his phone began to ring.

It had started. The calls, relayed from the TV station switchboard, were coming in. Not exactly thick and fast but in a steady trickle.

There were a number of calls from former evacuees and local children who'd been friends with evacuated children, saying that they remembered a Pat or a Mabel – sometimes separately and sometimes together. But none was admitting to a connection with Tailors Court.

Just as Wesley was starting to think the whole exercise had been a waste of time and resources, the phone rang again and he heard a tentative female voice on the other end of the line – an elderly voice, high-pitched and slightly quivering.

'Hello. I . . . I think I'm the Pat you're looking for.'

His grip tightened on the receiver. 'Can we start at the beginning? When you were evacuated to Devon what was the name of the house you stayed in?'

'I was evacuated in 1944 when the doodlebugs started and I was sent to a big house near Tradington called Tailors Court. It belonged to a Mrs Jannings.'

Wesley felt like punching the air in triumph. He'd found the right Pat at last. He asked the next question, trying to keep the impatience out of his voice. 'You wrote to a lady called Mabel? A fellow evacuee?'

'That's right. I invited her down here. I live in Buckfastleigh.'

'And she's staying with you?'

There was a moment's hesitation. 'She was but she left yesterday. She wanted to see some more of the West Country. I'm just calling to say that you don't need to worry about her. I saw her daughter on the telly and . . . I'm sure Mabel didn't mean to cause any bother. She . . .' The voice trailed off.

'Look, Mrs . . .'

'Beswick.'

'Look, Mrs Beswick, I'd like to talk to you as soon as possible. Would it be convenient –?'

'Why? I've told you Mabel's all right. Don't you believe me?' The woman sounded quite affronted, as though she imagined Wesley was accusing her of lying.

For the next few minutes he did his best to smooth the waters. Eventually he decided that the truth might just produce the desired result.

'This isn't just about Mrs Cleary. The skeleton of a child was discovered at Tailors Court recently and we think the bones date from around the time you were there. We need to talk to anyone who might be able to confirm the identity of the dead child.'

There was a long silence before Pat Beswick spoke again. 'I see.'

'Do you remember a land girl called Mary?'

'Yes.'

'And a man called Miles Jannings?'

'I knew who he was. He was old Mrs Jannings's son; he married a girl called Esther then he got killed in the War. I arrived after the others and he was dead by the time I got there.'

'Can you remember the names of the other children you were with?'

'Well, there was Mabel of course. And Belle.'

Wesley frowned. 'Is that all?'

'Yes. Just the three of us.'

'Look, I'd like to talk to you. Would that be all right?' Wesley spoke gently, reminding himself that this was an elderly woman who'd probably had little to do with the police before.

She hesitated. 'It's getting late now. Can't it wait till tomorrow morning?'

He looked at his watch. If he set off now it would be after nine-thirty by the time he reached her – probably past her bedtime.

'That's fine,' he said after she'd given him her address. 'I'll see you tomorrow.'

When she rang off he sat staring at the phone, listening to the dialling tone. Unexpectedly he felt rather excited at the prospect of meeting one of the Tailors Court evacuees face to face. Mary Haynes, the land girl, had spent most of her waking hours at Gorfleet Farm, working from dawn till

298

dusk, her mind occupied with courting the farmer's son. She had only used Tailors Court as a place to lay her head at night after a hard day toiling in the fields. But the children had lived, eaten, played and slept there. They would have known everything that went on.

His mobile phone began to ring and he looked at the caller's name. Rachel.

'I was just going to call you,' he said before she could speak. 'I've had a call from Pat. She lives in Buckfastleigh and Mabel's been staying with her. If you're still with Sandra, tell her her mum's OK will you?'

'I'll tell her. You sure the call was genuine?'

'Yes. She knew all about Tailors Court. Mabel moved on yesterday to do some sightseeing but I'm going to see Pat tomorrow morning.' He paused. 'Come with me if you like.'

'I might just do that. Look, Wes, I know I said I'd report on it tomorrow morning but I thought you'd want to know about my visit to Mary Haynes. Is the boss still there?'

'Yes.'

'I think I've got a name for the victim at Tailors Court. An evacuee vanished in 1943.'

'Was he called Charlie by any chance?'

'How did you know?'

'Mabel Cleary's reminiscences mention a kid called Charlie arriving at Tailors Court with a wooden car.'

'But Mary said he went to another billet. He came down to Devon from London with his cousin – a girl named Belle who was slightly older than him. She said he'd been unhappy and found a billet in another village but . . .'

'His own cousin wouldn't lie about something like that surely?'

'That's what everyone thought at the time, but around

the time Charlie disappeared Mary said John Haynes found a bloodstained knife and saw Miles with blood all over his hands.'

'It's a farming area. He could have been gutting a chicken or skinning a rabbit. There's nothing to suggest the blood was human.'

There was a long silence before Rachel spoke again. 'If anyone's in the frame for murdering that child surely it's Miles. He was seriously disturbed and Mary said he was obsessed with scientific experiments. I really don't think we need look any further. I think the bones must be Charlie's. He didn't go away like his cousin, Belle, said. But why should she lie?'

'Because she was involved somehow?'

'I don't know. Let's talk about it tomorrow, eh?'

Wesley said goodbye and put the phone down.

Pat Beswick had never had anything to do with the police before and she'd found it a disturbing experience.

She jumped when she felt a hand on her shoulder. Then she breathed deeply. Getting worked up about it wasn't going to help the situation.

She turned to face her companion and saw that Mabel was shaking. 'What will happen, do you think?'

Pat gave her a weak smile. 'I don't know. Perhaps we shouldn't have done it.'

'But I had to get away. I couldn't stand it any longer.' Pat saw Mabel's eyes filling with tears. 'What a mess,' she said with a sob. 'Do you think . . . do you think they'll put us in prison?'

'I don't know, Mabel. I really don't.'

CHAPTER 12

Transcript of recording made by Mrs Mabel Cleary (née Fallon) – Home Counties Library Service Living History Project: Reminiscences of a wartime evacuee.

One day in the summer Charlie went but we weren't told where or why. He just vanished one day with that toy car he always carried: Belle said it was the only thing he'd rescued from his house when it was bombed. She said Charlie had found another billet but I wasn't particularly bothered. He was a strange boy, not the sort I wanted as a friend – not like Otto.

Otto kept asking where Charlie had gone and Belle was quite nasty to him, calling him the usual names. But we hadn't time to think about Charlie for long because there was a wedding at Tailors Court. Miles and Ugly Esther decided to tie the knot before he went back to his unit. Not that it was a big affair and Esther didn't bother much with clothes so there was no big white dress made of parachute silk. But everyone saved their coupons so we had a good spread and Mr Haynes at Gorfleet Farm donated some of the cider he'd made. Mary got quite drunk and she was sick, but John Haynes looked after her.

Then Miles left and a couple of weeks later the telegram arrived saying he'd been killed in action. Why was there so much death around?

When Wesley eventually arrived home Pam met him in the hall, eager to know why he'd wanted Nanny Buchanan's details. When he told her, she stood there deep in thought.

'Surely someone in her position would have told the police everything they knew at the time,' she said.

Wesley knew this made sense but there was a nagging doubt in the back of his mind that wouldn't go away. 'If she didn't know that something she witnessed or over-heard was important she might not have mentioned it.'

Pam shrugged and he put his arms around her waist. The children were in bed already and, for once they were alone. At least until her mother Della decided to inevitably put in an appearance. Time to tell her about his day and the incident at Dalcott's cottage.

When he'd finished she broke away from him with a vexed look on her face. 'You shouldn't have gone there alone. You could have been killed. The killer has a gun, remember.'

He found her concern rather gratifying and he didn't spoil things by mentioning his assignation with Nuala Johns – although he rather feared that Neil might do the job for him.

The peace of the evening was shattered, however, when Della turned up at ten bewailing the fact that the latest man in her life had turned out to be a liar. He'd told her he was an unemployed musician but really he'd falsified his qualifications on his CV and lost his job in an insurance office and now he was expecting to move in with Della so she could keep them both. Pam told her to put her foot down. But by the end of the evening a large quantity of wine had made that foot rather unsteady so she ended up staying in the spare room.

During the long evening, Wesley had taken refuge from Della's dramatic revelations in the dining room, reading and re-reading the transcript of George Clipton's trial. The case against the doctor seemed watertight in every way but he still felt uneasy. He needed to reassure himself that the jury had reached the right conclusion. He needed to talk to Enid Buchanan and the locum, Dr Liam Cheshlare. He had asked Trish Walton to trace Cheshlare's whereabouts – if he was still alive – but she hadn't got back to him yet.

When he finally went to bed his mind was too active for sleep. He kept seeing James Dalcott's dead, staring, startled eyes and he kept thinking of Tailors Court and its strange history. Flesh Tailor's Court – the home of Simon Garchard, the self-styled physician, who had been so anxious to push the boundaries of knowledge that he'd resorted to murder and was hanged for his crime, as James Dalcott's father, George Clipton, had been.

He awoke on Friday morning, his head spinning with tiredness. Pam was already up, getting the children dressed and preparing herself for the day ahead. They were starting rehearsals for the Christmas nativity play next week, she told him over a strong coffee. Michael had landed the role of a sheep – not quite Joseph, but teachers' children can be shown no favours in the world of modern education.

Della staggered off to work on a strong black coffee and Wesley was the last to leave the house. He sat in the car for a while before starting the engine. He needed time to think.

Gerry was still working on the theory that Dalcott's shooting had something to do with the events at the Podingham Clinic – either the drug trial that had ended so disastrously for Carl Utley, or Oscar Powell's blatantly unethical conduct. There was also the possibility that Adam Tey and Charleen Anstice might have lashed out at the doctor they blamed for the loss of their child. But Wesley thought this unlikely, especially as Charleen was now pregnant again. Also, of course, they couldn't forget that Dalcott's death had come at rather a convenient time for his estranged wife and Harry Parker.

The person who'd locked him in that room at Dalcott's house had, presumably, gone there to look for something. Perhaps Roz was afraid that her estranged husband had already made a new will and had hidden it somewhere in the house without informing his solicitor. Or maybe the incident had something to do with the folder and the photograph hidden under Dalcott's bed. Wesley still couldn't get rid of the feeling that there was some connection between George Clipton's crime and the death of his son.

He drove to Neston, his mind only half on the traffic. The folder he'd found in Dalcott's house was open on the passenger seat beside him and when he stopped at the traffic lights he glanced over and saw that photograph: George and Isabelle Dalcott with the young locum, Dr Cheshlare, smiling in the background. Why did Cheshlare seem so familiar? Perhaps one day soon it would come to him.

Trish Walton greeted him when he reached the incident room and, from the keen expression on her face, he guessed that she had good news for him. But he was wrong. She'd been doing her best to find out what had become of Dr Liam Cheshlare, contacting professional bodies both in the UK and abroad in an attempt to discover where he'd gone after leaving George Clipton's practice, but she'd had no luck. Dr Cheshlare had disappeared off the face of the earth, Trish said in dramatic tones.

Wesley thought for a while before he spoke. 'Perhaps he gave up medicine. See if the name comes up anywhere else. Marriages or deaths. Criminal records.'

'If he changed his name, we're snookered.' It wasn't like Trish to be so pessimistic but Wesley knew she was right.

'He might have changed it because he thought being involved in the Clipton case would damage him professionally. He might have taken his mother's maiden name.'

Trish sighed. 'I'll see what I can do.'

He suddenly had an idea. 'As well as seeing what became of Cheshlare afterwards, can you find out what he did before he went to work with Clipton? Perhaps we'll be able to trace him through someone who knew him back then. Get all you can about him.'

Wesley could see the scepticism in Trish's brown eyes as she turned away.

'And check any deaths in that name too. It's always

possible that he's no longer with us,' he added as an after-thought.

As Trish hurried back to her computer to continue her desk-bound investigations, he looked round the incident room. Rachel Tracey was over in the far corner talking to Nick Tarnaby.

He watched Tarnaby walk away, head bowed, before he caught her eye and waved her over. She pressed her lips firmly together and marched across the room.

'Are you ready to visit Pat Beswick?'

'Yes.' She hesitated. 'It might be nice to put her in touch with Mary when this is all over.'

He could have sworn he saw Rachel's cheeks redden a little. Perhaps, he thought, Mary Haynes wasn't the only person of interest at Gorfleet Farm.

Rachel swept out of the room and Wesley watched as she lifted her heavy coat off the rack in the corridor outside. He hadn't had time to take his coat off since his arrival so he pulled at the zip to fasten it against the weather. He could see the rain landing in rivulets on the window. It was cold and wet out there and he wasn't taking any chances.

On the drive out to Buckfastleigh the windscreen wipers were working overtime and Rachel observed that it would be even bleaker when they reached the edge of Dartmoor. He knew she was making conversation but he didn't really want to talk. His mind was still churning over the facts of the two cases – the child at Tailors Court and the shooting of James Dalcott. He hoped that Pat would help him solve the first. As for the second, he was starting to experience that feeling of frustration he sometimes had in dreams when he was being held back from his goal by some unseen force. There'd been so many possible leads but none of them had come to anything. Perhaps the Clipton angle would be the same.

When he reached Buckfastleigh he saw that some shops had started to put Christmas displays in their windows, reminding him that time was speeding on. And the powers that be would be expecting results sooner rather than later.

Rachel found Pat's address easily enough. It was a small pink-washed semi-detached house of indeterminate age on a side road not far from the main street. The woman who opened the door was small and thin and reminded Wesley of a sparrow. Presumably she was in her seventies but the sprightly way she moved made her seem a lot younger. She also had the alert look of a good observer.

They were invited to sit and tea was offered and accepted.

'So you stayed in Devon after the War?' Rachel began. She tilted her head to one side, genuinely interested. Wesley knew that the woman would soon be telling her her life story.

'My late husband was in the navy and he was based in Plymouth. Then he got a job in admin at Devonport. We moved here when he retired. He died two years ago. Heart attack.'

Rachel made the appropriate noises of sympathy before asking her next question. 'You've kept in touch with Mabel all these years?'

Pat hesitated. 'No, we only found each other recently. My son got me on the Internet and I Googled some names. You know, from when I was evacuated. I only found a couple. A lad called Otto Kramer I knew from the village – he was Jewish and his dad was a doctor: they'd managed to escape from Germany somehow. Anyway he became a professor over in America so I e-mailed him and got a lovely reply. Then I found Mabel's name on a library website. She was taking part in some project – writing down her memories of being evacuated. There was a photo of her but the actual thing she was writing isn't on the website yet so . . .'

'Go on,' Rachel prompted gently. She glanced at Wesley who was sitting on the edge of his old-fashioned armchair, perfectly still.

'Well I e-mailed the library and they passed on my message. She wrote to me and I wrote back and invited her down here.'

'And now she's gone off sightseeing to Cornwall. Do you know where exactly?'

There was a short silence. Then Wesley heard a sound coming from the direction of the kitchen. Something being dropped on the floor.

Then suddenly the door opened. A small thin woman with grey curls and a beak-like nose stood in the doorway. Wesley recognised her immediately from the photograph her daughter had provided. He put his tea cup on the table by the side of his chair and stood up.

'Hello, Mabel,' he said quietly as Rachel put her cup down with exaggerated care and sat forward, her eyes fixed on the newcomer.

Mabel gave Pat a feeble smile. 'It's all right, Pat. I can't have you getting into trouble. You can get locked up for telling fibs to the police.'

'We've been looking for you,' said Wesley, immediately aware that he was stating the obvious but they were the first words that came into his head.

'I didn't know there'd be all this fuss and I didn't mean to upset our Sandra. I just wanted some time back in Devon with Pat. We've not seen each other for years.'

'But why the lie about you moving on?'

Wesley saw Pat and Mabel exchange a worried glance.

'Will we get into trouble for lying? Will we be prosecuted?'

Wesley could tell she was deadly serious. 'I shouldn't think so,' he said gently. 'We're just glad to find you safe. But I don't understand why you didn't tell us you were still here.'

Mabel took a deep breath, suddenly more relaxed. 'It was our Sandra,' she said. 'Always fussing, she is. I thought if Pat rang and said I was OK and I'd be back when I'd finished my travels ... If Pat had said I was here, I thought Sandra might come and spoil things.'

There was a long silence and the two women sat there like a pair of schoolgirls outside the headmistress's office, fearful of a scolding.

'You've no idea what she's like' Mabel continued. 'She calls round every day and then she rings me to ask what I've been eating. I have to hide the sherry bottle – she found it once and confiscated it. Said it was bad for my health. I mean to say, if you can't enjoy a tipple at my age, when can you enjoy it? I just got sick of it all so I came to see Pat.' She pouted defiantly. 'And now she's got the police looking for me.'

Wesley couldn't help feeling a modicum of sympathy for this woman with her bossy, controlling daughter. But there was something he needed to clear up. 'Well, Sandra's not entirely responsible for us being here, Mrs Cleary. I need to talk to you about a murder enquiry we're working

309

on. I told Pat over the phone that some human remains have been found at Tailors Court – the skeleton of a boy aged around nine or ten buried near the paddock.'

The defiance disappeared from Mabel Cleary's eyes and she nodded slowly. 'I remember the paddock.'

'We think the child was buried there in the early nineteen forties – around the time you were living there. Pat says she knows nothing about it but you were there before she arrived so I wondered . . .'

It was difficult to read Mabel's expression as she sank into the nearest chair and grabbed a tissue out of the box on the table by her side. She dabbed at her mouth absent-mindedly before twisting the tissue in her fingers.

'Did Miles Jannings kill the child, Mabel?' he asked gently, hoping the answer would be yes. If it was the long-dead Miles, then he could close the case and concentrate on James Dalcott's shooting. It had to be Miles, surely.

He held his breath and watched Mabel's face. She looked agitated, as though she was reliving painful memories, then she looked him in the eye. Her own eyes were the palest blue and he could see uncertainty there, even fear. 'I put it all out of my mind until I started doing the project at the library.' There was a long silence but Wesley knew she was thinking; wondering how best to put what she knew – what she'd suppressed all these years – into words. Rachel and Pat were sitting quite still, listening intently, neither wanting to break the spell.

'I didn't like it at Tailors Court much. Some bits were all right. There was a nice land girl called Mary billeted there – she was courting the son of the farmer she worked for.'

310

'Mary married John Haynes and she's still at Gorfleet Farm.'

Mabel gave a weak smile. 'That's nice. I would have liked to keep in touch with her but you go back home and . . . Lives change, don't they?'

'Tell me about the other people at Tailors Court,' he said gently.

'Well, Mrs Jannings was in bed most of the time. Sickly she was. And Miles. I kept well away from him, and his girlfriend – Ugly Esther us kids used to call her. They got married not long before he was killed.'

'Tell me about the other children.'

She frowned. 'There was me and a boy called Charlie. He was a bit odd. He used to follow Miles around like a little dog and sometimes they'd disappear for ages together.' She hesitated. 'It was a long time before I found out what they got up to, and then I wished to God I hadn't.'

Wesley said nothing. He let her carry on.

'Then there was Charlie's cousin, Belle. She was a spiteful bit of work – the sort who'd pinch you and tell tales to the teacher. I was a bit lonely there until Pat came, although I did play with some of the children from school.'

'I expect Charlie played with the other boys,' said Rachel.

Mabel shook her head. 'He just wanted to be with Miles. Hero worship I suppose. Then Charlie disappeared one day and Belle said he'd gone to another village; found another billet 'cause he wasn't happy. Perhaps one of the teachers at the school took pity on him.'

There was something in the way Mabel was talking that

311

made Wesley uncomfortable. Her voice was too bright, too positive. As though she was trying to convince herself of something. He decided to take a chance.

'That's not true, is it, Mabel? I think you know what really happened to Charlie. Charlie had a wooden car and a wooden car was found in the grave. I think Miles killed him. John Haynes saw Miles with blood on his hands around the time he disappeared. Perhaps it was an accident.'

Mabel's face contorted in horror. 'No.'

Pat stood up, walked over to her friend and put a liver-spotted hand on her shoulder in a gesture of comfort. 'It's all right, Mabel. Just tell them.'

Mabel breathed deeply and continued. 'Otto saw him too . . . only they said they'd have him and his dad locked up if he said anything.'

'Who did?'

There was a long silence.

'Otto's safe in America. Whatever it is, it can't hurt him now,' said Pat. 'What did you see?'

Mabel buried her head in her hands for a few seconds. Then she looked up.

'It was a Saturday so there was no school. I was playing outside and I saw Charlie and Belle going into one of the outbuildings – the old slaughterhouse they called it. Then I went into the village for a while and met up with Otto and when we came back we saw Miles with a wheelbarrow – there was something wrapped in old sacking inside it. Belle was with him and they were going towards the paddock. Otto asked what it was and Belle said it was none of our business.' She shuddered. 'And then she threatened to tell the policeman that Otto's dad was a spy if he didn't go away. She said she'd say she'd seen him signalling to ships and he'd be hanged as a traitor. It was all lies of course, but we knew that she was spiteful enough to do it.'

'What about Charlie?' Wesley was afraid he already knew the answer to that question but he felt he had to ask it anyway.

'I never saw him again after that. Belle told me and Otto to go away so we went back to the village. I think Otto was a bit shaken by what she'd said. After what he'd left behind in Germany I suppose he just wanted the quiet life.'

'It could have been an animal in the wheelbarrow,' said Pat. 'It must have been an animal.'

Mabel shook her head. 'That's what we tried to tell ourselves, me and Otto. That's what I've been telling myself ever since. Until I read in Pat's paper that they'd found some child's bones.' She looked up at Wesley. She looked like a woman who'd just seen a vision of hell.

'That's why you never saw Charlie again,' said Pat quietly, putting her arm around Mabel's shoulder and giving her a comforting hug.

Children who kill. It was something Wesley found difficult to contemplate and as he and Rachel drove back to Neston in the fine misty rain, neither of them spoke. Even when they reached the police station they walked to the incident room in silence.

Miles's accomplice, Belle, might still be alive somewhere. Had it been a deliberate act, Wesley wondered. Or had Charlie's death been an accident and they'd panicked and attempted to cover up what had happened? Then he

313

remembered the cut marks Colin had found on the bones and the whole scenario changed.

Somehow Miles had drawn Belle and Charlie into his dark and gruesome world – he had passed on the legacy of his twisted search for knowledge to a pair of young apprentices. And it was Wesley's job to find out the truth.

When he reached the incident room Gerry Heffernan was sitting at his desk, the file on James Dalcott's murder open on the desk in front of him. Wesley saw that he was flicking through it, deep in thought, and when he reached the crime scene pictures he stopped to stare at the images of the dead man, his face solemn.

Wesley sat down at the other side of the boss's desk with a heavy sigh. At least he had one piece of good news to impart. 'I've found Mabel Cleary.'

Gerry looked up. 'Good. You told the daughter yet?'

Wesley pulled a face. 'To tell the truth I think Mabel's come down here to get away from her. Let's just let her know her mum's safe and give Mabel a few more days of freedom, eh?'

Gerry touched the side of his nose. 'I get the picture.'

'And I think I've solved the case of the child's bones at Tailors Court. You're not going to believe this.'

'Let me guess. It was that Miles character.'

Wesley nodded. 'That's right. And it seems that a girl called Belle was involved as well. Mabel said she saw her with Miles on the day Charlie disappeared and he was taking something towards the paddock in a wheelbarrow. This was around the time a kid called Charlie – who was Belle's cousin incidentally – went missing and was never seen again. Shortly after this Miles left to rejoin his unit. There was another witness too – Otto Kramer, a German

314

Jewish boy from the village whose father managed to get the pair of them out of danger just in time.' He paused. 'Belle threatened to tell the authorities that his dad was really a spy if he said anything.'

Gerry raised his eyebrows. 'The innocence of child-hood, eh? And we think today's youth's bad. I wonder where this Belle is now?'

Wesley shrugged his shoulders. 'I'm still working on that one but apparently Otto Kramer's alive and well and living in the States. Pat's been in touch with him. Any developments in the Dalcott case?'

'I've got a nasty feeling that we've hit a bit of a brick wall on this one, Wes,' said Gerry despondently. 'I've sent someone over to have another word with the not-so-griev-ing widow and to ask Carl Utley some more questions but apart from that . . . And we've drawn a blank with Syd and Brian. There's no evidence that either of them has fired a gun in the past few weeks, if ever. And Brian swears blind that he saw an elderly person visiting the house at around the right time. He said he only caught a glimpse so the description's not much use. He couldn't even be absolutely sure of the sex.'

'Right then,' Wesley said, organising his thoughts. 'I'll make a start on tracing Belle. Unfortunately, Mabel and Pat couldn't remember her surname.' He looked at his watch. 'Pat gave me Otto Kramer's number in the States but he might not be up yet. I'll try him later.'

Wesley was keen to get the Tailors Court case tied up so he could give James Dalcott his full attention and he spent a few minutes in thought, contemplating his next move.

Then he had an idea. He took a local telephone direc-tory from the shelves at the end of the office and looked up

315

the number of Tradington Primary School. After a short conversation with the head teacher, he looked around and saw that Rachel was leaning over Nick Tarnaby's desk pointing something out on the computer screen.

Wesley walked over to them slowly and Rachel straightened herself up. 'Feel like going back to school?'

'School?' She looked at him enquiringly.

'I'll tell you about it on the way.'

Half an hour later they were sitting in the headteacher's office sipping tea from a couple of mugs designed to celebrate the school's centenary.

The head herself was a small round woman with curly brown hair who looked rather like a child's drawing. A yellowing book lay open in front of her and she turned the pages proudly. The entire history of Tradington Primary was contained in these pages, she told them. The school log book contained the details of all the evacuees who had joined them in the 1940s to escape the dangers of the big cities. Some had gone back home after a while, of course – their parents missed them or decided for some reason that they'd be better off with the family. Others had stayed for the duration. Some had even returned to Devon later in life and settled. For some it had been a happy time, their first experience of the countryside and its freedoms. Others, she said ominously, hadn't fared so well: they had been homesick or been billeted with unwelcoming families. But this wasn't the sort of thing the school log book recorded.

The head teacher looked at Wesley, curious. 'Could you tell me why you're so interested in our evacuees? It seems rather strange.'

Wesley told her about the child's skeleton and the possibility that some of the children evacuated to Tradington might be important witnesses. This seemed to satisfy the woman's curiosity and, to Wesley's surprise, she produced a box from a low drawer. Inside the box were several class photographs swathed in tissue paper – the school's treasures.

The head selected a black and white group photo of around a dozen children aged between five and eleven and passed it to Wesley. The children wore the wartime childhood uniform of hand-knitted woollies, knee-high socks and sensible shoes; shorts, grey shirts and ties for the boys and faded floral frocks for the girls. Wesley turned the photograph over and the handwritten legend on the back told him that these were the evacuees of September 1943. There were names there too: Mabel Fallon smiled shyly at the camera, her mousey curls held back with a hair slide. Belle Haslem was blonde and chocolate-box pretty which made Wesley think how easily looks could deceive. And at the end of the row was pale little Charlie Haslem who had fair curls and the look of a sickly child. These were the children of Tailors Court and somehow they looked just as Wesley had imagined. Pat, of course, had arrived some months after this picture was taken but on the back row stood a dark, intelligent-looking boy by the name of Otto Kramer – now Professor Otto Kramer.

'May I keep this?' he asked the head teacher.

But he could see from the look of horror on her face that she wasn't happy. 'Well, if . . .'

But Wesley took pity on her. 'I suppose a photocopy of both sides would do. And if I could have a copy of any pages in the school log that mention the evacuees . . .' He gave her an expectant smile.

The woman looked relieved. 'Of course, Inspector. I'll get that done for you right away.' She disappeared into the outer office where the school secretary was working, leaving Wesley and Rachel alone.

Wesley sat, staring ahead. He'd just heard or read something that changed everything but he couldn't think what it was.

'Something the matter?' Rachel asked.

'I don't know.'

'Is it something about the photograph?'

Wesley shook his head in frustration. Perhaps if he looked at the picture again . . .

He had to exercise a great deal of self-control not to grab the picture when the head teacher returned. He took the copy politely and thanked her for her cooperation. Before they left she tried to extract a promise that a community policeman would come and talk to the children but Wesley gave her his best apologetic smile and said it wasn't his department – although he furnished her with the appropriate phone number and said to mention Gerry Heffernan's name. He felt she deserved a bit of preferential treatment.

He let Rachel drive and he sat in the passenger seat staring at the photograph and the names of the children.

Rachel had just set off when he asked her to make a detour to James Dalcott's house because there was something he wanted to check.

Rachel didn't say a word. It was only a quarter of a mile to Dalcott's place and when she parked neatly at their destination, she turned to him.

'Well?' she said.

Wesley touched her arm. 'I'm just going to check out

318

something on Dalcott's family tree. It's still in the house. Are you coming in with me or are you going to wait here?'

Rachel grinned. 'I'd better come in and keep an eye on you, after what happened last time.'

The lead-grey sky was already darkening as they walked slowly up James Dalcott's garden path. There was a constable on duty at the door. Since the break-in, Gerry was determined that the intruder couldn't try again. Wesley nodded to the officer – the sort people mean when they say the policemen are getting younger – and asked him to open up.

As he stepped over the threshold he was glad of Rachel's company. When he'd been there alone he'd almost felt the presence of the murdered man; almost felt Dalcott's shock and terror as he'd realised that death had come visiting unexpectedly.

Putting this thought from his mind, he marched straight for the drawing room and found the folder containing Dalcott's family tree lying in the bureau. Wesley took it out and unfolded it carefully.

There are some moments – Wesley's mother had always called them 'eureka' moments – when everything begins to slot into place, and this was one of them. He was hardly aware of Rachel standing behind him looking over his shoulder as he whispered a triumphant 'yes'.

'Found something?'

He spread the sheet of paper out in front of him. 'Look at the maiden name of James Dalcott's birth mother – the woman his father allegedly strangled because she'd been unfaithful.

'Haslem. So?'

'The school photograph has the children's names

inscribed on the back. The evacuee Belle's surname was Haslem too. She was the cousin of Charlie, the child who disappeared – and according to Mabel, she might have had something to do with it.'

'Belle Haslem. And Dalcott's mother was an Isabelle Haslem. It must be the same person.'

'So she's the link between the two murders – the child's and Dalcott's – and she disappeared off the radar after the war only to reappear again as a teacher who married a local GP much older than herself.'

'Why should anyone want to kill James Dalcott over something his murdered mother may or may not have done when she was a kid?'

Wesley's excitement began to drain away. He had been so sure he'd found the answer but now Rachel's practicality was starting to make him doubt his own instincts. Gerry Heffernan had always been a devout believer in following your hunches. But was he right in this instance? Was Wesley reading too much into this unexpected connection between his two cases?

'Let's get back to the incident room,' he said, tidying the contents of Dalcott's family tree folder and tucking it underneath his arm. 'I want to show this to Gerry.'

CHAPTER 13

Transcript of recording made by Mrs Mabel Cleary
(née Fallon) – Home Counties Library Service Living
History Project: Reminiscences of a wartime evacuee.

*Mary was spending more and more time at Gorfleet Farm
and I hardly saw her. I missed her and I hated being on my
own with Belle. When the Americans arrived at the end of
1943 it was all very exciting. They were doing something
very hush hush down in Bereton, so everyone said, and all
the people from round about were sent away from their
homes – just had to pack up all their belongings and get out.
Looking back it must have been awful for them.*

*Then another girl called Pat came and things seemed OK
again. We used to follow the Yanks about whenever we saw
them and they always had a smile for us kids when they
stopped in their jeeps. They were very generous with what
they called candy and they had this friendly way of talking.*

We thought they were the best thing ever and they certainly took our minds off Mr Hilton's stories and Tailors Court. Belle had been really quiet since Charlie left and she wasn't even nasty to Pat which quite surprised me.

We never saw old Mrs Jannings much after Miles left because she took to her bed permanently and Miles's new wife, Esther, ruled the roost. When the telegram arrived saying that Miles was missing in action, Esther didn't seem particularly upset. She never took much notice of us evacuees. We were left to run wild. And some of us ran wilder than others.

We'd never heard any more of Charlie and Belle refused to mention his name. Belle hardly talked to me and Pat. But we didn't mind because now we had each other.

Roz Dalcott said goodbye to her customers – a middle-aged couple down in Tradmouth for a winter break – with a businesslike smile as they left the gallery. Like others they'd stared for a few moments at Harry's work and then moved on to something more cheerful. Perhaps Tradmouth was the wrong place for his sort of art. But she wasn't sure whether she could face a move to London. In fact the very idea made her feel a little sick. Perhaps she was the dull provincial type after all, she thought with a sigh as she began to tidy her desk – not that it needed tidying but it was something to do. With the baby on the way – and her estranged husband's violent death – everything had changed. And that nosy young copper wasting half an hour of her time this morning asking more pointless questions hadn't done much to help her mood either.

The urgent drone of the telephone on her desk made her jump. She pushed her hair back off her face and picked up the receiver. 'Trad Itions Gallery, Tradmouth. Roz Dalcott speaking. Can I help you?'

'Mrs Dalcott? This is Green and Talbot, the late Dr Dalcott's solicitors.' It was difficult to tell if the voice was male or female. She pressed the receiver to her ear and listened carefully. 'We've been going through our files and it seems that Dr James Dalcott left a sealed envelope with us shortly before his death and, as you're still legally his wife, it was thought it should be passed to you. It was misplaced, I'm afraid – put in a pile ready for filing – so I'm afraid we've only just found it. In the circumstances would you like me to let the police know or . . .?'

'No,' she said quickly. She could almost sense the caller's surprise on the other end of the line. 'No. It might be personal. I'd like to have a look at it first if that's OK?'

There was a short pause. 'Certainly, Mrs Dalcott. When would be convenient?'

She paused for a while to give the impression she was consulting a diary. She didn't want anyone to think she had too much time on her hands. 'Would later this afternoon be all right? About four-thirty?'

Once the arrangement had been made Roz Dalcott put the receiver back in its cradle and placed a protective hand on her abdomen.

Gerry Heffernan studied the school photograph and Dalcott's family tree. Wesley was glad to see that there was no trace of doubt on his face.

'It can't be a coincidence, Wes,' he said. 'But I think we've only got half the story. We need to find out more about what really happened to Isabelle Haslem.'

'We know what happened to her. Her husband strangled

her because she was playing away from home.' Wesley thought for a few moments. 'But Clipton always denied murdering her. Even at his execution his last words were "I didn't do it". And I'm finding it difficult to trace the locum, Liam Cheshlare – the one on the photograph I found at Dalcott's house. He was one of the main prosecution witnesses.' He paused. 'I'm going to talk to the nanny who found the body – she's due back from holiday today. She lives in Looe and I've asked Trish to keep trying her phone number. But I really want to speak to her face to face – it's only about an hour's drive.'

Gerry leaned back in his chair, an impish grin on his face. 'OK. I just fancy some fresh air and a trip out to Cornwall will do nicely. Pity the weather's not better. Have you spoken to Otto Kramer yet? You got his number from Pat, didn't you?'

Wesley performed a swift calculation in his head. Where Kramer lived was five hours behind the UK so he was bound to be up and about by now. He found the number, punched it out and waited. Eventually the phone was answered by a woman and when Wesley introduced himself and asked for Professor Kramer the answer was yes. He was in luck.

'Hello, Inspector Peterson. Otto Kramer speaking. How may I help you?' said a deep transatlantic voice that sounded surprisingly youthful. In Wesley's imagination he was speaking to a slightly older version of the dark-haired boy in the school photograph but he knew Kramer was in his seventies and probably suffering all the usual indignities of age.

Otto Kramer sounded interested rather than wary as Wesley gave a brief outline of the situation, wishing he could see the man's expression. When he'd finished there was a long silence.

'Hello, Professor. Are you still there?'

'Yeah. It's just a bit of a shock, that's all.'

'I know. And I'm sorry to rake it all up again. It must have been a difficult time for you and your father.'

There was another silence. 'Yeah. We were the only members of the family to escape from the Nazis. My mom and my sisters, they –' His voice cracked with emotion. 'They were taken to Belsen and . . .'

Wesley looked up and saw that Gerry was watching him. He turned away. 'I'm sorry' was all he could think of to say but it seemed so inadequate.

He heard Kramer sigh. 'Life goes on, I guess. So what is it you want to know, Inspector?'

'A lady called Pat Beswick gave me your number.'

'I've been in touch with Pat by e-mail. How is she?'

'She seems very well. As I said, we're investigating the murder of a local doctor – name of James Dalcott. We've discovered that his mother was one of your fellow evacuees – she lived at Tailors Court and her name was Belle Haslem. She had a cousin called Charlie who apparently disappeared in 1943. You remember a girl called Mabel Fallon at Tailors Court?'

'Sure. I remember Mabel. When Pat arrived they became great buddies.'

'Mabel told us you were with her when she saw Belle and a man called Miles Jannings behaving suspiciously. This was around the time Charlie Haslem vanished.'

'That's right,' Kramer said tentatively. 'I don't remember Mabel being with me – although it was a long time ago. But I certainly saw them with a wheelbarrow. There was something in it, something heavy.'

'A body?'

There was a moment of horrified hesitation. 'I never thought it was anything like that at the time. The place was full of heavy stuff. Sacks of feed and . . .'

'I believe Belle Haslem made certain threats to make sure you kept the information to yourself.'

There was another silence. 'If you've talked to Mabel, then you'll know what Belle was like.'

'Yes. But I wondered whether you could tell us anything more. Did you have much to do with Belle or Charlie?'

'I knew them but I can't say I had much to do with them. Belle wasn't the friendliest of kids and I recall that Charlie was more interested in hanging out with that soldier guy from the house than in mixing with the rest of us.'

'Miles Jannings?'

'Yeah, that's right.'

'Did Belle hang round with Miles too?'

'Sometimes. Knowing her, she probably thought he'd be useful to her in some way. She was like that.'

'Nobody seems to have a good word for Belle.'

'No,' was the enigmatic reply.

'She was murdered in 1957. Her husband was convicted and hanged.'

Wesley couldn't quite make out the reply but it sounded something like 'It doesn't surprise me.' But then if Belle had threatened and bullied the young refugee, the news of her death would hardly come as an unwelcome shock.

'What can you tell me about Charlie?'

When he answered he sounded as though he was choosing his words carefully. 'I remember he was an odd kid. He caught this field mouse once and he started killing it, very slowly. In the end I snatched it from him and put the poor thing out of its misery. I used to hear that he did things to other animals. I tended to keep well away from him.'

'Of course,' said Wesley with feeling. 'Had he any distinguishing features? Anything unusual about him?'

'Come now, Inspector.' Wesley could hear a smile in Kramer's voice. 'It was a long time ago. He didn't have two heads or anything – he was just an ordinary kid. I remember he had curly blond hair – a bit girly-looking, I guess.'

'What happened when Charlie vanished?'

'I'm not sure, to tell the truth. One day he was there and the next he wasn't. Belle said he'd been found another billet.'

'Did you ever think that the thing Miles was carrying in the wheelbarrow could have been Charlie's body?'

Wesley heard a sigh on the other end of the line. 'I didn't think so at the time. And I was a refugee, Inspector. When you're in that situation you learn not to ask too many awkward questions – especially when someone threatens to tell lies about you. I had no reason to disbelieve Belle when she said Charlie had left the village and I didn't make waves.'

'Just one more thing, Professor. Did you hear anyone talking about a man called Simon Garchard who'd owned Tailors Court back in the sixteenth century?'

'Now that I do know about.' Wesley could almost feel the relief at the change of subject. 'The man we were billeted with was a local historian. He told us all about Simon Garchard – my father was a doctor, of course, so he thought he'd be interested.'

'Did you share the story with your school friends?'

The professor thought for a moment. 'Yeah. I remember it gave me some cachet with my classmates.'

'I presume Belle heard the story?'

'She used to ask me all sorts of questions about it, her and the other kids. I admit I enjoyed scaring them with it. Body snatchers, murder and dissections – kids just love that sort of thing, don't they?'

'I know what you mean. Did you ever go up into the attic room?'

'Simon's workshop – that's what Mr Hilton called it. I went up there once but Miles caught us and went berserk. I never tried to go up there again, I can tell you.'

'Thank you, Professor. You've been very helpful.' After a further exchange of pleasantries, he put the receiver down. Perhaps he was getting his hopes up. Perhaps Charlie Haslem and the buried child at Tailors Court had nothing to do with Isabelle Clipton's death. Perhaps George Clipton, the cuckolded husband, had been guilty after all and he was seeing things that weren't there. Gerry Heffernan had always claimed that an over-active imagination was one of his failings.

He was about to make for Gerry's desk to tell him about his conversation with Otto Kramer when Trish waylaid him. She'd established contact with Miss Buchanan who'd just returned from Austria. She was in the process of unpacking so she'd be in for the rest of the day and she'd be delighted to talk to the police any time. Trish hadn't told her about Dr Dalcott's death. It was something that would be better said face to face.

When he arrived at the DCI's desk, Gerry Heffernan raised a hand in greeting. He looked like a man with a lot on his mind.

'You ready to visit Nanny Buchanan? Trish says she'll be in for the rest of the day.'

Gerry stood up wearily, stretching with his hands in the

328

small of his back. 'OK, Wes, let's go and see Nanny. But I bet you a tenner we'll hit a dead end.'

Wesley picked up his coat and waited while Gerry put his on, zipping it to the neck and saying that his lady friend Joyce had warned him to wrap up warm. Wesley had to smile to himself – Gerry, the scourge of Chief Superintendent Nutter, was a big softy when it came to the women in his life.

Even though the drive to Looe only took an hour it seemed long and arduous. As they drove towards Plymouth the sky was a uniform battleship grey and the normally lovely land-scape looked bleak and desolate. The favourable weather forecast proved to be a work of fiction and when the rain started Wesley drove on, headlights blazing and windscreen wipers on full. He was glad of the car heater. It looked cold out there.

After they'd passed through the outskirts of Plymouth and crossed the Tamar bridge into Cornwall, Wesley suddenly felt a little lighter, more optimistic. But as he parked up, he could see the dark, churning sea lapping angrily against the harbour wall and, once he was out of the car, the wind bit through his coat and the rain felt icy on his face.

'Looks a bit rough out there,' Gerry commented as he shivered.

Wesley didn't answer. He kept his head down and rushed down the narrow lane towards Nanny Buchanan's address – a tiny stone cottage with leaded windows and a low door that led straight onto the street. He was relieved to see a welcoming glow of light in the window.

'Come in, gentlemen,' Miss Buchanan said as soon as she opened the door. 'You must be frozen. Cup of tea?'

This was exactly what both men needed. They took their coats off as invited – Nanny told them sternly that if they didn't, they wouldn't feel the benefit when they went out again – and settled down by a roaring fire. There was no sign of unpacking and Wesley suspected it would have been dealt with already, swiftly and efficiently.

The first thing that struck Wesley about Enid Buchanan was her energy. She might be in her late seventies but she was rarely still, rushing to and fro to fetch tea and biscuits, making sure her guests were comfortable and rearranging any object she considered out of place as she went. She had short grey hair, cut for practicality rather than glamour, and intelligent eyes that missed nothing.

'I've been very lucky, gentlemen,' she began as she finally settled in an armchair by the fire. 'As soon as I retired from one career, I was asked to share my experience with a new generation, as they put it, and appear on television.' Her lips turned upwards in a conspiratorial grin. 'Actually one of my children – I mean the children I looked after; I always think of them as my own, you see – is now a senior TV producer and he was kind enough to think of me. Anyway that led to the publishing deal and, as you see, I'm still making myself useful. Nobody could ask for more, really, could they?' She smiled and Wesley noted that she had a wide gap between her two front teeth: some said it was a sign of good luck.

'They certainly couldn't, love,' Gerry said with what sounded like admiration.

'Now what is it you want to ask me? I must admit that my time with the Cliptons wasn't the happiest period in my life. The little boy, James, was a sweet wee thing but the mother . . . Of course when James came here I chose my words carefully. I didn't want him to spend the rest of his life

330

knowing that his mother couldn't give tuppence for him, did I?'

'James Dalcott came to see you?'

'Yes. It was just before I went to Austria. We had a lovely long chat. He seemed a nice man and I was happy he'd turned out so well after what he'd been through. Of course he asked me all about his mother's death and I answered his questions to the best of my ability. He's promised to visit me again when I returned from Austria.'

Wesley and Gerry looked at each other. She'd been away so she hadn't heard the news and it was up to them to break it. After Gerry told her as gently as he could, Enid Buchanan sat for a while, her hands folded neatly on her lap. Then she closed her eyes for a moment as if in prayer, and when she opened them she gave a small shudder. 'Have you any idea who killed him?'

'We're hoping you might be able to help us.'

'Of course. If I can.'

'What can you tell us about Isabelle Clipton?'

'I take it you've read the transcripts of her husband's trial?'

Wesley nodded.

'Well, I feel there's little I can add. She was a selfish young woman; only concerned with her own pleasures and not in the least bit interested in poor little James. I was very relieved when the Dalcotts offered to adopt him. Mrs Dalcott was Dr Clipton's sister. She was a very nice woman and she couldn't have children of her own.'

'It worked out well all round,' said Gerry.

'Yes. It did. Of course the reflected notoriety didn't do me any good at first but, after an awkward couple of months, I managed to obtain a new post with a family up in

Yorkshire – two lovely little girls.' The memory made her smile again.

'Have you kept any photographs of your time at the Cliptons?' Wesley asked.

Miss Buchanan stood up and walked over to a large bureau in the corner of the room; rather like the one he'd seen in Dr Dalcott's house. The drawers were filled with photograph albums. From the ease with which she found the right one, Wesley suspected they were all arranged carefully in date order – all her families; a life of being mother to other women's children.

She carried the open album over to the two detectives and sat down.

'This is James. He was a very calm baby.' She looked straight at Wesley. 'You think these pictures might help find his killer?'

'It is possible that his death's connected to something in his mother's past, yes.'

Miss Buchanan nodded and continued. 'This is Mrs Clipton with James.'

She pointed to a posed photograph of Isabelle Clipton, just recognisable as the adult Belle from the school photograph he'd seen. The child was sitting on her knee but she was holding him at arm's length and she didn't look comfortable in the situation. There was no love there, Wesley thought. Or perhaps he was just seeing what he wanted to see.

Miss Buchanan turned to another picture. Father and son this time. George Clipton was smiling and hugging the little boy sitting next to him. If anyone loved the child, it was his father. Wesley suddenly felt sad that George Clipton had never had the chance to watch his son grow up.

'What can you tell us about the locum, Dr Cheshlare?' Wesley asked, watching the retired nanny's face carefully.

Miss Buchanan frowned.

'You do remember him?'

'Oh yes, Inspector. I remember him all right.' The way she said the words made Wesley hopeful that she had something interesting to say.

'And?'

Miss Buchanan considered her reply for a few moments and cleared her throat. 'I'll tell you what I told James – he seemed very interested in Dr Cheshlare as well. Most of Dr Clipton's patients got on all right with him but on a couple of occasions there were . . .' She hesitated. 'How shall I put it? Murmurings.'

'There were complaints against him?'

She shook her head vigorously. 'Oh no, nothing as strong as that. It was just that he didn't seem very . . . well, in those days they would have said he didn't have a very good bedside manner. He wasn't a good listener, I'm told. Now I'm not saying that he wasn't dedicated. He was always reading medical text books. It was just that he didn't have much empathy with people. Not like Dr Clipton – he was very popular.'

'What was Cheshlare's relationship with Mrs Clipton?'

Miss Buchanan looked up sharply. 'Well, I don't think they were up to any hanky panky if that's what you mean. I made that quite clear to James too. In fact I believe they were related – I think that's how he got the post.'

Wesley and Gerry looked at each other. This was something new.

'You don't know how they were related?'

'I'm sorry, I don't.' She picked up the album again and

333

started to flick through the pages. 'Here he is,' she said, handing it to Wesley. 'That's Dr Cheshlare with Dr Clipton.'

Wesley studied the photograph. It was rather clearer than the one he'd already seen and once again he had a strong sense that he had seen Dr Cheshlare somewhere before, although he had no idea where or under what circumstances. He handed the picture to Gerry who stared at it intently.

'Did Dr Cheshlare tell you anything about himself?' Wesley asked.

'He never said much to me. He wasn't one for pleasantries, although he could be quite charming if he wanted to be. I wasn't any use to him, you see. I was only the nanny.' She said the words as a matter of fact without any resentment.

'Where did he live?'

'In a rented cottage about fifty yards from the surgery.'

'Did he mix with the Cliptons socially?'

Miss Buchanan considered the question. 'I saw him a few times talking to Mrs Clipton. And I had the impression they weren't just passing the time of day.'

Wesley leaned forward. 'What do you mean?'

'They'd sometimes whisper in corners as though they were sharing a secret. But don't ask me what it was. If they were related perhaps it was a family matter.' She hesitated. 'However, I'll tell you one thing. Dr Cheshlare was a liar.'

'How do you mean, love?' said Gerry.

Both men sat perfectly still, awaiting the reply.

'He lied about which hospital he'd trained at. He said he studied at Bart's in London. I trained as a nurse there and I never came across him. I thought I'd test him one day so I asked him if he remembered a senior surgeon there. He said he remembered him well and he agreed with me when I said what an old tyrant he was.' A mischievous grin spread across her face. 'Trouble is, I'd made the name up. There was no such surgeon. He'd never been at Bart's in his life.'

'So you're saying he was an impostor?'

'Like I said, he spent a lot of time with those text books – reading up on the job, I reckon. They say if you have enough confidence and you look the part, you can get away with anything, don't they?'

'So you think he might not have been a qualified doctor at all?'

The answer was a shrug.

'Did you mention your suspicions to anyone? Dr Clipton maybe?'

Miss Buchanan took a deep breath. 'I did as a matter of fact. But he said Dr Cheshlare was a relative of his wife's and he trusted him implicitly. He said no patient had ever complained about him and that he'd probably only agreed with me out of politeness.'

'Did you take the matter any further?'

She shook her head. 'Shortly afterwards Mrs Clipton was murdered and all hell broke loose, as they say.'

'Where was Dr Cheshlare when she was murdered?' Wesley asked.

'I said all this in court. When I found the body and I couldn't find Dr Clipton, I dashed to Dr Cheshlare's cottage. He'd just had his evening meal – I could see the dishes on the draining board. And I think he must have been preparing for bed because he was in his dressing gown.'

There was a long silence before Wesley spoke again. 'The victim was strangled but her face had also been disfigured. The murderer would have had blood on his clothes.'

'Yes. There was blood on Dr Clipton's clothes – but while I was at Dr Cheshlare's he said he went looking for his wife and when he found her he carried her upstairs and put her on the bed. He would have got blood on him then, of course. However, there was lots of other evidence against him, you know. And he had a very good motive, didn't he? That wife of his led him a merry dance and he just snapped.'

Enid Buchanan looked worried. After years of certainty she'd now been presented with the dreadful possibility that her evidence had helped to send an innocent man to the gallows.

'You say Cheshlare was wearing his dressing gown when you called,' said Gerry. 'But what if, rather than fancying an early night, he'd got undressed because he was covered in blood?'

'But why would he do it? He had nothing against Mrs Clipton.' Miss Buchanan straightened her back. 'If he was going to kill anyone because they found out he was a fraud, it would have been me.'

She had a point, Wesley thought.

'And besides, I don't think Dr Cheshlare was alone when I called.'

'Really?'

'I saw a woman's blouse draped over the back of one of the chairs – at least it looked like a woman's blouse. I think he was – entertaining. That would explain why he seemed so flustered, of course.'

'But you don't know who the woman was?'

She shook her head. 'Mind you there were those who said . . .'

'Said what?'

336

She pressed her lips together. 'Well, it was just gossip and I never repeat gossip.'

'Oh, I think it's OK in this case, love,' Gerry piped up. 'There's been many a good conviction secured by a good bit of gossip.'

Miss Buchanan nodded. 'Well, a woman was seen leaving his house on more than one occasion and one of the girls who cleaned for him said he had a secret wardrobe full of women's clothes. She reckoned he had a secret mistress but nobody ever saw her, as far as I know.'

'They might have been his,' Wesley said tentatively, glancing at Gerry. 'He might have enjoyed dressing up.'

'Anything's possible, I suppose,' she said, a smile playing on her lips. 'But it's not something that anyone considered at the time.'

'Did you mention this to James?'

She thought for a moment. 'I think I told him more or less everything I've told you. Although I was careful to use a certain amount of tact. I mean, they were his parents after all.'

Wesley began to stare at the picture of Cheshlare again. There was definitely something familiar about the man, if only he could think what it was. Or maybe it was his imagination. 'Do you mind if we borrow this picture? Our Forensic people might be able to enhance the image. We'll let you have it back.'

'Of course, Inspector. Please take it.'

Wesley took a plastic evidence bag from his pocket and carefully slipped the photograph inside.

'In fact I had a much better picture of Dr Cheshlare. I've always liked taking photographs – memories of people I've met. I don't think he knew I was taking it but anyway, I showed it to James and he asked if he could borrow it.'

'And did he?'

'Yes. I said he could keep it. Have you found it?'

'Was it one of him with the Cliptons?'

'No. It was just of Dr Cheshlare.'

'In that case we haven't found it,' said Wesley. 'Thank you, Miss Buchanan,' he said as he stood up to go, anxious to get the photo to the lab. Perhaps his luck would be in this time: perhaps this picture of Cheshlare was the key to the whole thing.

When Wesley's mobile began to ring, he was on the road. Gerry answered it and Wesley tried to make sense of the one-sided conversation without much success.

When he'd finished Gerry ended the call. 'Well, that's a turn up,' he said with a puzzled frown.

'What is?'

'You know you thought the kid in the grave must be Charlie – Isabelle's cousin who vanished? That was the head teacher of Tradington Primary. She's been doing a bit of research – ringing round other schools and that. Anyway, she said a Charlie Haslem enrolled at Stokeworthy County Primary School around the time he disappeared from Tailors Court. Belle told the truth. He did change his billet. Apparently it was quite common back then. Charlie's not our corpse.'

'So who is?'

Gerry shook his head. 'No idea. We'll have to do some more digging in the old missing persons records.'

Wesley drove on, saying nothing for a while. Then Gerry broke the silence.

'So if Charlie didn't die, and Nanny Buchanan's right about Dr Cheshlare being Isabelle's cousin . . .'

'Cheshlare and Charlie Haslem could be the same person.'

'Why the change of name?'

'Perhaps there was something in his past he wanted to hide.' Wesley suddenly gave a smile of realisation. 'Charlie Haslem – Liam Cheshlare. It's an anagram. Why didn't I see it before?'

'You weren't looking for it, that's why.'

'And he'd lied to Miss Buchanan about training at Bart's.'

'I've been thinking,' Gerry said. 'Why was Isabelle Clipton's face bashed in?'

'Maybe the victim wasn't Isabelle Clipton. Maybe they got it all wrong back then and she's still around. Maybe the dead woman was Cheshlare's mysterious girlfriend.'

Neither man said much until they reached the incident room. If Wesley was wrong, it would be back to square one.

*

Neil Watson had just been back to Tailors Court to bring the Persimmons up to date with his findings, which was really an excuse to have another look at the wall paintings in the upstairs room. He'd taken a colleague who was doing a doctorate in medieval and Tudor wall paintings along with him but he'd hurried back to Exeter for some unspecified social event. So when Nuala Johns's call came Neil was at a loose end and was only too glad to meet up with her at the White Horse.

Neil bought the drinks – a half for himself and a vodka and tonic for Nuala – and joined her at the table.

She leaned forward and touched his hand gently, a gossamer brush of skin against skin. 'I really need some help with my article – these skeletons at Tailors Court. I'm going for the early medical experiments angle. Body snatching and dissection. How the pioneers of medicine had to break taboos and go to extreme lengths to push the boundaries of knowledge. Does that sound sufficiently sexy to you?'

'Sounds fine,' he said before taking a long drink. 'When the bones have been examined, the vicar's going to rebury them in the churchyard.'

'Now that would make a great photo opportunity,' Nuala said with a satisfied smile on her face.

There was a pause in the conversation and Neil sensed that there was something on Nuala's mind; something that didn't concern archaeology.

'I wanted to see Wesley but I can't get hold of him. Any idea where he is?' She must have seen his expression of disappointment because her hand moved upwards to give his cheek a lingering touch. 'Not that you're second choice, of course, Neil.'

This woman was a flirt. But Neil was enjoying every minute, even though he had a strong suspicion that she was only using him to further her own ambitions and maybe get to Wesley.

'What did you want to see him about?'

'I've been talking to my gran. The police have been asking questions about the evacuees at Tailors Court so I'm going to try to trace them. I've got a friend who works for one of those probate researchers in London – he's used to tracing people who've disappeared into the wide blue yonder.'

'Good luck,' said Neil. His mobile phone began to ring and when he answered it he heard Annabel's voice on the other end of the line. 'I'm e-mailing you an extract from a book you might be interested in. It's out of print now but I came across a copy in the archives. It's a history of the village of Tradington by a man called Clifford Hilton.'

Neil thanked her and looked at Nuala who was watching him expectantly. 'Who was that?' she asked.

'Got to go,' he said mysteriously, enjoying her look of frustrated disappointment. Some people were just too nosy for their own good.

Roz Dalcott arrived at the offices of Green and Talbot, solicitors, just as they were about to close. She took the envelope from the receptionist then she left, closing the door carefully behind her, and stood on the pavement outside for a while, staring at the thick A4 envelope with her name on the front. *To be opened in the event of my death.*

She resisted the temptation to rip it open there and then and half walked, half ran back to her car, pulling her coat closely around her against the biting wind. After making herself comfortable in the driver's seat she flicked on the overhead light, unsealed the end of the envelope and pulled out three sheets of handwritten paper.

'*I'm hoping you won't be reading this,*' it began. '*But I've made certain discoveries in the course of my research into my family and I feel I must write them down here in order to clear my father's name. He died at the end of a hangman's rope but now I know he died an innocent man. I am leaving this with the solicitors in case I don't have the chance to complete my investigation and finally bring my mother's murderer to justice.*'

She read on, her heart sinking. James had been living in his own fantasy world, she thought as two photographs – one monochrome black and white, the other recent and coloured – fluttered out of the papers she was holding and landed on her knee. And what he'd written was surely quite impossible to prove one way or the other. She picked the photos up and looked at them. She recognised one of the faces although she'd only seen the person in question a

341

couple of times. But she had to acknowledge that the two people were certainly alike. However, if she went to the police, she might be making a fool of herself, and of James.

She turned one of the photographs over and saw that there were three names printed neatly on the back, one of which she knew but the other two were unfamiliar.

She made her way home and when she reached the flat she settled down on the sofa and read through the letter again several times. And each time the contents seemed less believable.

Perhaps, she thought, her estranged husband had been suffering from some sort of delusion brought on by the obsession he had with tracing his forebears. Or perhaps he'd been a little mad.

Harry wasn't there, which was a disappointment because she felt she needed to confide in someone. But she knew it would be better to talk to someone who'd known James well – someone who would confirm that what he claimed was nonsense.

She went through the possibilities. There were the other doctors in the practice – Dr Graham and Dr Fitzgerald – but she didn't like Keith Graham and she knew Maritia Fitzgerald's brother was one of the detectives in charge of catching James's killer so it might be inappropriate to take her into her confidence. But Evonne Arlis had been close to James and she was the sympathetic sort. She looked up Evonne's number, picked up the phone and dialled but there was no answer.

She put down the receiver and looked for the card Inspector Peterson had given her with his direct number at Neston Police Station. She began to dial but she stopped halfway through. She needed proof before she made it official.

342

CHAPTER 14

Transcript of recording made by Mrs Mabel Cleary (née Fallon) – Home Counties Library Service Living History Project: Reminiscences of a wartime evacuee.

The Yanks all left in June 1944. D-Day. They'd been practising for it over at Bereton and some people said there'd been a terrible accident and a lot of them were killed. I remember hoping it wasn't true. I'd liked the Yanks and it did seem quiet and dull once they'd left.

It was Pat who went home first after the War was over – her mum was missing her, she said. We promised to always keep in touch and we did for a few years. Then life got in the way. I got married and had our Sandra and those days at Tailors Court seemed a long way off.

When I left Devon to go back to London Belle was still there. Someone – it might have been Otto Kramer – said she had nowhere else to go and it didn't really surprise me

343

that nobody wanted her. She was so pretty but she was really nasty. I once bit into a lovely red apple and found a maggot in it and I suppose Belle was a bit like that – nice on the outside but bad on the inside. I didn't care that I never heard of her again.

Nobody ever heard of Charlie again either and I sometimes wondered what had happened to him. But I don't suppose I'll ever find out now.

When Pat and I wrote to each other we never mentioned Belle and Charlie. Some things are best forgotten.

When the telephone on Wesley's desk began to ring he picked up the receiver, his inner pessimist telling him that whatever he was about to hear would probably add to his workload and put paid to an early escape.

For a few moments he heard a muffled conversation, as though the caller had covered the mouthpiece and was talking to someone else. Then a female voice asked whether she was speaking to Detective Inspector Peterson.

'Who's that?' he asked.

'It's Sister Packham from Ward B6 Morbay Hospital. We have a patient here – a Mrs Esther Jannings. She was admitted earlier today and she keeps asking to see you. Says she's got something important to tell you.'

Wesley took a deep breath. 'OK, Sister. I'll be over as soon as I can.' Just as he replaced the receiver he spotted Rachel entering the office with Paul Johnson, deep in conversation.

As soon as Rachel saw him she walked over to his desk. 'Anything new?'

'I've made rather an interesting discovery,' he said, printing two names on a spare sheet of paper. 'Notice anything? You too, Paul.'

344

Paul came and leaned over Rachel's shoulder. After a few seconds he smiled with recognition.

But Rachel still looked puzzled. 'What am I supposed to be looking at?'

Wesley's eyes met Paul's and they exchanged a conspiratorial smile. 'The names Charlie Haslem and Liam Cheshlare – they're anagrams. Clipton's locum was Isabelle's cousin – the one who was evacuated to Tailors Court.'

Rachel looked him in the eye. 'So he could still be around somewhere.'

All the names and faces involved in the case rushed through Wesley's mind. But no man he'd seen seemed to fit. Dr Welman or Oscar Powell at the Podingham Clinic perhaps. Or Keith Graham, the retired senior partner at Maritia's practice. He stared at the only photograph he had of Cheshlare – he could be Graham. It was possible. He'd arrived late at Maritia's dinner party. Was it possible that he'd just come from shooting James Dalcott? Or Dalcott's neighbour, Len Wetherall – he was around the right age. It seemed unlikely but, in the course of his police career, he'd known stranger things happen.

But he'd given his word to the Sister on Ward B6 that he'd visit Esther Jannings so it was a question he'd have to contemplate later. He asked Rachel to go with him to the hospital and she fetched her coat without a word.

The cold, rainy drive in the dark from Neston Police Station to Morbay Hospital took them through the village of Belsham, past the vicarage where Maritia and Mark lived. There was a light in the front room window – but then vicars tend to work a lot from home. He sat in the passenger seat while Rachel drove, his mind overloaded with possibilities, knowing that the solution was staring him in the face and if he made just one more connection, everything would come into focus.

It was Sister Packham herself who greeted them at the entrance to the ward. In a hushed voice she told them that Mrs Jannings's condition had deteriorated since they'd spoken on the phone. The tacit implication was that Esther Jannings hadn't got much longer to go in this life. But she still insisted on talking to Inspector Peterson. There was something on her conscience that she had to share before she went.

When they arrived at Esther Jannings's bedside in the small private room off the main ward, her eyes were closed and her hair was spread out on the blue hospital pillow like a steel wool cloud. But as soon as the Sister announced their arrival the eyes snapped open and a claw-like hand emerged from the bedclothes and made a feeble beckoning gesture. Wesley moved forward and sat down on the bed.

'What did you want to tell me, Mrs Jannings?' he said softly.

Her bony, liver-spotted hand fluttered towards him and he took it in his.

'There are things I did. Things I was scared of the police finding out.'

'What sort of things?'

'It was me that told them to bury him.'

Wesley looked round at Rachel. She was standing at the end of the bed, watching and listening in silence.

'I didn't know what they were doing. I honestly didn't know.' Esther's voice seemed stronger now, as though their presence had given her new power.

'Tell me,' Wesley said almost in a whisper.

'I was round at Tailors Court looking for Miles when I heard noises from the outhouse and I went in. He was lying there all cut open.'

'Who was?'

'And Belle had this look on her face. Go on, she was saying. Go on.'

'Why didn't you tell anyone?'

'I was scared my Miles would get the blame. Everyone used to talk about him and the experiments he did. I told him it was really all his fault showing things like that to children.'

'Whose body was it?'

'I don't know, just a boy. I didn't look closely. It was horrible. I thought if the body was never found they wouldn't blame my Miles. He'd promised to marry me, you see.'

'Who killed the boy, Esther?'

'He was such a pretty child: looked so innocent, like a little angel.'

'Who did it?'

There was a long silence and for a few terrible moments Wesley was afraid he wasn't going to learn the name. Then Esther spoke again. 'Charlie,' she whispered. 'Belle said Charlie killed him.'

'What happened to Charlie, Esther?'

'I found him another billet later that day, far away from Miles and that Belle. I said it was an emergency.' She paused to catch her breath and all Wesley could hear was the faint hissing from her oxygen mask. 'When he came to see me at Palm View I never recognised him, not till he told me who he was.'

Wesley looked at Rachel. 'He came to see you? When was this?'

347

'After they'd found the bones. I don't know how he knew I was there. He made me promise.'

'What did he make you promise?'

'Never to tell and I swore I wouldn't. But I can't go with that on my conscience. I can't.' There was panic in her eyes, as though she knew that time was short. 'When he came today I was scared. He went when I pressed the button to call the nurse but what if he comes back?'

'Can you describe Charlie? Please, Esther.'

She formed the word 'no' with her parched lips. Then her eyes suddenly closed and her whole wasted body seemed to go limp, like a puppet dropped by its operator.

'That's enough,' said a stern female voice from the door. Sister Packham was standing guard, ready to shepherd them out.

Wesley looked at the woman on the bed. He could hear her breathing. It was shallow and rattling. He said goodbye to her, even though he was sure she couldn't hear him.

'Has she had any other visitors today?' he asked the Sister as she led them out of the ward.

'Yes. A lady. But she didn't stay long.'

His heart began to beat faster. 'Can you describe her?'

The Sister took a deep breath and gave a detailed description, right down to the shoes and handbag. She was the sort who'd make an excellent witness. He took the photograph of Isabelle, George and Cheshlare out of his pocket.

'Can you take a look at this photograph? If you cover up the hair can you tell me if there's any resemblance to the woman who visited Mrs Jannings yesterday?'

The Sister took the picture and began to study it

348

intently, her hand shielding the subject's hair. Then she handed it back.

'There is a likeness. Are they related?'

Wesley thanked her and left.

It was a Friday evening and the traffic between Morbay and Neston was bad. But Wesley was too preoccupied with what he'd just learned from Sister Packham to feel the usual frustration of the jam-bound motorist.

When he reached the incident room he asked whether anything had come in for him before making for his desk and switching on his computer. He decided to check his e-mails and found that there was just one jewel amongst the routine dross.

Neil had forwarded something that Annabel had turned up for him. It was an extract from a book by Clifford Hilton, the local historian who had taken the Kramers in during the War, entitled *A Short History of Tradington*. Wesley settled back and began to read.

The dark history of Flesh Tailor's Court came to a head in 1595 when Simon Garchard was arrested and hanged for the murder of a maidservant, Annet Raine.

But two years later, John Raine, shipwright and father of Simon Garchard's alleged victim, gave the following testimony to the magistrate.

'Master Philip Tanner threatened that he would kill me and cut me to pieces if I spoke against him so I was afraid to tell the truth but now I desire to bear witness to his evil actions and I beg your lordship's indulgence. When my daughter, Annet, was maidservant in the household of Simon Garchard, a physician and caster of spells, Master Tanner served as apprentice. Against the laws of God and man, this Garchard defiled corpses he took from the churchyard.

349

Garchard was hanged for the wicked murder of my beloved daughter but at his trial he swore that he was innocent.

Rather he said that Philip Tanner, eager for fresh flesh to use for his hideous and unspeakable deeds, did strangle my daughter and defiled her dead corpse, cutting at her innards. I did not believe Master Garchard's words, thinking he desired only to shift the blame and avoid the noose and another servant, Elizabeth Ryde, told the jury that she too saw Garchard with blood on his hands when Annet met her death.

But I now know what Garchard said was the truth for Tanner boasted of this deed at his house in Tradmouth when I visited him last Candlemass and found him in his cups, drawing pictures on his wall of a most terrible nature. He said that Garchard had used the dead buried some days beneath the earth in such a way but Tanner had wanted a corpse that was fresh and warm. He performed his foul deed in the byre near to the house and left her poor mangled body to be found by servants, knowing Garchard would be blamed and the woman Elizabeth Ryde he threatened with death if she did not bear false witness against her master.

I was afraid to come forward, sir, because he threatened to cast a spell upon my wife who was sick with the dropsy. But now she is dead, my lord, so I can tell all.'

Tanner, who was operating as a physician in the port of Tradmouth, vehemently denied Raine's accusation, saying Raine bore him a grudge because of a long-standing quarrel and, as Elizabeth Ryde was by now dead, she could not give evidence so no charge was ever made. However, Tanner was said to have confessed to the crime on his deathbed, although we can never really know the truth of the matter.

When Wesley had finished reading he found himself wishing that the mystery of the Tailors Court skeletons was all he had to worry about. There were times when he envied Neil. He looked at his watch, wondering what time he'd get home.

Then his phone began to ring.

Harry Parker had returned to the flat after an afternoon spent in the Tradmouth Arms with a group of local fishermen, and when he'd found the place in silence he'd felt a little uneasy. Roz never went off like this without telling him. But then he discovered the note she'd left, saying she'd gone out and she wasn't sure when she'd be back. The vagueness of the message bothered him slightly, as did the fact that whenever he tried her mobile, it went straight to voice mail.

It was dark now and it was starting to blow a gale out there. On the way back from the pub he'd seen the boats pitching to and fro on the churning water and he didn't like to think of Roz driving in this sort of weather; not in her condition.

He switched the TV on and sat there for a while, hardly aware of what was happening on the screen. Roz was out there somewhere and he had a terrible feeling – a premonition almost – that she could be in some sort of danger.

At one time Harry Parker had hated the police with every fibre of his being but now, when it came down to it, he knew they might be the only ones who could help him. He picked up the phone and began to search for the card the inspector had left. He had just located it when suddenly he noticed a photograph lying on the table.

He picked it up and frowned. There were three names scribbled on the back – names he didn't recognise – and he was sure it hadn't been there when he'd left the flat for the Tradmouth Arms.

He flopped down in an armchair and sat there for a while, staring at the phone, going through his options. Roz might have gone to see a friend and return any moment. But on the other hand, the uneasy feeling that something was amiss was refusing to go away. He studied the card in his hand and reached for the phone.

When DI Peterson answered Harry could sense his impatience, as though he were in the middle of something important.

'Is there anything else?' the inspector asked once Harry had confided his worries. 'Anything at all, however trivial?'

'I found a photograph of a bloke – old-fashioned black-and-white one with three names on the back. I wondered if it could have anything to do with –'

'What are the names?'

When Harry told him Wesley thanked him and ended the call.

Roz Dalcott didn't much like driving down single-track Devon lanes in the dark and there were moments during her journey when she wondered just why she was doing it. James was dead and they'd been living apart anyway. But over the past days he had been on her mind a lot. He'd been a good man. Maybe he hadn't deserved the way she'd treated him. Perhaps it was her uneasy conscience that was making her continue the enquiries he hadn't had a chance to complete. James had wanted to know the truth about his father and she told herself that it would do no harm to do a bit of preliminary digging. If she discovered anything relevant – which was doubtful – she could tell the police later.

She found the place without much difficulty and parked

352

the car on the muddy verge outside the house. She clambered out of the driver's seat, her large belly making her movements clumsy. The house squatted behind the low hedge that separated it from the lane; a small, low building with a light on in the downstairs window. After locking the car – you couldn't be too careful, even in the middle of the Devon countryside – she walked slowly up the path and when she reached the door she hesitated, her hand hovering over the door bell. Was she doing the right thing? Probably not, but it was too late now to turn back now.

Roz rang the bell and waited for a while but there was no answer. She reached out her hand and gave the front door a tentative push. It yielded to her touch and her heart pounded as it creaked open slowly to reveal a neat hallway, with watercolours of local scenes on the walls and a rich Turkish rug on the floor. Something, curiosity perhaps, made her step inside, calling a nervous hello.

The front room door was open and a pool of warm light spilled out into the hall. She moved forward on tiptoe and crossed the threshold. But where she'd expected a cosy living room, she saw something quite different. This was a room without the normal comforts; a room filled with books and anatomical drawings like the ones she'd seen long ago in James's old university text books. It was a room lined with shelves and on these shelves stood jars containing unspeakable things: body parts and foetuses; eyeballs and brains all floating like jellyfish in the liquid that preserved them from decay. Roz stood there staring in horror and curiosity, then her hand went to her mouth as if to stifle a scream.

Now she knew it had been a mistake to come and her first and only instinct was to flee. But as she took a step towards the door, she heard a sound in the hallway. Thinking the house was empty had been another mistake. And she feared that it was a mistake that she was about to pay for.

By now the incident room was half empty. Gerry had told most of the team to go home and get some rest which was exactly what Wesley wished he was doing, but he couldn't help worrying about Roz Dalcott.

The nearest person was Nick Tarnaby who was sitting at his desk typing into his computer.

He asked him to call the number of the Podingham Clinic. 'Urgently.'

Nick's expression gave nothing away as he made the call and asked for the name Wesley had specified. After a few minutes he walked slowly over to Wesley's desk with a sheet of paper in his hand. 'Not there but I got the home address.'

Wesley took the paper from him and examined it. 'It might be nothing but I want to get over there as soon as possible and I think I might need some back-up.'

He began to move and Tarnaby followed him out of the building. As they reached the car park, he heard a familiar voice.

'I've been waiting for you.'

Nuala Johns was emerging from the shadows wearing a trench coat, fashionably short with the belt pulled tight to emphasise the slimness of her waist, and a pair of high-heeled black leather boots. She had the look of a glamorous female private eye but that was probably the intention. This was all Wesley needed.

'I rang Roz Dalcott to see if she'd give me an interview,' Nuala went on, 'but her husband said she wasn't in. He sounded worried so I put two and two together. Something's going on, isn't it?'

Wesley felt his fist clench. 'Look, Nuala, contact the press office. I can't tell you anything.' He turned once more to his car.

'Come on, Wesley, you can do better than that. What's going on?'

He swung round. 'I can't talk to you at the moment. Go through the proper channels.'

He clambered in behind the wheel and, with Tarnaby beside him, roared recklessly out onto the main road.

Roz recognised the tall woman framed in the doorway. She'd met her before at a drinks party the previous Christmas. She tried to smile. 'I'm so sorry. The door was open and I –'

'What are you doing here?' Marie Shallech's voice was quiet but Roz detected a hint of threat behind the words.

'I wanted to talk to you about James. My late husband. You worked with him at the Podingham. Do you remember, we met at . . .'

Roz realised she'd begun to gabble. She often did when she was nervous and she was certainly nervous now. 'You see, James left an envelope with his solicitor – I've only just been told about it; I think they mislaid it or something.' She saw that Dr Shallech was still staring at her but she carried on. 'You probably don't know that James's father was hanged for murdering his mother. He'd started looking into the case and he thinks his father was innocent. He thinks his father's locum killed his mother. They were cousins and she'd known some secret about him; something he did when he was a child.'

355

'I don't see what this has to do with me.' The woman spoke quietly, almost in a whisper.

'James left a photograph of the locum and there were three names on the back of the picture. Charlie Haslem, which was the cousin's name. Liam Cheshlare, which was the name of the locum. And your name – Marie Shallech. Can you think why your name would be on it? And he left this photo of you.'

Fumbling, she took the picture out of her bag and handed it to Marie who took it and held it between her finger and thumb as though it was something dirty.

Roz took a deep breath, feeling a new wave of courage. If she didn't ask, she'd never find out. 'I think there's a resemblance between you and the man in the other photograph. Is he your brother, Dr Shallech?' Roz said. 'Is he still alive?'

But the question wasn't answered. Instead the older woman stood absolutely still, her eyes fixed on Roz's face. Then she spoke. 'Did you tell anyone you were coming here, Mrs Dalcott?'

'Roz. Please call me Roz,' she gabbled, suddenly aware that she shouldn't have come.

She took a step back. 'Look, the police think my partner's got something to do with James's death and I just want to know the truth.'

Marie Shallech's lips turned upwards in a cold smile. 'Let's go into the other room and sit down, Mrs Dalcott. I'll make us a nice cup of tea.' She turned and led the way back into the hall but she stopped at the door and let Roz go first. It looked like politeness but Roz had a sudden suspicion that she was blocking her escape route. Marie opened the door to the back room – a small living room with French windows at one end, shabby and furnished only with the bare necessities. Roz entered and sat down on a well-worn sofa then the door closed and Marie stood there, leaning on the door, staring at her.

'I wish you hadn't come here, Mrs Dalcott. I really do.'

Wesley drove towards Tradmouth, with Nick Tarnaby sitting silently in the passenger seat. After they'd driven about five miles down the unlit A road, Nick broke his silence.

'Isn't that the road you want – Hawkston?'

Wesley signalled right and took the narrow single-track lane, putting the headlights onto full beam. The car that had been behind them all the way from Neston also took the turning. It was following a good distance behind but Wesley was aware of the headlights in his rear-view mirror. A fox galloped across his path, turning for a moment to stare at the approaching car with bright, terrified eyes, but as he was driving fairly slowly, it managed to scurry away into the tall hedgerow to safety. A few yards later a rabbit with suicidal inclinations did the same; but again, it was lucky enough to escape.

Hawkston was little more than a hamlet: a handful of stone-built houses and a small village green. Wesley parked the car on the verge behind a small blue Toyota. He recognised the car. It was Roz Dalcott's. His instincts had been right.

He emerged from the car, stepping carefully over the muddy tyre ruts at his feet, and walked up the lane with Nick by his side, straining in the darkness to examine the house names. The one they were looking for stood at the end. Green View: not the height of originality, Wesley thought. There was a light on in a downstairs window and the two men walked up the path to the front door, unaware of the car that had doused its headlights and rolled to a halt just out of sight round the bend in the road.

Roz felt her unborn child move inside her as Marie raised her hand and, with a swift movement, her steel grey bob had gone. The hair left behind was cropped and thinning. The make-up she wore now made her look vaguely ludicrous – like a dame in an amateur pantomime.

Roz stared, unable to think of anything appropriate to say.

'It's something I've perfected over the years, living as a woman. I'd always enjoyed dressing as one, of course, and when it became necessary for Liam Cheshlare to disappear, I became Marie Shallech. And to tell the truth, I've rather enjoyed it.' Marie took a step forward and opened a drawer in a nearby side table. Roz felt herself gasp when she saw her take out the gun. She closed her eyes and said a silent prayer to a God she'd ignored since her Sunday school days.

'The human body is a wonderful thing, Mrs Dalcott.' Marie levelled the gun at her head. 'And so fragile. A perfect machine. It almost makes you believe in a creator, doesn't it? I dissected my first human body when I was ten.' She said the words with a matter-of-fact coldness that made Roz shudder. 'Would you like to hear about it?'

Roz nodded, welcoming anything that might give her extra time.

'My parents were killed during the war. A bomb dropped on our house during the Blitz. I saw their bodies.

They'd been blown to pieces; exploded into bleeding lumps of meat. And when they found me I was covered in their blood, trying desperately to reassemble my parents. I was only nine years old and I was trying desperately to bring them back to life.'

'It must have been awful for you,' Roz whispered.

Her sympathy wasn't acknowledged. 'Then I was evacuated to Tradington with my bitch of a cousin – to a house called Tailors Court. They thought it would do me good – make me forget.' She snorted. 'As if.' She paused for a few seconds. 'A soldier called Miles lived at the house. He'd seen some terrible things in the war too – comrades blown to pieces; men with bloody pulp where their heads should have been. We had a lot in common, me and Miles. And I shared his interest in science and experimentation. Only I took that interest one step further.'

'What do you mean?'

There was a mirthless smile. 'I don't expect it'll do any harm to tell you now. In fact some say that confession can be quite therapeutic. It's a simple story really: I was playing by the river with my cousin and a couple of other children. One was a local boy called Victor and he fell in the water – he was a sickly child, small for his age but he wanted so desperately to join in.' There was a long pause. 'I can't remember much about it but my cousin told me later that I'd held Victor's head under the water till he was dead. Of course everyone assumed he'd been swept away by the current and, as half the river was being used for military purposes, nobody was in a position to launch much of a search for a missing child. We hid his body then Belle fetched the wheelbarrow and we took him back to Tailors Court and . . . I'd spent a lot of time cutting up animals with Miles but I was desperate to see how the human body worked. Aside from my parents, who didn't really count, I'd only seen the pictures, you see. I wanted to see the real thing.'

'What pictures?'

'The ones on the wall in Miles's room. A boy called Otto Kramer had escaped from Germany with his father. They were staying with a man who knew a lot about local history and he told us how the house had once belonged to a doctor who was hanged for killing a woman and dissecting her body. He'd wanted to discover the secrets of life.'

'And is that what you wanted?' Roz said, surprised at her own boldness. But some instinct told her that she had to keep the conversation going, play for time.

'We took Victor into one of the outhouses.' The person Roz had known as Marie gave her a sweet but menacing smile.

'And nobody knew what you'd done?' She had to keep talking – strike up a relationship. Her life depended on it.

'It didn't stay a secret for long. Esther, Miles's girlfriend, found out and I was sent away. She contacted the billeting officer and said I couldn't stay.'

'But she didn't tell them why?'

'She just wanted me out. Besides, I was only ten. Not responsible, you see.'

'What's your real name?'

'The name on my birth certificate is Charles. Charlie. Charlie Haslem. But that's not important. Identity is fluid if you want it to be.'

'But you kept the same letters. They're all anagrams, aren't they? Liam Cheshlare. Marie Shallech.'

'Very observant of you. I found it rather entertaining.'

'So what do I call you?' She tried to sound casual, friendly.

'I prefer Marie. I've always been more comfortable as a woman.'

'Why did you kill my husband?' The gun dropped slightly, pointing at her pregnant belly rather than her head.

'James and I were related, you know. He was my cousin, Belle's son. I think obsession must run in the family. I became obsessed with scientific discovery and poor James became obsessed with proving his father's innocence. The two obsessions, of course, proved to be incompatible in the end.'

'How did he find out about you?'

'He told me he'd always been good at faces and he was given a picture that interfering nanny took of me when I worked as his father's locum. He thought he recognised me and when he began to delve into my background he found some discrepancies. I knew it was only a matter of time before the whole thing came out. I couldn't face prison, Mrs Dalcott, and being trapped in with all those criminals. Your husband was an honest man as I'm sure you know. He would have considered it his duty to bring me to justice.'

There was a thunderous rapping on the front door that made Roz jump. She saw Marie's eyes widen for a second in panic.

'You'd better answer that,' Roz said quietly.

But Marie didn't move. The arrival of the visitor – whoever it was – had only served to increase the tension. Roz saw the finger on the trigger twitch. She closed her eyes.

Then she heard a voice calling out the words 'Police. Anybody in?' It came from the hall. The front door must have been left unlocked, a small miracle which made Roz's heart leap with new hope. She wondered whether to call out but the gun was pointed straight at her so she decided not to take the risk.

'What's the point in killing me?' she said calmly, appealing to reason. 'If you go now' – she looked at the uncurtained French windows – 'you can get out and I'll tell them you left ages ago. Please. I won't tell them anything.'

Marie's eyes travelled to the gun. 'There are six bullets in here. Plenty to go around.'

Roz's few moments of hope were at an end and she suddenly felt cold.

Then there was a hushed rattle and she saw the door handle turning slowly.

Wesley stood outside the door to the back room. Nick Tarnaby had disappeared upstairs to check whether there was anybody up there. He could hear doors opening and closing above him and he guessed that Nick had drawn a blank.

He'd seen what he assumed was Marie's study – all those specimens preserved in formaldehyde. The sight of some of them had made him feel sick: a baby's severed limbs; various internal organs; a disembodied ear; an assortment of eyeballs. As he stood in the hallway staring at the tightly closed door, he had an uneasy feeling about what he'd find on the other side.

'Nobody up there, sir,' Nick Tarnaby said as he descended the stairs.

There was one place they hadn't looked. Wesley put his

hand on the doorknob and turned it slowly. But before he could push the door open, he heard a voice behind him.

'What's going on?'

He swung round and saw Nuala Johns framed in the front doorway, waiting for an answer.

Wesley took a deep breath. The woman had gone too far this time. 'Get out of here, Nuala. Go and sit in your car.'

She pouted. 'Oh, come on, Wesley. I won't get in your way. Promise. All I want is to be first with the story.'

Wesley took a step towards her. 'You heard what I said. Get out. Now.' He didn't raise his voice but he said the words with such conviction that he was sure she'd get the message.

'DC Tarnaby, will you take this lady back to her car?'

Nick took Nuala by the arm but before he could move away the closed door swung open.

Wesley turned, unprepared for what he saw. A tall figure in women's clothes with cropped hair and incongruous make-up was facing him, gun in hand. And the gun was pointing straight at him.

In the room beyond he could see Roz Dalcott cowering in a deep armchair, her body curled defensively. She was watching Wesley, her eyes pleading with him to do something.

He heard Nick in the hallway behind him talking in hushed tones on his mobile – probably calling out the Armed Response Unit, Nuala Johns having just slipped down his list of priorities. Wesley did a rapid calculation of how long it would take them to get there – the answer he came up with was hardly encouraging. He moved into the room and gently pushed the door closed behind him

'Dr Shallech, isn't it?' he said, fixing his eyes on the figure in front of him. 'Why don't you put that gun down and we'll talk about this?' He spoke calmly, struggling to keep any hint of nerves out of his voice.

A grim smile played on the painted lips and the gun remained in position.

Wesley hesitated. 'Is it Charlie? Charlie Haslem?'

He was relieved when an answer came. While there was communication, there was hope.

'That was a lifetime ago. I've been other people since then.'

'Liam Cheshlare?'

'Perhaps I underestimated our wonderful British Police Force. I thought you'd just lock up the grieving widow's disreputable new boyfriend and that would be that.' She jerked her head towards Roz, a gesture of disdain.

'Did James Dalcott find out you'd killed his mother?' he said. He had to keep talking. And in his experience there was nothing murderers liked better than to boast about the cleverness of their crimes. 'Why don't you tell me what happened?'

There was a short silence before Marie answered. 'My parents died in the war and I was evacuated here – but you'll know that, won't you?'

'Yes. And I know about what happened at Tailors Court.'

'I'd had no outlet, you see, until I heard the story of Simon Garchard and saw those drawings in Miles's room. I think Miles would have liked to do what I did but he lacked the courage. He limited himself to animals but I had no such qualms. When I tried to put my parents' bodies back together I found out we were just lumps of meat:

blood, bone and gristle. I wanted to discover the secret of life.'

'And you killed another child to find out?'

'Killing Victor was my fall from grace, my eating of the forbidden fruit. I was sent away to another billet while my bitch of a cousin stayed put even though she'd been involved in what happened. And then when the war ended I was fostered – sent from one home to another. I'm sure I wasn't a difficult child but a cloud seemed to follow me and adults whispered in corners so I couldn't hear what they were saying. Or perhaps I was imagining it. Anyway, there was no hope of me going to medical school so, since I couldn't pursue my . . . special interests, I worked in a hospital as a porter and used all my spare time studying and experimenting. Then one of the young doctors was killed in a road accident. His name was Liam Cheshlare – he used to joke that his name was an anagram of mine and I suppose you'd say he was a nice chap. But I hated him. He'd had all the privileges – he'd had all the chances I should have had.'

'How did you end up working for Dr Clipton?'

'I'd heard Belle had married a doctor called Clipton and when I saw he was advertising for a locum I decided to go along as Dr Cheshlare.' Marie held her head up proudly. 'I'd studied for years and I knew my stuff. I was as good as any of them.'

'So what did Isabelle say when you turned up?'

Marie gave a mirthless smile. 'I think she got a bit of a shock. But I'd already told her husband that we were related – that's what got me the job. To a man like Clipton it would have been bad form to question a relative's qualifications too closely. In those days gentlemen took each other at their word. Anyway, Belle had to keep up appearances for a while. But then she told me she found my presence uncomfortable and she threatened to tell her husband and the whole village that I was a fraud. She even implied that she might reveal what I'd done back in Tradington.' The smile disappeared and the eyes became hard. 'I wasn't going to let Belle control my life. She'd tried that before and failed.'

'So you strangled her?'

Marie looked uncomfortable. 'That sounds so brutal.'

'It was. So was the fact that you disfigured the face.'

'She laughed at me. She'd always mocked me and I found I'd had enough so I put an end to it once and for all. She deserved all she got really. Belle wasn't a nice person.'

Wesley hesitated. 'George Clipton didn't deserve to hang.'

'It was a matter of survival. Survival of the fittest.'

Wesley was searching for the next question to ask when he heard Nuala Johns's distant voice raised in protest followed by Nick Tarnaby's deeper tones, exasperated and struggling for control.

Marie had heard too. The gun was raised, levelled at Wesley's heart.

Wesley raised both hands, a gesture of appeasement. 'Why don't you tell me what you did after that? How did you become Marie Shallech?'

'After the court case Liam had to disappear so I became Marie. I became quite good at forging references and certificates and in the past the British have been far too polite to ask awkward questions so I was able to work in various private hospitals and clinics. And before you ask, I underwent surgery. I am a woman now. I am Marie – Charlie and Liam don't exist any more.'

'Tell me about James.'

An exasperated look appeared on Marie's face, as

though James Dalcott had been nothing but a minor irritation. 'Everything was fine until he became obsessed with his father's case. Do you know he'd even managed to find out somehow that Liam Cheshlare liked dressing as a woman? He said his old nanny had told him. He spoke to me at the Podingham Clinic and asked if we could meet in private about a personal matter – something to do with his father. He said he'd been trying to trace a Dr Cheshlare who'd been his father's locum and he wanted to see me. I thought it would only be a matter of time before he discovered the truth so I had to dispose of him before he took it into his head to expose me.'

Wesley heard Roz give a small gasp of horror but he carried on. 'Was it you who locked me in the room at Dalcott's cottage?'

'When I killed him I didn't have a chance to search the place properly because I saw the neighbour's car pulling into their drive and I couldn't go back until the police had stopped guarding the house. I needed to find the evidence he said he had – he'd mentioned a photograph. Not that I imagined the police would put two and two together but . . .' A smile appeared on the painted lips. 'I have to hand it to you, Inspector Peterson, you're more intelligent than the average plod. You're black, of course, which a few unenlightened people say is a disadvantage in life, but on the other hand your father is a distinguished surgeon; your mother's a doctor and so is your sister. You've had all the advantages I never had, Inspector Peterson. What I wouldn't have given to come from a family like yours. Do you think you deserve all the privileges life's given you?'

'Where did you get the gun?'

Marie glanced down at the weapon in her hand. 'It was

367

Clipton's old service revolver. I took it with me when I left. I knew it would come in useful one day, I suppose. George supplied the means for his son's death. Ironic that, isn't it?'

Wesley looked into Marie's eyes and saw a hatred that shocked him as her finger hovered on the trigger, preparing to squeeze.

The moment of tension was broken by a sudden commotion outside the door: a high-pitched voice telling someone to get out of the way and a deeper shout of warning.

The door burst open and Wesley heard the words 'Mrs Dalcott. I need to –' But Nuala Johns's words were cut off by a loud explosion. Wesley stood for a split second paralysed with shock. Then he twisted round to see Nuala lying on the floor, groaning.

Marie was standing, the gun still in her hand. Her eyes were staring at her handiwork. For a moment there was complete silence. Then she started to raise her arm again but before she could take aim Wesley flung himself forward and knocked her off balance. Another shot exploded somewhere and the elderly body he was pinning to the floor suddenly went limp.

He heard Nick Tarnaby's voice. He was crouching in the doorway, bent over Nuala Johns. 'She got past me – just made a run for it. I couldn't stop her.' He sounded close to tears.

Then there was the sound of police car sirens outside in the lane.

Gerry Heffernan had sent Nick Tarnaby straight home as soon as he'd been checked out by the doctor.

'Is Nuala Johns going to be all right?' he asked Wesley

now as they sat on a damp garden bench outside the cottage. The seat was slimy with lichen and the cold ground beneath their feet was carpeted with soggy leaves but at least it wasn't raining.

Wesley looked down at his hands. There were times he wished he smoked and this was one of them. 'Our intrepid girl reporter? Just a shoulder wound. She'll dine out on the story for years. Rachel's gone down to the hospital to take a statement.'

There was a pause before Gerry spoke again. 'I saw Rach going into the Tradmouth Arms last night. She was with that bloke from Gorfleet Farm.'

Wesley said nothing. Somehow he wasn't in the mood for station gossip.

'What about Roz Dalcott?' Gerry asked.

'They've taken her off to the hospital to be on the safe side but the doc doesn't think there's any damage to her or the baby.'

There had been a trio of ambulances parked outside the cottage. Now just one remained. As the life of Marie Shallech – alias Charlie Haslem – had been pronounced extinct, there was no particular urgency.

'Did he mean to shoot himself, do you think?' Gerry said quietly.

Wesley thought for a few moments before answering. 'I suppose she knew when she was beaten.'

'She? Wasn't her real name Charlie Haslem?'

'Yes. But she'd become Marie in more than name. Gender reassignment they call it.'

Gerry grunted. 'I had a call from Sandra Ackerley while you were out. Her mum's been in touch. They're travelling back home tomorrow.'

'Good. Wonder how she'll take the news about Charlie? This all began when they were evacuated together.'

'If you ask me, Wes, it began when he saw his family blown to pieces. He was just one more casualty of war.' He stood up and stretched, his mouth opening slowly in a wide yawn. 'Let's get back to the incident room. You ready for a celebratory drink?'

Wesley nodded, trying to summon some enthusiasm and failing. 'I'd better let Pam know I'll be late.'

Gerry began to walk towards the car and Wesley followed. He looked back at the cottage and felt rather numb. James Dalcott was dead and Nuala Johns was in hospital but he'd bow to tradition as usual and drink to the successful solving of the case. He took out his mobile phone and rang his home number.

Pam said it was fine. She'd see him later. But he could detect the disappointment behind the words. She'd had a hard day, she said – Christmas preparations at school. He made sympathetic noises and rang off.

'Look, Gerry, do you mind if I give the pub a miss?'

Gerry looked like a child whose friend had refused to come out to play. 'Well, I won't be staying long. Just going to show my face and get off. Joyce has got a hotpot in the oven,' he added coyly. 'Come on, you look as though you need a pint.'

Wesley nodded. Sometimes it was easier to follow the crowd.

CHAPTER 15

Transcript of recording made by Mrs Mabel Cleary (née Fallon) – Home Counties Library Service Living History Project: Reminiscences of a wartime evacuee.

There's something that's been on my mind for all those years. Something dreadful. I told Pat, of course, and asked her advice and she said that, in the circumstances, it would do me good to get it off my chest. When I recorded my reminiscences for the library there were things I felt I couldn't say. How could I let anyone know that I took part in something so terrible? Anyway, I've had a word with the people in the library and they said I could arrange for this part of my reminiscences not to be published even after my death. I said I wanted the transcript to go straight to Sandra, she'll just have to live with what I did like I've had to all these years.

The letter from Sandra Ackerley arrived with an avalanche of Christmas cards on the 23rd December. Since the post arrived after he'd gone to work, Wesley found it propped up on the hall table when he got home.

Pam gave him a passing greeting as she rushed in and out of the kitchen. He was just hanging up his coat when Neil appeared at the living-room door.

'I thought you were going up to Somerset for Christmas?' Wesley said.

'Tomorrow. After three days my folks get sick of my slovenly ways and chuck me out so I leave it till the last minute. Pam's invited me to dinner,' he said with a grin.

'I'd better give her a hand,' Wesley said half-heartedly.

'I've already offered. She says it's all under control.'

They went into the living room where the children were watching cartoons on the TV, sitting on the floor, transfixed by the bright moving images on the screen. Wesley flopped down in an armchair.

'I've got some news,' Neil said.

'What's that?' Wesley played with the envelope in his hand, studying the postmark. Orpington. Who did he know in Orpington?

'Remember Tony and Jill Persimmon from Tailors Court?'

'What about them?'

'Well, the article Nuala Johns did for one of the nationals stirred up a lot of interest so they've decided to open part of the place to the public – especially the wall paintings and the attic.' He grinned modestly. 'They've asked me to help them with the historical side – the story of Simon Garchard and all that. They're going to mount an exhibition in one of the outbuildings with artefacts found around the place and there's going to be a lot about Elizabethan medicine and Garchard's body snatching and all that. They're getting some grant from a heritage body and –'

'Have you heard from Nuala?'

'Can't get away from the woman.'

'She had a narrow escape.'

Neil snorted. 'She's bloody indestructible if you ask me.'

He turned his attention to the frenetic cartoon on the TV and Wesley began to slit the envelope open. There were several sheets of paper inside and he spread them out in front of him. A short handwritten note told him that the sender was Sandra Ackerley.

'*Dear Inspector Peterson. I'm sorry to tell you that my mother passed away suddenly a week ago,*' she began. '*I'm enclosing the remaining transcripts that she made for the local library together with one section that she asked not to be released until after her death. I'm sending it to your home address because I want the information it contains to stay between ourselves. I trust this will be helpful to you.*'

Wesley began to read with interest. Pat was mentioned often in these new pages – previously he'd only read accounts of the time before she arrived in Devon – as was Charlie's departure and the arrival of the Americans in South Devon to rehearse the D-Day landings. But it was the final page that made the chatter of the TV recede into the background. He held his breath as he read it.

I'd seen the old paintings on the wall in Miles's room. Belle took me in there and showed me – dared me to look. If it had just stopped there it would have been all right but Belle had to push things further as usual. Her cousin Charlie was really strange. He had blond curls and he looked like an angel but he'd seen terrible things which had affected his mind. That's why what Belle did was so awful. One day me and Charlie and Belle were down by the river and one of the village children – a weedy little lad called Victor – turned up and wanted to play with us. Anyway, he got into trouble when we were swimming and he drowned. Charlie was with him but I didn't really see what happened. Then Belle said why didn't we take him to one of the outhouses at Tailors Court that was never used. We'd seen the attic where Miles used to cut open the animals and we knew there were knives in there so Belle borrowed some of them; Miles was out at the time so he didn't know. Charlie was scared but Belle started teasing him and calling him names. She took the lead and the rest of us followed. Even me. She got Charlie to hold the knife and cut Victor open but as soon as he saw what he'd done he began to shake and then he started to sob and said he couldn't do it any more. He said Victor looked like his mum – I didn't know what he meant but later someone said he'd found his mum and dad's bodies blown to pieces.

Anyway, Belle said she'd tell everyone he killed Victor – she said she'd seen him do it and Charlie seemed to believe it himself. Somehow she managed to convince him that Victor hadn't drowned and that somehow he was responsible so that he'd do as he was told. I'm sure he hadn't killed Victor any more than I had. But Belle was so convincing. She was the strong one. She'd made Charlie cut Victor open and I'm so ashamed that I ran away instead of standing up to her. And when Ugly Esther found Charlie with Victor's body and thought the worst, she got Miles to bury him and clear up and had Charlie sent away.

Belle said she'd thrown Charlie's toy car into the grave which was cruel because Charlie loved that car – it was the only thing he'd brought from home to remind him of his dead family. But I still never said anything because Belle had drawn me in. She had this way of making people do what she wanted. I heard from the police that she was murdered back in the 1950s and they say Charlie did it so it looks like he got his own back at last. But an innocent man was hanged for her murder and they say Charlie killed that doctor who was going to tell the police what he'd done. Maybe if I'd spoken out none of it would have happened. I don't know.

I've lived with the shame of not saying anything for all these years and it feels good to write it all down. It's like a burden's been lifted from my shoulders.

By the time anyone reads this, I'll be dead. What is it they say? For evil to succeed all it takes is for good people to do nothing. I could have told someone and put a stop to Belle Haslem's nasty little tricks once and for all. But I didn't. I just hope people don't think too badly of me.

'What's that you're reading?'

Neil's voice brought him back to the present.

But before he could think up a suitable answer, he heard Pam's voice calling from the kitchen. 'Wes, can you come and give us a hand?'

He stood up and stuffed the papers in his pocket. It was almost Christmas. Pam always liked to light a real fire at Christmas; perhaps it was best if Mabel's confession went up in smoke.

EPILOGUE

Roz Dalcott looked down at the sleeping baby and felt an unaccustomed and shocking wave of love. Little Simon had been born with perfect timing on Christmas Day: it had been an easy birth which rather surprised Roz after all the trauma she'd endured during her pregnancy.

Harry had just left the ward, very much the proud father. However, as she gazed down on her son she felt a flutter of panic. He was the image of James. But she'd feared he might be. She'd done the calculations, keeping her conclusions from Harry in the hope that it might all go away. After all, she'd only slept with James once at the relevant time – in a rash moment of nostalgia for what they'd once had together – whereas she and Harry had been in the throes of fresh infatuation.

She put the baby carefully in the plastic cot next to her bed, thinking of everything James had discovered about his family. She closed her eyes and saw the shocking image that had haunted her since that night – Marie standing there with that cropped hair and hideous make-up. Marie pointing the gun at her belly. Marie who had been James's mother's cousin.

Perhaps there was bad blood in that family, she thought as she touched the cheek of the sleeping child who looked so like James in repose. And bad blood passed from generation to generation.

She lay back on her pillow, staring at the fluorescent light above. The child was Harry's, she told herself. Harry's. Nobody else's.